THE FALL OF
RHO-TORKIS
BOOK ONE OF
CHIMERA COMPANY

Tim C. Taylor

Theogony Books
Coinjock, NC

Chris Kennedy/Theogony Books
1097 Waterlily Rd.
Coinjock, NC 27923
http://chriskennedypublishing.com/

Publisher's Note: This is a work of fiction. Names, characters, places, and incidents are a product of the author's imagination. Locales and public names are sometimes used for atmospheric purposes. Any resemblance to actual people, living or dead, or to businesses, companies, events, institutions, or locales is completely coincidental.

Cover Design by Vincent Sammy.

Ordering Information:
Quantity sales. Special discounts are available on quantity purchases by corporations, associations, and others. For details, contact the "Special Sales Department" at the address above.

The Fall of Rho-Torkis/Tim C. Taylor -- 1st ed.
ISBN: 978-1648551239

For Cpl Taylor, 27th Field Squadron, Royal Engineers. He held the line.

Acknowledgement

The author wishes to thank all those who supported the making of this book. In particular, Vincent, Brent, Melissa, Michael, JR, Melissa, my brave redshirts, my real-life family, the Swan at Bromham for fueling my Monday-night scribbling with fine ales, and Tharg the Mighty for seeding the idea back in 1977.

Chapter One:
Osu Sybutu

"You know the Federation's touring all five hells in a handbasket when even the Littoranes fire on the Legion."

Sergeant Osu Sybutu glared at Yergin's back while the sapper sealed the final replacement pipe in the meltwater drainage system.

Did Yergin tense his neck and shoulders, knowing he had gone too far in his grumbling? It was impossible to be sure, swaddled as the man was in the thick padding of cold weather gear. In any case, legionaries were trained to think—it was what set the Legion apart from the Militia—and Yergin was only giving voice to a thought that had run through every sapper's mind in the unit.

"How's that, Yergin?" Osu challenged. He had no choice; Lieutenant Stuart wanted a lid kept on this particular train of thought.

A hush descended over the other sappers as Yergin abandoned his task and stood to face his sergeant. Sapper of the Legion Marc Yergin was an old sweat, though he was new to the 27th Independent Field Squadron (Legion Engineers), having only joined during their transit to the ice world of Rho-Torkis.

Osu could barely make out the man's features, shrouded as they were by his heated tunnel-like hood and glacier glasses, but he recognized a challenge in the set of the man's shoulders.

"At the very beginning, the Legion *was* Littorane, barring a few human kids. What went wrong, Sergeant? What in Orion's name are we doing here?"

"Were you abandoned in deep-cryo and forgotten about for thousands of years, SOTL?"

Osu itched to be checking on the work party perimeter guard, not lancing this boil, but he waited for an answer as if he had all the time in the galaxy.

"No, Sergeant," Yergin answered.

"I'm glad to hear it. We're not in the Orion Spur now, Yergin. You're talking about events over three thousand years ago that were written up centuries later by self-serving politicians who wouldn't recognize the truth unless it was covered in 1000-credit chits. I don't know why Littoranes rarely sign up to the Legion anymore, nor why the slime-munchers of this world hate us so much. So long as they keep away from Legion country, I don't care. And while it's true that Littoranes have fired upon us, the colonel says the individuals who did so were planted here by the Rebellion. As for why we are here...we're sappers, Yergin. And what is it that sets us apart as superior to regular Legion units? What is the fundamental underpinning of civilization that only we can be relied upon to get right?"

"The drains, Sergeant. We're out here beyond the isolation zone in order to fix the drains."

It was true. The 27th had inspected the surrounding area on the first day since their arrival that the snowstorms had cleared enough to move out from the ASI-39 dig site. When they had discovered the inadequacy of the meltwater drainage system, Major Cartwright had conveyed his professional opinion to Colonel Malix using every ounce of his considerable skill in creative cursing.

But that wasn't what Yergin had asked.

What *was* the Legion doing on this damned planet? Every legionary not directly involved in the dig teams asked themselves that question every day. And with two full brigades here, that meant a lot of jacks with time on their hands scratching their heads and wondering what was going on in the restricted areas of ASI-39.

What set Osu apart from all those scratching jacks was that he knew the answer.

Not even the lieutenant knew that.

He growled inwardly as he waved Yergin back to the task of sealing leaking collector pipes before reburying them in gravel. A little knowledge was a painful burden, and his sat heavily upon him as he set off to inspect the perimeter guard out in the surrounding trees.

Two thirds of the sappers were tasked with protecting the safety of the other third repairing the pipes, protecting them from the same Littoranes he'd just told Yergin not to blame for everything. Suited up in battle armor, the sappers of these assault sections were either on overwatch in the trees or patrolling farther out. The two armored wagons that had brought them here were monitoring surveillance drones and had their gun turrets active, all to watch out for the seven-foot long, six-legged giant newts that were officially perfect friends and hosts of the Legion.

In ancient times, Littoranes had built and crewed the Legion's navy. Now they had mostly retreated into themselves, desiring to be left alone to fight their endless religious wars and listen to the song of the universe.

"They're not to blame for everything," he told himself.

The newts hadn't even sabotaged the drainage pipes, as everyone had first assumed. That had been a far more deadly foe: the planet

Rho-Torkis itself. The gene-modified conifers all around pushed their roots through tens of meters of ice to extract nutrients from the ground below. Against that, even the tough flexi-ceramalloy of the pipes could put up only token resistance.

It wasn't exactly the first time in history that tree roots had played havoc with drains.

"We're ready to leave in five mikes," Osu told the lieutenant as the sappers began packing the gear away.

"Thank you, Sergeant."

The day's work felt like an anti-climax to Osu. He tried to tell himself that he'd earned a little boredom after the adventures of the previous posting—a skragg-ball mess of a world called Irisur—but he wasn't buying it. So it was with a vague sense of disappointment that he began checking Corporal De Ketele's orderly withdrawal back into the beetle wagons.

Without warning, Lieutenant Stuart looped him into an ongoing radio conversation.

"Please say again," requested the lieutenant.

"RILs have eyes on you," said Captain Ankhbayar. "RILs have eyes on your grid from all directions. We see twenty armed with light blasters and…tail clubs."

Osu's pulse quickened. RILs. Legion speak for Religious Insurgent (Littorane). So, it wasn't the Rebellion who was hunting them today. That was good, because Osu's religious belief was a match even for the most fanatic Littorane.

His religion was the Legion.

And it was his religious duty to smite the Legion's foes.

"They've reinforced their numbers over the last ten mikes," said the captain, "but they do not appear to be at ambush strength. My guess is that they will be taking a pot shot at you on your way home to make a point, and then fade away. But be prepared for anything. They're Littoranes. We see religious symbolism prominently displayed and nothing of the Rebellion's emblems. I would dearly like to know why they are attacking us, but I see nothing to indicate a reason. Safe journey."

* * * * *

Chapter Two:
Osu Sybutu

"Beetle-1 feels dead," Lieutenant Stuart informed Osu twenty minutes later on a private link from the other wagon. "Not the wagon, the SOTLs."

Osu boosted the signal to better cut through the rumble of the CEGP-2 "Beetle" Utility Wagon as it powered its way along the lakeside track, headed home.

The lieutenant laughed. "You'd think I'd served up month-old rat carcasses and ordered the men to eat every last morsel. Is Beetle-2 any more upbeat?"

The crew in the forward compartment of Osu's beetle were alert and pensive, thinking about what dangers the journey home might bring, and he assumed the other wagon would have the same atmosphere. The only issue here was the lieutenant's inexperience.

"Sir, I'd describe the men's demeanor as *professional.*"

"Good. I wasn't sure if I should try to rouse morale or whether in so doing I'd just make myself appear a pompous asshat."

A grin softened Osu's face. Stuart could never be the LT they'd lost at Irisur, but he'd as good as asked his transport sergeant for advice. He'd do.

"You're fine as you are, sir. I'll be sure to inform you when you're being an asshat."

"Make sure you do, Sergeant...Hello? What's this?"

13

"Beetle-1 slowing," said Krynox, Beetle-2's driver.

"Tree's blocking the path," added Jonson from the forward turret. "Freshly cut, it's an—"

"Ambush!" exclaimed the lieutenant.

The sound of splintering timber announced another tree falling to block their retreat.

"Get off the track and onto the lake," Stuart ordered.

The beetle weighed 48 tons unladen, and in its three articulated compartments, it carried not only its five crew, six sappers in work gear, and racks of equipment, but the aft compartment also carried an assault section of a dozen legionaries in armor. That was a lot of weight to drive over a frozen lake. But as the nose rose and the 36 Haisan-Linc Industries 71T motor cells crescendoed into a frisky whine, it wasn't the thought of falling through the ice that worried Osu.

"We're being herded," he told the lieutenant as the vehicles powered through the trackside foliage and over the moraine ridges, scattering rocks in all directions. "We're where the RILs want us to be."

"I know," Stuart answered. "I'm counting on it."

The vehicles moved onto the ice, which immediately began making the sound of shattering glass, although no cracks appeared on its surface. It was holding. But the cracking continued.

Twelve fat wheels on each wagon extruded new tire surfaces to maximize grip, and Beetle-2 accelerated away for the center of the lake. Krynox could selectively reduce grip too. In fact, Osu trusted him to pirouette the three sections of the armored utility wagon more gracefully than any ice skater.

Which was precisely what he might be called upon to do in the next few minutes.

Lake Gamma-37 lay across the southern perimeter of the isolation zone around the dig site. Shaped like a pair of fleshy lips, it was 1.6 klicks wide and 3 long, and was formed from freshwater accumulation that had frozen on top of a glacier. Now that Rho-Torkis was emerging from its long nuclear winter, the lake was no longer frozen all year round.

"Ice depth approximately four meters," said Zavage from signals and sensors.

Four meters! That was much too shallow. "Slow down!" Osu warned.

But it was too late.

With an extra ear-splitting crack, the ice beneath Beetle-2 exploded, sending a spray into the chill air to freeze before it splashed into the water lapping at the edge of what looked like a bomb crater. This was blowback: pressure waves forced by the beetle's considerable weight had reflected off the shoreline and erupted like a geyser.

"Angle your heading to the south," ordered the lieutenant, "and restrict speed to 15mph. We'll angle north. Meet at the lake's center."

Driving out onto a lake following a shallow angle to shoreline was standard practice on thin ice, but it felt ever more like they were dancing to a RIL tune.

"Contact," announced Stryker from the mid-turret. "Unidentified drones closing fast from the west. 400 meters."

"Dust 'em," instructed the lieutenant, a fraction before Osu could give the same instruction, albeit in more colorful terms.

The beetle's mid-section didn't just house blasting charges, micro-dozers, ice manipulators and the like; its turret housed a quad-barrel rapid-fire railgun optimized for anti-air defense. Then there were the four ordnance launch tubes, all of which now sent a missile whooshing into the air.

As the two beetles crawled across the frozen lake, a furious battle of maneuver took place in the sky above. The drones had multiple duct fans on 3-axis gimbal mounts, blast jets, and gravitic nudgers to lurch, spin on a fingertip, and bob up and down like a drunken uncle.

Even the trained human eye struggled to track them.

But the AL-6 missile boasted 200G acceleration and variable-thrust rocket nozzles that fed out from its base like a tubular river delta.

A sequence of aerial flashes marked the death of each drone. The whole process had taken four seconds.

"We cannot permit enemy aerial observation," said the lieutenant squad-wide. "However, I remind you that ground targets are not to be engaged with accurate fire without my permission."

"Understood, sir," Osu replied. "You heard Lieutenant Stuart," he added on Beetle-2's channel. "Make like you're the Militia."

All three sections exploded in jeers and hoots of laughter.

The two beetles were coming together again at the center of the lake when a line of ice plumes erupted in front of them.

"Contact! Contact! Wait out," called Narvik, Zavage's opposite number in Beetle-1, who was playing his part by allowing panic to edge into his voice. He wasn't fooling anyone who knew him, but BattleNet encryption had been designed by a largely Littorane team a long time ago. It was conceivable that the RILs were listening in on broadcast frequencies, and the Lieutenant didn't want his sappers to appear too confident.

The wagon drivers skewed their vehicles around, sliding out their rear sections before reapplying traction and powering away from the gap in the ice that had just opened up.

Osu trusted the maneuvering to the expertise of the drivers. He had other concerns. "Turrets, report!"

"I can see water through the trench," said Jonson in the forward turret.

"Indirect fire inbound on our position," said Zavage. "Coming from the west."

Osu grinned, able to try out the newfangled system on these up-rated beetles. "Lima Victor Delta," he said.

The Low Velocity Deflector system deployed over each of the three compartments. They looked like pitched roofs made from wire netting, but as bombs rained down, the wire contracted like twitching muscle just before each projectile impacted. A combination of locally applied repulsive charge and the released tension of the wire deflected some bombs away, and those that exploded in the netting were kept well away from the Beetle's upper armor. Damaged netting was no problem. When the party returned to base, they would simply slot in replacement LVD panels as required.

"Looks like they're tossing homemade explosives," ventured Jonson.

"Even without the snowshoes over the roof," said Stryker, "they would be nothing to worry about."

"Forget the roof," said Osu. "What's happening to the ice?"

Before they could reply, low-slung figures emerged from the tree line near the western shore. Littoranes. Immediately, the giant newts used their long tails like slingshots to fire a volley of objects hundreds of meters away into the path of the wagons.

"Give those RILs something to stir them up," ordered the lieutenant from Beetle-1.

Osu grimaced, uncomfortable with what he knew Stuart was asking him to do. If you bore arms against the Legion, the Legion would kill you without delay or hesitation. Didn't matter whether you were a Federation citizen or acting on behalf of an external power. That simple equation had kept the Federation together for 3,000 years, but now the beetles would do something different. Even if only temporarily, it still felt a perversion of the Legion ethos.

He tapped the forward turret cage occupied by SOTL Jonson. "Turret one, *tickle them.*"

Jonson sent twin lines of heavy blaster fire into the shoreline, causing the RILs to scatter among trees whose lower branches were catching fire. And the highly visible bolts of induced plasma made it obvious to Osu why the purple-green needles of the trees were alight: the gunner was firing over the heads of the enemy.

But not entirely. Jonson dipped the stream of bolts for a moment and alien screams pierced the woods.

"Sergeant," said Zavage. "The ice…the bombs aren't targeting the vehicles. They're cutting through the ice."

The volley of slingshot bombs landed in a ring around the two wagons, surrounding them in a sheet of fire and ice.

Plasma grenades.

The fire was soon overcome by dense eruptions of steam that condensed almost instantly into an impenetrable fog that wiped out all visibility.

Krynox flung the legionaries hard against their straps as he slewed the wagon around to avoid the melting ice.

"You command the wagon," Osu told Lance Corporal Aronov and headed aft, unclipping his helm from his belt while he set his earpiece to a private link to the commander. "We need to take these RILs seriously. Recommend deploying assault sections immediately." He jumped over the violently moving inter-compartmental joint and into the mid-section.

"Agreed," replied the lieutenant. "But we're bait and that's always a dangerous game to play. We cannot show too many teeth, Sergeant. Deploy your assault section. I will keep Beetle-1's in reserve."

"Understood. Out."

"Told you so, boys," said De Ketele on the squad channel when Osu reached the aft compartment. A dozen legionaries in combat armor sat waiting to deploy. "We're about to stretch our legs."

The noise of cracking ice had been a constant accompaniment since driving onto the frozen lake. It suddenly grew into an ear-splitting sound, as if the fury of an ice god was being vented upon the wagons of the 27th.

The deck fell away like a plunging dropship, sending Osu tumbling across the compartment until he grabbed onto the base of the turret cage and clung there. The aft compartment was bobbing up and down, and the deck was now a steep incline up to the joint with the midsection. Metal ground in protest against metal.

"Hey!" called De Ketele. "Who ordered the ice bath?"

"No offense, Corporal," Krynox told the exfil master over the bulkhead intercom. The wagon throbbed with power as Krynox made the engine rear up like a struck horse. "But I thought assault section could do with a wash."

The heavy wagon lurched forward and came to a halt, all compartments on the ice. For now.

"Gonzalez," said Osu. "Let me see."

The rear gunner jumped out of his turret and Osu took his place, using the twin joysticks to swing the armored bubble around, thankful that they'd been upgraded to Mark 3 Beetles with expanded turrets big enough to be used by legionaries in armor.

Fog still hung in the air, but it had dispersed enough to see the jagged gap cut around the wagons. At no point was it less than five meters across. They were on an ice floe in the middle of the lake. Trapped. Just where the RILs wanted them.

He called down into the compartment, "Assault section will deploy."

The exit ramp crashed down onto the ice, raising a fringe of hissing steam from its heated edge. While his team rapidly deployed onto the ice, Osu adjusted his helm to get a closer look at the shoreline, but the only movement was the black smoke curling up from the burning branches.

With both wagons stationary, even the sound of cracking ice had vanished, leaving the legionaries in an eerie silence.

He shook his head. "This is too easy," he muttered, but the lieutenant still wanted him playing the part of vulnerable prey—a role he suspected was no longer an act—and so he remote-activated one of the smokers he'd mounted himself under the mid-section.

"Grymz," he said over the radio, "standby to deploy an ice management team on my signal."

"Sculptors ready," the sapper replied, raising a laugh from Osu.

The Corps of Legion Engineers worked *with* the landscape whenever they could, and on a world such as Rho-Torkis, that meant using the ice. Ice berms, ice causeways, ice buildings, ice breastwork, ice roads: they were mostly built using diggers, dozers, and graders, but the finishing touches were often added by ice manipulators.

Legionaries being legionaries, training on this vital equipment usually produced humanoid figures with unfeasibly exaggerated body parts, but a few of the sappers had the talent to create impressive ice sculptures.

Marc Yergin in particular. Last week, he'd sculptured in intricate detail an eight-foot-high screaming guinshrike, the eagle analog that had been the symbol of the Legion since time immemorial.

Grymz had told Osu that there was something profoundly poetic in creating an object of such beauty, knowing it would inevitably melt into oblivion.

Osu didn't know about that. There was no time for poetry in *his* soul. Not when he had his work cut out keeping his SOTLs out of mischief.

Through the scratched transparent armor of his turret bubble, Osu could see sooty smoke belching from the device he'd activated beneath the vehicle. "Come get us," he muttered as he took a last look at their surroundings. "We're wounded. Vulnerable. And I haven't got all day."

The RILs weren't playing ball. They'd vanished. But they were still around…*somewhere.*

He jumped down to the deck, slapped the waiting Gonzalez on his back, and jogged off to join the legionaries on the ice.

Despite the seemingly chaotic skidding of the wagons, there had been method to the drivers' mayhem. Each three-section beetle had been parked in a curve. *The wagons had been circled.*

Using the vehicles as cover, the assault section legionaries outside had their PA-71 railguns ready for action, scanning for threats. Front and rear turrets rotated as their gunners searched for RIL targets, praying that the officer would show mercy and allow them to unleash destruction upon the newts. Mid-section turrets watched the skies.

Come on…They're not even flinging bombs. Why not?

"Stay alert," he warned the sappers. "If the RILs are going to move, this is when they'll do it."

Osu waved at Grymz's team and they came down the exit ramp, dragging two ice manipulators on hover frames. To the uninitiated, the devices looked like man-sized metal cylinders sprouting several articulated hoses, but to Osu they were something much simpler: a route to safety.

Taking four legionaries of the assault section with him, Osu escorted Grymz's ice sculptors to the edge of the ice floe where they set to work. Beneath the white spray of ice splinters and steam they were kicking up, they were creating ice out of moist air and lake water. Within a few minutes, they would have sealed the gap and the beetles could drive away.

Unless the RILs stopped them, of course.

And yet, still, there was no sign of attack.

He thought he'd heard them move—a sigh, like wind whistling through the trees. But it couldn't be. The sound was coming from beneath the ice.

From the water.

"Get back from the edge!" he screamed.

The Littoranes leapt out of the water, lifted by powerful flicks from their muscular tails, firing their dripping blaster rifles before they'd even landed on the ice.

Osu saw sappers go down before the wild onslaught of blaster bolts, but whether dead or going to ground, he couldn't tell.

He sighted a Littorane—range, ten meters—who'd reared up on its hind legs and was about to hurl a grenade with one rubbery front limb while the other sprayed blaster fire at Beetle-2. Three rounds spat from Osu's railgun, severing the gray amphibian's arm at the shoulder, causing it to ululate in horror as its severed limb fell to the ice, still clutching the grenade.

Littorane screams announced legionary railgun flechettes finding their mark, which was very obliging of the newts because against the brightness of the turret fire, he could barely see what was happening. Osu panned his weapon left and put three rounds through the center mass of another attacker.

He glanced across at the unarmored workforce. They were firing back with sidearms. Some had definitely been hit but getting the wounded out and treated was De Ketele's role. For the moment, Osu's job was to shoot RILs.

The grenade in the lifeless alien hand went off, making Osu tense, but it was a smoker, throwing inky blackness into the air over the newts, although the device fell back into the water, nullifying most of its effect. More grenades went off behind him. He chanced a look and saw the roofs of both beetles enveloped in artificial darkness.

Unable to see, the turret gunners ceased fire.

Meanwhile, Osu was searching for targets to service among the tangle of dripping tails and gray limbs. He realized with a shudder that the Littoranes had worn what looked like heated wetsuit jerkins over their trunks, but heads, limbs, and tails were protected against the deep freeze conditions by nothing more than the circular metallic tattoos they favored.

"Gives us something to aim for," Osu told himself, but in truth he was troubled by the way the newts had adapted so readily to the conditions on this ice world. It meant they could exploit the terrain in ways that wouldn't even occur to the Legion.

But they hadn't won this time. They were all dead or dying.

"Sierra 1-5-6, Sierra 4-1-0, do you need support?"

Lieutenant Stuart was calling him over the general broadcast channel. Why wasn't he using direct comms?

He noticed his helm's alert overlay was flashing a warning message at the bottom of his HUD: *suit comm system damaged*.

The RILs had shot him and he hadn't felt anything. It was a common problem with blaster bolts, which killed their targets by warping the air into plasma, not through kinetic impact. His comms were on the fritz, but he'd still come out of it better than the big aliens heaped on the edge of the ice, with sightless eyes, seared flesh, and gills flapping feebly.

"Sierra 1-5-6, Sierra 4-1-0…"

Osu assessed that *this* attack had been neutralized. He knew that was what he was supposed to tell the lieutenant, but he was tired of holding back the 27th's true strength. The Legion wasn't designed to fight insurgents. This wasn't the kind of war he'd trained for.

"…do you need support?"

But the officer's orders had been clear.

"Sierra 4-1-0, this is Sierra 1-5-6 I do not require support. Beetle-2 call signs, keep alert for RILs playing dead. They look retired, but we can't risk what looks like newt blood turning out to be exploded packs of fish sauce."

"That would have to be a fuck-ton of fish sauce," said a nearby legionary.

One of the newts moved!

Osu put a round into it.

The newt shook away the bodies of its comrades and charged. At Osu.

What the hell just happened?

He let out half a breath, expelling the question of how the newt was unhurt along with his spent air. He steadied the red dot of his helm's sighting reticle on the flat Littorane head and eased back the trigger.

The charged rails of his PA-71 spun a flechette tipped with NG-enriched supermetals, propelling it out the muzzle at two klicks per second in a plume of ionized air. His combat armor absorbed the bulk of the recoil kick that could shatter the shoulder of an unprotected shooter. Even so, the distraction of the recoil slap was enough that he couldn't tell where his dart had gone. Not at the target, that was for sure.

Osu couldn't miss at this range. The reticle had lied to him. Or the galaxy had gone insane. Either way, this was not good.

The Littorane hissed in defiance and kept coming.

It didn't seem injured at all. How had it survived the fire the legionaries had poured into it?

Switching to iron sights, Osu was about to fire a burst at point-blank range when he realized that he hadn't missed at all. Other rail-gun rounds assailed the RIL and sparked fire as they deflected off an invisible barrier surrounding the alien.

Force shield!

Flicking on its safety catch, Osu dropped his rifle and prepared to meet the threat, suddenly very conscious of how massive Littoranes were.

By the Five Hells! How did it get a force shield?

The newt dug all six limbs into the ice and stopped, just four feet from Osu.

"Knives out," he shouted, drawing his own foot-long blade and advancing warily on the Littorane, who watched him through enormous dark eyes. The fat, fish-like lips that stretched the full width of its mouth parted and lifted. The damned newt even raised a fleshy eye ridge.

Is that thing laughing at me?

PA-71s couldn't defeat this ancient and rare military tech. But this had to be the porous type of shield—it had to be, or else it would be punching a hemisphere down into the ice. And with the porous type, the training manual said you could ooze through the barrier and gut the enemy inside. Could be a few bruises by the time he got home tonight, though. He grinned. Didn't matter. He knew just the right person to rub them better.

"Come on," he taunted the RIL as they began to circle each other. "Let me show you how I fillet fish."

"Odd Beetle-2 call signs, overwatch," ordered De Ketele. "Even Beetle-2 call signs, knives out and close on hostile."

Why was De Ketele repeating…?

The warning message in Osu's helm switched to: *suit comm system total failure.*

A plume of spray erupted from the water a short distance away, stirring the smoke where the grenade had fallen in. Under cover of this distraction, Osu seized his chance and lunged at his opponent, but he'd come in too fast and bounced off the force wall, rolling back along the ice and coming up to rest on one knee with blade out.

But the bulky amphibian wasn't interested in him. It was using its tail to swat away circling legionaries like flies.

Meanwhile, the plume rising from the water had firmed into the form of a curved tunnel carving its way through the smoke on the water's edge. Inside that bubble was another Littorane. This one had a spiked club attached to the tip of its tail.

It barreled through the line of armored legionaries, who fired on it to no effect, and carried on to the work party of ice sculptors who ran for safety. But it didn't chase them. As it flicked back its tail while still on the canter, it was obvious this newt had come to smash the ice manipulator machines.

But one SOTL hadn't abandoned his equipment.

"Hey! Fish head!" called Yergin. "Watch this!"

The RIL turned to face the man. Yergin fired his plasma pistol in its face.

Unlike the hypersonic darts that traveled too fast for the human eye to track, the ball of plasma seemed to scorch through the air in slow motion, spreading out over the force shield as it curved around the RIL's face.

Dazzled, Yergin's assailant swung its tail at the annoying human.

A good hit with an armed tail tip could smash through light vehicles, batter legionaries inside the best combat armor, and would have had no trouble ending Yergin, except the SOTL was no longer there. He was sprinting for one of the ice manipulators, ducking under the tail as it came over and sliding along his side on the slick ice until he was where he wanted to be.

The RIL charged Yergin but was enveloped by heavy blaster fire from one of the turrets that must have freed itself from the smoke. It was a powerful light show. Energy weapons would never penetrate its shield, but the newt was blinded.

Osu was supposed to be in a melee himself, but his opponent didn't seem to regard him as a threat and was engrossed in the other fight.

"That's right," he said to himself as he crept up. "Keep watching the show."

Trying to imagine he was landing face first on a soft sea of bubbles, rather than 300 pounds of hostile amphibian, Osu tipped himself onto the Littorane. The force shield pushed back, but not hard. He began to sink through.

"It's a dead newt walking."

Osu looked up at the unexpected voice and saw SOTL Zy Pel riding the Littorane's tail and holding a bloodied blade aloft. It was unlike anything Osu had ever seen: twin crescent blades with a neon green edge.

"Poison blade," explained Zy Pel.

Poison? Since when had the Legion ever authorized the use of poison? It wasn't just the weird blade; there was a lot about Hines Zy Pel that was nonstandard. One day, Osu would get to the truth of the man's story, but first they both had to survive the Littorane attack. With Osu still not quite through the force shield, its wearer shook itself, ridding it of the two legionaries like human fleas.

It raced for its comrade who'd attacked Yergin.

But Yergin was no easy prey.

The sapper had penetrated his RIL's force shield and was sitting on the ice manipulator canister while gripping the base of the newt's tail as if riding a highly pissed off alligator. Bending low across the alien's back, he was firing a weapon. At first, with all the violent motion, and with Osu jogging off to assist, it was difficult to see what Yergin was trying to do.

And then it became clear.

The weapon he was firing…it was the manipulator hose. He was aiming it at the RIL's head like a flamethrower. Or, rather—Osu corrected himself—as an ice thrower.

Yergin, you're a genius!

A thick spear of ice shot through the RIL's throat.

Yergin wriggled into another position and sculptured a fan of ice that burst out of the newt's chest.

"Jump!" screamed Osu a second before the newt he'd been fighting slammed into its comrade that Yergin had speared with ice.

Yergin did jump. But just as the force shield made it difficult to get inside, so it made it difficult to exit in a hurry. He bounced off the inside of the invisible barrier.

The two force shield bubbles slammed into each other like extreme bowling on ice. Osu's newt transferred most of its momentum to Yergin's which went spinning off the ice and into the water, taking a flailing Yergin down with it. Osu's newt followed, slithering off the ice floe with a trembling body and half its limbs limp.

It seemed Zy Pel's poison was working. Not that its usefulness was going to lessen the reaming out he'd earned for carrying an unauthorized weapon.

Osu began organizing Yergin's rescue.

But the sapper bobbed back to the surface, which brought a sigh of relief to Osu. He had no desire to send people under the water if he could avoid it. The newts *owned* that zone.

Strong hands reached down and hauled Yergin wet and shivering out of the water.

While De Ketele updated Osu on the casualty situation—two being treated inside the beetle for blaster wounds—Grymz used the surviving ice manipulator to first melt the ice that had formed on Yergin's clothing and then jet warm air over him.

"If you're offering salon service, Corp," Zy Pel said to Grymz, "I could do with a shave and haircut."

Yergin gave a shaky laugh. Osu expected Grymz to offer a piece of his mind, but he said nothing. What was it about Zy Pel that let him get away with murder?

As Yergin walked off to the warm beetle, Osu looked over the edge at the half-built ice bridge. Legionaries could hop across, but it was nowhere near enough for the beetles.

"Strengthen the bridge," he told Grymz. "De Ketele, organize overwatch. My comms are fried. I need to speak with the lieutenant in person."

De Ketele didn't reply. He shrugged and pointed behind Osu.

"I'm here," said the lieutenant.

Osu looked around to see not just the lieutenant but everyone out of both beetles, including two sappers on stretchers.

"It is not necessary to work further on the bridge, Grymz," said the lieutenant. "We're still bait and must not appear impregnable."

Osu didn't like what he was hearing. The newts had force shields. What other surprises had they in store? It was one thing to take an inexperienced officer out to fix the drains, but this had become a serious battlezone.

"Seeing as I'm off-grid," Osu said, "I'd better stick with you, sir. De Ketele, take my place. The men are yours now."

They made it safely across the half-built ice bridge without incident, abandoning their wagons with ramps sealed tight and false smoke now billowing from both of them.

With eyes and weapons covering every potential avenue of attack, including from below the ice, they initiated a tactical withdrawal to the north.

When they were half a klick from the far shore and the lure of cover in the trees there, the Littorane army made its move.

And it *was* an army.

The newts emerged from the trees and crossed the southern shoreline onto the lake. Osu estimated four hundred RILs, protected by armored pads and armed with blaster rifles. Their tail tips were fitted out with maces or slingshot holders like catcher's mitts in which they held homemade bombs. With their six limbs splayed out from their heavy, low-slung bodies, they dashed across the ice with menacing intent…and high speed.

"Reckon they bought it, sir," said Osu.

Littoranes were masters of close quarter combat. If they had force shields that allowed them to close with impunity, they wouldn't need their firearms to wipe out the legionaries.

"Let them close," said the lieutenant.

"If they're shielded," Osu advised him, "we need to secure our egress across the north bank. We need to do it now."

"You're right," replied Stuart, bringing his rifle up to his shoulder. He fired three rounds. A klick away, two of the RILs went down, sending ripples of disruption as the tightly packed newts stumbled over their fallen comrades.

"Shields don't seem to be a problem," stated the lieutenant cheerfully, and Osu began to believe that this might still be the one-sided contest they'd all hoped for. Sure, the RILs were heavy-duty bruisers, but their complete disdain for spacing revealed they had the tactical awareness of an unruly mob. This was going to be a turkey shoot, just with oversized turkeys armed with blasters.

"Nonetheless," said Stuart, "take four armored men and secure a route off this lake into the northern tree line."

Tapping the shoulders of Zy Pel, Heidl, Bulmer, and Urdizine, Osu led his team across the ice to the north bank a few hundred meters away.

"I'm hoping you can see through the trees, Urdizine," said Osu through external speakers. "I can't see a thing."

The Zhoogene sapper gave the trilling laugh of his species. "Your human sight is limited, but that's why legionaries wear helms."

"Maybe," said Zy Pel, "but some of us humes have eyes in the back of our heads. Everyone else, keep scanning the north bank. Sarge, you need to look behind."

Osu turned and saw.

Shit!

The enemy was raising dripping equipment through the gap in the ice they had blown when they'd first revealed themselves. The contraptions looked like large portable solar panels angled back and mounted on ski sleds.

The RIL column advancing from the opposite shoreline flowed around this gap in the ice and formed up behind the equipment panels, which had closed into a line and were being pushed at speed toward Stuart and the main mass of legionaries.

PA-71 volley fire raked the enemy mass. Bright flashes sparked in front of the panels, but the RILs behind were completely unscathed.

"Portable shield generators," murmured Osu to himself. "Who's supplying them with this? Even the Legion doesn't have this tech anymore."

And it got worse. Some of the RILs had detached from the main group and were trying to gain access to the abandoned beetles. Holy Azhanti! If the enemy could get into the turrets...

"Movement," said Urdizine. "In the trees to the north."

The legionaries didn't wait to get a clearer look. PA-71s spat hypersonic darts into the trees, shredding needles, bark, and Littorane flesh.

Screaming blaster fire scorched through the air from the trees. *Tchewww...tchewww...tchewww.*

At this 300-meter range, the deadliness of the enemy blasters was blunted, but amid the blaster whine came the crack of slug-throwing rifles.

"I'm hit," said Heidl. "Arm wound. Bullet. Non-critical."

The return fire from the trees ceased abruptly.

"Hold position," Osu ordered. "If there are still hostiles active, closing only makes their blasters more effective."

He took a knee and scanned the shoreline and the forest a short distance beyond. There was no sign of the RILs, but he spotted movement a hundred yards east of the position the Littoranes had fired from. A couple of small cylinders rolled out of the trees and onto the ice. One flashed gold, the other red.

The colors of the Legion.

"Hold your fire," said Osu. "Friendlies are in control of our exit route."

Finally! It's begun.

"Keep any wounded RILs alive!" shouted Zy Pel into the trees he'd been shooting at moments earlier. "Moving down range," he added for the legionaries as he sprinted for the shore. "Try not to shoot me."

Osu let him go. "Heidl, what's your status?"

"Full range of motion. Hurts like it's been sat on by a lardy Jotun."

He took a look at the black column of death thundering toward the lieutenant's position behind their impenetrable line of force shields. The weight of the RIL mass was making the ice crack like thunder. It would be tempting to call in a fire mission to blow the ice beneath them, but there were legionaries too on the ice.

Even so, he downgraded the RIL threat. "Heidl, report an update to the lieutenant and seek assistance from medics."

"Yes, Sergeant."

"We will advance to the tree line," Osu told Bulmer and Urdizine. "Confirm targets before firing."

"Sergeant," called Heidl, "the LT wants you with him."

He's not the LT, thought Osu angrily. The LT died on Irisur. As good as murdered by the Militia but it was me who failed his mission.

"Sergeant?" prompted Urdizine.

Osu waved on the Zhoogene legionary. "Go. Take Bulmer with you and don't let Zy Pel do anything too stupid."

"Captain Estrup just sent us her compliments," announced Lieutenant Stuart when Osu jogged over to him. "I've been invited to the 302nd's mess tonight."

The RILs were close enough now that in order to be heard over their battle cries, Stuart's external speakers were cranked so high they were distorting.

The legionaries had their knives fixed to their PA-71s as bayonets, waiting for the onslaught. The momentum of the newts, though…if they slammed into the legionary line, they would sweep through the 27th's detachment like a bulldozer.

SOTLs were beginning to glance anxiously at each other. He didn't blame them. De Ketele would be steadying them, though.

The lieutenant didn't appear concerned. In fact, he sounded pleased with himself. And with good reason. Captain Marianne Estrup, 2nd battalion, 302nd, was notoriously difficult to impress, but that hadn't stopped the 27th's CO, Major Cartwright, from trying ever since the squadron had arrived on Rho-Torkis.

Osu cursed Estrup silently. What the hell are you waiting for?

Throughout the Federation and beyond, the Legion had a reputation.

The truth was that the Legion's federal budget had been assaulted by the Militia and their political allies since the dawn of time, in theory to bolster the *People's Army,* as the Legion's enemies liked to call the Militia when they wanted votes in the Senate, but mostly to line their own personal accounts.

The reality was that the Legion operated ancient equipment kept going by cannibalized parts, duct tape, and fighting spirit. Powerful weapons from ancient times were hoarded and kept secret from the Militia. Or maybe that was just a rumor.

Since a decade ago, when the scandal of corruption had erupted at the very top of the Legion's own ranks, the death grip on the Legion's funding had tightened.

But none of that had been enough to take away the Legion's reputation. Not yet. If you crossed the Legion, you died.

A very simple equation.

No warning. No mercy. And even without the equipment it deserved, the Legion was highly effective at killing its enemies.

The RILs on this planet had forgotten that.

A lesson had to be taught, and the Federation must see its delivery.

No one had expected the RILs in such numbers, or to be so well equipped with precious equipment the Legion would dearly love to claim for its own.

No one had been sure the party of sappers would be ambushed on their mission to fix the drains.

But it had been judged a possibility, an opportunity for the Legion to kill its enemies. And so the 302nd brigade had deeply embedded its 1st battalion in the area around the 27th's maintenance mission, and 2nd battalion around the route from Camp Faxian.

Tunnels and observation posts had been prepared in secret during the dark of the night—no easy matter in this frozen ground—requiring all the 27th's engineering skill. The 302nd had occupied them three days before.

Hiding.

Waiting.

The ambushers were to be ambushed.

So why wasn't the 302nd firing?

The force shield panels spread out, leaving gaps between them.

A deluge of newt blaster fire flew out at the 27th, sizzling the air. But the fire was wild. The RILs were hellbent on closing and smashing the legionaries, tail to face.

Osu picked a target and sent a burst of flechettes into the newt who dropped and spun along the ice, tripping the crush of RILs flowing through the narrow gap.

Along the line, the result was the same, as legionaries— Lieutenant Stuart among them—poured accurate fire into the first of their foe to emerge from behind the force shields.

But the gaps between the shields widened all the time, and behind them waited hundreds of the alien warriors itching to kill. They were mere yards away.

Suddenly, the momentum leeched out of the enemy mass.

Osu took out a RIL to his left who was upon them, swinging its tail at one of the SOTLs. The dead newt's swing clattered the legionary onto the ice.

It was the only foe to make contact with the 27th's line.

Thunderclaps punched the air from the distant north and south shores of the lake, a thunder god smashing his mighty hands together into the mass of RILs. Smiting them.

The surviving newts at the front of the attack began looking behind to see why their comrades were no longer following.

The sight they faced was of RILs being shredded by railgun fire. Farther out, at the western shoreline, they would see pinpricks of blue-tinged fire—the characteristic muzzle flashes of PA-71s ripping the air into plasma.

It was the northeast and southeast edges of the lake that interested Osu most. They were also studded with PA-71 muzzle flashes, but from each direction there was one much larger gout of flame.

"Captain Estrup sends her apologies," remarked the lieutenant. "The southern GX-cannon jammed, and she deemed it necessary to wait until she could deliver the dramatic panorama she requires."

Azhanti! The 302nd had GX-cannon!

Osu took out a lone RIL looking desperately for an escape route.

There weren't any. Not inside a GX crossfire.

The fearsome infantry support weapons were relics of the Orion Era. Meticulously maintained, almost venerated, over thousands of years, the official report would make no mention of these legendary weapons lest the Militia claim them for their own. But the grim sight of their destructive effect...that would be shown throughout the Federation.

There would be image capture experts working on the massacre as it was taking place. And in a day or so, they would take the sickening sight of frozen RIL corpses heaped on an ice lake and turn it into an iconic vision of the fate that befell all enemies of the Legion.

The usual idiots would decry the Legion as evil, that legionaries gloried in slaughter. That wasn't true, but the Legion wasn't there to be liked. It was there to hold the line.

And if it ever failed in that holy mission, then those carping about Legion brutality would be clutching the guts spilling from their bellies, wondering how the galaxy had suddenly become so unfair.

As for the images, they would serve to reinforce the Legion's reputation.

Cross the Legion. You will die.

But who was really confronting the Legion here? The RILs had gotten what was coming to them, but someone had set them up.

Whoever you are, you'd better start running.

At least, that was what Osu tried telling himself, but he couldn't quite believe it. Someone with deep resources and influence had instigated this.

Someone with an agenda.

Whoever that was, Osu didn't believe they would be running. More likely, they would see this as an opening skirmish in a campaign. It would get much worse for the Federation before it got better.

Osu's spirits didn't lift after they left the lake under the control of the 302nd and set off for Camp Faxian in the beetles.

"It's quite the mess, Sarge," said Zy Pel, accosting Osu as he was passing through the mid-section on the way to checking on Heidl's wound.

"Speak clearly, SOTL," Osu snapped back, in no mood for Zy Pel's games.

"What I meant to say, is that it would be easier if we knew why we were fighting. I interrogated one of the RILs. Didn't get much, but you should see this. *Privately*."

They set a helm-to-helm deep-link and Zy Pel replayed a recording of his interrogation.

A Littorane lay curled on its side among the red-stained snow scattered with green needles. Where the RIL's torso thinned into tail, its flesh had been blasted away to reveal shattered tail vertebrae. It must have been in agony, but it was prepared to talk nonetheless.

"You die why pointless?" said Zy Pel. "We Legion, Littorane. Human main allies from time of Shepherd-Nurture your-queen are. Together strong alliance make still. Why you try kill me?"

The RIL stared up at Zy Pel, who seemed from the camera angle to be crouching in the snow. It drew in deep wet-sounding breaths but did not immediately reply.

If Zy Pel hadn't felt this footage was important enough to pass on, Osu would have assumed the RIL hadn't understood the human words.

When Far Reach Federation was first settled, widely available translator systems meant language had not been a barrier between Littoranes and other races.

Now, however, successfully speaking to Littoranes involved a pidgin language stemming from the archaic versions of English and Littorane Standardized Military Dialect used in the time of the Exiles. With the furious rate at which Littorane groups had spun out from the original Exiles and diverged, even if anyone still understood how to reprogram the translators, it would be a challenge to keep up with the linguistic drift. It was so immense that Littoranes from different systems often used this human pidgin to converse with each other.

The RIL gave a long, gurgling exhalation and spoke. "We truth have. Blasphemer terror men. We know. Know we do of evidence Khallini-man via."

"Evidence no no!" said Zy Pel firmly. "Liar Khallini-man. Lady Indiya of Goddess we follow still. Blasphemer no. Liar Khallini-man. Holy war good. You war stupid. You war blaspheme. Goddess angry. Tell evidence Khallini-man."

"Truthspeak now. You die. You lie. You death big." The RIL shuddered, and then lifted itself up on its front limbs and spat blood over Zy Pel's helm.

"Your Indiya offended the Goddess," said the alien in perfect modern human speech. "For two thousand of your years. All those who follow her will die. The Legion must die. This, at the lake, is just the beginning."

"I don't believe it," said Zy Pel. "You're being used."

But the newt's only reply was to reach with a trembling limb for its blaster, which was several feet away in the snow. Might have been a lightyear away for the critically wounded RIL.

"Don't!" shouted Zy Pel, lurching forward to kick the blaster away, but as he did so the Littorane reached suddenly for something slung beneath its torso.

Two legionaries out of sight blew its head off with their PA-71s.

The world looked even bleaker than normal to Osu. This had been only the second day since they'd arrived on Rho-Torkis when the planet hadn't seemed to be actively trying to kill them with blizzards and rad-storms. The locals had taken up the weather's slack, and if they were convinced that the Legion was the enemy, then today's slaughter on the lake would only encourage them to further violence.

"Good work, Zy Pel. I'll pass this on to the lieutenant with my report. The RIL talked of Khallini-man. Is that the name of a person? Do you have any idea who that might be?"

"I don't know."

Osu gave a disappointed grunt. Sometimes Hines Zy Pel knew secrets no regular legionary had a right to. The man denied having ever been in Legion Special Missions, but it was a denial that lacked conviction.

"You know more than you're admitting, Zy Pel."

His expression changed to one that Osu had never seen before. One of awkwardness. Pain. Loss. Was this the real Hines Zy Pel he was seeing for the first time?

"You're right, Sarge. I have speculations. Nothing more than that. But speaking of them could get you killed real fast. Pass the footage up the chain and let others speculate. And, Sarge, whatever you might think you know about my past, it doesn't mean anything. I'm a sapper of the Legion. Nothing more. I swear that to you on my honor and the honor of the Legion."

Osu held his gaze for a few seconds and then nodded. Zy Pel's words would suffice.

For now.

* * * * *

Chapter Three:
Osu Sybutu

The mood in the general chow hall at Camp Faxian was rowdier than normal, but Osu wasn't ready to join in yet. He sat on the end of a table staring pensively into his empty food tray. Despite his hunger, he hadn't joined the long queues for the food hatches that were still functioning. There was someone he was hoping to accidentally bump into.

For the moment, he was glad that preparing an official account of the day's events had kept him apart from the men in his troop. There was so much going on—so much, he suspected, that had barely begun—that he needed to spend a little time working these dangerous thoughts through his head.

Three thousand years before, the Exiles had settled at Far Reach in the Perseus Arm of the galaxy, cut off forever from Earth and the Orion Spur by unimaginably vast distances. In those far-off days, many of the first settlers still referred to themselves as the Human Legion as if it were a single unified entity.

It wasn't.

In its first decades, the fledgling Federation had battled for survival against both the harshness of alien ecosystems and then slave raiders and invasion fleets. The need to work together today, or die apart tomorrow, had taped over the worst of the cracks. They even gave themselves a new name—the Amilxi—and for a time, individuals of all species, religions, and political persuasions pledged themselves to this new identity.

And when the Federation could at last breathe easy, free for a time from existential crises, the cracks in its unity had been ripped apart in blood and bullets.

It was after the first nukes had started flying, and after asteroids had already been towed into orbits that would suck them down into planetary gravity wells, that the rival leaders of the Federation paused, their heads collectively knocked together by those old enough to remember a distant time when the factions had stood shoulder-to-shoulder in the War of Liberation.

The asteroids were diverted into safe orbits.

Seals were replaced on the nukes.

And the deep split that had caused the exile in the first place was acknowledged in a new constitutional settlement.

Military forces split along factional lines. The Far Reach Militia took responsibility for system planetary defenses and protecting against internal disorder. Their supporters were allowed to retain their dominance over the Senate and Council.

The other faction was renamed the New Human Legion, although that name was soon simplified to the Legion as the Federation began admitting planets populated by species native to the Perseus Arm. It became the Far Reach Federation's mobile strike force, and a balance to the Militia's political influence. It was the Legion who had held the line in the war-filled centuries that followed, and the Legion who had then taken sword and fire deep into the home sectors of the Federation's external enemies.

There hadn't been a war for over a thousand years. Neither inside nor outside the Federation's borders. Not unless you counted the Gorgantheletta Eruption, and that had thankfully been constrained to a single world.

And there were many who muttered that perhaps the consequences of peace were not all benign.

Over time, the authors of the constitution had thought the divisions of their era would gradually fade into irrelevance.

They hadn't.

The Militia had become so corrupt that Osu regarded it as an enemy of the Federation. And the Legion had been starved of funding for so long that if the Federation should ever again face an invader, they would find their doughty Legion had turned brittle.

And then, a decade ago, the treachery of Legion First General Clarke swept over the Federation like a breath of fetid air. Before that day of infamy, the Legion had known it was the only stalwart institution in the Federation because it was incorruptible. Its honor shone like a beacon of hope in the mire of degenerate pessimism. Not all citizens loved the Legion, but even those doubters trusted it to do what it felt was right.

Until Clarke, the Commander-in-Chief of the Legion, had been discovered passing military secrets to foreign powers.

The years since then had been a febrile darkness. These were the end times. From the songs and stories of popular culture to hushed conversations in bars, everyone in Far Reach talked of an inevitable cataclysm to come. Precisely what form that cataclysm would take was a matter of wild speculation, but few would deny that the last days of the Federation in its current form were around the corner.

Utter drent.

That's what Osu had thought of the chunder-brained, defeatist talk.

Until the posting to Rho-Torkis.

Until today.

"I hear you cooked up a little drama out in RIL country."

Osu looked up into the grinning face of Sergeant Nydella Sanderson of 4th battalion, 83rd Brigade, who'd sortied out from a passing group of friends.

"I..." Osu started, then gave up talking and grinned instead. Nydella was the reason he was sitting hungry at the table, and not queueing for the food hatch. But he'd been so deep in thought, he hadn't noticed her.

He shrugged. "Nothing we couldn't handle."

Nydella arched an eyebrow. "Really? I hear you had to get your arses pulled out of the fire by the 302nd. The three-oh-second! If that's not humiliation, I don't know what is. You should have stuck to digging ditches."

"You're just jealous because SOTLs can send flechettes downrange just as well as you, but we've got skills on top that are completely out of reach of you ass scratchers. For a start, you'd need to understand words with more than two syllables."

Howls of derision launched from Nydella's friends.

"Ditch sniffer."

"Wedgehead."

"Tunnel Tester."

But it was all in good humor, and she waved them away and took a seat opposite Osu.

Whatever she had been about to say, she thought better of it. Her serious face came into play. "Hey, Sybutu! Cheer up, man. You didn't lose anyone today."

He forced a smile. "No, not since Irisur."

She grabbed his forearms, and he found himself looking into her dark eyes.

Sanderson was a robust no-nonsense legionary, which was exactly how Osu liked his women. But Nydella was different. Special. When she chose to deploy them, her open smile twinned with twinkling dark eyes could penetrate his hardest mood and bathe his heart in warmth. No one else had ever been able to do that.

But her eyes weren't smiling now.

"Irisur was months ago," she told him. "You are not responsible for Lieutenant Szenti's death. But today you *were* responsible for your SOTLs. As you will be tomorrow. And the day after. Osu, I'm not saying forget Szenti. Just put his memory in the right slot, okay?"

He shook his head. "It's not just the LT. The mess on Irisur...I can't be sure, but I think it's happening here too. We didn't just encounter a rabble with a few old rifles today."

"I heard. Holy Azhanti, Osu. They had force panels."

"What's going on here?" he growled. "The others aren't concerned yet, but you and I know—"

She dug her fingers into his arms. "We know *nothing*."

Osu freed his hands and crossed them behind his head, trying to look casual. Man, his arms hurt! "Fair point," he said with a shrug, because with all these inexplicable things going on, there was one rock-solid certainty. The secret they shared needed to *stay* secret.

He had been stupid. He could have gotten them both killed as intruders. But that night had been wild, and there was no point asking what he had been thinking of because the reason was sitting in front of him.

The mission of the two infantry brigades, and now the 27th engineers too, was to protect, support, and isolate the military archaeology going on four klicks to the northeast of Camp Faxian. Area of Special Interest 39.

The two brigades acted as border guards, boots to pound ASI-39's security perimeter, but not welcome on the inside where the final zone of security was provided by Strike Shoal Seven, an elite unit of the Legion with—perhaps ironically—Littorane personnel.

What better way to show off to the boots with the pretty eyes that followed his every move than to enter the forbidden zone? ASI-39 itself?

In truth, it wasn't quite as impossible as Sanderson thought.

Before the Legion took an interest, local archaeologists had dug up a few pre-Federation artifacts at a place they had named the Grove of Serenity. When the Legion took over, pressing many of the archaeologists into military service, the first team here had dug a few ditches and levies as required and started plugging in portable power generators, adding piecemeal to the infrastructure with no thought of how big an operation this would eventually become.

Eventually, someone with a little sense realized the generators running through the same power grid, already stacked far beyond safety limits, would not support the big jump in power requirements for the next phase of the operation. That's when they called in the 27th.

And not a moment too soon. It was obvious to the most junior SOTL that it was a miracle ASI-39 hadn't yet drowned, collapsed, or burned down in an electrical fire.

While the 27th worked in the blizzards of the initial weeks of its deployment, trying to first make the grove safe before expanding, Osu had gotten to know the lay of the land, including the many conduits and buried channels the SOTLs could use to move around the site without the howling winds beating them to death. As to what the archaeologists thought they'd found, he'd been no more the wiser.

But that night, two weeks ago, it had suddenly felt right and proper that he and Sanderson should find out. With luck fueled by copious brandies—and amplified by the ancient urge to impress someone hot—Osu had led her to the grove's secret heart.

The only secrets they found there were each other, and that was more than enough, all thoughts of discovering cold artifacts flushed away by the joys of discovering warm flesh. As they were enjoying each other in the heat and shelter of a power junction hut, the floor had suddenly shaken beneath them. Osu had glanced up to see the power throughput monitor on the console above his head was nearing critical. What the hell was all that power needed for?

With warm protective gear back on, they left the hut to confront a wondrous sight.

Beneath gentle snow flurries, the ground nearby had revealed itself to be giant ice-covered panels. These slid aside to expose a cavernous underground area like the hangar of a capital warship, although there was only one vessel they could see. Presented to the nighttime sky, an artifact that strongly resembled a small starship was being raised on a pedestal from the depths. Its front section was 120 meters long, and it looked as if its conventional cylindrical shape was made of metal. Three sweptback angular wings bristled with gun ports. The hull also sprouted segmented protrusions of what looked like bleached bone the length of a human arm. These bone hairs dangled limply.

The weirdest aspect was the rear. The ship had a 100-meter long tail in a slight S-curve that rested on the pedestal. It looked flexible and blubbery, like a Littorane's, and indeed like a Littorane warrior it ended in a spiked thagomizer club.

They watched in awe as the ship awoke.

A blue glow emerged from the hatch in its hull through which fat power cables snaked. The bone hairs stood erect and then bent upward to point at the sky.

Its long tail twitched.

"Let's get out of here." Osu started to get up.

Nydella held him back. "It's beautiful."

"*You're* beautiful." He pointed at the alien ship that surely was the explanation for all the excitement over Rho-Torkis. "That down there—that's *danger*. It's something we never saw. It's something we never discuss. Understand?"

"Sergeant Sybutu," she said with drunken solemnity, "often the most beautiful things in the galaxy are also the most dangerous."

"Okay. You're dangerous, Sanderson. And—I guess I like it. But I like avoiding a court-martial even more."

"Oorah," she said offering a hazy salute. "Take me home, Sybutu."

They both took a last look at the ship. Its tail stopped twitching and started extending, stretching back a good twenty meters.

Suddenly, the hut behind them exploded into a cacophony of electronic alarms and the rattle of isolators kicking in as the power feeding into that thing below tripped emergency shutdown protocols.

The light in the ship's interior winked out, and they noticed the power hum by its sudden absence. The portable spotlights on the ground were on a different circuit and they illuminated the ship's death throes as its bone hairs fought for the sky, and its tail-tip flicked aggressively in what looked like a combat strike.

It fought for about ten seconds before sinking down onto the pedestal.

Osu had the sense the ship had fallen unconscious.

Sanderson must have felt the same because she murmured, "I wonder what it dreams of."

Technicians and officials emerged from their hiding places into the hangar space. The recriminations over what had gone wrong were loud enough to reach the witnesses who had no business being there.

In the confusion, the two lovers had made their escape.

Osu was pried from his memory by a smile that stretched to sparkling eyes. "Want to talk about it?"

Knotted muscles relaxed. His worries fled. There were many things about Nydella Sanderson he admired and enjoyed, but most of all, she knew when and how to listen. But that wasn't what he needed now.

He shook his head. "First, I need food. Damned cold makes me hungry. It's beers with the wagon crew in the Washington Drift Bar at 20:00 hours. Want to come?"

She gave him a look of pure innocence that fooled absolutely no one. "It's 17:00 now. How high are you planning to heap that food tray? Unless you're considering death by gluttony, you should have a few hours to kill before 20:00. I could suggest a suitable after-dinner activity to fill the time."

Osu looked away, reluctant to appear too serious. "You mean more to me than someone to kill time."

He glanced back at her face, fearing she would be backing away from his words, and equally worried that she was delighted by them.

"I know," she replied with a noncommittal smile.

His processor block trilled. With an apologetic shrug, he snapped in an ear stud.

"Go for Sybutu."

"You have been summoned." It was far below freezing outside, but the chill in Squadron Sergeant Major Vyborg's voice was colder still. "Get yourself to the colonel's office. Now!"

"Do you know why, Sergeant Major?"

"I was hoping you could tell me. Think, man, what have you done?"

Sanderson gave him a look of sympathy.

"I don't know, Sergeant Major."

"Oh, good," said Vyborg in a voice that sounded the polar opposite of good. "I do so love it when my NCOs present me with a *fucking mystery*."

"Maybe it's good news," Osu replied before adding quickly, "On my way. Sybutu out."

He looked at the serving hatch and Sergeant Sanderson with an equally distraught sense of loss.

"I'll bring snacks when I join you tonight at Washington Drift," she told him. "Now go."

He snatched a kiss and tried to smarten his uniform before facing the colonel.

* * * * *

Chapter Four:
Osu Sybutu

Newly promoted Lieutenant Colonel Malix had arrived on Rho-Torkis on the same transport as the 27th, taking up the position of executive officer to Major-General Levesque, the commander of all Legion operations in the system. The man's promotion irked Osu's sense of justice because Malix had been the XO to Colonel Lantosh on Irisur, and no one should be rewarded for the way that ugly business had turned out.

And yet here he was, looking settled in his padded chair behind the second-swankiest desk in Camp Faxian.

Lieutenant Stuart and Squadron Sergeant Major Vyborg were present too. Stuart sat down when Malix gestured for them to do so. Vyborg remained as tautly erect as an orbital elevator cable.

So did Osu, who tried not to breathe and wished invisibility upon himself as he looked for clues as to why he'd been summoned. Had he and Nydella been spotted at the dig site and the consequences had only now reached him? If so, things would go very badly for both of them.

He hadn't spoken to Lieutenant Colonel Malix since Irisur. It had been Malix who'd ordered him not to intervene in the betrayal of good people, but it was Osu who had obeyed those orders and stood aside when he could have made a difference. His choice to make a mockery of the LT's sacrifice.

As for Vyborg, he had shrink rays blasting out his eyes that made Osu feel two-inches tall.

Only Lieutenant Stuart seemed oblivious to the atmosphere that was as charged as a spinal mount railgun.

"Stuart," said the colonel conversationally, "I asked you to drop by because I want to borrow Sergeant Sybutu and some of your half-troop for a special assignment that will take about a week to ten days. I've already cleared it with Major Cartwright. I just wanted to give you a chance to voice any concerns."

"I'm curious as to the task," said the lieutenant, "but if the major's okay with it, then I'm sure I can work around the temporary absence of Sybutu and…how many men?"

Out the corner of his eye, Osu saw Malix pause to consider his answer.

Azhanti! The colonel hadn't thought of that?

"Five," he answered, turning to Vyborg with a questioning look. "Sergeant Major?"

Vyborg's face reddened. The enlisted personnel belonged to him as far as he was concerned. Malix was the senior staff officer on the planet, but that didn't give him leave to 'borrow' Vyborg's people on what looked like a spur of the moment whim.

The sergeant major cleared his throat. "May I ask for what purpose, Colonel?"

"I regret I cannot say. Sybutu demonstrated the ability to work independently back on Irisur. I have a task that is somewhat clandestine in nature, and I feel that to dispatch him without an officer will attract less attention."

"Is that wise, sir?" asked the sergeant major in a tone that made very clear his view on this matter.

"We shall see." The colonel's expression suddenly went as hard as stone. "Are you making an objection, Sergeant Major?"

"No, sir. Not at this moment."

"Splendid." Malix was all smiles again. "Just a little adventure for a few days and then we can all get back to normal. Sybutu, wait here so I can brief you personally. Thank you, gentlemen."

The other two saluted and marched away, leaving Osu alone at the mercy of the same officer who had ordered him to betray the honor of the Legion.

* * *

"Relax, Sybutu."

Osu didn't fall for the man steepling his fingers behind his desk. When a lieutenant colonel told you to relax, you knew your life had just taken a seriously wrong turn.

"So what if we're ruffling a few feathers?" said Malix. "We have a job to do, and you're going to make it happen. You will take five men with you and travel unobserved to a location in the capital where you will deliver a coded phrase to this contact."

He pushed across a photograph showing a human male dressed in smuggler chic. Even from the static image, the man oozed charm, but he revealed something else too: purple eyes. The man was a mutant.

"His name is Captain Tavistock Fitzwilliam, and he's a free trader of flexible legitimacy. Let's call him a smuggler for simplicity's sake. You deliver the message and then return here without incident, after which no one will speak of this again."

Osu kept his demeanor blank, but the questions were raging inside him. His officers in the 27th gave the appearance of having waved through the colonel's bizarre orders, but the squadron sergeant major would not let this drop easily. He'd be lodged in an ambush point close to the colonel's office where he'd be waiting to pounce on Osu and interrogate him. Vyborg would suspect him of conspiracy in this affront to proper conduct. His sappers as undercover spies? Osu would rather face a crusading army of newts than the sergeant major on the warpath.

"Make sure one of the men you pick is Hines Zy Pel."

Osu's mask must have slipped because Malix added, "If there is a problem, I expect you to speak."

"Is Zy Pel a Special Missions operative, sir?" There. He'd said it.

"You'll have to ask Colonel Lantosh. Even after they bumped up my rank, I still don't have clearance to see Zy Pel's full personnel record. Make of that what you will."

"But you must have put feelers out…"

Malix gave him a cold stare.

You're trying to decide whether to hang me from a whipping post or answer my question. Well, it was your decision to have me lead an undercover team, Colonel. Let's see whether you trust your own judgement.

The colonel seemed to decide on the latter option and softened half a degree. "There was a Hines Zy Pel who died in the Defense of Station 11. Or so the official records tell us. I have reason to think that our Hines Zy Pel is the same man."

"But…Station 11 was twelve years ago. According to the personnel record I've seen, my Zy Pel is in his mid-20s."

Malix put his hands up in surrender. "I know, I know. The other Hines Zy Pel was 42 when he was KIA."

"He's 54? Can't be the same man. Impossible."

"For you and I, Sybutu, that is true. But away from the core worlds, I've encountered mysteries that defy explanation. Don't discount the possibility. Keep an eye on him. For the moment, he is a vital asset, especially given the nature of what I have tasked you with. However, if you ever suspect him of an agenda that undermines his duty to the Legion, then I am ordering you to kill him before he realizes you suspect him."

Kill Zy Pel in cold blood? That wouldn't come easily.

"Acknowledge," the colonel demanded.

"Yes, sir. If Zy Pel appears to be turning, I will kill him."

"Do you remember Colonel Lantosh's words when she was arrested on Irisur?"

Talk about a sucker punch to the gut! Osu remembered everything about the incident when the Militia arrested the CO for standing up to the corruption endemic on that world.

It was Legion philosophy to respond to defeat or reversal with immediate counterattack. Lantosh and Malix's response had been the most un-Legion like possible.

"Yes, sir. She told us not to act. To let the skraggs take her without resistance. Without the Legion retaliating."

"No," snapped Malix. "She did *not*. She ordered us to let her go without retaliating *until the right moment*. This *is* the right moment, Sybutu. This message you will carry. You're doing this for the colonel."

Malix's words set loose a turmoil of emotions in Osu's breast that he didn't fully understand. He wept tears of rage, something he hadn't known was possible.

The colonel stood. "This is the moment when the Legion holds the line. Can I rely upon you, Sergeant?"

Osu saluted. "To the ends of the galaxy, sir. No matter what."

* * * * *

Chapter Five:
Osu Sybutu

L ike all legionaries, Osu kept a grab bag ready in case he had to move out at a moment's notice. So it was less than thirty minutes later that he and his five chosen men reported to the small armory room just off Vehicle Park 8.

Malix had said they needed to pass for civilians. That was obvious, but the consequences were a shock. Gone were their armor, helms, and PA-71s. In their place, blasters, a rifle, swords, and a collection of mismatched fetid armor pads and electro chainmail covered in heavy, mud-stained, tattered cloaks.

No self-respecting civilians would look like this, but they could always pass for Militia.

Osu was last to leave, delayed by the need to confirm with the colonel that, yes, they were ready to set off and, no, they would not communicate with anyone, going completely off-grid until the mission was completed.

As he left to pick up his transport, looking and smelling like a barbarian, he found the passageway blocked by De Ketele.

"What's up, Sergeant?"

"What do you mean?"

De Ketele flinched. "Don't treat me like a fool."

"Sorry." The silence hung heavily as Osu thought of the right words to explain without compromising OpSec. He found none. "Look after the guys," was all he could say.

De Ketele's eyes widened. "You *are* coming back?"

Osu placed a hand on his friend's shoulder. "Of course."

He froze. It hadn't occurred to Osu that he might not return in the few days Malix had suggested. The message he'd been given was intended to unlock a powerful unknown. In the face of such uncertainty, even a few days away from Nydella suddenly seemed like an age. The separation was bad enough but went with the job. It was leaving without ever saying what they meant to each other that cut him.

"Do me a favor?" he asked De Ketele.

"Anything."

"Tell Sergeant Sanderson that I'll come back to her. Tell her...tell her I love her."

If De Ketele's eyes were wide before, now they practically exploded. "Azhanti, Sybutu! What in Five Hells is going on?"

"I don't know. Honestly. But something bad's headed our way. Stay sharp till I get back."

"Damn right I will." They clasped arms and locked gazes. "I'll tell her. I swear."

Osu nodded. He knew he could rely on De Ketele.

But it still stung to leave in secret without even saying goodbye to her.

Oh, she'd understand. He dared hoped she'd even wait for him. But after leaving the LT behind forever on Irisur, it felt like he was now doing the same to Nydella.

De Ketele slapped him on the back and walked off without another word.

* * * * *

Chapter Six:
Osu Sybutu

Urdizine gunned the motor of his bike, whooping as he sped away through the half-finished meltwater conduit. The gravitic repulsors of the modified civilian bike were pushed out of phase by the unevenness of the surface, making a painful beating noise that pounded Osu's skull like merciless electro hammers.

Crazy Zhoogene. The Perseid natives with the waxy green skin were as much plants as men, which made their deep love of engine vibrations pulsing through their bodies all the more ironic.

Osu called after him before he disappeared into the darkness of the tunnel. "There will be plenty of time to tear up the ice once we clear the base. Button it up for now, Urdizine, and get your green ass back here."

The wayward legionary turned his bike in a lazy circle that had him riding halfway up the curved wall of the tunnel. His headlights picked out a rat, which froze before scurrying through a gap in the wall.

"Sergeant's right, Greenie." Stryker sounded even more rebellious than usual. "We've a vital mission to perform. And that's bugging me, Sergeant. You've spoken drent and smoke since we left camp. We're to pass on a message? That's why God gave us encrypted radio comms. And, for that matter, short orbital hops to get from one point on a planet to another without having to ride a damned bike through the ice storms. What are we really doing?"

"We're holding the line," said Zy Pel. "That's right, eh, Sarge?"

Osu ground his jaw. He'd let Stryker blow off steam because he knew that's what Tavarius Stryker needed before he'd cool and see sense. He didn't need Zy Pel's help.

"Damn right," said Osu. "This is Legion business. I don't understand the half of it, but it *is* Legion business."

"And that's all any of us need to know," added Zy Pel in a tone that said the topic was closed for good.

"What, are we Militia now?" Yergin decided it was his turn to challenge. Osu cursed silently. He was losing them already. Probably his own doubts were surfacing. The Legion wasn't used to following a leader who didn't believe in what they were doing.

"Quiet!" hissed Zy Pel. He tilted his head, listening. "Someone's coming. Go dark!"

They switched off their headlights, plunging the tunnel into absolute darkness. Osu still couldn't hear anything, but a few moments later, Urdizine whispered in his ear. "I hear them too. Boots. Marching."

"Legionaries?" asked Osu of the inky blackness—unlike the Zhoogene, he couldn't see in the dark without his helm.

"I don't think so. Maybe. It's strange. Can't figure it out, but they aren't Littoranes."

Osu thought hard. Who could they be? He couldn't think of a single answer that he liked. He grabbed the ball he had kept ready in his cloak pocket. "Peeper out," he whispered as he threw the device into the tunnel.

The peeper bobbed along the tunnel, keeping a few inches above its floor and relaying mapping data to Osu's goggles. He drew the long hood of his cloak down over his eyes to limit any light emission. The peeper too would be keeping itself to the shadows, passing back its findings via a tight-beam microwave link transmitted along microscopic relays it left along the way.

When the 27th arrived on Rho-Torkis and assessed the area around the dig site, Major Cartwright had drawn deeply from his well of curses to describe the inadequacy of the drainage. A huge amount of energy was being used to power the dig site itself. What did the garrison think would happen when that energy reached the snow and ice of the surrounding area, and on a planet that had recently flicked on the fast thaw?

When operational, the meltwater channels they were passing through would be the permanent solution.

A few hundred meters up ahead, the central tunnel they were transiting through began splitting into offshoots like a delta system, a design intended to reduce flooding from the outflow. Nearly a full klick away, up one of these side channels, the peeper found the source of the noise.

Osu sighed with relief. He didn't know what he'd expected to see, perhaps a rebel army or an invasion by an alien power such as the Muryani. Even in the false light image sent by the peeper, it was clear that they had encountered legionaries marching back to the camp.

Zhoogene hearing was incredible, but at this distance, even Urdizine's ears weren't entirely reliable.

They were just legionaries. Nothing more.

Nonetheless, they were legionaries who would shoot first and ask questions never if they encountered unauthorized civilian intruders in ragged cloaks, mounted on hover bikes.

"Follow my lead," said Osu. "It's a Legion patrol. Dismount and set bikes to stealth mode."

They pushed their bikes into a different side channel, hurrying to get there before the legionaries emerged into the main tunnel.

As Osu monitored the advancing unit, he began to side with Urdizine's first impression. Something was wrong with this image. The soldiers wore Legion armor and most of them carried PA-71s. Even their spacing was textbook. But their movements were awkward in a way that Osu couldn't put a finger on. It was as if they were trying to act drunk but making a hash of it, which made no sense at all.

At first, he tried to tell himself that the strained jerking movements were those of exhausted legionaries at the end of a forced march. But he knew that was a lie.

Who the hell were they?

What were they?

"Camp Faxian can take care of itself," Zy Pel whispered as the strange legionaries passed by into the main channel, apparently oblivious to the close encounter.

Behind his goggles, Osu's eyes narrowed. Did Zy Pel suspect them too? How could he possibly know?

Annoyingly, Hines Zy Pel was right again. The colonel had told them not to stop for anything. Not to report back for any reason, no matter how strange or dangerous, until the message was delivered.

The area was guarded by seven battalions of legionaries. To bolster numbers, they'd even drafted in an ad hoc unit of Militia, scraped from dregs across the planet.

Militia...His spirits fell. Could these be Militia masquerading as legionaries?

Too many unknowns. But Osu had all the certainty he needed: a clear mission objective.

"They've passed us," he said quietly to the others. "Time to push on."

"One thing first," said Stryker. "We *are* legit, right? I mean, after what Clarke did, hiding from other legionaries is not a good look."

It would be easy to answer yes and tell his squad to shut up and get the hell out of there. It would be harder—but still easier than the full truth—to say that he wasn't sure whether they were acting legitimately in the eyes of the Legion's sector commandant and leave it at that. But Osu figured his men deserved a proper answer.

"When Colonel Lantosh was arrested on Irisur," he said, "she told us to wait before we got our retaliation in. Well, now we're done waiting."

"Holy Azhanti, Sergeant," exclaimed Stryker. "Why didn't you say so in the first place? So, let's hightail it outta here already. We've got a message needs delivering."

* * * * *

Chapter Seven:
Osu Sybutu

"The contact is a small-time smuggler called Captain Tavistock Fitzwilliam," said Osu, scanning the trees below their hideout through his binocs. "Last known location is Bresca-Brevae. The capital."

"He?" queried Urdizine. "Do we have a confirmed and stable gender?"

"Yes. Male."

"*Human* male?"

"Kind of." Osu lowered his binocs. "He's a mutant."

He turned round to assess the reaction of his team. A lot of people had no time for mutants, but he didn't sense protests brewing. Stryker and Zavage had their faces turned away and glued to their own binocs, watching the approaches from other directions. They'd used camo-sheets to cover the hollow scooped out of the dying glacier, which made it too dark within for his team to see each other's faces well, but the others seemed to register a quiet buzz of excitement, not disgust for mutants.

"And we stay off-grid," added Yergin. "No matter what. Copy that. We stop for nothing. Copy. So why are we camped in a snow hole instead of riding these bikes the hell outta here?"

Because every time Osu thought of the legionaries in the tunnels, foreboding lashed at him. But he wasn't ready to share his paranoid fears.

"I want to know if we're being followed," he answered, which was true. "It'll be dark in two hours. We set off then."

"Storm's coming on the horizon," added Zavage. "That'll cover us."

Yergin narrowed his eyes and stared at Osu. He knew something wasn't right. But the two men also knew they could trust each other. Yergin shrugged and looked away, untroubled.

Osu returned to his observation of the camp four klicks away.

When the 27th had arrived on Rho-Torkis a few weeks ago, they had come in during a blizzard that had thrown fist-sized ice balls around like it was a public stoning. On other planets, the shuttle would have abandoned the approach or shifted to a landing site with better weather.

But on Rho-Torkis, a ferocious ice storm meant a good day.

Today was the first day of truly clear skies since their arrival, and the world had taken on an astonishing beauty. The upper atmosphere was still heavy with soot from ancient nuclear fire, which meant that even two hours from sundown, the skies were a deep coppery red unlike anything he'd seen on other worlds. Melting ice and snow made a playful tinkling sound as glistening drops flowed and merged into rivulets and miniature streams. The blanket of moist snow created such a fiery glare that your eyes would burn and visibility would be zero without the smart-filtering of their glacier goggles.

He'd seen the pictures from space. The planet looked like a red ball of heated metal.

And Camp Faxian in the evening light was spectacular. It was laid out as a pentagon, with walls coated with ceramalloy that looked like burnished red gold. Cylindrical towers stood proud at the vertices of the outer defenses, each topped by a domed cupola from which projected a heavy 288 cannon. It was a dream of form and function.

Even the landing pad where the 27th had arrived in such foul conditions now looked peaceful, with neatly lined up shuttles shining like hot jewels.

And inside this impregnable fortress was Sergeant Sanderson.

They say you don't fully appreciate what you have until it's taken away.

Well, he'd never exactly *had* Nydella. But he had a shot of making something with her, and he knew now how precious that was.

When they returned in about ten days. Their reunion would be...*monumental*.

He laughed at the prospect, but even as he did so, he packed away thoughts of homecoming. He had a job to do first. Thinking about her would not help him to come back safely.

The moment he withdrew his binocs, his eyes registered movement at Camp Faxian. All five turret cupolas were traversing.

The guns were moving inward.

"Legionaries sighted," Zavage announced. "Between northeast edge of glacier and the tree line. Infantry moving north armed with PA-71s and one SLM-B missile launcher. I see a dozen, but in these trees, there could be a lot more."

Friendlies or hostiles? All Osu could be certain of was Malix's orders to stay unobserved. "Zy Pel, add your eyes onto the infantry. Stryker, you're with me putting eyes on Camp Faxian. The rest of you, be ready to move out."

Back at the main base, the turrets had finished traversing inward. There were no other signs of unusual activity. If sirens were blaring or shots being fired, they should hear it from their location. If there was a BattleNet call to arms, he was plugged into the general broadcast frequency. But there was nothing. Perhaps this was an exercise. Every system had to be tested sometime.

"Something's bothered the infantry," said Zavage. "They're conferring."

Osu shifted position and trained his binocs on the soldiers in the snow field at the base of the glacier. Looked like an officer was giving orders. An officer pointing excitedly at Camp Faxian. Beyond them, dark figures could be glimpsed headed north through the trees, not toward the camp but in the direction of the dig site itself. They had the outlines of legionaries, but the way they marched wasn't right. Some jerked like marionettes, while others possessed an uncanny smoothness to their movements as if they were slugs oozing along a slime trail. And they were bunched too, the awkward ones following those with smoother movement.

"Zavage, Zy Pel, notice anything strange about that infantry?"

"Yeah." Zy Pel spoke with relish. "They aren't legionaries."

"Speculate. What are we facing?"

"Rebels in captured suits," suggested Zavage. "If those newts were given force shields, why not give humanoids Legion armor?"

Zy Pel wasn't listening. He threw back his hood and sniffed deeply at the frozen air. He shook his head and replaced the hood over a face already burned red by the brief exposure to the cold. "Don't know," he said. "Can't be sure."

Before Osu could question the man further, they ducked instinctively in the deep hollow as the clear skies cracked with thunder.

"Aircraft inbound from western horizon," Stryker announced. "Twelve Saturn bombers with Falcon escorts. I estimate forty fighters."

Below their concealed position, the suspect legionaries were staring at the incoming aircraft, mostly in a very un-Legion level of consternation. The soldier with the personal missile launcher was one of the few to act like a professional. He dropped his tube onto the snow and began to swap out his load, pulling a round from the store on his back.

It was painted with a blue band. *Surface-to-air munition.*

The man took a knee and readied to fire at the incoming aircraft.

"We've got to help." Stryker sounded shaky.

"Keep it together," snapped Osu. "We stay on mission."

"Why aren't they firing?" said Zavage.

Good question. The camp had anti-air defenses that would extract a high blood cost from the Saturn bombers if they dared to attack. Missile strikes would have to penetrate a formidable point defense grid backed up by the other smaller forts that surrounded the all-important dig site.

So why weren't they firing?

The throb of powerful engines resonated in Osu's chest. The Saturns were coming in low for tactical bombing. Either their pilots were suicidal, or they had a reason to be so confident.

A few missiles rose from the legionaries running to man the camp defenses, but it was a pitifully ragged response. Below Osu's position, the soldier with the SAM ready seemed to realize that his unit was not the target and held his fire, jogging for cover in the trees.

Even through the optical wizardry of his goggles and binocs, it was difficult to see what was happening in the air as the fast-moving aircraft screamed in against the backdrop of a huge sun setting in a blood red sky.

A fireball bloomed overhead. One of the attackers had been dusted. Fighter or bomber, he couldn't tell.

But if it was difficult to see the results of the battle in the sky, on the ground it was hideously apparent.

The turret guns thundered as they fired upon their own camp.

Accommodation blocks exploded into a twisting plume of dust and flame.

Two turrets combined fire to blow out the southern wall from the inside.

And all around, legionaries were running, shooting back, and trying to coordinate a defense in a crazy situation where friend had become foe. Mostly, though, they were dying.

Another thunderclap announced yet more aircraft entering the battle as the first wave of Falcons screamed in, shooting plasma bursts at ground targets, not only in the main camp, but burning up the secondary forts too.

Plasma guns were usually only effective in space, because in a planetary atmosphere, you had to close to within spitting distance to get maximum effect. But with the air defenses off-line, that's what the Falcons were doing, coming in so low over the trees that their crowns were flattening before diving inside the camp walls and hurling gouts of burning plasma over helpless legionaries.

The treacherous main guns paused to avoid hitting the aircraft. Then they resumed fire the moment their target zones were clear.

Not one of the northern turrets, though. It collapsed, toppling outward and throwing up an enormous dust cloud.

And maybe the legionaries weren't entirely helpless. The air crackled with small arms fire from Camp Faxian. Two of the first wave of Falcons emerged from their strafing run with smoke belching from their engines. One exploded as it tried to regain the air; the other crashed into the trees, which began blazing with fire, despite the cold and ice.

Another of the camp's main guns fell silent, fingers of smoke curling up from the turret.

The others continued to rain destruction.

Osu's team was stunned into silence. His every instinct screamed to disobey orders and go to the aid of their comrades in the camp, but what could they achieve?

The bombers were almost over the target zone.

"Colonel's Retaliation, Colonel's Retaliation, this is Colonel's Remorse." The voice came over the general broadcast frequency. "Do not respond to this message. Proceed to objective without deviation."

The voice was automatically neutralized to make identification of the speaker more difficult. They hadn't exchanged call signs for this operation, but this had to be Malix himself.

High in the sky, bombardiers rained down bombs.

Bombs, not missiles? Fuck! That could only mean one thing. Nukes.

"Colonel's Retaliation, Colonel's Retaliation, this is Colonel's Remorse. Do not respond. Proceed to objective without deviation. Colonel's Retaliation—"

Someone threw Osu to the bottom of the hollow a moment before the first of the bombs hit Faxian.

Even with eyes squeezed tightly shut behind his goggles, the explosions were so intense, so bright, it felt as if an army of powerful flashlights had been switched on inside his skull. Giant hands slapped his brain and pummeled the air out of his lungs. He sensed a wave of heat howling overhead, but the hollow protected them from the worst of it. In fact, he realized, the hollow had probably saved their lives.

All of them were staring at the bikes and their toxicity sensors. If they started flaring rad-alerts, then all of them would die from radiation sickness long before they reached Bresca-Brevae and this Captain Fitzwilliam.

The seconds ticked by. The bikes stayed silent.

Through lungs seared and bruised, the legionaries began to breathe more easily.

They might not live out this day, but it wouldn't be radiation that killed them.

Osu looked out over the devastation.

Mushroom clouds expanded over holes in the forest where the secondary forts had stood. A much larger column twisted over Camp Faxian, its cap expanding lazily into the bloody sky.

"Nydella," he groaned.

Of the five outer walls of the base, two were blown out completely. Where moments before they had been gleaming like burnished gold, now they were scorched and dull.

Incredibly, Osu could see a few dazed survivors moving through the ruins.

Survivors…Nydella might still be alive!

"We've got to help them," Stryker screamed. He jumped onto his bike and drove it off the edge of the glacier.

* * * * *

Chapter Eight: Osu Sybutu

Osu Sybutu's world had broken.

The heat from the irradiated firestorm he called home licked at his face through the opening in his cloak's hood.

The main guns had turned inward.

In the woods below his position on the glacier's edge, phony legionaries swarmed north on an unknown agenda.

We have been betrayed.

And Sapper of the Legion Stryker had just ridden his bike off the sheer edge of the glacier.

"Sarge!"

Osu didn't know what to do next.

Hic manebimus optime.

Hold the line.

Hic manebimus optime. The legionary motto.

The Legion had excavated a desiccated language—long dead even before the Scramble for Earth—and found a saying they had made their own.

We are here. That's what the words meant in the original Latin. We're gonna make a success of this place. And we ain't budging for nobody.

These were history's earliest recorded words spoken by a legionary. *The first legionary*...It made for a good story, and the Legion lived for its ancient tales of glory, even those borrowed from the ancients: the Czech Legion and the Romans.

That suited him just fine because Osu was Legion to his core. Cut him open, and you would find the guinshrike emblem stamped onto his bones.

Hic manebimus optime.

Hold the line.

He steeled his nerves and forced himself to look into the mushroom cloud above Camp Faxian.

"We are Legion," he told it. "We're not done here. We're just getting started."

Then he scrambled out of the hollow so he could lay his body over the edge of the glacier and look down.

Until very recently, a single sheet of ice must have covered the entire region, but as the climate warmed and the ice receded, it had left behind a block on top of a rocky outcropping that dropped forty feet to the forest below.

Osu watched, horrified, as Stryker completed a near-vertical descent. He'd picked the man for his bike handling skill, but this was something else. Stryker had dipped his ride's nose and was surfing a cushion of repulsive force down the base of the slope. At the bottom, he sprayed snow over the figures in legionary armor as he kicked down into an abrupt halt.

If anyone else had attempted that, they'd have broken their necks. Only one problem. Although the soldiers Stryker had joined in such a dramatic arrival had appeared as stunned by the air attack on Camp Faxian as Osu's team, that didn't mean they were friendly.

Actually, that wasn't the only problem. Zy Pel was gesturing to the west where a gray army was swarming across the cleared zone around the camp and advancing on its ruins. They were newts. Hundreds, maybe more. And they were gunning down anything that moved.

First things first. Since Stryker hadn't broken his neck, they'd better go rescue him.

Urdizine and Yergin were already on their bikes, ready to take the longer way down to join Stryker.

"Wait! Don't let yourself be seen."

The two on the bikes looked around at Osu as if he'd gone mad.

"I know that's legionary combat armor down there, but I don't know who or what is wearing it. We will hope they're friendlies but assume they're not. Zavage, join Urdizine and Yergin. Work your way down their right flank. Zy Pel will do the same with me on the left. I want a closer look before we reveal ourselves."

Osu was activating his bike when they were all blown flat against the snow. Enemy Falcons screamed over their heads heading east, their force keels bending trees and raising a cloud of fine snow in their wake.

The sappers dusted themselves off and descended the slope with their bikes in stealth mode.

During the Orion Era, equipment running stealth mode had been completely invisible to the eye and even to the most powerful sensors. It sounded fanciful today, but the accounts of the tactical doctrine that resulted were so detailed that Osu believed them. As he circled left, with Zy Pel following in the footsteps his boots had punched into the snow, the bike's motor ran near silently. Osu held it by the handles, putting its snow-camo body between him and the suspicious legionaries.

This was the extent of stealth mode in the modern era.

Whoever Stryker had ridden into, they were more interested in him than in keeping watch. Osu was within a hundred yards and still hadn't been seen. Stryker was gesticulating and shouting at the mystery soldiers, unable to understand why they wanted to head north and not west to help any survivors at Camp Faxian.

They certainly didn't seem alert enough to be intercepting comms. "Zavage," Osu called over the radio. "What's your status? Over."

"Inside tree line due east of Stryker. We saw a few stragglers deeper in the trees, but whoever they are, they look like they've moved off to the north."

Without warning, the soldiers around Stryker sprang into life, leaping onto the sapper and dragging him off his mount and into the snow.

"Zavage," radioed Osu, "move your team in and grab our man. We'll cover."

Using their bikes sideways-on as cover, he and Zy Pel sighted targets in the uneven struggle going on in the snow. Stryker was doing his best to give his attackers hell, but whatever they really were, they wore Legion armor with muscle amplifiers, and they outnumbered him five-to-one.

What made Osu hold his fire was their reaction after they had Stryker upright in the snow with arms and legs pinned. They just held him there, as silent and as motionless as Stryker's occasional lunges for freedom would allow.

Waiting.

Waiting for what?

Not waiting for anyone to come rescue their captive, that was for sure. A single bike approached silently from the tree line beyond. They didn't appear to notice it. But Osu did. He noticed the absence of the other two bikes even more. *Where are they?*

"This is Zavage," came the answer over the radio. "We've sighted more of them in the woods. Estimate company strength. So far, they seem more interested in getting north quickly than engaging us, but we're keeping an eye on them while Yergin moves in to snatch Stryker."

From the forest to the north emerged three figures in legionary armor. Osu took the one in the middle to be an officer. Stryker's captors shuffled him around to face the 'officer,' pulling back his hood to reveal Stryker's snarling face.

"That's right," Osu muttered to himself. "Keep your eyes on your boss." Then in a clear voice he added, "Zy Pel, when Yergin moves in, take the shot on the officer."

"I have the shot," replied the team's marksman. "Holy skragg...not again!"

Osu couldn't see what was getting Zy Pel worked up.

But there was no time to ask. As if the situation weren't already weird enough, the VIP walked to within touching distance of Stryker and removed her helm.

She was a Kurlei. Gray, narrow face with razor-sharp cheekbones, oversized eyes, and empathetic head fronds like metal-sheathed fishy dreadlocks. Same rare species as Zavage, who would flirt with anything carrying a pulse, irrespective of species or gender, but was so terrified of the females of his race that he would lock himself away rather than encounter them.

Yergin gunned his bike and sped in to make the rescue.

Osu steadied his blaster sights on one of the Kurlei's escorts and whispered, "Zy Pel, take the shot."

As soon as he heard the crack of the slug thrower rifle next to him, he pulled on his blaster's trigger. Bolts sizzled through the air, but Osu already knew he'd missed and so too had Zy Pel.

A pressure wave was pushing from behind, ramming his cheek against the saddle of the bike he was using as cover. Then a scream of protesting air assailed his ears as a flight of fighters flew low overhead in pursuit of the aircraft who'd destroyed his home, the oversized force keels revealing them to be FVA-7 Spikeballs.

He picked himself up from the toppled bike he'd sprawled over and resighted on a confusing scene. The Kurlei's escorts had picked themselves up from the snow and were trying to protect her with their bodies, facing outward at the new threats. Those who had grabbed Stryker now opened up his clothing, baring his chest to the Kurlei officer who was rubbing her face in the man's flesh.

What was she doing? He couldn't take the shot; she was too close to Stryker. So he poured blaster bolts into one of the escorts.

Beside him, Zy Pel was muttering in horror. "Not again. Not again. Not here. Not now." But he kept it together enough to put three rounds into the other escort, who staggered back.

Exposed now, the Kurlei officer was revealed as a creature from hell. Its jaw had extended until its chin was now a sharp spike. But it was her teeth that transfixed him. She was sprouting huge canine fangs before his eyes. As she licked her growing fangs with her long tongue, she opened her arms as if in prayer and sniffed greedily at the frozen air.

She appeared oblivious to the weapons fire. Her only desire was to sink those fangs into Stryker's flesh.

Yergin flew in at speed, spraying the group with blaster fire and knocking the ring of captors around Stryker into the snow. Osu and Zy Pel poured fire into the enemy who had been thrown clear of Stryker.

But it was not over yet. At this range and against legionary armor, Osu's blaster was not delivering kill shots, and Zy Pel's rifle was faring only a little better. Yergin was deadlier, firing into armor weak spots at a range measured in mere inches.

From the woods over to the east erupted scattered bursts of blaster and railgun fire. It sounded like Urdizine and Zavage were too occupied to help any time soon.

"We need to get closer," said Osu, and mounted his bike, ready to drive into the fray.

The enemy seemed confused by the sudden close quarters combat, but not the Kurlei. She employed the renowned athleticism of her race to jump through the melee as Yergin kicked and fired his way through to Stryker. She landed on Yergin's bike control panel beneath the handlebars, facing the sapper.

Zy Pel—the man who would keep calm in the direst circumstances, more than any legionary Osu had ever known—gave such a scream of horror that Osu's blood turned to ice.

Osu abandoned Zy Pel, driving his bike straight at the enemy.

Yergin's advance had stalled under the blows of railgun stocks raining on his head. Stryker had his hands around the Kurlei's waist, trying to tug her away from Yergin's bike, but she kept an unbreakable hold around Yergin, her face buried inside his cloak as if feeding upon his flesh.

"No!" yelled Zy Pel as Osu slammed his bike into two of the enemy with a sideswipe against the backs of their knees.

The Kurlei raised her head, licking Yergin's blood from her fangs with a long tongue. The fronds in her head were erect and quivering, and Osu could feel the emotion of raw triumph she was broadcasting through them. As he stuck a blade through an enemy's neck, he could also feel the moment when her confidence changed to confusion. She snapped her bloody jaws at Stryker's hand, which he snatched away just in time. She used the space she'd won to sniff the air and then stare into the distance. She was staring directly at Zy Pel.

A rifle report rang out from the sniper's position, quickly muffled by the snow and trees, as Zy Pel put a round through the Kurlei and blew her alien brains out.

At the officer's death, the enemy appeared stunned, confused.

"Yergin, get him out of here," Osu shouted, taking advantage of the confusion to put coldly murderous fire into the false legionaries.

Yergin recovered his senses and hauled Stryker up to ride pillion behind him. They sped away, passing Zy Pel and heading back to the hollow they'd scooped out from the top of the glacier.

Osu drove off on a looping curve that put a little distance from the group of phonies who were by now dead, wounded, or too confused to fight. Then he circled back, savaging the area with his bike's blaster cannons until no one was left alive.

Covered by Zavage and Urdizine who had emerged unscathed from the trees, he retrieved Stryker's bike and set it to auto follow.

As they raced back to rejoin the others on the glacier, the red sky made a fiery backdrop for an uneven aerial battle. Legion Spikeballs tore into the fleeing enemy aircraft, bullying through the escort fighters and cutting a swathe of destruction through the bombers that had almost escaped to orbit.

Even at this distance, the fireballs blossoming in the upper atmosphere from the dusted bombers cast sharp shadows along the tree line.

Osu prayed that not a single enemy aircraft would escape.

They regrouped in the hollow. Osu saw immediately that it wasn't Stryker who was the most shaken by the experience; it was Yergin.

With Zavage, Stryker, and Urdizine mounted on their bikes and providing overwatch, Osu knelt in front of Yergin under the cover of the camo-sheets. He was shaking—and not from the cold. His eyes were wild, and he was sweating despite the ice, but when Osu took a closer look at the wounds the Kurlei officer had inflicted on his chest, they were bloodied scores, but they were far from the deep gouging wounds Osu had expected. She seemed to have sunk the tips of her fangs beneath Yergin's skin and moved them from side to side, but no more.

Had she used venom? It was a good thing she hadn't sunk her fangs into Stryker too.

"Skragg!" screamed Yergin. "Holy Azhanti, they were vampires, man! Alien vampires. They fucking bit me! I'm gonna turn into one of them."

"There are no such things as vampires," Zy Pel told him with calm finality. "But..." He looked away. "I've seen things that are much worse."

Yergin grabbed his shoulders and drew him down till their foreheads were almost touching. "Is that what we're facing, brother? This nightmare you met in your past? Tell me it ain't so."

"Maybe." Zy Pel shook his head. "Almost certainly not."

"Suppose it was," said Osu. "What would you advise then?"

Zy Pel gave him such a look of pain and loss that Osu took a step back. With a visible effort, he calmed himself and reached for a med-kit. "This isn't what I saw before. But if it were, we would need to watch you, Yergin. Give it an hour to get on our way and then…"

Yergin shook him by the shoulders. "C'mon, Hines. What? Decapitate me? Stake through the heart? Spit it out. C'mon, man!"

Zy Pel started cleaning Yergin's wound. "There's no such thing as vampires, okay? I encountered an alien cult once at a place called Azoth-Zol. They bit people to make them more pliable. Some kind of mind-control shit. But their victims were aliens, and you're Marc Yergin. You may be a borderline case, but technically you classify as human."

His words calmed Yergin a little but had the opposite effect on Osu. That Kurlei had sniffed out Zy Pel, and his scent had confused the hell out of her. There was much more that Zy Pel wasn't saying.

While Zy Pel applied an active dressing, Osu tried to calm Yergin further. "Mind control drug administered through false fangs," he said. "As alien freak cults go, that's pretty mild. How long after being bitten did the effects surface?"

"An hour," Zy Pel replied as he stowed his med-kit.

Zy Pel's words were spoken casually, but Osu took them seriously. Within an hour, he would ensure Yergin would be restrained and under armed supervision. First, they had to get out of there. Fast.

"Are you all in denial?" It was Stryker, who had slid into the hollow to join them.

"Get back to your position," Osu snapped, beyond furious.

But Stryker only glared back. "De Ketele," he said. "Krynox, Grymz." He peered at Osu. "Sanderson," he whispered. "Newts in protective rad gear are assaulting what remains of Camp Faxian. Fires are still burning, and the air is thick with blaster bolts. There are hundreds of damned newts. But there must be survivors too, though not for much longer unless we do something. And here you are talking about vampires. You're in denial! Let's go help our friends, already!"

"I don't like it any more than you," said Osu, "but the colonel trusted us with a vital mission. And we *will* carry it out."

"Is that it?" Stryker roared. "Is that our skragging response? Everyone we know either died or will do soon, and we let those RILs get away with it?"

"I think this is bigger than the RILs," said Osu, raising his voice for the benefit of Zavage and Urdizine, who were doubtless listening in from their watch positions outside. "Bigger even than Camp Faxian. We won't forget this, I promise you that. I swear we will send a multitude of newts to meet their precious goddess, but first"—he cast a worried look at Yergin—"we need to move out."

"I'm still Marc Yergin. What about you, Sarge? Are you still Osu Sybutu or did those nukes mutate you into a vampire hunter? Because I know the real Sybutu would never abandon his comrades."

"The real Sybutu gets the job done," Osu told him. "However hard the route I have to take. The same goes for any true legionary. That's why none of us are going back to Faxian. We're heading east to complete our mission."

"Anyway," hissed Zy Pel as they stowed the camo-sheets in their bikes. "They are *not* vampires."

"Maybe not," Yergin replied, "but whatever the hell they are, they're still out there. They're close by and they're coming for all of you."

"Stop that crazy talk!" snapped Osu. "We get through this nightmare by acting like professionals. We are not Militia. We are not RILs, rebels, or bandits. We are sappers of the Legion and this is where we prove it, by holding the line."

"I'm *not* crazy," growled Yergin. He accelerated away, hard, heading southeast off the glacier and disappearing into the eerie glare of the red sky and burning legionary base reflecting off the snow.

"I know they're surrounding us," Yergin shouted, his receding voice cracking. "I can *smell* them."

The air snapped as streaks of fire hit the upper atmosphere, punching shockwaves that transmitted down through the clouds. They were warships coming in hot, bigger craft than the fighters that had been scrapping. All hell must be breaking loose in orbit.

But there was enough to worry about down here in the snow.

"Get him back," ordered Osu, as he adjusted his goggles to search the skies.

The fiery streaks resolved into mid-sized freighters. Jump-capable, maybe a dozen crew, and with so many modifications in the centuries after they'd rolled off the production fab-plants that their configuration was effectively random. They were the kind of ships you would see dotted around any port. The kind that went unremarked.

Perhaps the Legion was imposing an orbital interdiction, and these were traders with something to hide.

Legion Spikeballs screamed after the freighters in pursuit, their fuselages dotted with the narrow force keels that gave them half their name. The other half of the Spikeball designation came from the four beam generators that curved around their bodies to combine in a central nose spike. These lanced energy beams at the freighters, whose shields flared briefly before safely dissipating the weapon strikes.

Freighters with shields? Smugglers weren't shy about making a few after-factory alterations. To emerge unscathed from that kind of firepower, though...even for the Smuggler's Guild, that meant serious mods. Those ships had military-grade shielding. What were they really? Troop transports?

The Spikeballs broke away to engage a wing of mismatched and mostly obsolete fighters just emerging from orbit.

Up ahead, Yergin was laughing. It was a demented sound, almost a cry of pain. "Follow me," he yelled in a voice that sounded little like the friend Osu had known these past four years.

The glacier the bitten man was crossing descended gently to the southeast with sharp drops to the north as it fell away to the forest, and to the south where it butted against the Great Ice Plain.

The light was dying, the bright red skies being swallowed by the gray maw of a storm advancing aggressively from the south, so it took a moment for Osu to resolve the awful sight in front of Yergin.

Blurry white figures were rising out of the snow. They formed a horseshoe several ranks deep, blocking the exit from the glacier.

Osu raced to catch up.

The sappers opened up with bike cannons on the blocking soldiers. Some went down, but not nearly enough. Yergin wasn't firing; he was head down and speeding for the center of the enemy formation.

The air above the bikers rippled as railgun flechettes cut through, but despite wearing Legion armor and firing PA-71s, the enemy were clearly no legionaries. They fired wildly. Or perhaps they were firing deliberately high. For now.

Osu desperately sought options.

A few hundred meters behind the enemy, the glacier fell away in a sheer drop, with the promise of cover in the forest beyond. Stryker had ridden off a similar drop and survived. Could anyone else?

"They want you alive," screamed Yergin. "Follow my example. Don't let them take you."

Yergin pushed his bike even harder, its engine rising in pitch until it screamed. He kept going. The powerplant shrieked like a banshee—he must have disabled its safeties.

"Yergin!" Osu screamed. "Don't do it!"

"Gonna take some dirty vamps with me," he screamed as his bike rammed the enemy, knocking several flying before its nose pitched down, caught in the snow, and began a high-speed tumble, scything through the phony legionaries like a boomerang drone.

"Grab him," shouted Osu, speeding through the other bikes and heading for Yergin. With so much snow and so many bodies thrown into the air—and the whine of the bike motor like screeching nails running along the inside of his skull—he couldn't locate his friend. But he was in there somewhere.

A fireball erupted as the powerplant on Yergin's bike blew, and Osu was off his bike and flying through the air.

Once again, the bogus legionaries were slow to react. Zy Pel wasn't.

"Yergin's bought us an exit," he shouted as Osu mounted his fallen bike. "Use it!"

They raced through the gap Yergin had blown through the enemy ranks, kicking, stabbing, and shooting the dazed survivors who threatened to block them.

In the flickering light of the burning bike, Osu slowed to scan the snow, hoping against all the odds that Yergin had been thrown clear. He hadn't. Osu saw his burning corpse steaming in the snow. His friend was beyond rescuing.

"I'll keep them safe," he promised Yergin. "No matter what we're really facing here."

Osu saw a flash on his bike armor, inches from his thigh, and felt the tiniest of nudges as a flechette round deflected away.

"Gotta go," he told Yergin and threw his bike forward.

Rounds zipped past him, but, within moments, he was inside the howling snowstorm rolling in from the plain and being beaten by balls of ice pummeling him like fists. The others slowed down and allowed their engine heat to radiate so he could find them with the IR overlay on his goggles.

They altered their bikes to limit their emissions in case they were being followed. Doing so robbed them of performance, but with visibility so poor that the legionaries couldn't see the ground, it made sense.

Instead of riding off the glacier's edge into the howling gale, Osu ordered his team to turn right, taking them behind the enemy who had halted to lick their wounds. The wind caught snatches of shouted commands to the beaten soldiers to pick up their boots and head north.

Soon, though, the voices fell away and they were left alone in the whiteout with only the dots in their goggles to reassure them that they were still together.

After a few klicks, the storm blew out and they seized the chance to get clear off the glacier. Following Stryker's instructions, they accelerated off the edge of the ice cliff to make it easy to keep their mounts balanced. Osu misjudged it and had to throw himself clear of the bike. But both of them were undamaged after their fall into the accumulation of fresh snow and headed off for the shelter of the trees as the storm rolled back in.

Here the dense tree canopy protected them from the worst of the howling gales and replaced it with a muffled silence. But as they drove beneath the pines, they had to dodge falling piles of snow that slid off laden boughs.

Osu preferred the violence of the storm out in the open. It was something he could fight. The way the world closed in on them inside the forest felt suffocating. The ghosts of those he'd lost that day seemed to cling to the trees, and he was glad when nighttime soon fell. Darkness was a form of sensory deprivation he was much more familiar with.

They encountered no one.

No birds. No Littoranes. No one friendly, but also no zombie legionary vampires or whatever the hell they'd encountered out there.

If the image of nuclear fire hadn't seared itself so strongly into his memory, it would be easy in this oppressive silence to start believing they had imagined the disaster they'd escaped. De Ketele, Colonel Malix, the new lieutenant, and Nydella…he was certain they were all dead, along with everyone he'd known who wasn't with him, wrapped in cloaks and riding bikes through the night. It was a deadly fact waiting for him in the darkness like an underwater mine, but he hadn't yet felt its emotional impact. Yergin was different. It was Yergin's death he struggled to process the most, the image of

Yergin's burning corpse he kept seeing lying on the forest floor out the corner of his eye. And the way he had claimed to smell the enemy—the same way their Kurlei officer had sniffed out Zy Pel.

If Osu survived this mission to make a report, he would paint Yergin as a hero who had sacrificed himself to buy his brothers an exit. The horrifying truth was that Yergin's terror of what he might become was so powerful that Osu was sure he would have blown his bike anyway.

Osu suspected the other survivors in the party were consumed by similar thoughts. Or maybe they were sucked into a different private hell. In any case, they pressed on in silence, willingly numbing themselves with the mindless task of threading the hoverbikes through tree after tree.

"Yergin was right about one thing," said Zy Pel, breaking the silence on the first rest stop. With Zavage keeping watch, they sat in a circle of their bikes, munching on ration bars without enthusiasm. "He was my brother. I miss him already. But if those freaks we encountered were what I found at Azoth-Zol, then...he's better off dead."

"I'm not in the mood for anyone talking drent," shouted Osu in an instant rage. "You said it was mind control. And it only worked on aliens. It's obvious to everyone here that you're freaked out by whatever it is we're facing. You! The unflappable Hines Zy Pel who laughs at any suggestion that he was SpecMish, and then proves he is with the skills and hoarded kit that makes regular legionaries like us look like junior cadets."

"I was trying to calm Yergin. Finding words to cool all your heads. It's still only a hunch."

Osu got to his feet and glared at Zy Pel. He was uncomfortably aware of his hands. They needed to hit something. Or someone. "I am in charge here, SOTL. You *will* share what you know. Next extended stop, you will tell us everything. In the meantime, if these freaks are who you suspect, is there any intel you might care to share with your surviving brothers that improves our odds of staying alive a little longer?"

He shook his head and then looked away. "I'm sorry."

Sorry? He didn't look it! Zy Pel took a battered leather pouch from the inside of his cloak and drew out his clay pipe and tin of synth-bac. Ignoring his NCO standing over him, he tamped leaves into his pipe bulb.

If it were anyone else, Osu would have snatched the pipe away and thrown it into the night at such insolence. But there were multiple levels at which he didn't want to escalate conflict with this man.

He did so anyway, but selected a different angle of attack. One Zy Pel wouldn't see coming.

"We've got more mysteries than we can cope with," Osu told the group. "We move out in three mikes." He stared at the man happily puffing away without a care in the world. "Let's see if we can solve a few before we do. You with the pipe! Are you the Hines Zy Pel who supposedly died on Station 11?"

Zy Pel froze for several seconds, the pipe clamped between his teeth. "That doesn't matter now."

"The hell you say!" Stryker erupted with anger. "My best friend got bitten and blew himself up. The main guns at the base turned inward and nearly everyone we know is dead. I've seen zombies wearing Legion kit, newts in rad-gear who knew this attack was coming, and bombers that miraculously snuck through the orbital defense system. No one's told me what's so important about these damned dig sites, or why the colonel gave us an off-grid mission like we're some hard-ass secret agents. Maybe he chose us because buttoned-up jack-head legionaries are the most unlikely spies ever, because we always do everything by the book and once we join the Legion family we never interact with outsiders except to shoot them or drink at their bars. The idea of undercover SOTLs is so ludicrous, no one would ever suspect us. The colonel was either an idiot or a genius."

He stood beside Osu and joined him in glaring at Zy Pel. "I don't know who I can trust any more, Hines. Right now, I'm not trusting you."

Zy Pel took a long draw on his pipe. He rolled the smoke around his mouth as if trying to capture the last lingering taste of a pleasure now lost.

"Yes," he replied. "That was me on Station 11 back in '87. There wasn't much of me left after we had beaten off the final wave of assault droids. Half of me was rebuilt, rejuved, and augmented." He took another puff on his pipe. "More than half, actually. And mostly with advanced techniques I don't understand myself, but a few of my repairs came straight out of the Bronze Age."

He pulled back his hood and then used both hands to draw apart the skin on his neck to reveal a gleaming plate underneath. Zavage brought closer one of the dimmed glow stones they were using to stave off the dark of the forest.

Beneath false skin, was a curved plate of an orange-brown metal.

"They used to call me Bronze." Zy Pel blinked—almost flinched at the sound of his old name. "Though that's not what it's made from. It is primitive, though. I think they put it there to remind me who it was who had rebuilt me. Who owned me."

"And who was that?" pushed Stryker.

"SpecMish. They owned me for a few years. Then I was kicked out for…reasons."

"Theft, hacking, extra-judicial dustings." Stryker held out his hands. "I'm just repeating the rumors."

"Everything you think you know about the Special Missions Executive is a calculated lie. They are not the paladins of the Legion you see on the holo-dramas. I have my reasons for my actions, and I'd do the same again. What I did, and why—trust me—you really don't want to know."

"Almost time to go," said Osu. "But I want one more answer out of you, Zy Pel. SpecMish seems to me like the kind of operation no one gets busted out of. If you ever retire, you do so permanently. And yet here you are, drawing your pay as a sapper of the Legion."

"Now that," said Zy Pel pointing the mouthpiece of his pipe at the other legionaries in turn, "is why our sergeant is the one person who can get us through this skragg-pile of a mess in one piece. You're right, Sarge. I was kicked out but allowed to live. That never happens, which means someone is keeping me on a long leash. Who? I don't know. And I'll give you another answer for free. Yergin was convinced he'd been bitten by vampires, but I know for a fact that's not what they are. I could smell them too, though not as strongly as Yergin could."

"You?" Osu shook his head, but he couldn't shake away the sense that Zy Pel's latest inconsistent story was finally hitting a rich vein of truth. "You were bitten?"

"I was." Zy Pel busied himself with stowing his pipe. "I'm one of them, after a fashion. And I know what they're after, too."

"The ship," Osu found himself saying.

The others shot a bewildered look at him, all except Zy Pel who gave him a scan of appraisal.

"What ship?" pressed Stryker.

Osu never understood why people talked of their cheeks flushing hot with shame; his felt cold. He almost apologized. "The dig site. All over the sector, we knew there were buried signs of a great war that ended thousands of years before our ancestors arrived at Far Reach. Then the Legion pressed scattered teams of archaeologists into military service and upped the scale of operations a thousandfold. We all assumed they'd found something. I can only guess about what that might be on other systems, but I do know what they found here at ASI-39. Sanderson spotted it when we were…I guess I was trying to impress her. It's like nothing you've seen before. Midsized—120 meters from bow to stern and a hull covered with what looked like bone hairs. And it wasn't a twisted wreck. It was powered. Maybe even space worthy. I think the phony legionaries were headed for the alien ship. That's their objective."

Stryker laughed. "Security around the site is tighter than the defenses around a federal senator's private bank vault. And you snuck in to impress a girl?"

"Not just any girl," Osu replied. "Sanderson."

"She was a fine legionary," said Stryker. "And so are you, Sergeant. Mr. SpecMish here is right about one thing. Even when you're playing hooky, you're Legion to the core. Now, let's get out of here."

Osu was a hypocrite for keeping such a secret while condemning others for keeping theirs. Stryker knew that—they all did—but

Tavarius Stryker possessed the precious ability to easily brush aside issues that weren't about to kill him. Matter closed. Move on. Osu, too, pushed away any sense of guilt or shame. Not because it was easy, but because he had to.

The others, though, shot him looks of disdain as they formed up, ready to move out.

Only Zy Pel kept his thoughts guarded.

And Urdizine, Osu realized. The Zhoogene hadn't said a word during their stop.

Whatever was eating Urdizine would have to wait. They first had to survive Rho-Torkis and its Great Ice Plain because Bresca-Brevae lay at the far side, about 260 klicks away.

They had rested near the eastern border of the forest. As they pushed on, the trees thinned and the pelting of snow dropping through the needles stopped altogether. The snowstorm had ended.

It was dawn when they reached the edge of the forest and looked out upon the ice plain that stretched to the horizon. The rising red sun transformed the ice-scape into a sheet of polished fire.

There were no signs of ambush. No indication of life in any form once the trees stopped. It was a barren land, but that's what Osu was counting on. His route took them due east for three days, never passing closer than twenty klicks to a geographical feature significant enough to appear on his map. No one would find them here.

They set off into the endless sea of ice, wondering what horrors this new day would bring.

Osu was right. Their appearance into the ice plain went unnoticed.

But a few hours later, a patrolling micro-drone spotted the dying remnants of their heat trail and began a stealthy pursuit. And when it reached the party of five humanoids on hover bikes, its algorithms processed its observational data and categorized the party as hostile.

The drone was too dumb to conceptualize the idea of hostiles as anything more than a category in an enumerated data class. It could not feel hostility itself, any more than it could recommend a search and destroy team should intercept. It simply radioed back what it had found.

But the operator who received the transmission was a far more complex being who was not only capable of feeling hostility but sparked with excitement as he called for a search and destroy team, because he would join the chase himself.

* * * * *

Chapter Nine:
Osu Sybutu

"What are we going to do about the spy drone?" asked Zavage.

"The *alleged* spy drone," countered Stryker, who was huddled next to the Kurlei in the bivouac of camo sheets stretched between the circled bikes. "I haven't seen any drones. All we've picked up are two tight-burst transmissions, and the last was over an hour ago."

"What else could it be?" asked Zavage. He sounded distant from within the shadows of his hooded cloak. They all did.

"We will assume it's a drone for now," said Osu, "but that's not the most urgent question. What are we going to do about you, Urdizine?"

Everyone looked at the Zhoogene legionary whose answer was a groan of pain that had been held in for far too long.

"Sorry, Sergeant. Think I caught a fragment of Yergin's bike when he blew it up. Thought it would self-heal. Didn't want to be a burden."

"Injuries are to be reported and assessed. It's my place to decide whether you are a burden, SOTL Urdizine. Not yours. What's your status?"

"Shrapnel caught me upper-left abdomen. This armor I'm wearing smells like boiled slug hide but it managed to soak up most of the energy. I thought the hydraulic bands that underpin my muscles would push it out. They haven't, which means the fragment must have worked its way into the bands themselves. Someone needs to take a look who's skilled in Zhoogene field treatment."

"That would be Jonson and Bulmer," said Stryker wistfully. "None of us is skilled in patching up talking shrubbery like you."

"There's a Militia base forty klicks northeast of here," said Osu. "Fort Iceni. We could detour and drop you off."

"Allow the Militia to poke inside me?" Urdizine sounded indignant. Beneath his hood, the stems growing out the top of his head would be waving angrily. "I've a better idea. There's a town ninety klicks to the east called Raemy-Ela. It will be a much shorter detour and I can make it that far. Believe me, I'm not as fragile as you humes. All I have to do is harden my hydraulics around the wound. Can't do sit-ups, and I dread each bowel movement, but I won't die on you."

"You and your hydraulics," murmured Stryker. "If we're operating under cover, we should be using codenames. *Hydro*. That's your cover, Urdi."

"Hydro," Urdizine repeated, testing out the name. He laughed and immediately winced in pain. "Don't make me laugh. You're killing me. *Hydro*. Hey, it's not bad."

Why didn't I think of that?

Osu beat himself up. There hadn't been time to stop and consider such practical details, but of course that was no excuse.

"Good thinking, Stryker," he said. "If we really are being followed by a drone, it will have cameras, and in clear daylight it may be able to lipread. You will each have a cover name and from now on, we use them exclusively until I say so. Even inside your own head, think of your comrades by their codenames. Use your new name when thinking of yourself because one slip could make the difference between success and failure."

"*Old Guard* was my call sign on Irisur," said Stryker. "That works for me, but what about frond-head?"

Osu regarded SOTL Vol Zavage. "You're Teep because no one believes that thing you do with your head is anything other than telepathy."

The Kurlei sighed. "You humes are as predictable as always."

"If only that were true, Teep," answered Osu. "Zy Pel has to be Bronze and...Yergin. He earned a name, and it's Michelangelo for his beautiful ice sculptures. Maybe *Angelo*. Yeah, that sounds more practical."

A somber silence came over the bivouac as they dipped into memories still raw.

"Hydro," said Osu, "relieve Bronze on watch."

"Wait," said the Kurlei whom Osu told himself to think of as Teep. "There's someone still unnamed. We need a name for you, Sergeant, and you can't name yourself. That would be bad luck."

"I've already decided," Osu replied. "Figured luck's been so bad, nothing we can do will make it worse. Call me...*Sanderson*."

A few minutes later, with the wounded Zhoogene outside on watch, replacing Bronze—Osu was trying hard to stick to the codenames, even in his own thoughts—it was time to make further decisions.

"I need to get that crazy walking plant seen to properly," Osu informed the crouching circle of sappers. "That town he mentioned is too far away, so I intend to change course and head directly for the Militia at Fort Iceni. If hostile forces are tracking us—and I think

they are—then this should flush them out. It's only a half day's journey to Fort Iceni. We'll force the issue then reassess Hydro's state. If
he's worsened, I'll order him to seek treatment at Iceni. If he hasn't,
we'll make for Raemy-Ela together."

"I don't want to go anywhere near the Militia," said Stryker. "I
don't trust the treacherous skragg-wipers."

"And me?" Osu spat. "Do you think I can ever forgive them for
Irisur?" He took a deep breath. "Let's hope it doesn't come to that."

It was difficult to be sure beneath the hoods of their cloaks, but
the others appeared troubled yet acquiescent. Not so Bronze. Having
initially recoiled at his new name—as if it invoked a ghost from his
past who still haunted him—he settled into the ritual of filling and
lighting his pipe without the slightest sense of urgency.

Should have called him Stove, Osu mused.

"Have you something to say?" he challenged Bronze as the sapper blew his first plume of smoke.

"Yes…*Sanderson.*" Bronze spoke Osu's codename with obvious
disapproval. "How are we to defeat any pursuers?"

"Ambush."

"Good. Urdizine should be in the ambush party."

"Urdi's wounded," said Stryker. "I mean, Hydro."

Bronze clamped his pipe between his teeth and raised both hands
in supplication. "The green man is my friend too. I want him well. I
want the frenzied panic on your faces when he comes into season
again—when the weeds in his head bloom and cause mayhem because for a few days everyone succumbs to an insanity in which
green is irresistibly sexy. But we watched thousands die in seconds.
We can't bring them back by shielding a single life. They're gone.

Ambush duty's dangerous, is all I'm saying. Hydro is not too good at traveling right now, but he can still fire his weapon."

"If Hydro dies in the ambush," said Osu, "that removes one obstacle in the way of our mission objective. Is that your point?"

"Of course it is. Look, Hydro is a Zhoogene. He's outside on watch in the howling winds, but he can still hear every word we're speaking. Would you like me to ask him in, so he can volunteer?"

"Very well," said Osu. "Bronze, you lead the ambush party. Take Hydro and Stryker. Zavage, that leaves just you and me. Oh, hell! Zavage! Teep! Hydro! No, this isn't going to work. Zy Pel, your name has the potential to flag alerts far beyond everyone else here. You stay as Bronze. I will be Osu or Sybutu as everyone prefers. No one is to call me sergeant. That leaves, Urdi, Zavage, Stryker, and…Yergin. Commo talk is to be sloppy. Do like the Militia. We've ten minutes to figure out how to make that drone think we're still traveling as one unit before we move out. Destination: Fort Iceni."

* * * * *

Chapter Ten:
Lep Clynder

The three surviving targets rode their bikes in a tight column, headed directly for the Militia base twenty klicks away. Their leader was making the same distinctive gestures he'd been using since Lep had first picked up their trail when they'd emerged from the forest. He would sweep his arm or point as if indicating locations, but most of all he twisted around periodically to check his party was still cohesive, even though there were only three left after whatever had befallen them at the bivouac.

Target-1, Lep had designated the man, and he was reassured by the target's consistency, because precious little else made sense about the targets.

Lep peered into the viewer and tried to focus the drone's image. It was a hopeless task. The snow had started to fall once more, and since the event at the targets' bivouac, interference had been cutting static through the picture.

He couldn't even be sure that Target-1 was a *he*. But back when the image had been clearer, the PatRec system had decided the leader was most likely male human, so that's what Lep would run with.

Taking point, Target-2 had a slighter frame. Working assumption: human female. Lep's biggest question was the identity of Target-3. It seemed too short to be the wounded Zhoogene, but on the other hand, it was hunched over and rigid, exactly how a Zhoogene would be if its filthy alien body began locking up.

Even so, Target-3 had literally not moved a muscle in hours. It was a macabre thought, but as Lep studied the snowy scene taking place about twenty klicks northeast of his warm GPC-4 hover carrier, he began to think the rigid figure in the tattered cloak had been dead for some time, their corpse frozen solid and carried to its final destination by a bike on autopilot.

Sod it! They were Cora's Hope Division—supposedly one of the Rebellion's elite units—and his reconnaissance drone couldn't tell its operator whether a surveillance target was alive or dead. They were supposed to turn the galaxy upside down with equipment like this?

He tapped the image of the rigid biker and gestured for medical assessment.

Text appeared in the status window.

Supply higher fidelity surveillance data.

Lep banged on the monitoring system. "What you think I'm doing?" he grumbled at the stupid thing.

He had the whole scout-upgraded sensor suite wrapped around him. Heavy banks of interpretative quasi-intelligences topped up with monitors and status displays. The others quipped that his station was a nerd mech, and it *did* feel like he was wearing mechanized armor.

Fat lot of good it was doing them now.

"Problem, Technician?" asked Ensign Zywroal from the front of the carrier's personnel compartment.

Technician First Class Lep Clynder glanced jealously at the dozen scouts riding with the ensign. Most of them had dozed off, and he couldn't blame them in the smooth ride and gentle hum of the

GPC's gravitics. They had nothing to do until the lieutenant finally decided where she would make her move. Or maybe she would never make her mind up, and the scouts wouldn't be woken until they were required to stroll down the egress ramp and back into the forward operating post. There they'd pat themselves on the back and congratulate themselves on a job well done before going to grab a coffee and cake.

Was there a problem?

Yeah. The drone didn't work, and this military operation had been far too easy. But the truth wasn't what officers wanted to hear.

"I'm sorry, sir," Lep told the ensign, but also Lieutenant Nwyhypnaguran who was pretending to ignore him but would be listening in on every word. "I still can't say why, but something is wrong about the picture I'm seeing."

"But you have no new information to convey," said the lieutenant from her command position just behind the pilot and co-pilot.

"No, sir."

"Something's bugging Clynder," said Zywroal. "We might do well to follow his instincts. Recommend we change course and intercept targets one through three before they get too close to that Militia outpost. We can always return to the bivouac site after."

"Stay calm, Zywroal." There was an acid edge to Nwyhypnaguran's voice. She did not appreciate the unsolicited opinions of her subordinates. "We proceed as planned to the bivouac site. Technician Clynder will monitor the three active targets via the drone while we investigate the two inactive ones in person. May I remind you, Ensign, that our role here is to acquire intelligence. I wish to know who these people are, not to kill them. Their extermination is a task for the pacification forces who will follow."

Lep stuck his head into the monitoring system and kept his stupid mouth well and truly shut.

* * *

When he judged Lieutenant Nwyhypnaguran to be engrossed in the scene outside, Lep took his chance and raised his head from the feed streamed to his monitor by the drone twenty klicks away, and looked instead at the bulkhead screens showing what was happening outside the carrier.

The GPC was circling around the spot in the Great Ice Plain the targets had used to set up a bivouac stretched across their bikes.

It looked like an explosion had ripped their shelter apart. What had caused it? Lep didn't know. The surveillance feed had gone dead for a few minutes. When it had restored, a crater had appeared that hadn't been there before, and the three targets—who were still being tracked by the drone—were already riding north as fast as their bikes would take them.

Had the targets been attacked? Certainly, no member of Cora's Hope Division would abandon their comrades without good reason, but Lep had flown the drone around the site and it had not been obvious that the fleeing targets were in any immediate danger.

The carrier looped around a scene of destruction frozen into permanence by the cold.

Two humanoid corpses sprawled just beyond the lip of the crater. Their loose cloaks were frozen in the act of billowing in a wind that had died away hours ago.

Already, Lep was beginning to fear the cold of Rho-Torkis more than the prospect of the inevitable Legion retaliation that would come, perhaps within days.

The two bikes also looked frozen into place. The blast must have thrown them up and dropped them on their rears, resting against the side of the crater. They appeared caught in the act of pulling a near-vertical wheelie—not a bad trick for a hover bike.

"Hey! That one moved," said Uxham. "The body farthest to the east. Its hand moved."

Lep followed the scout's pointing finger to one of the bulkhead monitors.

All he could see was a body whose contours were softened by snow.

"Been eating those special cakes again, Uxham?" piped up one of the other scouts.

But whoever it was, he didn't get the laughs he was after because everyone was watching a hand raising feebly out of the snow.

Uxham was right.

The figure rolled out of its snowy covering and waved pitifully for help. Then it lay still, its last energy reserves spent.

"An excellent turn of events," said Lieutenant Nwyhypnaguran. "I had feared the corpses would prove too frozen to extract much information. Pilot, circle us around that wounded target. Remain cautious and pull out immediately if anything smells wrong to you. If I judge this scene is as innocent as it appears, then we'll set down a hundred meters away and, Zywroal, you will secure the area before approaching the target."

"Sir, I think the live target is the Zhoogene," said Lep. "Movement is all wrong for a human. We know it's been wounded since we first tracked it."

"So," said Nwyhypnaguran, "they've left behind their wounded. Whoever we're facing clearly has no honor. And you, Clynder, are supposed to keep your eyes on the drone feed! If you disobey orders again, it will be you who's abandoned out there in the snow."

Lep gave a vague apology, but his mind was too busy filling with horror to worry about the lieutenant's threats.

If the Zhoogene was here, who was Target-3, twenty klicks away?

He glanced back at his monitor. The display was blank except for a dangerous message.

No input feed. Reconnect device.

"Sir!" he snapped, but before he could give his warning, one of the other scouts beat him to it.

"Movement! Below us. Inside the crater."

"Bugging out!" announced the pilot as the smooth hum of the engine suddenly roared, throwing Lep against his restraints.

Helpless, he watched as two hostiles emerged from concealed hollows in the sides of the crater and punched the controls of the two bikes without bothering to mount them.

They'd timed their appearance to perfection. The speeding hover carrier passed over the firing arcs of the bike cannons as they spat blaster fire into the air.

Impacts rippled along the GPC's underbelly.

And then the craft shuddered in the air as the gravitics blew out.

That was the problem with gravitics. Always had been. Put as much armor as you like elsewhere, but gravitic vehicles would always be vulnerable to attack from underneath.

Which was why 2nd Regiment had upgraded their ride to the GPC-4c "Fat Belly" variant. It maneuvered like a drunken Littorane out of water, was slower than praise emerging from Nwyhypnaguran's lips, but had layers of armor bolted between the deck and the bank of gravitic motors.

They lost all lift and skimmed across the ground in a blinding spray of snow.

Nervous glances spread like a disease, but although the gravitics had blown, the belly armor held. They were shaken, and immobilized. But they were unhurt.

And spoiling for revenge.

"Alpha Section, man the gun ports!" bellowed the ensign. "Beta, ready to deploy. Final check."

While half the squad began calling out that they were ready to charge down the ramp, the rest opened the armored shutters in the bulkheads and poked out their blaster rifles, seeking targets.

They were already too late.

One of the hover bikes had ridden up a ramp built into the side of the crater, and was sailing through a hurried volley of blaster fire before landing on the GPC's roof. The rider even had his face exposed, wearing a hat, and—of all things—he had a long smoking pipe clenched between his teeth.

Lep couldn't believe what he was seeing in the external cam feed. Who were these devils?

"Keep that ramp closed," said the lieutenant. "The hostile on the roof is obviously intending to shoot us as we disembark."

A ripple of fear passed through the scouts, Lep included.

"Stay calm," roared Sergeant Nialeg. "The buggers have crippled our motors. That's bad. But the carrier's armor is still solid, our guns are hot, and our rifles are ready to make an accounting. That's also bad...*for them*. And if that idiot on the roof hasn't broken his neck in the landing, he's wasting his time. He'll never get through the roof armor. We'll burst through the roof hatches and catch him in crossfire. For purity!"

"Purity! Purity!" replied the scouts.

Lep didn't join in, too busy using his station to flick through the external cam feeds, looking for targets for the carrier's autocannon pods to service. But there was nothing.

"Er...Sarge?" queried one of the scouts readying to deploy through the roof hatches. "Can you smell something? It's—I don't know...ozone?"

An instant later, a circular disc of foam dropped down onto the scout's head from a hole that had miraculously appeared in the roof.

"Frags out, rebels," said a man's voice as two grenades followed the—

It's a boarding patch.

The thought just had time to register in Lep's mind that he was seeing a piece of ancient military technology from a long-dead era before the grenades went off, and the Fat Belly hover carrier became a fat-bellied slaughterhouse.

* * * * *

Chapter Eleven:
Osu Sybutu

"**S**o, speak!" Osu demanded of the sullen rebel.

The squatting man kept his gaze down at the ice beneath his boots, ice turned red by a ruby sky approaching dusk.

It cast a demonic glow on the interrogation proceedings, but also softened the bloodstains on the rebel's greatcoat. Maybe that would loosen him up.

He said nothing.

Was he still in shock? Zy Pel...*Bronze*...had said that when they'd pulled the only survivor out of the wreckage of the rebel carrier, he hadn't resisted, but he'd screamed uncontrollably. They'd had to gag him before setting him riding pillion behind Stryker.

Osu wasn't convinced this was shock. Time for another line of attack.

The man started shivering.

"Stryker, set the bikes to throw some heat. We won't learn anything from an icicle."

"You won't learn anything anyway," the man grumbled.

"All we really want to know is what the hell is going on with this damned planet," Osu explained. "Is this an invasion? Are we in a civil war now? And why in the Five Hells was a military unit sent to kill us? *Us!* We represent an interstellar mining corporation. Who the hell did you think we were?"

The man shuddered, and this time it wasn't the cold. "We saw...things. Horrors in the woods. Creatures that cannot be. We thought that's what you were, and we followed you because we needed to know what we were facing. The guys call them vampire jacks. They had Legion equipment, and they looked like normal people on the outside. But they weren't. They bit!"

"We aren't certain what they are," said Bronze. "But there are no such things as vampires, and *we* don't bite."

The rebel looked up with interest for the first time, peering inside Bronze's hood. "It's you. The rider with the breach patch. I didn't know such things existed any more. Why would a miner carry around a treasure like that?"

"They wouldn't," said Osu, "but Bronze here is a merc. He runs our escort team, and what pit of thieves he might visit to buy his toys is the kind of question I know to avoid asking."

"Let's say I believe you," said the rebel. "You're not vamps. You're not military. What are you going to do with me?"

Osu shrugged. "It depends on the answers you give. Is it the Rebellion's intention to seize mining rights on Rho-Torkis for itself?"

"No, of course not."

"Then we aren't enemies. Tell us what's happening to Rho-Torkis, and I'll set you free."

The rebel withdrew into himself to consider his response. He flinched when Bronze stretched out a gauntleted finger and traced the unit patches on the man's lacerated greatcoat.

"You're a scout," Bronze said. "2nd Regiment, Cora's Hope Division. Says so right here on your shoulder. We assumed you were with the Rebellion, but you're Cora's World regular troops. I heard the situation had gone absolutely to drent in your system but is Cora's World exporting its insanity now? Is Cora's World trying to become Cora's Empire?"

"I stand with the Rebellion," insisted the rebel. His face fell. "My world has descended into hell. We got away in time. It's why we need to forge a new Federation where the bonds between all strata of society are strong. It's time to start again."

"Like you did on your homeworld?" Bronze gave him a contemptuous grunt. "I was briefed. You had your own little homespun political revolution, didn't you? You didn't need vampire cults or alien invaders, the madness came from within you. All it took was the usual slime-spined Militia who will turn a blind eye to anything for the right price, and a heap of totalitarian bigots who deluded themselves they were creating a pristine new world order. *By any means necessary.* I bet you cheered them on, rebel scout. Until one day you woke up and found yourself atop a mountain of corpses—those who had to die because they hadn't sung out the political mantra with sufficient fervor. Ideological purity is a madness that won't stop until your planet's a ghost world with two final survivors stalking each other, looking for an opening to kill the last betrayer of the narrative."

"You don't believe any of that speech, do you?"

"No? Every civic center on your planet has a place of public execution where political enemies of the new world order are put to death on the hour, every hour, every day, forever."

"It's true," the rebel admitted. "The movement was betrayed. That's why we sided with a Federation-wide alliance of liberation. The Rebellion. This time we will get it right."

"Easy," Osu snapped. "Both of you. Don't mind Bronze, he snaps worse than he bites. Look, why not tell us your name? We already know your unit. See, I'll tell you ours. That there is Urdi. He's Zavage, and Stryker is standing outside."

"They sound like code names."

"Some. But they're the mercs. I'm a geologist. My name's…Sybutu. What's yours?"

"Lep. Lep Clynder."

"Well, Lep. I still don't know what we're up against here. I thought the Rebellion was a political movement with a military wing whose existence it denied, not that anyone believed you. And here you are, regular troops from Cora's World nuking a peaceful planet, murdering thousands within seconds."

"I'm ex-Legion," said Bronze. "Whatever you may think of the corrupt skragg-necks and aristo-hats who run the stinking Federation, most legionaries are decent folk trying to do the right thing in a galaxy where acts of decency are condemned by a sea of haters as reactionary deviance."

"I've nothing to do with that," Lep said hurriedly. "We're Scout Company. We come in quietly. Take a look. Get out. If all goes well, no one gets hurt. No one's supposed to know we're even there."

"Don't mind him, Lep," Osu reassured the scout. "Though I don't blame him for smarting at what you did to the legionaries."

"I didn't do anything. I have never fired a weapon in anger. I swear it!"

Osu held up his hands. "Okay. I believe you. I'm just saying that I'm the one in charge here, not the merc—who, by the way, was kicked out of the Legion and with good reason—and all I need to know before I can let you go is your intentions here. Is this an invasion? A raid? Are there rebel authorities who will maintain the rule of commercial law, or should I hightail it to the nearest spaceport and evacuate my team? Give me a reason to set you free, Lep."

"I cannot say."

Osu stared at Lep, considering his next move. It didn't look as if the rebel was going to say anything else of use, but Osu wasn't ready to give up just yet. "Do you have someone special to return to, Lep?

Someone who would miss you if we hadn't pulled you from that personnel carrier?"

"Alyssa," he replied. From inside his jacket, the rebel pulled out a holo-wallet showing a smiling young human woman and practically shoved it in the faces of everyone there inside the ring of warm bikes.

Lep seemed eager to establish a human connection to his captors. It had the opposite effect on Osu's scorched soul.

"I expect she's worried about you," he said acidly.

"Yes," said Lep. "Terrified."

"But you know she loves you and that helps get you through. That so?"

He nodded.

Osu laughed. It was not a happy sound. "I envy you that. My girlfriend's name is Nydella. I never had the guts to tell her that I loved her. Seems stupid, really. I've always been too scared I'd scare her away."

"You should take courage," said Lep, relieved to be making this connection. The others looked away grimly. "Trust your feelings."

"Yeah. I should have."

The rebel froze. Doubt clouded his eyes.

"Shame you nuked her."

Osu drew his plasma pistol and burned a hole through the rebel scout's head.

He stared at the corpse for a few moments after it had slumped to the ground. Then he glared at the others, daring someone to criticize his state of mind, even his ethics. Several look thoughtful, but none spoke.

"We have a mission," said Osu. "That man got in our way. His life was forfeit the moment he took up arms against the Legion."

"You don't have to justify yourself to us, Sergeant," said Zavage.

"Contact!" shouted Stryker from outside the circle of bikes. "Skragg! We're surrounded."

"Federation Militia," announced an amplified voice before Osu had even grabbed his blaster and peered over his bike. "Put down your weapons or die."

"Sorry, guys," said the failed sentry, but Osu didn't blame Stryker. Even as he watched, soldiers rose out of the snow like winter-camo zombies rising from a graveyard. He estimated thirty, and more were appearing every second.

One giant of a man threw off his camo-cloak and stood ten feet away from Osu, as if a herald awaiting the reply to take back to his master. Over his chain armor, he wore a huge cloak of fake animal fur. Beneath a metal helmet steaming in the cold air, the man's beard was plaited and set with beads. If Osu had harbored any doubt that this was indeed what passed for a soldier in the Militia, the man's rifle was slung over his huge shoulder. His weapon of choice was a war hammer, which he swung impatiently.

"Hold your fire," yelled Osu, though he stayed behind the cover of the bikes. "We're Legion. Everyone stand down. We're on the same side. We're Legion."

"We know you're Legion," said the pale-skinned Viking herald. "We overheard your little chat after you executed the rebel scout."

Militia troopers approached the bikes casually, with rifles slung.

Osu lowered his weapon to the ground and stood erect with arms in surrender. "We're on the same side."

The Viking shook his head and clicked his tongue. "Now, that's where we have a problem. Your typical Legion arrogance means you lack attention to detail." The troopers were leaping over the bikes now. "You see, the two statements contradict each other. Let me spell it out. You can be Legion, or you could be on the side of the

Militia and the Federation. But you can't be both. Legionaries, you see, are traitors."

"Don't shoot them," Osu ordered his team, and checked that the others weren't going to put up a brief resistance. "And don't believe anything that comes out the mouth of these prison scum."

"I'm glad you're Legion," said a woman who'd perched her butt on the nearest bike and was watching Osu with her head resting in her hands. He sensed a quiet lethality about her that reminded him of the SpecMish man currently going by the name of Bronze.

She pulled back her hood to reveal an unnaturally white face completely covered in tattoos: roses weeping black blood.

"Killing is normally such an ugly business," she said. "Every death is a wound to the soul for soldiers like you and me, Sybutu, and you *are* a killer. I can tell that poor Lep Clynder was not your first kill. The lives we take…even for killers like us, it seems so slight at the time, Sergeant, but each one festers and never heals. Have you learned that yet?"

She hopped off the bike and sauntered over, laughing like a child. She looked up at him clicking her tongue. "Which is why it's such a relief that you turn out to be legionaries."

Dread crept along Osu's spine. Troopers were walking behind him, but he couldn't see. He couldn't turn around. And when he tried to cry out a warning…he voiced only silence.

"Legionaries, you see"—she covered her head once more—"are different. Killing you won't leave an ugly residue. In fact, it'll be fun, and boy, do I need some fun."

She reached up and plucked something from his neck: a small dart which she presented in front of his eyes before storing in a pouch in her coat.

"Let's see if this has worked, shall we?"

She poked him in the sternum with a single digit and over he went, his body completely rigid.

His head hit the ground hard, but he barely felt a thing.

"No peeking," said the Militia trooper before someone unseen secured a hood over his head.

They'd paralyzed him. He could see nothing through the hood, smell only leather and sweat, and had only a vague sense of being dragged along the ground before being dumped into a vehicle, although they could be phantom sensations he'd imagined to fit with his expectations.

His ears, though…they worked only too well. The tattooed woman, who volunteered her name as Trooper Lily Hjon, would not shut up. She spent the entire journey to Fort Iceni telling him the many ways she was going to enjoy torturing him.

Osu had some personal experience with torture. Enough that he could tell from her whispered details that she had a whole lot more.

And she knew that the most harrowing torture was often the simplest.

"You're their sergeant," she told him a hundred times in variations of the same cruel barb. "They look to you to keep them safe. And did you? No. You let them be captured without a fight. And now they'll suffer for your failure."

The journey to Fort Iceni was not long in distance, but it felt endless to Osu's soul, because the yapping tattooed trooper was right. He *had* failed his team. Better all around if it had been he and not Yergin who'd bought the others an exit through the phony legionaries.

But even the longest journeys end eventually. He felt a jolt as their transport halted. Then a burning pain in his neck and a merciless tingling in his extremities.

They had arrived, and he was recovering.

Whatever the Militia had planned, they had made a mistake in not killing him straight away. A mistake they would pay for.

Hic manebimus optime.

He was Osu Sybutu.

He was Legion.

And he would *never* give up.

* * * * *

Chapter Twelve:
Osu Sybutu

Osu rolled his shoulder blades against the boulder, trying to soak up every last morsel of heat from the rock into the naked flesh of his back. He felt his blood pumping hard in its attempt to transfer the life-sustaining warmth—modest though it was—to his chest, his face, and his numb arms that dangled uselessly over his head, brushing the icy stone ground of this accursed courtyard.

He couldn't hold out much longer.

The resolve not to tell the Militia anything still held, but his interrogator had yet to ask him a question. At the beginning, Lily Hjon had declared she had no interest in extracting information from him, only pain. He had thought her words an interrogator's gambit, but so far it was looking as if she had spoken truly.

So far, his battle had not been a test of wills with the Militia trooper, but a rerun of a more ancient battle: man against the elements.

After stripping him naked from the waist up, a mob of troopers had chained him upside down to a rounded boulder that had been warmed to stretch out this rearguard action against the cold of Rho-Torkis.

At least he was spared the sight of his body succumbing to frost-bite, because his eyelids had frozen in place and his blurry eyesight was icing over.

A last wave of anger shook his body, rattling the manacles securing his ankles to the rock.

Immediately, he cursed his weakness. He knew any sounds he made would summon *her*.

Sure enough, he heard the familiar footsteps approach, and then hands in insulated gloves lifted his head away from the rock and into the cold.

Gently, she huffed her hot breath over his eyes, releasing them from their icy coating. The warmth that had passed through her lungs smelt of cigarettes and coffee, and he realized that she must be sitting nearby, enjoying the entertainment of a slow death. Perhaps through the windows of a mess hall.

Were others watching him too?

And what of his comrades? He hadn't seen them since the Militia had taken them from the ice plain. Were they in the same courtyard at Fort Iceni, chained to other rocks?

He tried to call out to them, but his chest and throat were frozen solid.

Hjon shushed him like a child...or—strangely—even the intimacy of a lover. Drawing back her hood, she wiped away his slushy tears with her warm cheek. Then she stood back, and her tattooed face clarified in his vision.

Expecting this to be his last chance, Osu tried to make sense of Trooper Lily Hjon. The words she flung with abandon sparked with a spiteful cruelty that didn't match her face. She seemed dulled by tragedy that she tried to cover with sarcasm and tattoos.

Osu wasn't fooled. This was a woman performing a role. Militia Trooper was not what Lily Hjon was meant to be.

She could be cast into the Five Hells for all eternity for all Osu cared, except that just maybe this untapped restlessness he sensed in her was a last straw for him to clutch.

Still grasping the back of his skull, Lily moved closer until all he could see was an upside-down pair of feminine eyes.

"Is there something you wish to ask me, Sergeant?" She spoke in ecstatic gasps, as if aroused by this interplay.

Osu wasn't buying any of it.

Her falseness gave him hope, but the biting cold was all too real.

"Wh…wh…why?" he stuttered. With his brain and his lips so numb, it was a supreme effort to say even that.

"Why?" she echoed, and then let his head drop to crack against the boulder. "Because despite your pretty, dark flesh, I can never ignore that you're still Legion. And even if you haven't wronged me personally, there's plenty enough guilt attached to those of your order who have. The deaths of you and your men will not even begin to compensate. Especially not after what you did to Raven Company."

Osu wanted to ask what she meant, but the cold had him too strongly in its grip, and he watched her depart through misting eyes.

But she hadn't abandoned him to his death. He couldn't see, couldn't move, but he heard the ringing of metal on metal and the hum of a power unit starting.

She returned, bulkier than before and holding something.

He jerked in his chains as a sudden whoosh of flame lit the cold air of the courtyard. She was carrying a flame projector.

"Let's see if we can warm you up," she teased, releasing another gout of fire from the weapon's barrel.

She was a couple of feet away and the warmth from the flames was invigorating. He felt his strength return.

"Why?" he repeated. "Militia and Legion, we can work together."

Hjon pointed the barrel at him, leaving the muzzle between his eyes close enough to sear his brow. "Not anymore."

"Ahhh! But we can. I've done it." He smelled his flesh smolder. "Hnnnnn! At my last posting."

She dropped the barrel, and Rho-Torkis immediately supplied a soothing balm of icy chill to his tortured flesh. "You are not a good liar."

That was true. He had been part of a joint Militia-Legion operation on Irisur, but it had taken only hours before each side had trained their weapons on the other.

Lily had gone!

The cold had already leached the heat away from the burn on his forehead, and he was ready to beg for the flamer's return.

Where was she?

The flame thrower unleashed a long burst nearby.

From behind.

"Tell me when you're warm enough," said Hjon cheerfully from the other side of the boulder, before hurling more fire at the rock.

He could feel the surface warming between his shoulder blades.

"A bit more?" she teased. "You got it." She poured more flame into the boulder.

"That's enough," Osu shouted. His back was now slick with sweat.

"What's that?" Hjon called. "That's not hot enough?" She played fire over the stone.

"Stop!"

"More hot?"

Lily was laughing now, and when Osu began thrashing his body, trying to keep his flesh away from the burning rock, her laughter grew louder.

"Please!"

She ceased her laughs and powered down her flame projector.

"Better," she said bitterly and walked away, leaving Osu shackled upside down across a boulder that was rapidly cooling, but not quickly enough to prevent him screaming in agony.

* * * * *

Chapter Thirteen:
Vetch Arunsen

Five Days Earlier

Vetch Arunsen ran into the courtyard with the stupid fat fingers of his left hand struggling to fasten the strap beneath his helmet, while his right kept the haft of his war hammer close to his body. The weapon's sling mostly did a good job of holding it securely, but even in its collapsed state, his melee weapon of choice had a nasty habit of battering his kneecaps when he sprinted.

He sensed a slowing down of the stream of troopers racing to Raven Company's assembly point near the punishment area that could be viewed from the chow hall.

Upon the walkways and watchtowers, he saw sentries moving with a bored shuffle. Wrapped up tight in cold weather gear, they feared neither the bitter cold of Rho-Torkis nor the assault of an enemy. They weren't even afraid of their officers.

No, sir. This was not a base under attack.

Vetch knew exactly what this call to arms really was: another meaningless exercise in keeping Raven Company on its toes and its troopers miserable.

He slowed to a jog and let his helmet straps dangle freely. They were barely noticeable in the great mass of his beard anyway.

What he couldn't do was look his comrades in the eye. Raven was not like the other companies in the Fort Iceni garrison. They were fair game for every petty torture its officers could devise because Raven was a punishment company. It was everyone else's duty to make Raven suffer before it could ever hope to atone for its crimes.

He took his place in the front rank of his squad and cursed the guilt that washed over him like it always did. Raven Company's plight was an injustice, of course. Legion misunderstanding and arrogance had been seized upon by a corrupt Militia officer as an excuse to dump them here on Rho-Torkis.

Captain Solikin-Goh watched her company assemble from the top of the south gate.

How much did the Raven's new commander know about the real reason for the company's presence in Rho-Torkis? They hadn't been posted here to be punished; they had been sent here to die for the crime of knowing too much.

And he, Sergeant Vetch Arunsen, knew more than all of them, because he was the one who had provided the excuse for Raven Company to be punished.

They'd been sent here to die in the ice of Rho-Torkis because of him.

Well, bugger that!

Vetch had never been good at rolling over and being a victim.

He would be the one to get the Ravens reinstated in a place of honor.

But how to do it? That was proving tricky to figure out. And every day the endless cold and the mindless routine made it more difficult to think.

The captain descended the steps from the top of the south gate, looking unbalanced with her folded wings adding considerable bulk beneath her coat. Something had gotten the Gliesan excited and Vetch found himself hoping she didn't slip and break her neck. He was surprised to find himself care. Solikin-Goh had been promoted directly from ensign—scarcely knowing more than which end of a rifle went bang—but at least she appeared dedicated to restoring Raven Company's good name, no matter how many of its personnel had to die to achieve her aim.

"Bet the captain's itching to unfurl her wings and glide," said Lily from the other end of the front rank.

Vetch gave a little chuckle at Lily's comment. It was true. Gliesans were a race of gliders who had a bizarre dislike of descending steps. To them, it was like an embarrassing bodily function. Nature intended them to glide; steps were a convenience you used when no one was watching.

"I'd like to see her try," said Meatbolt from the rear rank. "Reckon her wings would get frostbite before touching down on the floor."

"Button it," Vetch growled.

Meatbolt was a good lad and would do well, unless his unguarded mouth got him chained to one of the punishment boulders and his frozen corpse left there indefinitely as an inspiration to the others.

"Sorry, Sergeant."

Vetch grimaced. He was going to have to teach the youngster when to shut up very soon.

Too late. As Solikin-Goh took a place in front of her assembled company, Vetch's platoon commander, Lieutenant Shen, turned his head around to scowl at the ill-disciplined enlisted ranks behind him.

Shen ran his withering stare over his troopers, making them quail under its intensity, quelling all disorder through an all-consuming mix of respect and fear for their platoon commander.

At any rate, that was probably what was running through Shen's little head.

But if that really was the effect he thought he was bringing out in his troopers, he was an even bigger fool than he looked.

Like the other troopers, Vetch wore a comm headset beneath a heated fabric hat that kept the frostbite from his ears. A metal helmet perched on top; in his case, one with cheek plates and a crest that could have come straight out of the Bronze Age if not for the pair of helmet lamps.

The heated hat was so bulky that the helmet's eye cut outs opened onto his forehead. And it wasn't just him. With their randomized great coats, helmets, and other equipment, the other troopers looked like vagabonds standing in lines.

Not so Lieutenant Julius Shen. His helmet was a highly polished silver affair with an elegantly curved rim, modeled on ancient European Renaissance designs from Earth. His comm unit was integrated with the helmet, as was an advanced impact energy dissipation system, and climate control that included the ability to blow warm air over the ears, which were uncovered despite the intense cold. It was so highly polished that the captain had ordered him to add a fabric covering for operational use, lest its reflection advertised his unit's position.

Vetch knew that he himself looked like a scruffy barbarian.

Better that than look a complete arse.

"Troopers of Raven Company," announced the captain in her high-pitched Gliesan voice, which made her words very clear. "Thanks to our sharp-eyed sentries, I have wonderful news."

Vetch groaned. This sounded like a new and exciting way to get her company killed.

"Tomorrow morning you were due to embark on a convoy of trucks that would transport you to the new guard post in the perimeter around the ASI-39 dig site. There you would have established the post, readying it for Legion reinforcements due in a few weeks. Troopers, it is not often that the Legion begs the Militia for aid, so it was natural that I volunteered us for this notable role."

And we were duly lumped with it, thought Vetch. No one else would go near such a sucky job. So what have the sentries found to change all this?

"It was an opportunity to show the Legion we are as good as them. Better, in fact. To the south of us, at this very moment, a large body of legionaries is marching west across the Great Ice Plain in the direction of Camp Faxian. Marching! Why would they march if not to assert their mettle in front of us? I believe this is a test, and I do not intend for us to fail it. Therefore, we shall eschew our motorized transport and will march alongside our rivals and allies."

We? I bet you won't be joining us on the march, Captain.

"Ravens, you are designated a punishment company. I will seize every opportunity to prove you can rise above your mistakes on Lose-Viborg and demonstrate your true worth here on Rho-Torkis. Now is your opportunity to repay my faith in you. Ravens, we move out in thirty minutes. Liberty or death!"

* * * * *

Chapter Fourteen:
Vetch Arunsen

When Raven Company set out into the snow to join with the legionaries, the air was crystal clear and sharp as a blade against any exposed skin. The freshly laid snow crunched beneath their boots with an obscene spitting sound. Within minutes, though, the western horizon darkened in anger and blew snow into their faces. Swirls of pitiless white brought land and sky together into a featureless hell.

Snowstorms on the Great Ice Plain could last for weeks, but mercifully this one blew over in less than an hour. By then, the troopers had lost all sense of direction and found themselves a mile to the east of Fort Iceni and, luckily, in the marching line of the legionaries headed west.

The troopers fell in with their rivals, saving their energy by stepping into the footsteps the jack-heads had flattened into the snow. At least, the humanoid ones did.

Trooper Ndemo-327-Cerulian—her name usually shortened by her comrades to Enthree—was not humanoid. The progeny of Muryani traders, Enthree was a hairy, six-limbed insectoid whom Vetch was attempting to inject with the rightful Militia sense of heavy cynicism. She soon gave up on following the humanoid footsteps and punched her hoof-like feet through the snow in time to a very different gait.

135

"I hold many questions about Fort Iceni that I cannot resolve," she announced to the crisp air. "Most of all, I do not understand why it is located in the middle of this great mass of featureless ice and snow, many miles from any other settlement."

The legionaries they were marching with gave no more reaction to Enthree's words than they had to any of the troopers. It was as if the troopers who had joined them from Fort Iceni were ghosts, manifesting as ephemeral shades to those elevated to the legionary plane of existence.

By contrast, Enthree's squadmates hopped into closer trails of footprints to better hear the latest episode of the squad Muryani's special brand of naivety.

"The locations of other Militia garrisons are considered with great care," she continued. "They might be close by the local center of political power. Perhaps guarding the mouth of a river, the main spaceport, or a major junction on a key trade route. None of those are so for Fort Iceni."

"I don't care where they put a base," said Meatbolt, "so long as it's somewhere that has proper roads. And people. People are good."

"In my experience," offered Lily, "if the Militia does something that makes no sense on the surface, then there's a hidden reason that involves money."

"Fair point," Meatbolt responded. "Got to be to do with the minerals."

Vetch glanced at the young human trooper. Even in his padded white cloak, the great bulk of Meatbolt's torso was obvious. Clearly, his veins ran more purely than most with the blood of the ancient titans who had served as Legion Marines back in the Orion Era. It wasn't just his physique, but his martial temperament also fitted with the tales told of those long-ago legionaries.

He had high hopes for the boy, but Meatbolt had a lot to learn first. And quickly.

"How do you figure that?" Vetch asked. "Everyone knows this region is rich with deposits. There's Leezore, xonryllium, holmium, and probably a rich seam of that gunk Enthree rubs on her hooves to stop them from splitting."

"They are *not* hooves," the alien insisted. "I possess foot-hands, and I do not understand why you mock my regime of dutiful hygiene. You insist we keep our weapons greased with the correct low-temperature lubricants. What's so different about my moisturizers?"

"Suit yourself, Trooper," Vetch replied, trying not to laugh. "All I'm saying to our budding young geologist here is that the ten feet plus of permanent ice covering the ground is kind of a problem."

"Is it?" Meatbolt sounded pleased with himself. "I reckon some aristo-hat staff officer already owns the land rights. They ordered Fort Iceni to be built here, and then put themselves in a stasis pod for a century or two. When the world thaws, they'll wake up to find the land worth a fortune, and a Militia base nearby to ensure their ownership rights are protected."

The squad crunched onward. And if they were like Vetch, they were all stunned by the longest statement Meatbolt had ever uttered that wasn't on his usual topics of food, sex, or firearms.

"You know," Vetch said, "that's actually pretty smart, Meatbolt. It might even be true. But I'm shocked. Shocked, I say, that such cynicism can escape those innocent sweet lips of yours. Where could you possibly have learned such skepticism?"

"Err," Meatbolt replied, confused. "You and Lily, Sarge. Mostly."

Vetch added 'Beginner's Guide to Irony' to 'How One Keeps One's Dumb Mouth Shut' on the list of things he needed to teach Meatbolt.

Suddenly, the going underfoot got a lot easier. Vetch guessed that the Ravens had been following a group of Legion stragglers who'd lost their way and been forced to break a fresh trail through the deep snow. Now they had rejoined the route of the main column where the snow had been flattened by the passage of many legionary boots.

Thousands.

Up ahead, the marching column stretched beyond the horizon. A few individuals stood out against the white background like an army of distant ants, but mostly the winter-camo legionaries were invisible; it was the highway they'd flattened out of the snow that betrayed their enormous numbers.

From her cozy gatehouse vantage point, Captain Solikin-Goh had given Vetch the impression that she'd seen a company of legionaries and wished to force a favorable comparison with her own Ravens.

A company? This felt more like a brigade. And if the Legion was swallowing its pride and asking the Militia for a company to fill a shortfall in its numbers, how come an entire brigade appeared that wasn't in any Table of Organization and Equipment that he'd been briefed on.

An entire brigade not on the TO&E? Even for the Legion, that was seriously odd.

If he were in command of Raven Company, he'd be on the radio to Major Yazzie, urging her to rouse the colonel out of bed and ask him to find out what the hell was going on.

Only problem was, Vetch wasn't the Raven's boss, and Solikin-Goh was back at base relaxing her wings in her warm quarters.

He glanced across at the trooper who had once been a company commander, and on this planet too.

"You need to go through the lieutenant," she told him.

All he'd done was glance Lily Hjon's way, but the disgraced former officer knew precisely what was on his mind. "It's the only way. Sorry, Vetch. It's your duty to do this."

He took a deep breath that burned his lungs with cold. Lieutenant Julius Shen's uncle was a major-league aristo-hat, with palaces, seats on the boards of several interstellar corporations, and, yes, the formal hats that looked like stacked Shinto temples inlaid with priceless jewels.

The fact that his nephew was stuck in the position of a lowly lieutenant said a lot about Shen's lack of competence and ambition. Maybe it also spoke of a limit to the Militia high command's willingness to permit the service's officer corps to become a laughing stock.

Perhaps, but even if Shen was a lowly platoon commander, he was still *Vetch's* platoon commander.

While Vetch searched for an angle that might prompt Shen into action, Meatbolt started waving his arms excitedly. "Watch this!" he cried. Before Vetch could stop him, the youngster was marching in lockstep with one of the legionaries, matching the jack-head stride for stride.

Sort of.

Vetch frowned. Now he saw one of his own troopers in such direct comparison with one of the legionaries…something about the way the jack-heads were marching wasn't right.

"These legionaries move strangely," said Enthree.

Orion's balls! If even the big bug could see it, then something must be up.

"Maybe we've stumbled across a Zhoogene unit," suggested Deep Tone.

"No such thing," said Sward, the only Zhoogene in the squad. "And even if there were, these drones don't move like my people. I think they're drunk."

Drunk? Outside of their bases, the Legion was always as sober as a Littorane priest. If they were drunk, then they sure as the Five Hells were not legionaries.

Vetch clicked his tongue twice to activate his headset. "Lieutenant Shen, this is Arunsen. Request switch to channel 13."

"Legionaries are never drunk outside of their burrows," Lily replied to Sward's comment while Vetch listened for the lieutenant's reply on his headset. "As children, future jack-heads can pass as normal people. But then, during the Legionary induction, a prophylactic is inserted up their arses, which is infused with the quintessence of arrogance and will release slowly throughout their lives, protecting them from the dangers of humility. With this sense of superiority throbbing in their backsides, it's no surprise they walk funny."

Lily made Vetch chuckle, which was unfortunate because he was still laughing when Shen replied.

"What is it, Arunsen?"

"Request we switch to channel 13, sir."

"This had better be good. Switching…"

Vetch lifted up his helmet to turn the channel selector switch on the side of his headset.

"Are you even there, Arunsen?" Shen obviously didn't realize the lesser members of the People's Army had clunkier switch gear.

"Yes, sir. It's the legionaries. Something's wrong. The entire squad is telling me the jacks aren't acting right, and where the hell has this brigade sprung from? The existing garrison at ASI-39 is only brigade strength and they're requesting Militia reinforcements. So who is it we've stumbled across in the snow by accident? Do we actually know who we're marching with?"

"*Something* is wrong." The radio signal faithfully carried the contempt in Shen's voice. "Some. *Thing*. If you have a matter to report, Sergeant Arunsen, then you will use *specifics*. Numbers. Directions. Facts! Don't distract your superiors with vague feelings that are probably a result of crashing blood sugar because you haven't stuffed your fat gut in the past hour. They are legionaries, Arunsen, and we are following them to the security zone around ASI-39. If I catch you suggesting otherwise, then I will have every member of your squad flogged, and I will make sure to let them know who to blame for the scars on their back. Am I clear?"

Another snowstorm was rolling in from the western horizon. Already it was swallowing the extent of the column they were marching with. It didn't change the facts, though. And although it would cut visibility to a few feet, it wouldn't make the slightest difference to their platoon commander's ability to see what was going on around him.

Even in a perfectly clear day, he was blind to almost everything.

Vetch conceded defeat. For now.

"Yes, sir. I understand. Arunsen out."

"Problem?" Lily asked as he switched his comm back to the squad channel.

She'd been listening to his side of the conversation. By the looks of the faces pointed his way, they all had.

"Certainly not," Vetch proclaimed cheerfully. "Lieutenant Shen has ordained that furthermore there are to be no problems."

"That's decent of him," said Lily. "Are you saying the lieutenant has cured the galaxy of insufferable jack-heads?"

"He has. And if you imagine you are walking in legionary footsteps, or that we are not alone out here in the ice and snow, then you are to report for psych eval as soon as you get back to Iceni, because whatever you *think* you see are but phantasms."

Enthree regarded him through the rectangular eyes of her stretched head, which was topped ludicrously with a taped-on helmet. "I understand why two groups with similar roles would feel a natural sense of rivalry, but—"

"It's more than that," interrupted Lily. "The next war we fight is far more likely to be against the Legion than it is your Muryani Empire."

"It is *not* an empire. Nor is it mine. I was born a Federation citizen."

"If you say so," Lily replied. "The Federation is better off without the Legion. In fact, it's better off without the Militia too. Scrap them both and start over. It's the only way."

"Thank you for your candor, Trooper," replied the alien. "If we are to be billeted with the Legion, it is important I understand the subtleties of our enmity and our insults. For example, why do you name them jack-heads?"

"Another time," Vetch snapped, worried about the heaviness of the blizzard that was almost upon them. "That's enough talk about the Legion. Stick close to me. You too, Meatbolt. Meatbolt? Damnit! Where are you?"

"But, Sergeant Arunsen, if we are to work with the sodding jack-head skragg-wipes, then I must understand them better."

"What Vetch means to say," Lily told Enthree, patting her on the flank, "is that he's done talking about the Legion for now. Try the sarge again in a few hours when his patience has recharged."

Vetch ignored them, trying to spot Meatbolt among the marching legionaries.

Enthree snapped her elongated jaw. It was such a deafening sound that even under his hat and helmet Vetch could have sworn a field railgun had just fired.

"Very well," said the Muryani, "but please now be serious. These people we march with concern me greatly."

Vetch and Lily looked at each other. "You're right," she said. "It's like their minds are spaced out on warp blast. I'd ask them for a few pods to pass the time—purely for morale purposes, you understand—but legionaries don't do pharmacological recreation. Their tiny heads would explode if they tried anything that went against regulations because that would offend their precious Empress."

"Empress?" Enthree queried. "There is no such individual as an *Empress*."

"Yes. Yes, there is. The Empress Indiya. Dead two thousand years or more, and even if you dug up her bones and reanimated her, she wouldn't recognize that title. That's what they call her now, though. I bet half these jack-heads have her image inked into their skin." He sucked in a chilly breath, breathing in the first flurries of the approaching blizzard, and muttered, "That's if they really *are* legionaries."

He slapped the Muryani on the shoulder. "Thank you, Enthree. You're right. Something's wrong, which is why I'm worried about Meatbolt. Stay sharp, everyone, and keep close. Here comes a Rho-Torkis welcome."

The blizzard hit them hard, whipping snow high above their heads, and gusting winds that threatened to topple them over. In such a whiteout, their missing trooper had well and truly disappeared.

Around them, the blurry shadows of the legionaries shortened their stride and leaned into the wind, but continued to march with a confidence in their bearing like an army of ants following a pheromone trail. The opaque visor on their fully enclosed helmets was not just designed by Legion techs to intimidate; there were HUDs on the inside that would show the location and status of their squadmates on a tactical map. Vetch imagined they also had a big red arrow that said, "March this way, jack-wipes!"

The troopers followed the legionaries, knowing that if they didn't, they would quickly lose all sense of direction. As a last resort, the general processor blocks in their backpacks could give a compass bearing, but they weren't ruggedized for use in the deep freeze, and Vetch didn't fancy the idea of removing his thick gloves to operate the damned thing, only to find the extreme cold had glued his finger to the screen before shattering the device and taking a frostbitten digit with it.

No, they had to stick with the jack-heads for now. Captain Solikin-Goh had better be right in her assumption that they were headed for ASI-39.

All he could see were shifting outlines of people who might be members of the squad.

And might not.

He didn't like this situation one little bit.

"This is Sergeant Arunsen," he bellowed into the gale. "Call out!"

"Sward."

"Deep Tone."

"Lily."

"Enthree."

"What in the Five Hells are you doing?"

"Meatbolt?" It definitely had been Meatbolt's voice the wind had carried to him. "Meatbolt! Answer!"

At first, the only reply was the howl of the wind, but then: "Get away, you freaks!"

Vetch had a clearer fix on the trooper's voice this time and headed Meatbolt's way.

"Sarge! Help!"

The storm calmed temporarily, the veil of snowflakes lowering to reveal a bizarre sight. Three legionaries had Meatbolt's arms pinned behind him, presenting his bared neck to a fourth who had removed its helmet. The trooper's eyes were wild as they gazed in horror at the legionary's mouth…or, more specifically, his *teeth*. The mad jackhead wore false fangs and there was no doubting what he intended to bite.

"Well, well," Vetch shouted.

The legionaries snapped their heads to regard him, snarling.

"Some kind of vampire cult ritual killing." Vetch shook his head. "And in the Legion too? Who'd have thought it?"

"Sarge!" Meatbolt sounded frantic, but Vetch wasn't a fool. He was stalling for backup.

Except it wasn't coming.

The legionaries seemed to have decided Vetch wasn't a threat and tightened their grip on Meatbolt. The biter closed in.

Taking a step toward the one with fangs—which looked very re-alistic, he admitted—Vetch asked politely, "Please let my friend go."

When the bloodlust wasn't gripping him, it was Vetch's way to be courteous in battle. If he ever met his ma in the afterlife, he intended to explain and justify every kill. He would be able to swear on his soul that he had never committed murder, and wherever he could, he would offer an opportunity for the other side to back out. He even tried not to cuss, except when he was really fucked off. Or drunk.

And in case he ever met his loser of a father in hell, he had given strict instructions to all his comrades that when he died, he should be buried with Lucerne. He figured that if he were going to hell anyway, he could at least acquaint dad with the business end of his beloved war hammer.

A good man went into the afterlife shielded by the positive karma of his good deeds. Vetch wasn't a good man; he intended to go armed.

But he didn't intend to go anytime soon, which was why he'd left his PPR-3 blaster rifle slung over his shoulder and began swinging Lucerne before he'd even finished his plea to let his friend go.

Almost two seconds passed in silence.

War hammers took a little work to bring into play.

The fanged legionary hissed like an angry snake.

Certainly, none of them apologized or offered to let their captive trooper go, which was all that mattered as Vetch swung his hammer through the crisp air in an arc that would intersect with the head of the nearest jack-head holding Meatbolt.

He felt the jolt in his shoulders at the moment of impact. It was sharp and painful, a sign that the legionary was wearing a helmet under their hood. Or *helm*, as they liked to call them because, naturally, a jack-head was too special to wear a mere *helmet* like the rest of the galaxy.

Vetch couldn't help but grin. A legionary helm offered good protection against blaster bolts, shrapnel, bullets, and burning plasma. Against Lucerne, though, it offered little protection. The man's brains had just been pulped inside his skull.

Meatbolt threw off the two legionaries pinning him and rushed the jack with the teeth.

Meanwhile, Vetch carried on his hammer swing over his head, building up speed as he brought it low and then swept up beneath the chin of the next legionary in line, who was too busy readying his rifle to realize the danger he was in.

The man's PA-71 charge pack sent electric juice into its rails, but before he could fire, Lucerne's studded metal head thumped into the base of his chin and snapped his neck back so far that the rear of his *helm* was touching his spine.

In skilled and untired hands, war hammers made superb melee weapons, but there was still a lot to be said in favor of weapons that only required you to point and shoot.

As Vetch recovered his hammer into a neutral ready position, Meatbolt was trying to wrest control of the legionary-vamp's PA-71, while the remaining jack was pointing his rifle at Vetch's center mass.

Bugger!

"Liberty or death!"

The Militia battle cry came from all around, as if being uttered by the blizzard itself.

148 | TIM C. TAYLOR

Blaster bolts sizzled through the air, followed by the reassuring shapes of Raven Company reinforcements.

Vetch dropped Lucerne and dove to one side.

The jack fired but missed, distracted first by the cries of the charging Militia troopers, and then by the multiple blaster bolts that crackled like persistent lightning over his visor.

Legion helms were good protection against blaster bolts. But at such short range, that protection only went so far.

The visor exploded, the legionary's head with it.

Still, the jack had Vetch in his sights. He should have blown darts through him but hadn't.

How very un-Legion-like.

The blizzard was closing in again, but Vetch could see that Lily was organizing a defensive ring, and the fanged jack was on the ground.

"Are we boring you, Meatbolt?" he asked of the crouching young trooper, trying to snap him out of the shock that seemed to have uncharacteristically gripped him.

Meatbolt drew his coat closer around him. "Sorry, Sarge, it's just..." The trooper stood and shook his fists in rage. "Those skragg-stuffing jack-heads. They *bit* me!"

"Just their deviant way of showing affection." Vetch scanned the battlespace, expecting to see blaster bolts zipping through the snow. He should be hearing the whine of railguns charging and the crack of grenade explosions. But there was nothing. It made no sense. All around them, legionary HUDs should be flashing news of the dead jacks.

"Lieutenant Shen this is Arunsen. Request you switch to channel 13."

"Why are you trying my patience, Arunsen?"

Stupid dope. Channel 13 was the only channel the jacks shouldn't be able to eavesdrop. "Sir, request you switch to channel 13."

"Why?"

Blaster bolts sizzled through the falling snow. "Why? Because the legionaries are trying to kill us," he shouted over the open channel. "Raven Company. Raven Company. Legion is hostile. Disengage. We are betrayed. Withdraw to the east."

A humanoid shape loomed out of the snow. Vetch smacked its knees with Lucerne and it fell. "And don't hesitate to smash a few jack-head skulls on the way."

He swung Lucerne around his head and down into the twitching figure at his feet.

It stopped moving.

"Militia, to me!" he bellowed. "To me, troopers!"

Raven personnel formed a wedge around him.

They were bunching. Too close.

Before he could shout at them to put some space into their shape, a heavy blow glanced off his helmet, making him stagger back.

Head ringing, he felt out the wound with fat, gloved fingers. There was a new groove cut through his crest and one of his beautiful helmet lamps had shattered.

"Right! Who broke my bloody lamp? You'll pay for that."

Red berserker mist descended. Vetch no longer cared what his mother would say to him in the afterlife.

"Kiss my hammer!" he screamed. With Lucerne high, he charged the jacks who'd ruined his helmet.

* * * * *

Chapter Fifteen:
Osu Sybutu

Now

She came for him again.

The burning pain of the flame-heated rock hadn't lasted, sucked away by the cold, leaving Osu with surface burns that had soon cooled.

That was a good thing about the sub-freezing temperatures.

The bad was that the cold was also sucking away Osu's life.

His torturer had misjudged him, though.

He wouldn't break. He wouldn't beg.

But he also wouldn't survive much longer.

Maybe that was why she'd come for him at the end—to finish him off herself. Lily Hjon struck him as the kind of killer who would rather suck his dying breath into her lungs than let Rho-Torkis take him anonymously in the night.

Osu laughed sourly. All that death he had witnessed at Camp Faxian. Malix...Sanderson...and then Yergin. Somewhere along the line, he had convinced himself that if he could get the message out to Captain Fitzwilliam then their deaths would have meaning.

Such a lie. It was obvious to him now. A bitter one too, because his team hadn't even gotten halfway to their destination. But here their journey was about to end.

"I don't approve," said the torturer.

Wait—was that his torturer?

He tried to squeeze clarity into his blurred vision, but to no avail. The woman who'd spoken certainly hadn't sounded like Lily.

"It seems you have had the pleasure of becoming Trooper Hjon's personal project. Lily was just playing with you before we were ready for your interrogation."

"Per...Play?"

"Hjon has her issues. Playtime with her can be fatal, and she went too far with you, Sybutu."

The woman wasn't alone. She commanded a group, he realized, as she began gesturing instructions. "Take him down. Clean him up, and for pity's sake, put some warm clothing on the man. This is a disciplined Militia facility. Not a Fraxxan brothel. In the future, no one is to be chained to these rocks without my explicit approval." She hesitated. "Or the colonel's."

Osu sensed people around him. They acted as if they were releasing him from the manacles, but he was too numb to feel anything.

"My name is Major Shinto Yazzie, and I am executive officer here. I want answers from you, Sergeant Osu Sybutu of the 27th Independent Field Squadron, Legion Engineers, based out of Camp Faxian. I expect to get them. Lily Hjon may appear somewhat...*unconstrained* in her actions, but we lost six good people to Legion railguns a few days ago, and your commanders deny these murders even took place."

"All dead," said Osu, confused. Did this major not know what had happened at Faxian?

As he was being gently lowered from the rock, he whispered, "We were betrayed."

"Don't speak here," Yazzie hissed hurriedly. "I will listen with an open mind, Sybutu. But if I don't like what you have to say, I will have you and your friends chained on these rocks and I will flay you to death myself."

* * * * *

Chapter Sixteen:
Osu Sybutu

"There's no denying the evidence of your bio ID, Sergeant."

Exasperation colored the Militia officer's words. "You are Sergeant Osu Sybutu of Third Troop, 27ᵗʰ Independent Field Squadron. A sapper of the Legion, no less." Yazzie pursed her lips, and Osu decided that she wasn't frustrated by his refusal to speak, as he'd first assumed; she was irritated to be confronted with a time-wasting idiot.

Yazzie took his empty cup and replenished it from the flask of warm Pryxian brandy she kept decidedly on her side of her desk. For a moment, he weighed his chances of grabbing the flask itself, but when she pushed his cup across to him, he settled for gripping it between both hands and tipping a small quantity past lips still numb with cold despite the wondrous warmth of her heated office.

The brandy burned briefly as it drained through his throat, but the sweet warmth that spread through his chest was heavenly. Even the brandy-infused air he exhaled through his nose thawed the inside of his skull.

Yazzie gave him a minute for the liquor to warm him before proceeding.

"So, Sybutu, why did we find you a few klicks from Iceni pretending with charming ineptitude to be..." She raised her hands to

155

156 | TIM C. TAYLOR

the ceiling. "This is a point on which I am still unclear. Just what is your cover meant to be? Are you pretending to be bike pirates? Is this some form of performance art?"

It wasn't easy with the numbness mixed with crazy tingling from every nerve ending, but Osu did his best to clamp his mouth closed.

"Your comrades say you were to deliver a message. What could that be, I wonder? RILs are arming themselves, and we already know you encountered uniformed Cora's World rebels, so all land routes must be considered dangerous. Why, then, did you not simply radio your message? The global comms network is down, and every Legion station on the planet and above it is refusing to answer our hails, but that doesn't explain why you didn't use an old-fashioned radio signal. Cyphers do work, you know. Usually."

Yazzie barely gave him a chance to reply before continuing. "Clearly, yours is a message so vital that you must deliver it in person. And since this message is meant for someone outside of the ASI-39 perimeter, my guess is you were headed for the main spaceport at Bresca-Brevae. There your contact would relay the message off system."

Osu made himself concentrate on the brandy-warmth reinvigorating his body and not on the Militia woman who was penetrating his secrets with such ease. How the hell did she know all that?

Major Shinto Yazzie was not easy to ignore, however.

Outwardly, her physical appearance was unremarkable: average height and build for a female human soldier who kept herself fit. Unlike Lily Hjon, if Yazzie had any inked skin, she kept it hidden beneath her sharply pressed blue jacket with the silver-braided frogging and high collar. She boasted less jewelry and even less makeup than the Viking friend Lily had introduced while he was chained to the rock. Vetch, she'd called him. That particular oaf had worn eye shadow, and to the mob of freaks that called itself the Militia, he was a sergeant.

Yazzie was different. From her steely gaze to the neatness of the bun of hair at the rear of her head, everything about her spoke of discipline. She worried him more than Lily Hjon ever could.

"And now we reach the biggest question of all," said Yazzie, her gaze running over him like X-ray search beams. "It's a long way home, but I'm setting off tomorrow."

Osu half blinked. He swallowed. And then he froze every muscle. *How the hell did she know Malix's recognition phrase?*

"Your discipline is admirable, Sergeant. There may yet be hope for your mission. However, you are clearly not trained in clandestine operations. Your reaction to that phrase was obvious, which begs the question of why Lieutenant Colonel Malix would entrust such a vital message to a SOTL like you."

Osu said nothing, but he was screaming inside. *How does she know?*

"You will be relieved to hear that none of your comrades has revealed a thing. I was using guesswork to fish for a response. Remember what an easy pool you are to fish in, Sergeant. It might save your life one day."

But you know the code phrase. That's no guess.

"It's also *my* recognition phrase, Sergeant. I have a signal phrase too that I am to pass up the chain to my contacts when the time was right. Clearly, it now is. I expect Malix gave you another phrase to pass to your contact?"

"What connection do you claim with the colonel?" asked Osu.

"Malix? I've never met the man." She leaned across her desk and looked him closely in the eye. "I was recruited by Colonel Lantosh."

Yazzie sat back, smiling at Osu's astonished reaction. "Rally your mind, Sybutu. Insurrection, civil war, treachery, rebellion, invasion…I don't know which of these we are currently experiencing on Rho-Torkis. The only information channel I trust at the moment comes from the patrols I send out from Iceni. Nonetheless, I can tell you, Sergeant, that the galaxy has *not* gone entirely mad. These are not necessarily the end days. History is a process. That's what we are told by those who wish to diminish the very idea of heroes. Most of the time, I believe they're right, but we know that there are also times when the fate of worlds, even of entire species, depends on the decisions of a few heroes. We of all people should know that. If it were not for heroes of the Orion Era, none of us would be here. Humanity would have been terminated.

"Is there room for heroes in your philosophy, Sergeant Sybutu? Lantosh, Malix, and myself—we consider ourselves patriots. Some may even call us heroes because we saw beyond the process, beyond the centuries-long attempt to homogenize and diminish us so that the peoples of the Federation might be more malleable for those who would own us. Easier to fleece."

"I've served under heroes," Osu replied, although he was thinking of his old half-troop commander, Lieutenant Szenti, rather than Malix or Lantosh. "I tell myself that they don't always have to die pointlessly."

"If they didn't take risks, they wouldn't be heroes. And some challenges require a far greater test of bravery than simply charging the enemy guns alongside our comrades. Here you are, Sybutu, drinking my brandy, unchained and unguarded in my office, and I am taking a huge risk by revealing our recognition phrase. If that fell into the wrong hands, it could unravel the band of patriots who might be the last chance for Far Reach to avoid descending into oblivion. I could be torturing you for all you know about the legionaries who attacked my troopers. I could have you killed because the secrets you now know about me could mean my death. But Colonel Malix trusted you, and for that reason alone, I am going to put my faith in you and give you a choice."

"Let me guess, Major. You're giving me a chance to be a hero."

"If you like. You can remain uncooperative, or you can choose to trust me in return. I already possess all the information you have with the exception of the identity and location of your contact, so it shouldn't be too big a leap for you."

"You want me to cooperate? How?"

"You will shortly undergo a formal interrogation. You will tell everything you know about why the Legion has locked us out of every planetary system and killed six of my troopers. You will tell my interrogators how it can be that the Cora's Hope Division is here on Rho-Torkis and openly supporting the Rebellion. You will report concisely and fully because later tonight you will escape. After an unfortunate delay, I will send a detachment to recapture you. The lieutenant in charge will not know of the deception, nor will the troopers. Only the sergeant. You've met him. Vetch Arunsen is his name, and he's a better man than he realizes."

"Is he in your group of hidden patriots?"

"No. Not yet, at any rate."

"And we are to evade your recapture attempts, which your sergeant will ensure fail?"

The major swallowed hard. "Not exactly. The sergeant will escort you to your destination."

"You keep mentioning your sergeant will do this and deliver that. What about the lieutenant?"

For the first time, Yazzie looked troubled. "The lieutenant is a problem that you and Arunsen must resolve between you."

Azhanti! Did she just ask him to murder one of her own subordinate officers? What kind of monster did that? And if she could kill one of her own, it would be even easier to murder his legionaries.

"It is good that the notion troubles you," said Yazzie. "It is something I must wrestle with for the rest of my life, and yet if you discussed Lieutenant Julius Shen with members of his platoon, your conscience may not be so sorely tried. In any case, the matter of how to deal with the lieutenant is one that you must resolve with my sergeant as you see fit."

The Militia major seemed to think that all was settled.

She was wrong.

"Your plan is flawed," said Osu. "I've worked on a joint Militia-Legion operation before. On Irisur. It lasted less than a day before we started shooting at each other. It won't work."

"I know all about Irisur, Sybutu!" The major's eyes narrowed in quiet fury. "And the part *you* played in that debacle. Perhaps Lantosh and Malix were wrong to trust you, but interservice rivalry between Legion and Militia *must* be resolved. Are you the one who's hero enough to rise above it? I don't care about your personal feelings, Sybutu, and I don't care that it's *hard*. Grow some stones and think of your true loyalties. *Make* this work."

Osu shook his head. "Wishing something is true doesn't magically make it so. Legion and Militia…it's like taking a lion's head and crafting it onto the body of a donkey. The two just don't fit together."

"Lion and donkey." Yazzie curled her lip. "Which one of those two beasts represents the Legion? Oh, don't bother replying, man. Your hubris oozes like poison from every pore. Let me tell you something that Malix and Lantosh would say to your face if they were here. You legionaries have a lot to learn from the Militia."

Yeah, we do, Osu thought. Such as what a degenerate military organization looks like from the inside.

"Lion and donkey," said Yazzie in a more conciliatory tone. "You'll have to work on a better combination, but you're right in part. You must learn how to work with Arunsen in this chimera of a team."

"Chimera, sir?"

"An ancient concept from the depths of the Orion Era. Mythical creatures that are two beasts in one body. It is a shame that your work must remain secret, because a chimera would be a beacon of cooperation in this catastrophically cynical galaxy."

"These chimeras sound like freaks to me. They're not going to impress anyone."

"It will when you make it work, Sybutu. You and Arunsen to- gether. Only the two of you will know your true mission. Your *joint* mission. You will proceed to the destination where you will deliver your message. You will do it together and be *seen* to do it together by your contact, because it will come from both myself and Lieutenant Colonel Malix. Furthermore, once you have exchanged recognition phrases, you will identify yourselves to your contact by the code name I have assigned your joint team. That name is Chimera Com- pany."

Like that's ever gonna happen. Osu had finally figured Yazzie out. The Legion might have been systematically starved of funding for centuries, a mummified shell of its former self, but its reputation had survived largely intact. Major Yazzie was a Legion wannabe. She'd probably tried to join but been rejected. And now she maintained this bubble of relatively disciplined order within the chaos of the Militia and dreamed her chimeric fantasies.

Good for her. But if she imagined this Chimera Company would work, then she was madder than Lily Hjon.

Osu stood and gave Yazzie a crisp salute—Legion style: three-fingered to acknowledge their former Legion comrades left behind long ago in the Orion Spur. "This isn't Irisur, sir. This time, I'll make it work. I'll...*we'll* make Chimera Company a success you will be proud of."

She stood and returned the sloppy Militia salute. "On behalf of Far Reach Federation and the entire Amilxi civilization, I pray you do so. Good luck, Sergeant."

* * * * *

Chapter Seventeen:
Shinto Yazzie

Yazzie watched Sybutu go, escorted back to his incarceration a changed man. Well, not *that* changed. If he thought his little speech at the end had been convincing, then he was an even more conceited fool than she'd thought. The jack-head would say anything to get his team out of Fort Iceni and then ditch Arunsen's escort at the earliest opportunity.

Sybutu couldn't see it yet—maybe he never would—but recruiting so many of the Militia's enlisted ranks from the scum of the penal system brought in many skillsets that most legionaries lacked. Lying convincingly was one of them.

So was recognizing a lie when you heard it.

She'd deployed the falsehood that Lieutenant Shen would lead the pursuit, and it had worked as she'd hoped. She should be able to sideline Shen, to keep him at Iceni and ignorant of what a part of his platoon was really up to off base. But first she had another knuckle-headed soldier to recruit.

Sybutu and Arunsen. She chuckled at the thought. The men were like two rounds in the same clip.

Just too blind to see it.

* * * * *

Chapter Eighteen:
Vetch Arunsen

The viewing window in the northeast watchtower radiated cold over Vetch's face, which was fixed to the heated eyepieces of his sentry viewer. According to the reticule display, he was sweeping the glorified binocs across the northern approach to Fort Iceni in a standard search pattern, but Vetch would feel a whole lot better if he had landmarks to actually *see* where he was looking.

In the light winds dancing over the terrain, everything was white mixed with a dash of gray. He switched to IR mode, but it was even worse.

Sky.

Land.

Near.

Far.

Everything was a featureless blur.

After the skirmish that had left six good Militia troopers dead, Vetch had learned to fear this landscape. The mysterious legionaries had appeared out of a blizzard and disappeared in one too. What was lurking out there now on the ice and snow?

Two days later, the comms blackout had cut them off altogether from the outside world. It was as if the planet itself had swallowed them up, the landscape now an openly declared enemy.

He'd been left with the sense that danger lurked on the horizon. And those dangers were watching him.

The sense of being observed was unbearably strong at the moment.

Maybe his subconscious was telling him he'd seen something?

Vetch ceased his musing.

Yeah, that made more sense. His brain was playing tricks on him, but it was trying to help.

He tightened his concentration and reversed his search sweep, hoping to see something he'd missed the first time.

It wouldn't be difficult for an enemy in an insulated cloak and heat dissipator to make it near impossible to be seen from the watchtower. Was someone out there in the snow watching Vetch through their own binocs?

Waiting for the right moment...

"Sergeant!"

Vetch gasped and nearly jumped out of his skin, sending the pintle-mounted viewer spinning.

It was a gasp, not a scream, though anyone who didn't know him might mistake it for such.

He turned around and looked into the amused face of Major Yazzie.

"I know Raven Company was set up to be scapegoats," she said. "Back on Lose-Viborg."

The door to the observation room was shut. Vetch's comrades had mysteriously disappeared. And the fort's executive officer—who had never felt the need to speak directly to him before—had just spoken some incredibly dangerous words.

Not that he believed her, because the major had never lifted a finger to correct the injustice. She could easily have made their position at Fort Iceni a more comfortable one without allowing the extra duties, constant scorn, and endless petty punishments.

Yazzie gave him a searching look. She seemed to be on the brink of making a decision. A dangerous one.

Vetch knew all about *those* moments.

"I've done all I can for you," she said.

Liar.

She raised an amused eyebrow.

He groaned inwardly. Vetch was a proud man, but he knew he had many failings. His face, for example. Like it or not, his features spoke eloquently of his thoughts and emotions. Far better than his tongue did.

Lily had let it be known that no Raven was to play Vetch at cards when there was money on the table. Anyone who took advantage of Vetch's lack of guile would answer to her.

"I would understand it if you found my words hard to believe, Sergeant. I've decided to take your company's punishment designation at face value and treat you accordingly. It's unfair, I know, but that's too bad. Embrace the suck, Arunsen, because I'll tell you what's even more unfair. It has been intimated to me that you and Trooper Hjon should not survive your posting to Rho-Torkis. And the urgency with which your *non*-survival is requested tells me you know much that my superiors would prefer hidden."

Vetch said nothing. Invariably, it was the best approach to a conversation with an officer, and this particular one bothered him because he hadn't figured her out yet.

168 | TIM C. TAYLOR

Major Shinto Yazzie was executive officer for Fort Iceni, the biggest Militia base on the planet. Given that on most days the most taxing decisions made by her superior, Colonel Bock, was whether to get out of bed in the afternoon, or wait till the evening, that put her in a position of great authority.

She was a human who was just the right side of forty, according her official bio. Vetch didn't put much trust in that. He believed what his eyes told him. Beneath her overcoat, she held herself with poise and strength. Yazzie was old enough to have puffed and bloated during years of overindulging in gargantuan feasts of fine food and drink, topped up by indolence, footstools, and personal servants.

Many of her peers had done just that, but not Major Yazzie. Unlike Captain Solikin-Goh, if she had commanded the detachment sent on foot to Camp Faxian, she would have marched with her troopers. Probably berated them for not keeping up, too.

In short, she looked like the most dangerous category of Militia officer. A professional to her core.

In fact, he told himself, she could fit straight into the Legion. Probably had intended to but had gotten distracted and went into the wrong recruitment pod by mistake.

"I see you are considering the true merit of the officer you see before you," she told him. "It is good that you do so. You're going to need to make up your mind about me tonight, Arunsen. Bear this in mind. I know you must have encountered officers who are not fit to wear the uniform of the Militia. If I played their games, you would be dead already, and so would Hjon. But that is not my way, and we all know what can happen to Militia officers who choose a policy of decency and honesty. I'm sure that former Captain Hjon has told you all about that."

"Yes, sir. Lily might have mentioned it once or twice."

"I bet she has." Yazzie paused, and then nodded. "Which is why it pains me to say this, Arunsen, but tonight I wish your squad to play the role of the discredited and incompetent failed unit you are supposed to be. I'm requesting dereliction in your duty."

"Requesting, sir?"

"Yes, *request*, Sergeant. Oh, I could order you, of course, but that would be worthless. I need your...cooperation in a delicate matter."

"Would that be the kind of cooperation that is synonymous with collusion? Or illegal conspiracy?"

"That's the point, Arunsen. It's for you to decide the answer. You need to make a choice."

Vetch weighed his options.

It didn't take long. He hadn't any.

It wasn't just that Yazzie was now claiming to be their secret protector. If the major were so inclined, she could have him and Lily executed within the hour without so much as blinking.

They both knew that. All the same, he wasn't good at rolling over.

"Only one question, sir. You have a reputation as an officer who does things the right way. By the book, at any rate. And now you pull this...*dereliction* thing. Seems out of character, Major, and that makes me nervous. You're not doing this for money, are you?"

"No, I'm not."

Questioning an officer so directly would normally have severe repercussions, but Yazzie only looked amused. The unfamiliarity of this new ground made Vetch queasy, but he pressed on with his inquiry.

"In that case, Major, which side are you playing for?"

Far from a sharp rebuke, she seemed delighted by this question. He felt like he'd just passed a test.

"Chimera Company," she said. The name rolled a little awkwardly off her tongue, as if unfamiliar to her. "I'm doing this for Chimera Company, and I think, Vetch Arunsen, you have just joined."

* * * * *

Chapter Nineteen: Vetch Arunsen

Deep Tone looked up from his book. "Everything okay, Sarge?"

"World's not ending today, Deep. Go back to your book."

That was all the plasma gunner needed to lean his chair back against the wall next to the heat of the oil stove and reimmerse himself in his slate, the rest of the galaxy forgotten. Darant was the squad's book addict. Looked like he'd made a convert.

"Err…the door, Sarge?" prompted Darant. "You're letting out the heat."

"No, Darant. I'm letting *you* out. Man the viewer in the upper floor. The major's just impressed upon me in person that we need to keep our eyes peeled. Now I'm impressing the same on you. Get up there. You join him, Sward. Five-minute rotations."

"Sergeant," they both acknowledged with obvious reluctance. Vetch didn't blame them. They had just been about to finish an eight-hour shift on watch and peering out into the endless white was mentally exhausting.

They shut the door behind them on a relaxed scene.

Rynter was scanning the approaches through the same model of viewer that Vetch had been using in the floor above. To keep her concentration, she was calling out what she was seeing to Green

Fish, who was sitting beside her, with a blanket wrapped tightly across her shoulders.

Other than Deep Tone stuck in the book he'd borrowed from Darant, everyone else was playing cards at the wooden table near the primitive stove.

"I'm teaching Meatbolt how to bluff," Lily announced. "Care to watch, Sarge? You might learn something."

Vetch smiled. No matter how bad things seem to get, he thought to himself, there's always farther to fall. This group of happy rascals is what I'm going to risk, thanks to Yazzie's games.

Meatbolt had already forgotten his physical wounds from the encounter with the weird legionaries. He'd been bitten, but not deeply. His primary injury was the minor frostbite on his neck from its brief exposure to extreme cold. The sheer strangeness of it all had shaken Vetch, but Meatbolt had shrugged it off with the ease of youth.

Did that mean Vetch was getting old? *Thirty wasn't old. Was it?*

He beckoned Lily over with a nod.

"Seriously?" she responded. "I've money resting on this."

He gave a quick shake of his head.

"Don't touch a thing, kid," she told Meatbolt and walked over to Vetch.

"This is business," he told her quietly. "No messing. Straight answers. I need your assessment of Major Yazzie."

She crumpled her face into a pained expression. "Vetch, she reminds me of myself three years ago."

"Do you know her? I mean, from before."

"I do not. Vetch, I pointed the finger of justice at the people running this planet. Their crimes were all quietly forgotten, and I was busted for spreading the truth. My guess is that Sector High Command wanted to keep scandal away from Rho-Torkis for a decade or two. That's why they fed in officers who wouldn't cause scandal, out-of-favor losers such as Solikin-Goh who lacks influence, or our glorious Lieutenant Shen who lacks the imagination to dream up schemes of corruption. I expect they wanted to balance the dross with a few counter-examples of competence."

"Such as Major Yazzie."

"Sergeant, I've got a card game growing cold. Cut to the chase. Do we have to trust Yazzie with our lives in some crazy operation you barely understand?"

"Er…yeah. Looks that way."

"Then trust her."

"Cheers, Lily. I already have, but I feel ten times better for your support. Sorry for ruining your card game."

"But you haven't ruined it…*yet*. Oh, crap."

Vetch waved his arms for attention. "Hey, everyone! Card game's over. Book down, Deep Tone. Rynter, bend your ears this way. We've got a job to do. You're not gonna like it, but you'll just have to trust me."

Vetch could have done without the sea of long faces.

"And trust me too," added Lily, standing by Vetch's shoulder as he addressed the room.

"Deal us in, Sergeant," said Meatbolt. He broke into a belly laugh and made a show of dealing cards onto the table, just in case anyone had failed to appreciate his wit.

Vetch grimaced. *Don't laugh at your own jokes. I'd better add that to the list of things I need to teach this pup.*

"What's the play?" asked Deep Tone.

"Role play." Vetch grinned. "Let's say that Lily here has been caught playing naughty games chaining up helpless jack-heads for her deviant gratification."

"Excuse me, Sergeant," said Enthree. "Is this an accurate representation of our situation, or have you started the role playing already?"

Muryani! Vetch was never sure whether they were being serious or sarcastic. "Just roll with it, Enthree. Please. Now, because Lily has been bad, as a punishment we all get to pull double sentry duty tonight." Groans came from the viewing platform. "Just for clarity. The double duty is really happening. We are about to come off shift…and then go straight back on again. But this time, we get to pretend that we're hopeless incompetents."

"If you guys want to chip in," said Deep Tone, "I know where I can lay my hands on a small barrel of Laleucan gin. Should help us play our parts more convincingly. After a few glasses of that, an armored division could blow its way through the front gates, and you'd never notice."

Everyone laughed, Vetch with them. It was just as well they were starting off in high spirits, because this was going to be one hell of a night.

* * * * *

Chapter Twenty:
Osu Sybutu

Osu took a last look across the walkways and the watchtowers beyond, satisfying himself that he was all alone in the chill embrace of the nighttime winds. A sudden gust made him grip the wall, bracing against the lethal trickery of Rho-Torkis as it tried to nudge him just a handful of short steps off the wall to dash his brains out on the courtyard so very far below.

At Camp Faxian, walkways were fully enclosed, with embrasures facing inward as well as out. Anyone breaching the gates would find themselves in a deadly crossfire from defenders on the walls.

Would have, he reminded himself. Faxian was now irradiated rubble.

But it had once been proud and strong, unlike Fort Iceni, whose design resembled a Bronze Age hillfort.

Trust the Militia to do half a job.

And half a job was exactly what they were doing tonight.

When Osu and the others had removed their hoods a short while before, they'd found themselves in a watchtower room with their bikes, food, ropes, and most of their equipment.

Most of it.

They lacked their rifles, and as much as Osu respected his comrades, and the quad-barreled bike cannon, that was going to be an issue.

A trooper had shouted through the door to get their jack-headed asses over the walls and wait for their weapons before clearing the hell away.

Osu wasn't waiting much longer.

He stuck his head over the wall and looked down the rope to locate Zavage. The alien sapper was descending the last few feet, a ghostly figure in the goggles' low-light enhancement.

It was a long way down.

And once down there on the ground...then what?

Osu didn't question Legion officers when summoned to their august presence; he kept his mouth shut, nodded in the right places and figured out what kind of trouble he'd landed in afterwards. He'd reacted the same way in front of Yazzie, but the more he thought on it, the less he trusted her. They'd play along with the escape act but as soon as they were away, he had no intention of rendezvousing with her Militia 'escort.'

The rope jerked as Zavage jumped off onto the ice at the base of the high wall.

No more waiting. Time to get out of this mad place.

He threaded his hands around the rope, and mentally prepared to climb over the top and swing out onto the wall.

It would mean trusting to his grip. The knot tied to the mounting clip on the inner wall had to hold his weight too. As did the clip attachment into the wall. And the rope itself...

Osu calmed his racing heart.

I can do this. I did it on Irisur. I can do it here. After the count of ten...

A few deep breaths, and he was counting down.

The others could do this.

His legs were like soft rubber, but he abandoned his count and clambered onto the top of the wall.

"Ah," said a voice from the east watchtower. "You're still here. It's just as well you're so scared of a little height."

Osu dropped back onto the walkway. It was the Viking— Vetch—walking over, carrying a canvas-wrapped bundle in both hands.

As the trooper approached in the darkness, and his appearance became clearer, Osu shook his head at the sight.

Everyone knew that most Militia troopers 'enlisted' by being press-ganged from the jails and the gutter. But they'd gone too far with this one. Beneath his shaggy fur cloak (Osu began to question whether the fur was fake) a frill of lead plates jangled against the man's chainmail. These were weights to be inserted into the head of the archetypal Militia weapon, which was slung between his legs with its haft telescoped up.

A war hammer.

Even the man's helmet had metal cheek pieces and crest spikes straight out of the most ancient Earth civilizations. It was a miracle it wasn't sprouting horns or horse's hair.

"You're Sybutu?" said the Viking.

Osu nodded, and the man tossed across his bundle.

Skragg, it was heavy! Osu staggered back and nearly fell off the walkway. But it was worth it. The bundle contained their weapons.

"On second thought," said the barbarian, "I'll help you lower them. Once you're down safely, I'll untie the rope. I suggest you head north-northeast for the first mile or two, because that's safely inside our watch zone. Where you go then is your business."

Was it? Yazzie had talked about an escort. But this brute didn't seem to know about that. He *knew* he could never trust the Militia.

"Why are you helping us?" asked Osu, trying to tease open the Militia's intentions.

Vetch shrugged enormous shoulders. "A fair question. In fact, I asked myself the same one because—and let me be very clear on this point—I don't want to help you. I'd rather crack your skull open and fry your brains for my supper."

"Then why don't you try?" Osu decided the Militia man was being serious about his cannibalistic desire and started unwrapping the bundle. He'd read that eating the organs of defeated opponents was commonplace in the most primitive societies. And in the Far Reach Federation, you didn't get much more primitive than the Militia.

"Try? Why don't I *try?*" The trooper gave a deep bass laugh. "You have a lot to learn, jack-head."

"You know what? I don't care why you're doing this. I doubt you're capable of understanding yourself. Just help us get away, and you won't see us again."

"If only. Somehow, I doubt that."

On top of the weapon bundle was a sealed paper document. He had no idea what that was about and didn't care, because beneath it was something useful: an HC2 blaster rifle. Short barrel. Lightweight. Perfect. Osu snaked his hand inside the covering and gripped the buttstock. He would prefer not to shoot the man dead. But whether Vetch was alive or not made little difference to him.

"Really?" sneered the Viking, crossing his arms in Osu's peripheral vision. "You jack-head bikers might be a pack of treacherous, fuck-monkey skrangets, but it looks like we're gonna be a team for this mission."

Osu drew out the blaster and flicked on the charge pack. He felt the fizz of power through the trigger guard.

"Chimera Company," said the Viking. He didn't sound any more impressed by the idea than Osu.

But the legionary didn't care. He was the one with the gun. That's what mattered. And the muzzle was pointing at the trooper's feet.

"So you've spoken with Major Yazzie," said Osu. "I don't care. Clear off!"

The Viking planted his feet a little wider. "The major told me to let you ugly lizards get away. That's all I know. But I'm not stupid."

"You could have fooled me. I've just given you a chance to back out safely and yet here you still are."

"Oh, shut it for a minute, will you? The major's playing a very dangerous game here, so I'm not surprised she's keeping us in the dark until the last possible moment. Here's what I think she's not telling me. The fun and games tonight are about more than getting you out of her hair. She wants you to *get* wherever you're supposed to be going and *do* whatever it is you're supposed to be doing. It's clear you can't do either without being chaperoned, which means she'll want to give you an escort. Shall we guess who that might be?"

Hushed cries came from the base of the wall. "Sybutu! Are you okay?"

With the blaster pointed at the Viking, Osu leaned over and replied with a heavy whisper. "I've picked up an unwelcome friend. Just scraping him off my boot. Wait for me down below."

Urdizine would hear that; none of the others would.

"Back off," he told the trooper, leveling the blaster at him. "We don't need an escort."

"Course you don't, mate. Oh, and Lily says to say hi. I expect you'll be seeing her soon. Now, were you wanting me to help you get your weapons and your carcass down safely, or are you too proud to be scared of heights in front of me?"

"I'm going to count to five," said Osu with calm menace. "And if you're still here when I get to five…"

"You wouldn't make it. My snipers are listening in on every word. They'll kill you at four. But that would make a lot of noise and make the major cross, so why don't I just leave you to it?"

At last, the Viking moved off, back to the watchtower entrance. "Oh, and take care unwrapping that bundle," he called over his shoulder. "Lily spotted the major slipping a secret note in for you. Just wave if you need help getting down."

Osu waited, rifle at the ready, until the man disappeared into the watchtower.

"I hate the Militia," he said through gritted teeth.

The probability that he was under observation spurred him past his fear of heights. After tying the weapon bundle into the rope cradle they'd used to lower the bikes, he sent the rifles down the wall. If he'd accepted the Viking's help, it would have been a less noisy and bumpy descent, but there was a principle at stake here.

Then he abseiled down himself, sliding down the rope in his eagerness to get away from Iceni and its unruly denizens.

"Was that a friend of yours?" asked Zavage when Osu's boots hit the blessed firmness of the ice.

"No," Osu replied. "He's no friend of ours. Whatever reason they had for helping us was all about Militia internal politics. It's not our concern. Now, let's ride!"

They set off north-northeast and were quickly swallowed by the night.

"Boss, they may be dumb troopers," said Stryker after a few miles, "but we have to assume they planted trackers."

"Counting on it," Osu replied. "We'll worry about that at dawn. For now, keep riding."

They veered east, keeping their heading well away from Osu's true target: Raemy-Ela.

The night raged at their escape, sending a wind in pursuit that seemed to whisper one word: *Chimera*.

Yeah, well, the chances of Osu working with the Militia were as likely as running into a mashup monster with the head of a moose on the body of a giant snake.

Nonetheless, he urged his team on without a break, desperate to put distance between them and Fort Iceni.

Chimera Company.

Nah. Never gonna happen.

* * * * *

Chapter Twenty-One:
Vetch Arunsen

"You're a disgrace. All of you." Major Yazzie wore a path through the light snow covering the courtyard as she trooped the sorry line of incompetent Militia sentries, stopping directly in front of the man on the end wearing a black fur cloak and Thracian helmet. "But especially you, Arunsen."

Vetch stared over the top of the major's head, his gaze fixed at a point directly in front of him on the south wall.

"I had hoped your poor record on Lose-Viborg was a mistake. A one-off. Not to be repeated." She tracked her glare across the line, treating each of them to a blast of her disdain.

All through this display, Yazzie had pointedly ignored Shen, who was technically a part of the parade line, two steps to Vetch's right.

It's going according to plan, Vetch told himself. And it was true. It was going according to the *major's* plan. Vetch and his friends had as good as pleaded guilty to a serious offence that could get them executed.

This was often the way in the Militia. The officers took the credit when the troopers did good work. And when they didn't…well, the officers would have tried their best, but the troopers let them down.

Shen was being ignored altogether as an inconsequence, which suited him on this occasion. Captain Solikin-Goh was watching this charade in silent shame, shrunk so deeply inside her winter coat that her heavily shadowed features made her look like an undead night shade.

Snow began to fall, muffling the stamp of the major's boots as she trooped the line once more.

The thump of a heavier set of boots added to Yazzie's stomp. Vetch couldn't turn to see who was striding their way. Who was it? Solikin-Goh melted further into her coat, and Yazzie stopped to look.

Surely it can't be...

But it was. Puffing slightly with the exertion, the rotund form of Colonel Bock appeared, wearing a bell-jar greatcoat stiff with gold embroidery.

"This platoon's performance is a damned disgrace," declared the colonel. "Go clear up your mess, Lieutenant Shen."

Shen blinked as if somebody had set off a firecracker up his ass.

Yazzie was far more composed. She merely looked as if she'd been slapped by a wet fish.

Vetch didn't give any reaction. It was all going to drent before they'd even gotten started. So, situation normal. Besides, he was too intrigued to see how Shen would react to worry about whether they would have to bring the idiot along.

Even with the muffling snowflakes gently settling on the drama, the courtyard seemed to amplify the noise of Shen swallowing hard followed by a pathetic little sigh.

Nonetheless, Shen managed to screw up his courage and squeak out, "Right away, sir."

Shen paced up and down the disgraced security detail. Vetch, Lily, Enthree, Meatbolt, Darant, Rynter, Deep Tone, Green Fish, and Sward: he glowered at each in turn.

"You can count on me, Colonel," he said. "I'll make sure those legionaries are apprehended or these troopers will die trying. Er…what backup will I have?"

"Backup, Lieutenant?" Colonel Bock gave a warning growl. "I don't understand the question."

"What I mean, Colonel, is that once I've led this worthless group of disgraces to locate the escapees, what forces will I call in to apprehend them?"

"None, Lieutenant. Have you not been paying attention? We're cut off. I can't even make contact with my supply agent in the capital, and I certainly cannot spare troopers I need to defend Fort Iceni. After you locate the legionaries, you apprehend them. You, Lieutenant Shen. *You.* Bring at least one back alive for interrogation."

"But…They're legionaries. They're dangerous."

"Then be *more* dangerous." Bock regarded the junior officer, pursing his fat lips as if relishing the prospect of a sumptuous banquet.

Man, the colonel must really hate Shen, Vetch thought.

"Are you telling me you are unable to carry out your orders? Or are you *unwilling?*"

He might've been a dumb officer who'd parachuted his way into his post, but even Julius Shen knew there was only one correct way to respond to such a question. He puffed his chest out, attempted to look martial, and gave a crisp salute. "No, sir. We'll bring in that treacherous scum. Dead or alive."

"Make sure you do," the colonel replied. Under his breath he added, "Or don't bother coming back."

The senior officers marched away, leaving Vetch and his friends with the stunned lieutenant.

Only Vetch knew it so far, but it looked as if they had all joined Chimera Company, Shen included.

He looked at the man, whose mouth was flapping like a landed fish. Yazzie's plan would never work with this encumbrance, and Vetch had placed his squad all in with the major. Which meant Shen needed to be kicked out, and fast.

A chill breeze caressed his face, and he sensed his ma looking down from heaven. But she could trust her boy, because Vetch knew that he couldn't murder the lieutenant in cold blood. Probably not even in the heat of the moment.

So how *was* he going to solve the problem of Lieutenant Shen?

* * * * *

Chapter Twenty-Two:
Bronze

His headset chimed, a warning from his bike that was redundant because Bronze had already seen the flashing red section on the terrain map displayed between the handlebars.

Bronze was impressed. These custom bikes had mil-grade forward-facing terrain analyzers. Mines, hidden shooters, rotting carcasses, and thin ice would all show up—or in this case, a dip in the ice hidden by the covering of snow.

The hollow probably wouldn't do anything worse than cause the bike gravitics to cough and splutter, but Bronze was taking point, which meant it was his job to keep the ride incident-free.

He banked left, giving the dip a wide berth. The four bikes behind followed his lead, trusting Hines Zy Pel, the mysterious special missions operative to keep them out of trouble.

No one knew the real truth behind the man. Bronze, as they called him now—irony of ironies. They were far too trusting, but for now at least they were right to trust him.

The bikes weren't *that* good, though. Even after wiping his hand over his thigh to clear the worst of the snow from his glove, it took several attempts to gesture over the console to split the display so he could check their heading.

Bearing 062°. Still making for the coordinates Sybutu had given them after they had gotten a few klicks from Iceni.

Sybutu still hadn't explained the coordinates. The man was keeping far too much to himself, not because of a need-to-know basis, but because clamming up seemed to be the NCO's natural response to being out of his depth.

You've become a problem, Osu.

Bronze lowered his scarf for a second. Just enough to allow a blast of freezing air to shock some clarity into his tired mind.

Osu was far from the only problem they were facing. It was time to start solving them, but which one first?

The RILs, the Militia who had turned against them, or the full-scale rebel assault? Then there were the Invaders with a capital 'I'—the ones who seemed intent on securing the ship that had remained buried for thousands of years. Was it theirs?

He shuddered at the thought.

At least the Invaders were a foe he'd faced before and survived, but someone had ripped apart the Legion defenses from the inside and left Camp Faxian practically defenseless. And where was the Legion's orbital response? After the initial appearance of the Spike-balls...*nothing*. There had been no distant thunder of kinetic torpedoes dropping through the atmosphere against rebel ground targets. No sign of Legion aircraft.

Rho-Torkis was supposed to be a Legion bastion. To neuter it so effectively required betrayal at the highest level. This must be his primary objective: to report on this betrayal.

What a mess!

But to make an informed report, he needed the help of the sappers. Whether Malix was part of the Legion betrayal or had discovered it too late was a question Bronze would soon have to decide, but for now it suited Bronze to play along with the others.

Bronze...

It wasn't the first time he'd worn that name.

The persona felt surprisingly comfortable, wrapping itself around his shoulders with the ease of an old lover, not as poisoned by the bitter memories as he'd expected.

Careful, he told himself. You are not that Bronze. Not the one who let Sarah die at Azoth Zol.

No, Bronze was only a name now. And the Hines Zy Pel he was playing at the moment should have no trouble in deciding his course of action.

First, he had to sort out Sybutu. And he knew exactly which of the sergeant's many buttons to press.

"Urdizine?" Bronze spoke quietly into the icy air that whipped past, carrying his words in his wake. Only the wounded Zhoogene could hear them—if he was alert enough.

"Urdi, I need us to stop. I need to set the Sarge right. I'm worried about him. About you too. Can you get him to stop?"

Urdi's reply came over the radio twenty seconds later when an inhuman grunt of pain escaped the clamp of his lips.

"Urd!" exclaimed Stryker. "You okay, buddy?"

The Zhoogene attempted to reply, but his words were too overcome by his grunts of pain.

"Hold in there," said Sybutu. "Circle the bikes. I'm calling a halt."

* * * * *

Chapter Twenty-Three:
Vetch Arunsen

"You see, Sergeant?" said Shen after they'd put three swift klicks from the south gate. "All that Saruswine training I put you through paid off. I knew it would."

Foresight on the part of Julius Shen seemed unlikely in Vetch's worldview, but he admitted the lieutenant had been right by accident. The man had a knack for riding and the Saruswine were the only mounts on Rho-Torkis that wouldn't shatter into a thousand shards of frozen beast the moment you sat on them.

"Where to now, I wonder?"

Shen spoke as if in passing, but it was obvious he had no idea where to begin searching for the legionaries.

Normally, they would call for orbital observation. But visibility through an atmosphere choked with snow clouds and radioactive dust was always atrocious, and as far as anyone could determine, the orbital network had vanished. They had a pair of drones, but they were no use without knowing where to send them across the featureless ice plain.

If Yazzie hadn't given me rendezvous coordinates, I'd have no more idea than this pinhead. The jacks had better be headed there or we're dead meat.

192 | TIM C. TAYLOR

With a flick of the reins and a kick of his boot, Shen wheeled his shaggy white mount around until he faced his subordinate. Like Vetch and Lily, he was mounted on a juvenile: fast, skittish, fearless of danger, and unable to resist opportunities for grazing.

"The legionaries we encountered before were headed west," said Shen uncertainly. "Perhaps our targets are too. Back home to Camp Faxian. Maybe they're massing there with their rebel friends."

"They didn't look like friends when we captured them."

The heat bath from the lieutenant's Renaissance helmet allowed his face to go uncovered. Shen used this to give Vetch the full benefit of his sneer. "And you believed them, Sergeant?"

Orion's balls! What a piece of drent. Vetch bit his lip. He was depending on far too many people keeping to a plan he only partially understood. "My hunch is that they're headed east, sir."

"A hunch? You would risk our careers on *guesswork*?"

Vetch's mount shook himself impatiently and turned his head to regard him through the black hemisphere of an eye. It blew lines of steam at him through the dozens of slits cut into a nose that looked like a glazed doughnut the size of a human head.

Vetch hated the animals. Despite the thick mat of hair that covered the Saruswine, any sudden movement was like pounding Vetch's buttocks with war hammers. And they had only just set out.

He detested riding.

He was no fan of the lieutenant, either. "Sir, if our quarry started from Faxian, then they were headed east when we captured them."

"And if they were *returning* to Faxian, then they were headed west."

Vetch's heart leaped. They were both talking about Camp Faxian as a fixed point of Legion certainty. As the most strongly defended place on Rho-Torkis, that had made sense until a week ago. Since then they had seen the flashes of explosions on the western horizon, a brigade or more phony jacks marching that way, and signs of orbital battles. Despite his thick fur coat, he felt his bones chill. They knew absolutely not-a-skragging-*thing* about what was going on around them. For all they knew, Camp Faxian could be a smoking ruin flying a rebel flag.

All he was sure of were the rendezvous coordinates.

"West," Shen stated. He sounded confident now.

And the rendezvous point was east-northeast.

"Sir, before we make our decision, do you think we should…" Vetch faked a nervous cough. "I mean…Hjon is our most experienced officer. Obviously, she can't be in command—she's at the very bottom of the command tree—but that doesn't mean she can't help you make decisions."

Shen recoiled at the abhorrent suggestion. If Vetch had suggested he smooch one of their steeds on their muscular, prehensile lips, the lieutenant would have taken it more stoically.

But Shen had just enough spark of cunning to realize how useless he truly was. Not that he'd ever admit it.

"No," he replied. "I don't need advice from her. However, Hjon was stationed here previously. Perhaps I can draw out a course of action from her local knowledge."

Without waiting for the officer to finish speaking—figuring this was as good as he'd ever get from that moron—Vetch turned his shaggy beast around and headed for the rearguard, passing on the way the four adult Saruswine who between them carried eight troopers and lashings of equipment and animal feed.

"Oh, no!" said Lily as he drew alongside her.

"Shen wants—"

Lily leaned out of the saddle and beat him about the head with her riding prod, smacking him hard enough to make his helmet ring.

"Lily. Will you stop that? Listen! I know where the jacks are...*headed*."

Damn! She'd ridden off. The long hind legs lifting her Saruswine's rear and heading over to Shen in only a few bounds. Vetch cursed himself for not telling her earlier about the rendezvous.

It was too late now.

By the time he'd caught up with them, they were already arguing. Lily stopped to slap Vetch on the back of his head. "I was a captain," she raged. "I knew this world. I can't say I'm pleased about what they did to me, but you know what? I *like* being a trooper. Leave all that politics and backstabbing shite to the officers. I'm done with it." She turned from Vetch to Shen. "I don't want to lead. Get it?"

"No one said anything about leadership," sneered Shen. "Don't get above your reduced station, Hjon. However, you do have specialist knowledge."

"The lieutenant requires your advice," said Vetch when the other two resorted to glaring at each other in silence. *And the major requires me to ditch you, sir. How are we to manage that, eh?*

"I do not require advice from anyone," said the lieutenant.

"Of course not, sir," Hjon responded in that innocent voice she loved to put on for idiots. "Look, sir—and you too, Sarge—you figure out between yourselves how you want to run this show. That's your problem, fellas. Leave me out."

"Careful," snapped Shen. "In these exceptional circumstances, I am magnanimous enough to cut you a lot of slack. Be warned! Even I have my limits."

"Oh, drop it," said Lily, ditching the innocent voice for one laden with contempt. "You're out of your depth, Julius. Even taking a leak first thing in the morning without peeing on your boots is quite an achievement for you, and that's in the warmth of the fort. Do you even know how to do it out here without your extremities snapping off?"

"Trooper! How dare you?"

"How? Because you need me more than we need you."

Vetch was waving frantically at Lily to calm thing down. Everyone was hearing her insubordination.

Shen puffed his cheeks out. He looked like a three-year-old in a tantrum. "I will not tolerate any of this—"

Lily silenced him with a cutting motion. "Yes, you damned well will, Shen. Listen, you piece of shit. I do not want your position. I don't even want rid of you. I am no threat to you, Julius, unless you *make* me one."

Shen went silent; Vetch ceased flapping his arms. It was far too late now. Lily had just crossed a line. She'd threatened an officer.

"What do you mean?" Shen asked in an ominous tone.

"Oh, wouldn't you like to know?" Lily replied, once more in her innocent, singsong voice. "I know things about you, Shen. *Bad* things. If any mishap befalls me, people will know what I know, and unlike me, those people would relish the chance to ruin you. I can be your greatest asset. Who knows? I might even be able to make you look good. Or I can destroy you. Which is it to be?"

A hostile silence stretched out between the lieutenant and the disgraced captain.

Vetch looked behind at the party but his spirits only chilled further. All the other troopers were taking a sudden interest in the

196 | TIM C. TAYLOR

splotchy chocolate, straw, and white colored fur of their adult mounts, or looking into the distance, as far away from Lily and Shen as possible. All except Enthree. The Muryani trooper had a single adult Saruswine to herself. Usually, her riding position was to lie prone along its back, but now she rode erect with the front of her coat undone. Her species didn't possess ears; they 'heard' by picking up vibrations through their body hairs. The damned alien had bared her hairy chest to listen in on every word. Loving it too, most likely.

He turned back to regard Shen, whose lips had thinned and puckered inward like a stretched sphincter.

Oh, crap. Vetch reached beneath his shaggy coat to unsnap one of the lead weights that would slot inside the head of his war hammer. He couldn't. His fingers were trembling.

Sorry, Ma. I didn't want to kill him. Honestly.

"Splendid!" Lily announced, oblivious to Vetch's murderous thoughts. "I'll accept your silence as acquiescence, Julius. So, if anyone is still paying attention, this is what I recommend. Our fugitives are headed east-northeast. It's obvious."

Was it? Did Lily know about the rendezvous? Yazzie had only told Vetch and the jack-head sergeant. Leastways, that's what the major had said.

Come on, Shen. Listen to Lily. Vetch unsnapped the lead wafer and slotted it into Lucerne. *Please!*

"East-northeast," Shen agreed. "Of course it's obvious, though not to my idiot sergeant who urged me to head west. Still, it's useful to have my thoughts confirmed."

Idiot sergeant? Vetch sighed with relief. He could take such lies and insults all day and night, so long as the party was headed on the right bearing.

"Hurry up," urged Shen. "You've wasted enough of our time as it is, Arunsen." With a flick of his reins, the lieutenant sped away, his mount's hind legs spraying snow over Vetch and Lily.

Vetch growled.

But he unlocked the lead weight in his hammer and locked it back onto his belt before snapping the reins.

The young Saruswine buck reared up on its strong back legs and let out a howl that would carry for miles.

"Woahhhhh!" screamed Vetch as he found himself riding the shaggy creature through the air.

From the neck down, a Saruswine's body resembled a super-heavy rabbit with hind legs designed to leap to enormous heights.

And excited young bucks loved to leap...

The landing knocked the breath out of Vetch. He lost hold of the reins but gripped the animal's fur just tightly enough to hang on as the creature bounded after Shen.

Deep within its chest, the beast rumbled powerfully enough to make Vetch's legs shake. On every exhalation it gave a lengthy squeak of pleasure.

Vetch's butt clenched in anticipation of the lengthy torture it foresaw in its near future.

Please slow down please slow down please slow down.

But the creature wouldn't. And neither would Shen's.

It was an hour before the two Saruswine tired and turned around, sniffing the air to acquire the scent of the rest of the expedition they'd left far behind.

"Exhilarating, don't you think?" exclaimed Shen. The madman was genuinely joyous.

Vetch didn't answer. He was too busy figuring ways he could ride his Saruswine without his thighs or backside touching anything. Walking back was an increasingly tempting prospect.

* * * * *

Chapter Twenty-Four:
Osu Sybutu

"Honestly," Urdizine insisted, "the pain was only because my hydraulic bands had loosened. I need a few minutes more for them to harden. That's all."

Osu nodded, but he wasn't sure what to believe anymore. "Didn't anyone look at your wound at Fort Iceni?"

"Yeah." The Zhoogene looked away. "Told me to embrace the hurt—painkillers would have made me loosen my bands, maybe fatally. They were going to remove the shrapnel this morning. That's what I really need."

Osu's mouth gaped. "Holy skragg! I'm sorry."

"Don't sweat it, Sybutu. If you'd left me behind, they would be interrogating me now like they did to you."

Damn! How could he have known that his wounded man had been so close to treatment? *It probably wouldn't have made any difference,* Osu told himself. Probably. He realized he was too cold and tired to think through such complex questions.

The legionaries were squatting inside a ring made of their bikes with their heated seats set to maximum. When they'd first entered the Great Ice Plain, they'd secured camo sheets over their heads that had trapped the heat and shielded them from the wind. More sheets had been lain on the ground to make them snug as anything.

But the sheets had been lost in the encounter with the Cora's World rebels. Now they were five men in thick coats getting their butts frozen off.

Literally.

The cold was relentless. Even with the sun up for two hours now, it felt as if invisible tongs coated with liquid nitrogen were reaching up from the ground and clamping around his buttocks.

The only upside was that the intense cold had slowed some of their metabolic processes. So far, none of them had needed to relieve themselves since fleeing the Militia fort, but the horrific prospect of needing to do so at some point without even the camo sheets was beginning to crowd out other thoughts. He wasn't the only one developing a bathroom obsession, he was sure.

What a life!

Other than the need to give Urdizine a chance to harden his alien body, this stop, though, was about bodily input rather than output.

Osu rolled the frozen lump of rations around the inside of his cheeks, keeping it moving so as not to burn his soft tissue.

Duck in plum sauce, it said on the wrapper. The plums were a downright lie. And as for the duck, it was a species that had been left behind in the Orion Spur 12,000 light-years away. Whatever the paste's ingredients, the first dollop he'd squeezed out the mouth of the packet had at least been warm. Now that it was frozen solid, he'd had to snap it off in sections.

Zavage had laid his food on top of his heated bike to keep it from freezing. Osu made a note to do the same next time.

A nagging thought thawed out of the frozen ether and pressed against Osu's mind.

He stared at the Zhoogene. "What did you mean by being inter-rogated 'like me?' Didn't they question you at all?"

Urdi shook his head.

"They locked us up tight, warm, and safe," said Zavage. "It's ob-vious that your experience was different. It seems to me that whatev-er games were being played at Fort Iceni, it was all about you."

It was all about him.

Was it?

He hadn't the luxury of time or warmth to figure that out. They had to keep going.

"Five minutes. Then we move out."

"Or ten," said Bronze. "We still don't know where we're going. Or why."

"There's no time."

"Oh, c'mon, Sarge. I thought we were going to Raemy-Ela. Since our green man still needs fixing, I don't understand why you've set us going in the wrong direction. We're headed for coordinates that the map says are a random nowhere in the icy wilderness."

Although the SpecMish man's words were friendly enough, Osu heard an undertone that was accusing him of letting his team down.

Osu reached for an angry retort, but none would surface because Bronze was right.

What was wrong with him? Ever since Faxian, Osu had been run-ning. Even chained to that damned boulder, or locked in his cell, he'd still been running inside his head.

From what?

Nydella's death? Yergin's?

Then it hit him in the gut.

He winced.

The Legion.

He was running from the Legion itself, because the institution he'd trusted with his life for so many years was…rotten!

The main guns that had turned and fired on Faxian.

The ease with which the rebels had gotten through the orbital defenses.

Someone had destroyed the Legion presence in the Rho-Torkis system within minutes, and they'd done it from the inside.

"I'm still struggling with the concept of Militia capturing legionaries and then subjecting them to interrogation," said Bronze. "We're still two branches of the same Federation military. What did they hope to learn from you?"

"They thought we were…*biters*."

"And you convinced them that you were a vanilla SOTL and so they let us go?" Bronze laughed. "And just for fun, they made us climb down the walls on a rope?"

"No," Osu replied. "We had insider help. There was a Major Yazzie. She seemed to already know everything we're doing. She let us go and gave me this." He reached into his coat and drew out the sheet of paper he'd found bundled with the weapons. "These are coordinates for a rendezvous point. Yazzie said she'd send us help."

"Wait!" said Stryker. "We're not friends with the Militia now, are we? Tell me we're not actually going to make that rendezvous."

"The hell we are," said Osu. "That's our current heading, but we'll double back before we get there and make for Raemy-Ela like we said in the first place. Hang on there, Urdi. We'll get you sorted."

"And the trackers?" prompted Zavage.

"If the Militia planted something on us," Osu replied, "then that suits me fine for the moment. We'll deal with them next stop. Okay, breakfast's over, ladies and gentle-creatures. On my honor, I'll tell you everything I know before we reach Raemy-Ela, but first, we need to get away. Zavage, you're on point. Urdizine, you slot in behind our team empath. C'mon everyone, let's ride."

* * * * *

Chapter Twenty-Five:
Vetch Arunsen

Vetch cleared his throat loudly. "Lily Hjon, you are a dirty sneak."

The accused looked up from the tracker disk she'd secured to the ice.

And then returned her attention to the device.

"And ineffective," he added.

Lily frowned, but otherwise ignored him, making slight adjustments to the little concave dish of the signal collector.

He planted a boot in the snow to either side of the tracker and crossed his arms. "Running off every time we stop to rest the mounts." He shook his head. "Not very convincing. Especially not from someone like you with the constitution of a war droid, but I suppose it was enough to fool our glorious leader. So…this is your *hunch*? A tracker?"

"Uh-huh. Yazzie told me to put a transmitter inside their sergeant."

"And you've kept this secret…why exactly?"

"It suits my purposes to keep Shen in awe of my preternatural abilities."

He shrugged. "Fair enough. Works for me."

"Not anymore, it doesn't." She started folding up the device. "I thought I was being thorough. I desensitized the jack sergeant's skin and covered up the incision with some light burn scars."

"You lost the signal?"

"Me? I didn't lose anything. Either the signal is being jammed—"

"Or it's no longer transmitting. They cut it out of him."

Having folded the equipment through more dimensions than seemed possible, Lily slipped it inside a tiny coat pocket. "It seems the pretty boy sergeant is not as stupid as he makes out."

"He could be dead," Vetch suggested hopefully. "Or eaten."

"You are also a hopeless sneak." Lily got to her feet and scowled up at him. "You arranged a rendezvous with our phony quarry. One you don't want to keep. If you want my help, you need to explain what's happening."

"Well, yeah! I've been trying to. We also need to…make a decision about Shen."

But Lily was already striding away, back to where the others were tending to the Saruswine. "Leave Julius to me," she proclaimed into the air.

"I can't," Vetch muttered. "I got us stuck on this ice ball. Shen's my responsibility."

"Sir, we're headed the wrong way," Lily told Shen when they rejoined the main group.

The lieutenant bristled.

"Why would our quarry head northeast?" she said. "That heading only leads to an icy nowhere, followed by impenetrable polar nowhere. I only suggested it because Sergeant Arunsen told me to."

I did what now?

Shen fixed Vetch with a glare. "I suppose you have a suggestion, Hjon?" His voice was icier than the terrain.

"Of course. They're headed for Raemy-Ela. They have a wounded man who needs medical attention, and that's the only place they'll find it. No marine left behind. That's what they used to say in the Legion back in the Orion Era, and the jacks still tell themselves that."

"Is this true?" Shen asked Vetch.

"I…" Vetch clammed up. He wasn't a party to whatever Lily was playing at. Hitting things with a hammer was his specialty, not scheming.

"Arunsen, you are busted to trooper." Shen turned to Lily and gave her a sly grin. "And you, Hjon. I heard your desire to remain a humble trooper. I have therefore decided to award you a field promotion to sergeant."

He enjoyed her irritated silence for a moment before continuing. "And if we don't find them in Raemy-Ela, I'll shoot you both myself…with pleasure."

Vetch gave a bitter inward laugh. Between them, they'd messed Shen around so much that whatever happened from here, he would be planning on how best to execute them.

It was time to freeze off his moral qualms. He would have to do something about Shen and do it soon.

* * * * *

Chapter Twenty-Six:
Vol Zavage

From his position in the middle of the bike convoy, Zavage soaked in the calm resonating from his fellow legionaries. It was the rush he always felt when the tension around him released. It was better than the calm after sex, though he adored that too. Sometimes he felt frustrated that the humans and the Zhoogene could never fully understand the pleasures of an empath.

Even Rho-Torkis itself indulged the Kurlei legionary in his good mood. The clear skies brimmed with brandy-tinted light reflected off the endless white that stretched to the horizon as if they were traveling across an immense white sapphire.

The humans never stopped believing his empathic abilities—which in practice he'd greatly amplified by the power of diligent observation—were a front for the kind of telepathy that allowed deep access inside another person's thoughts and memories. Such feats were almost possible in deep relationships with others of his own kind, not that he had any personal experience of such things. Lengthy friendship with other species, though, did often lead to a greatly strengthened empathic link.

Zavage had known Stryker and Urdizine the longest, and he felt their shift into optimism as a strong tingling in his kesah-kihisia, the frond-like empathic organs that swept back from his head. Or fish dreads, as De Ketele used to call them.

His mind instinctively scrambled away from memories of Fredrick De Ketele and the others who had died at Camp Faxian; it rested instead on his sergeant.

If he had known Sybutu for as long as Stryker and Urdizine, Zavage felt sure the sergeant would be the one filling his fronds with pleasure, because he was the one who had unburdened the most in the past hour.

Which was just as well, because Sybutu had been close to cracking.

His kesah-kihisia wilted, and the pleasure he'd felt was briefly replaced by the remembered smell of flesh burnt to smoldering embers: his comrades reduced to ash dancing in the wind.

The bombing of Camp Faxian...Despite the distance from which he'd witnessed the event, the tsunami of emotion as the lives of so many of his comrades were snuffed out at once had been a psychic blast that still resonated in his fronds.

He teetered on the edge of the trauma the events of Faxian had blasted into his memories, and scrambled back to fresh memories, made just an hour earlier.

They'd been shivering inside the circle of bikes as three EMP grenades went off.

The more paranoid amongst them had worried that the Militia had planted trackers in the bikes. They might also be in the equipment or clothing. Perhaps they'd been tracked since before they'd set off from Faxian.

None of them could tell, and with the bike systems and weapons hardened against electromagnetic pulses, who was to say that any hypothetical tracker could not be similarly hardened?

But there had been a visible and immediate result to the electromagnetic pulses. Shackles had unlocked in Sybutu's mind, and he'd explained everything over short-range radio as they'd set off on a new heading, to the southeast and Raemy-Ela.

Sybutu had become a leader once more, and the future was beginning to look exciting.

Zavage checked the auto-follow self-diagnosis on his bike and satisfied himself that the separation distance remained optimal. Reassured, he settled into the pleasurable anticipation of reaching the capital. The prospect of mingling with such a rich diversity of civilians made his kesah-kihisia grow plump.

Even the Littorane town of Raemy-Ela held the prospect of exotic new empathic sensations. But this remote backwater, lost within an endless white desert, was also a serious test. Later in the mission they might have to pass undetected through a hostile capital seething with RILs, and maybe even rebel soldiers. First they must show they could pass without notice through Raemy-Ela.

Maybe the guys were a little *too* relaxed.

"Hey," he said over the squad channel. "Keep it together, legionaries. I can feel your minds getting sloppy. Don't. It won't be easy in town."

"Zavage's right," said Sybutu. "Except on one thing. We're miners, not legionaries. Remember the cover story at all times."

"Sorry, boss," Zavage replied. "Listen up. We're still a day out from Raemy-Ela. Playtime's over. Time to go to work on our cover."

Dismay washed over him from the others. "Holy Azhanti! I felt that!

None of you believe you can operate under cover except Bronze, and he doesn't believe the *rest* of us are up to it. Hell, he's the most scared of us all, on account of us being such incompetent jerks."

"I prefer the term *inexperienced* jerks," Bronze replied.

"Whatever."

"*Untrained* jerks would do just as well."

"So, train us, spy boy."

"Zavage's right again," said Sybutu. "I don't want us to sneak Urdizine in and sneak out again. I want us to try out our cover to the full. Bronze, is that realistic?"

"For sure. You can try anything you want. Doesn't mean it won't get us all killed, though. Tell you what. I'll train you as best I can, and when we get within an hour of Raemy-Ela, I'll tell you what I think you're capable of."

"Then you'd better start now," said Sybutu. "Because ready or not, Urdizine needs attention, and that means we're going in anyway."

* * * * *

Chapter Twenty-Seven:
Lily Hjon

"The trick, my friend, is to act like you belong here. As if you were born here, lived your entire life here, and fully intended to die here—though not necessarily in the near future. It's *everyone else* who needs to doubt that they belong."

"You're spouting drent again, Lily." Sward did that delightful Zhoogene thing where they huff indignantly but sound like a sneezing kitten. "Look around. This is not one of your human settlements."

Downtown Raemy-Ela had been laid out in the kind of grid pattern familiar to human town planners for at least five thousand years. But its seven heated roads marked this metropolis as distinctly Littorane.

The streets had a steep camber and wide side channels that pooled gently flowing streams of water against high curbs. Littoranes wallowed in these pools: luxuriating in the rare late afternoon sun, but not relaxing so much that they couldn't get out the way when the occasional truck splashed through the water, seemingly careless of how many citizens were crushed beneath balloon wheels.

It was just as well the traffic was rare because the narrow streets were narrowed further for tall vehicles, which had to drive along the middle because of the numerous wooden archways that stretched overhead. The arches varied in height and width according to an alien architectural aesthetic that escaped the two Militia troopers who had been sent in to scout the town.

Lily waved at a pair of Littoranes taking an interest in them from the shadows on the other side of the street. The ground was heated here, and the archways and banners reaching across the street between the upper levels of neighboring buildings went a long way to keeping the wind out and the heat and humidity in. Even so, she wore her thick coat, though unbuttoned and with the heating switched off. The temperature at street level was barely above freezing.

According to ancient history, population centers on the Littorane homeworld were in tropical lagoons and the littoral waters of warm, shallow seas. The locals here, though, were content to bask in the coolness of Raemy-Ela wearing nothing more than tunics of rubbery scales, and ornamental bands around the tips of their tails.

"Lovely day, isn't it?" she called out to them.

"It's not us they're interested in," said Sward.

The Zhoogene was looking down a side street at three humans who seemed to shrink from the attention behind their companion: a bulky Tallerman.

"You see, Sward? It's not the big newts who need persuading that we belong here, it's the other outsiders." She gave the other party a glare and murmured, "Who do they think they are? Coming into our town—"

"Forget them," Sward interrupted. "I hear a human voice. Two hundred yards ahead. Male. Clipped. Sounds military. It's our target!"

Lily couldn't see anyone, but Sward's hearing was sharper than any human's.

"Keep walking like we belong here," she told him.

A man exited a building a couple of hundred yards up the street and headed left up a side alley. An angry snort came from the doorway before it was slammed shut.

"Never underestimate the ability of the Legion to annoy sentient beings of all descriptions," Lily observed as they neared the turning.

Sward halted. "Shouldn't we report back?"

Lily sighed.

Dear Vetch. The messes you get me into…

She grinned.

According to the official version of events believed by Sward and the lieutenant, the troopers were here to bring back their quarry, dead or alive. Preferably the former. But that wasn't what Vetch and Major Yazzie had in mind.

Not at all.

"We can't lose the lead," said Lily, picking up the pace in pursuit. "We follow."

She turned into the cross street and almost bumped into her quarry who was consulting a handheld device with a large screen.

Crewcut dark hair and dark skin. Modest height but broad across the shoulders. Without his thick coat and hat, his physique was clearly visible and matched Sergeant Osu Sybutu's.

Neat.

She'd enjoyed him so far and hadn't any intention of stopping now.

"Well, look who I've found," she announced.

Sybutu turned to regard her.

The tinted glacier goggles incorporated a nose guard that obscured his face, but the way he looked at her like she was a piece of dirt felt mighty familiar.

Beneath his open camo greatcoat, his quilted tan jacket sported a pair of large breast pockets outlined in red trim. Over the right one was a rectangular patch displaying a white lozenge stretched across a red background. The emblem of Cora's World.

"Who are you?" asked the man. He sounded nothing like Sybutu.

This was a genuine rebel soldier!

A circular badge over the left breast depicted a red flame escaping a razor wire ring: Cora's Hope Division.

"We were wondering the same question," said Sward, coming from behind and resting his hands possessively on Lily's shoulders. "We were here first," he insisted drunkenly. "Hello? You're a soldier? Tell me you're not here to steal our mineral rights."

"I'll tell you who I am," said the rebel. "I'm the person demanding you explain who you are."

"Go fuck yourself," said Sward, squaring up for a fight, though with a wobbly swagger that implied copious quantities of alcohol were sloshing through his interior hydraulics.

"Hey!" Lily slapped Sward's face. "Just because he's human, doesn't mean I'm going to jump him. Stop getting so jealous. I was just saying hi to the nice soldier man."

"Really?" Sward's blinking and staggering was a fine portrayal of inebriated confusion. Lily was impressed.

"Really," she assured him, checking out the corner of her eye that the rebel was acting annoyed and not about to get all shooty.

Lily stood on tiptoes and kissed Sward.

Despite the relative heat of the town, her lips were still a little numb with cold. Not Sward's, though. She removed a glove and stroked the tight green slab of his cheek. His skin was cool and waxy, but his lips were peppery hot.

Sward relaxed into the kiss, devouring her as only a Zhoogene could.

From what felt like a great distance away, she felt Sward's hand clasp her butt. He parked it there awkwardly, like a hand-shaped piece of equipment clamped to a magnetic attachment point.

If his embrace was unconvincing, there were no worries on the kissing score. Her lips responded to his every whim, but it was the taste of him that was so addictive. She ran the tip of her tongue along the inside of his lips where he tasted of spiced lava. Shocks of pure sensation shot through her tongue and flushed her cheeks and throat. They grew in intensity but kept just the pleasurable side of pain.

Her ears filled with distant moans, and it took a long time before she realized they were her own.

All part of the act, she told herself.

"Will you cut it out!"

Sward released her from his lips. Breathless, she regarded the Cora's World soldier. He had removed his glacier mask and she saw he was younger than Osu, with a finely chiseled nose, and a hint of aristocratic blue in eyes filled with horror.

"That," he said indignantly, "is a sight no one should have to see. You expect that kind of thing among aliens but for a human to do that with a xeno?" He shuddered. "Who are you? Show me ID."

"ID?" Lily exclaimed. "This is Rho-Torkis, not bloody Zeta-Arcelia. Why would we carry ID? I'm Lily and this here's Sward.

We're traders in mineral rights. Now, it's your turn, soldier boy. Who are you and what gives you the authority to say drent like *show me ID?*"

The rebel squared his shoulders like a jack-head. "This region is now under the jurisdiction of the Pan-Human Progressive Alliance. An administration office will be set up in Raemy-Ela in a day or so. You must report there by the end of the week to be processed and allocated ID credentials. If you possess weapons, they will need to be surrendered."

"Panhandlers?" said Lily incredulously. "You Panhandlers are annexing planets now?"

"Watch your tongue! We're merely liberating this world and setting up a base of operations. The shortened term is 'the Rebellion', and you would do well to remember that if you want to avoid some very painful re-education."

"But...but you're Cora's World regular soldiers," said Sward.

Careful, Greeny. It took all of Lily's willpower to avoid hissing a warning at her Zhoogene companion who had forgotten to act drunk. He also seemed to have forgotten that they'd already seen Cora's World scouts. That was the problem with Sward: all instinct and no details.

She rather liked that about him, but this was not a time to appreciate his gloriously simple nature.

The rebel was looking at the Zhoogene through narrowed eyes. "I'm a billeting and requisition officer," he said slowly, looking for a reaction.

"But if you're staying here..."

Lily took advantage of the temporary halt in Sward's thought processes as he pondered the implications of the rebel presence, sweeping up for another kiss before he said something *really* dumb.

"Leave the politics to the soldiers," she whispered when she broke for air. "We're just here for the Leezore and xonryllium. And...*having a good time.*"

She closed her eyes and advanced on his intoxicating lips once more, her tongue tip in the vanguard.

But she tasted only cool air.

With his hands on her shoulders, Sward gently pushed her away.

"The rebel has gone," he explained.

"Good. It's just the two of us, lover."

Sward whispered into her ear. "We are not lovers, Sergeant Hjon. I like humans, but not in that way. I find your species sexually repulsive, and I hope you feel the same way about mine."

She winked at him. "It's Lily to you, pal. And consider your hopes dashed. Same as most daughters and sons of Earth, Zhoogenes make me hot. Always have. You have no idea how many of my favorite dreams feature you as their star, Sward."

Like the Cora's World rebel a few minutes earlier, Sward stared at her with horror in his golden eyes.

Then they both collapsed into laughter, supporting each other to keep from falling onto the sidewalk.

"Panhandlers, eh," said Lily. "Let's hope Sybutu and his friends aren't already here, because if they are, the hopeless buffoons will blunder right into them."

"Yeah, that's a complication we don't need. Let's get back to the lieutenant."

"Hold. Think about it, Sward. This could get messy. Forget the jibes about the Legion being perfectly behaved war drones. If you were a jack-head under a lot of strain and you reached a town where you thought you were safe for a day or so, where would you go?"

"A bar."

"Right. Now imagine you're a rebel soldier, fought your way through orbital defenses, made a landing against defended territory. Probably lost a few comrades in the past few days. For the first time, you're off duty in a town where you're safe. Where would you go?"

"I take your point," said Sward. "Let's find a jack and kidnap him before the Panhandlers kill them all. You should have been kissing that human rebel, Lily. He would deserve it because his friends are going to do our dirtiest work for us. We'll be returning to Iceni in a few days as heroes."

Lily screwed her face up. This latest mess Vetch had dumped on them was turning into farce.

Sward's eyes widened. "Uh oh. We...we don't want the jacks dead, do we?" He shot his words at her like an accusation.

"You heard what the colonel and the lieutenant told us."

"Lily!" he warned. "I'm not an idiot."

"Fine. We need to keep our legionary friends safe, and I answer to Vetch, not Shen. Though he'd better get his bloody act together and take charge."

"That's what I thought," said Sward. "I'm not stupid. I'm just...not human. I think differently."

"Got it. Guess that makes me a xeno-bigot same as that Panhandler. Soz. Whatever. Come on, let's go find ourselves some drunken jacks before they all get themselves killed."

* * * * *

Chapter Twenty-Eight:
Lael Kayshen-Oeyl

Even on this frozen world, over 10,000 light-years from the warm embrace of the ancestral waters, the Goddess provided her followers with lakes and rivers to swim, and fish to hunt.

The light from underwater lamps picked out iridescent purple scales from the bearded eels circling above Kayshen-Oeyl's head. The fish were confused by the brightness of the underlit ice that capped the frozen lake, mistaking it for sky. She drifted through the water watching as several extended their jaws into cylinders and flicked their tails. But instead of leaping clear of the water and scooping up mouthfuls of hovering insects, they bumped against the underside of the ice, thrashed their tails angrily, then dove for the depths.

Kayshen-Oeyl flicked her long tail and set off in pursuit, easily outpacing the native fish she had selected as prey. She stretched out her neck and snapped her jaws, biting off the tiniest morsel of the eel's tail, which she spat out in disgust as she allowed the creature to dodge sideways and escape into darker waters.

Some people actually ate the foul things, but even when cooked with the finest seasoning, they tasted like putrid slime. But for a little sport on the swim back from work, bearded eels were awesome.

"We greet you, Kayshen-Oeyl," called a voice in the darkness.

It came from three young unmarrieds of the Lael clan on the way home from the underwater farm, likely on a mission to ingratiate themselves with her in their quest for patronage.

"We are eating out tonight," said one Kayshen-Oeyl identified as Lael Hrish-Ek. "We're celebrating my promotion. Will you join us?" The farm girl thrashed her tail shamelessly as she approached. "There will be entertainments."

Kayshen-Oeyl barrel-rolled while she considered the request. The carousing of young unmarrieds was usually raw as hell, and she was sorely tempted. By the Serene Song, she deserved a little debauchery, but this was not a time to be seen relaxing—not when the clans were so perturbed by the human crisis.

She blew a long trail of remorseful bubbles. "I regret I must attend a xeno-political briefing this evening. But I wish you congratulations on your advancement, Lael Hrish-Ek, and a blessing upon your revelries tonight."

"The regret is all mine," Hrish-Ek replied. With a burst of speed, she drew alongside and allowed her tail to slide brazenly over Kayshen-Oeyl's before racing back to town as if a monster were snapping at her tail tip.

Kayshen-Oeyl floated in stunned silence at the retreating youngsters, and then laughed to see her claws were out.

I seriously need to loosen up, she told herself as she hinged up her claws and swam around in a tight circle, flattered by the flirtatious junior.

But she was tense, and if the clans really were about to face a crisis over the humanoids, then their best minds had a duty to keep themselves supple.

She swam through the proud industrial architecture of the mineral filtration hoops and parked herself in the Place of Beauty.

It was small and unassuming in comparison with a great Place of Beauty, such as were dotted around the temples of Bresca-Brevae. Here, the Lael maintained a circle of polished rocks in which engines of artistry produced unending streams of bubble statues.

"What matters is not the opulence innate to the artwork," Kayshen-Oeyl explained to the silent rocks, "but what the art lover brings into being through the act of observation."

She was adept at this. In ancient times, she told herself sometimes, she could have trained for the priesthood. It was said that the high priests could do more than observe the ebb and flow of the universe, but inject themselves into the current so that they might drift out of time and perceive the near future and the deep past.

Kayshen-Oeyl wasn't *that* talented, but she was what passed for an adept in the modern age. She closed her eyes and sent pulsing shivers down her tail so that its tip beat a hypnotic tone in the water. The Place of Beauty grew steadily more vivid in her perception. Her soul connected to the warp and weft of the universe, and the conceit that she was an independent being sloughed away into the cold lake water.

She floated within the Song of the Goddess. Not merely existing there passively, but singing her own contribution to the infinite complexity of its harmonies.

Suddenly, her collar trilled with a high priority comm alarm.

And then, when she didn't immediately respond, it vibrated annoyingly.

She opened her eyes on the Place of Beauty. Once more, the layered harmonies of the universe were hidden within the mundanities of rock and water. Of eel and ice.

"Go for Kayshen-Oeyl," she acknowledged.

"My apologies, I hope I haven't disturbed you. I am Tamxil Vinishin-Sknorr, a name I don't expect is familiar to you."

"On the contrary, I know you as a midranking member in the Heart-Strand of the Tamxil clan. Your expertise is in xeno-contract law."

"I perceive you are as well-briefed as I was informed. That is well. I request your aid in the humanoid crisis."

This town-dwelling Tamxilite requests my aid? Calling me out of the deep? Who does the rascal think he is?

More importantly, who does he think I am? The Lael clan is not the servant of the Tamxil.

"Honored cousin, are you angry with me?" he said. "I apologize for the forwardness of my communication."

"We are not cousins, Tamxilite."

"Lael and Tamxil *are* related. We share ancestors."

"Distantly."

"And we share none at all with the humans and their lookalikes. The humanoids are killing each other. These could be the opening skirmishes in a civil war. We must push differences aside and unite for our mutual protection."

"Which our clan leaders are already doing. Why do you discard protocol and call me so directly, Vinishin-Sknorr?"

"Our clan leaders bicker. They are too proud, too set in their ways—too *old* to respond to this crisis."

For the first time in her life, Kayshen-Oeyl wondered just how private their secure communications network really was. Conspiracy theorists and malcontents contended that the network was monitored by the authorities.

That question had been academic until now. If anyone was listening in for proscribed thoughts, this Tamxilite had just triggered the biggest.

"They meet to discuss humanoid activity across Rho-Torkis," said Vinishin-Sknorr, "but they do not *act*. Honored cousin, even if you were inclined to do so, your clan cannot hide under the ice among your farms and industrial workings. The influx of outsider humanoids to Raemy-Ela is already underway. Three groups have arrived since yesterday. We must learn their intent and, if necessary, confront them."

"The whole of Rho-Torkis is overrun with the humanoids who work the deep ocean scavenger mines."

"Not this far inland it isn't."

"Not hitherto," Kayshen-Oeyl replied contemptuously. "These humanoid invaders, do they advance from building to building, slaughtering the townsfolk with blaster rifles? Has the town been pulverized by artillery barrages?"

"You would not jest if you knew what I do."

Kayshen-Oeyl stared at the smooth ring of rocks, contemplating the threshold she was about to cross. If anyone really was listening in, then so far only the Tamxilite had revealed forbidden thoughts. Yet, although Vinishin-Sknorr was annoying, he was also right: the paramount echelon of the two clans had led them well but were proving unresponsive to rapid change.

Besides, the hints of secret intelligence and righteous conflict were so exciting they sent jolts of electricity along her spine. "Enlighten me," she said in a haughty tone.

The Tamxilite had the audacity to laugh at her. "The humans have deployed nuclear weapons on each other. Soldiers of the Rebellion have landed—apparently unopposed—and even now their logistical scouts are in our town demanding accommodation and other resources to station their troops. Here! In Raemy-Ela! We are to suffer an occupying force."

"We are to be conquered? Surely the Tail-Strands will wage war before surrendering to the humanoids."

"Our Tamxil Tail wishes to drive out the humans. But our Heart says no because the human soldiers come bearing financial bribery and the promise of great wealth in return for cooperation."

"That sounds like conquest by means other than guns," said Kayshen-Oeyl.

"My thinking exactly. We must..." Vinishin-Sknorr paused and continued in a calmer tone. "Too much of this is speculation. The Rebellion extols a political ideology of openness and equality. It is possible that they speak honestly."

"Do you believe that in your spine, Tamxil cousin?"

"No. But I acknowledge that I am less than fully informed."

"Your words are dangerous," said Kayshen-Oeyl. "Compelling too. But you have not yet asked anything of me."

"One group arrived shortly after dawn on hoverbikes. They claim to be miners, or more accurately traders in mineral exploitation rights. One is requesting access to the town authorities to discuss mineral rights."

"Speculators, then. Did this human comport itself like the executive of a Zeta-Arcelian mega-corporation?"

"Hardly. They all looked like bandits to me, including the male who sought to make contact."

"Humans usually do. But it is possible that you only saw the speculators' mercenary escorts. I presume you wish me to deploy my expertise in human languages to interrogate them?"

"Yes."

"And our seniors are unaware of this?"

"The human directed his inquiries at me, and now I am directing mine at you."

"Where is this human?"

Vinishin-Sknorr cleared his throat and spoke in formal mode. "Lael Kayshen-Oeyl, I invite you, as a guest of the communal habitation of Raemy-Ela and the Tamxil clan, for an evening drink at the Vengeance of Saesh Tavern. It will be my pleasure to supply you with fine drink and sustaining victuals. And if you should encounter a talkative human there, well, it is only natural that you should seek to practice your linguistic skills on the drunken fool."

"Do they still serve brackling pie at the Vengeance?" she inquired.

"Of course. The finest on Rho-Torkis."

"Order the food now, honored cousin. I will be there in twenty minutes."

* * * * *

Chapter Twenty-Nine:
Lael Kayshen-Oeyl

Why the hostelry was named Vengeance of Saesh was a strangeness that made sense only to the townsfolk of the Tamxil clan. Despite the violence of the name, the interior ambience was simply yet sweetly scented. The victuals were renowned even amongst her Lael clanmates who generally kept to the lake and the environs of Raemy-Ela.

She looked longingly at the steamed-up window that looked out onto the floating and underwater bar areas. The pools were deep and well heated here, the stock of ornamental fish delightful.

Maybe later. For now, she must keep to the dry area to mingle with the outsiders, some of whom were from xeno races.

Such as the human male who sat on a couch on the far side of the table, sitting on it like a bench, rather than lying on it as Kayshen-Oeyl did with hers.

He stared at her through those slitted human eyelids that gave her the creeps. His narrow mouth switched from speaking to ingesting the beer in his tankard. Goddess! Those humans knew how to drink.

"Listen, Sybutu," she told him, when she judged by the up-and-down motion of his eyebrows that he was signaling her to speak. "You are hardly the first to propose the use of orbital mirrors to accelerate the melting of the ice. You have yet to convince me why such a project would be conducted at Raemy-Ela."

"Rivers. Raemy-Ela was founded at the confluence of three rivers, and there is your critical advantage. There are many areas rich with minerals on Rho-Torkis, but the safe drainage of the ice melt presents a massive engineering problem. The river that flows out of the Raemy-Ela basin can carry water more effectively and cost efficiently than any artificial drainage system. And when the ice has gone, the mineral extraction and processing will require a constant supply of water—fed by your upstream rivers. Last, and best of all, Raemy-Ela is a fine town, but nonetheless a small trading settlement on the edge of a barely inhabited wilderness. Grow now, before the ice melts and more investment and settlers arrive on this world. Get first mover advantage by the use of our orbital mirrors, and in thirty years, you and I will be toasting our success here at the Vengeance accompanied by the sound of lucrative activity at the dockside. Just think of it. Raemy-Ela could be one of the major trading ports on the planet." He shrugged his shoulders. "Or it could stay a small town on the edge of nowhere."

"Not everyone will relish the prospect of expansion," Kayshen-Oeyl replied. Her mind, though, was filled with the imaginary sights and smells of portside bustle. Of prestige for the Lael clan, and, yes, for the Tamxil too.

"That is your decision, naturally."

Kayshen-Oeyl returned to the present and sniffed at Sybutu. Strange how the human appeared so relaxed at the prospect of a rebuff for the vision he'd sold so powerfully.

"And if your clans prefer the mineral wealth of this area to remain undeveloped, then you and I will know that the exploitation rights are worthless. Sell them to me for a modest price and I will sell on to another rights trader who does not know this. There will be a generous share of any profits for those individuals who made a sweet deal possible."

"What are you, Sybutu? A trader or a mining engineer?"

"Both." The human bared his teeth. "That's the beauty of it. I can win both ways. So can you."

Kayshen-Oeyl reached for her drink but the moment she'd taken the tankard from its holder, a drunken oaf slammed his body against her couch so hard that a little of her beer spilled.

She tipped out most of the rest herself.

"He appears legitimate," she snarled in Littorane at the inebriated fool, taking care to use modern regional vernacular.

The clumsy male—who, of course, was Vinishin-Sknorr—dipped his body submissively and crooned in an apologetic tone, "Did he mention the Rebellion?"

"No!" she yelled, lifting the upper half of her torso to vertical. She shoved her tankard at the cowering male who took it and slunk away to have it refilled.

"My apologies for the interruption," she told the human in his tongue when she lay once more along the length of her couch.

"No harm done," Sybutu replied. "The rate they're knocking back their drink, I expect my own team will be making a nuisance of themselves too before the day is done."

The prospect of associating with more humans gave her a jolt of distaste, but she'd spied only two more at the Vengeance. It wasn't enough of an infestation to spoil her evening's entertainment. "Tell me more about the wealth in the ground beneath our feet," she said, licking her lips. "Sell me a vision of a glorious future."

* * * * *

Chapter Thirty:
Bronze

His knowledge of the local Littorane dialect was non-existent—he hadn't even known the names of the clans until he'd started working the patrons of the Vengeance—but he knew enough Core Littorane to see through the charade of the spilled drinks.

The locals had been checking Sybutu out, and Bronze was pretty sure his sergeant had passed the test.

He sucked in the smoky air and set off in search of Stryker. In contrast to his sergeant, Tavarius Stryker was failing his test big time.

Bronze discovered the sapper in a gaggle of drinkers. They were perching on stools that lined one side of the tiled passageway leading to the west bar. The legionary was the center of attention, spinning a drunken tale that enthralled his modest crowd of admirers: a Gliesan, two Littoranes, and a human.

It looked as if Bronze would have to wade into the group and grab Stryker like a naughty child staying out late, but the drunken SOTL was alert enough to notice the cloaked human nursing his drink a short way up the corridor. Stryker quickly wound up his tall tale and came over.

"Hey, Bronze," he said, leaning against the wall.

"I told you to throw up your drink every time you visit the bath-room," Bronze said, not looking up from his tankard. "Spill it too if no one's looking. *Never* get drunk under cover unless you plan to do so in advance, and you should only ever do that if you're truly secure in your setting. Getting drunk professionally is an advanced skill. Not for noobs like you."

"Go skragg yourself. It's a Littorane town in the middle of nowhere. No one bad will come here."

"You need to be able to respond to anything in all environments. You *never* know what will happen next."

Stryker at least had the grace not to answer back.

"Stick close so I can keep an eye on you," Bronze told him. "Let's check on the boss."

They had to wait as a party of screaming Littoranes squeezed past. Bronze flicked on his radio. "Zavage, this is Bronze. You still sober?"

"Until someone relieves me, of course. Urdizine's in recovery now. Medics say he'll be conscious within thirty minutes. And after that...Well, let's see. Am I missing anything at the tavern?"

The Littorane revelers having passed by, they hurried along the corridor. "Sybutu's sales pitch is going down well. I suspect he's done more to keep Urdizine safe than any of us. Stryker..." Bronze growled as he opened the door to the main bar. "Stryker is wasted."

"Yes," said Zavage, "but am I *missing* anything?"

"What he's referring to," Stryker explained on the same channel, "is womenfolk. You old dogfish, Zavage. I've never met anyone like you. Any age past maturity. Any species...oh, except your own, of course, who scare the hell outta you. Any condition. It's all the same to you so long as they're female. Well, bad news for you, my friend. You'll have to start being more open-minded. I've checked and there are only guys here."

"Are you sure?" Zavage queried. Boy, did he sound disappointed. "Even the Littoranes?"

"Err…" Stryker shrugged. "Littoranes? I don't know."

"You see the one talking with Osu?" said Bronze. "Her nostrils have a crusty, sulfurous look. She's female. And the one handing her a tankard? His have an umber sheen."

"Hey, guys!" Zavage complained. "Not fair. I'm not seeing any of this."

"Patience, my friend," said Stryker, swaying as he scanned the room. "The boss will relieve you on Urdizine watch soon. I'm making a recount and you're in luck. If you like girls with six legs, a four-foot long tail, and nostrils on top of their snouts, then there's plenty of female company for you to enjoy. The real question, it seems to me, is why the hell they would have any interest in *you*."

"Is that a challenge, human?"

"It is."

The main door to the porchway opened, and Bronze watched out of the corner of his eye as two humanoids entered the bar.

Stryker stared.

"Well," he said, "too bad you're not here, Zavage. Just arrived— one Zhoogene male and a human female. Just taking off her hood. Let's take a look at…hellfire!"

"What? What is it? Don't do this to me. What's she like?"

"Zavage," Bronze said carefully. "She's got a shifting tattoo over her face. A rose on each cheek weeping black blood."

"Oh…*her*?" Zavage said, his voice trembling with anticipation.

Bronze shook his head in disbelief. What *was* he going to do with these amateurs?

And more immediately, they'd been discovered. What did Lily Hjon want with them? He checked for the poison blade secreted in his jerkin, a relic of the earliest Orion Era Marines. Whatever she wanted would not be good, but he was ready for her. Because regardless of the name he currently went by, he would always be Hines Zy Pel. And that meant he was ready for anything.

Bring it on…

* * * * *

Chapter Thirty-One:
Osu Sybutu

"Who is she?" asked Kayshen-Oeyl.

"Who?" asked Osu.

"The woman human."

"The which what?"

"A female of your species. She winked at you."

"Did she?" Osu made a show of looking around the bar and suddenly noticing Hjon.

The Littorane snorted. Amused, he thought. "May I ask you a personal question, Sybutu?"

"If you must."

"Do you have a mate?"

"No."

"I begin to perceive why. You need to be more observant, my friend."

"Oh, but I am. Orbital-magnetic surveys. Diabase folding patterns. The latest portable ion exchangers. These are the kinds of things that attract *my* attention."

"You are incorrigible, but I like you, Sybutu." The Littorane reached over the table, drink in hand. They banged tankards together. "I will make the appropriate communications. It will take a day or so. Will you wait in the town?"

Osu was acutely conscious of the two Militia troopers circling his position. Hjon obviously had something she wanted to say to him. Too bad. He had no intention of hearing it.

The Littorane cleared her throat just as a human would. "Sybutu! If you could keep your mind on our business affairs for just a little longer…"

"Sorry. Yes, we'll be here. If not me, then one of us. My boss—tough as an old bean he is—is a Zhoogene. Took some shrapnel when we were attacked by bandits and one of our party got killed. He's not going anywhere—"

Suddenly, Lily Hjon was straddling his lap, wriggling and grinding. She threw her arms around his neck and hauled her lips up to his ear. "You do realize there's a rebel battalion billeting here?"

Osu froze.

"Oh, yeah," she continued cheerfully. "Ran into a Cora's Hope staff team organizing accommodation. I don't think Raemy-Ela is the best place for your wounded soldier, do you?"

"It's too late," he whispered back. "The medic started operating on him an hour ago. He has to stay here for a few days."

"Perhaps. You were very naughty running away like that, but now that we're here to look after you, we could take your Zhoogene with us."

Osu thought that through. The rebels he'd seen so far were from Cora's World, probably the greatest stain on the Federation's reputation. Settled by an intolerant political sect, after centuries in which all dissent had been purged—whether real or imagined—its leaders had turned on non-humans as the last bastions of offense against their purist orthodoxy. All xenos were driven out. It was only the treaties signed with other worlds in the sector, guaranteeing passage and resettlement to the new refugees, that permitted most to escape with their lives.

It was the Militia—the likes of Arunsen, Yazzie, and the annoying tattooed woman in his lap—who were pledged to make such tragedies as Cora's World impossible. Yet they had watched and done nothing.

At least that meant the soldiers of Cora's World would treat all aliens of whatever species with equal contempt. When you know for a fact that all xenos are filthy aberrations, it's hard to tell them apart.

The best strategy was to leave Urdizine here. To leave him alone so the rebels couldn't connect the largely human party on bikes with the green alien in the hospital.

"What's your problem?" Hjon teased. "World not moving along straight lines for you, dear?"

"Far from it." He shoved her off his lap. "It's very simple. I want nothing to do with you or your kind. Go away!"

She came from behind, pinning his upper arms against his sides and rested her chin on top of his head. "We're friends now, Osu. Allies."

"We're neither. Take your hands off me. Just being within ten feet of you makes me want to burn all my clothing and spray myself with delousing agents."

"Oww!" Her hands flinched as if burnt. "Such passion! Such heat!"

He got to his feet and saw that Bronze and Stryker were already squaring off against Hjon's Zhoogene companion. "We can never work together," Osu told her. "We're not like you. We are proud…"

He bit his lip. Damn that woman. She had gotten under his skin. He'd almost said the word *legionary* in as public a place as possible.

"We are *professionals*," he declared instead.

"Professional whats?" she said. "I'll leave you to figure that out."

She led the Zhoogene out of the bar.

"She claims the rebels are already here," Osu whispered to Bronze when the troopers had left. "I have to take that seriously. I'll warn Zavage to keep out of sight, and you take this big lunk with you and follow Hjon. You got that, Stryker?"

The legionary squared his shoulders. "Yes…" The word 'sergeant' tottered on the tip of his tongue before emerging decisively as 'boss.'

"On second thoughts," Osu told him, "you stay here where I can keep an eye on you. Sit down and keep quiet!"

Osu began an apology to his Littorane contact as he took his seat, but the couch where she had been lying was empty.

"Did she buy your act, boss?" asked Stryker.

"I'm not sure." He pulled at his chin. "I guess we'll soon find out."

* * * * *

Chapter Thirty-Two:
Bronze

Outside the Vengeance, the alien streets were deserted of humanoids. As for Littoranes? If you wallowed in the curbside pools, you would find plenty, but they weren't Bronze's quarry.

He rushed a short distance in the direction of the main street, but there was no sign of them.

He had the feeling he was being observed, and not just by the Littorane citizens.

Think! he urged himself as he retraced his steps up the side street, moving more slowly now.

The intel they'd picked up inside the Vengeance portrayed the Raemy-Ela area as an alliance of two clans. The Lael controlled the underground rivers, the lake, and the forest, while the Tamxil were the town dwellers. There was plenty of fraternizing between the two groups, but from what he'd heard, most of it took place in the zone around the town proper, where the fancy heated roads turned into ice trails, and the buildings became simpler and lower. The hinterland wasn't just where Lael fraternized with Tamxil but with outsiders too.

Other than officers, he doubted any of the Militia soldiers would be wearing uniforms and insignia. They could easily pass for bandits, mercenaries, or the kind of scum who would seek out remote destinations to hole up, far from the prying eyes of the authorities.

And according to the drinkers in the Vengeance, such undesirables would naturally base themselves in a sprawling complex of fighting pits, taverns, stables, and trading kiosks to the west of downtown. The place was known as the Thousand Sorrows.

He rolled his eyes. Littoranes had strange ideas about what made a name sound attractive.

No matter. Thousand Sorrows. It was the only lead he had, and he went all in. Picking up the pace, he walked up the pavement, turning left into the first cross street and then broke into a run.

The sappers thought his Special Missions experience gave him almost magical powers of surveillance, killing, and persuasion. It was nonsense, of course. It was the quality of equipment that allowed SpecMish to do things regular folk thought impossible. Most of it had been secretly hoarded since the Orion Era, but not all. In any case, he was nearly out of gear liberated from his old role.

He whistled cheerfully. Sometimes, all you need is legwork.

Bronze looped around the streets, thanking the town planners for the heated pavement that made this possible at a run, and came back in the direction of the main street, farther to the west than his starting point. In the last few hundred yards, he slowed, and then concealed his advance, using doorways and the wooden archways that crossed over the street.

Still got it, he thought to himself. From behind the cover of a dumpster, he watched Hjon and the Zhoogene pass in front of him, heading west out of town.

Bronze waited in the shadows, grinning when the two troopers looked behind to check if anyone was following.

You're looking the wrong way, skraggs.

His quarry stepped up the pace. Only a fraction, but Bronze noticed it. Had they seen him? Impossible.

But their wariness was a problem, because they were almost at the edge of town. Beyond, the wind was whipping up a mist of snow. If they made it that far, his best bet was to make his way directly to the Thousand Sorrows, rather than try to follow through the whiteout.

Movement!

He'd spotted something in his peripheral vision. Turning his head ever so slowly, he brought two humanoid figures into view. They were edging their way along the main street, after Hjon and the Zhoogene, hugging the archways as he had done. These were Cora's World soldiers. Rebels.

Hjon turned suddenly and stared behind.

The rebels froze, hugging cover.

Not bad, Bronze thought. *Probably scouts like the one I pulled out of the hover carrier.* The rebels were carrying Levinger L6 "Atrox" blasters, good weapons that had the accuracy and range to waste the two Militia troopers before they could escape into the snow cloud.

Hjon and the Zhoogene broke into a run.

At first, the rebels didn't move, but Bronze did. He took advantage of the rebels' focus on the Militia to creep closer to them.

Hjon stopped and turned again. She was checking whether she had flushed out any pursuers by her apparent flight. The rebels hadn't fallen for that trick; they waited for the troopers to walk on before they resumed their pursuit.

By then, Bronze was in position. He tossed his last two EMP grenades high into the air. They arced over the rebels' heads, managed to miss the wooden archways and landed just the near side of the road's center line.

The grenades were un-primed, but the sound of their impact got the rebels' full attention. They snapped their heads around and looked in horror at the two cylinders rolling down the cambered road toward them.

The scouts knew what they were, all right.

They ran and dove for the ground, splashing into a curbside pool.

By then, Bronze was ready for them. He slashed with his Orion Marine blade, slicing the twin crescent tips through the spine of one. Without waiting to see the result, he immediately rolled over the wet streaming road to the other, ducking beneath a blaster bolt and lashing out with his knife hand to stab the other rebel in the throat.

He heard Littorane shouts in the distance, but he didn't have time to see where they came from.

The first rebel was thrashing in a pool of water already turning red. The other had dropped his rifle, both hands clutched at his ruined throat.

Bronze gave them both a merciful end. Methodically but quickly, he disarmed the rifles, wrapped their straps around the rebels' necks. Then he dragged their bodies by their collars over to the dumpster.

He picked them up and threw them inside, taking care not to allow blood to drip onto the sidewalk.

On the road, the stream of bloody water was already draining away in the self-washing streets.

Bronze hurried back to the main street to find the troopers gone, disappeared into the cloud of white.

Littorane shouts to halt came from the main street to the east. Bronze pretended not to understand and vanished into the side streets.

They pursued him, of course, but there was only one person Bronze had ever failed to hide from.

Her name had been Sarah.

She was dead now.

But he still couldn't hide from her.

* * * * *

Chapter Thirty-Three:
Ndemo-327-Cerulian

Enthree unbuttoned the underside of her shirt to better hear the happy sounds of her friends, comrades, and objects of observation. Lacking any specialist auditory organs, the Muryani trooper instead constructed a soundscape through hairs all over her body. With the extreme cold of the Great Ice Plain requiring thickly padded clothing, she'd been practically deaf since they'd left Fort Iceni.

"I never thought I'd miss them."

The speaker, Meatbolt, was sitting beside her. Now that she had uncovered her listening hairs, she heard his words with enhanced fidelity. Unfortunately, it also meant the sickness of his scent also assaulted her with enhanced clarity.

The scene at the bar should be joyous. Outwardly, it was. But the trooper known variously to her Raven Company comrades as Enthree, the Praying Mantis, or the Big Hairy Bug lacked the ability of the humans and near-humans to carouse at an instant's notice.

The team had a mission and it was an important one. She couldn't ignore that, but she didn't understand the attitude of her humanoid comrades as they had settled into their accommodation at the wonderfully named Thousand Sorrows on the outskirts of Raemy-Ela. They acted as if they were celebrating the end of the mission when it had barely begun.

Humans!

She didn't understand them but learning to do so was her job: the mission her Expansion handler had initially given her, and it was still her duty. She was here to learn of the humans and report back.

Her task had seemed innocent enough, until her handler had learned of her posting to Rho-Torkis. After that, everything changed. They didn't tell her much, of course, but she suspected the Expansion saw her as their most important asset in the whole of the buffer state the humans called the Far Reach Federation.

She was more than an observer of the humanoids; she was also their friend. Enthree worried about them.

The new officer, Lieutenant Shen, acted as if in leading the detachment to the Thousand Sorrows his job was done. Kulm, his predecessor, had been a most rude individual, but at least he had been a professional soldier. Enthree had taken it as a personal affront that Lieutenant Kulm had groveled to his new commanders since the day they had landed on Rho-Torkis, begging to be transferred away from Raven Company.

His replacement was next door in a private reserved room, enjoying a hearty meal. Shen appeared content that Hjon and Sward were scouting downtown in search of the legionaries, and the others were doing as they pleased in the public bar, acting the part of traders, or whatever they were supposed to be. Shen hadn't been clear on that point.

It had fallen to Arunsen to post Rynter and Deep Tone outside as guards, and send Green Fish to the stables to watch their equipment and Saruswine mounts. In the bar, that left Darant reading his book, Vetch a brooding presence contemplating a tankard on his own table, and Enthree to keep Meatbolt under observation in his dying days.

On reflection, she realized this was not a full celebratory party, but it still felt uncomfortably inappropriate to give the appearance of relaxation. If this were an Expansion expedition, Muryani Marines would have already sealed off the town and would be flushing out their legionary quarry. Not sitting in a bar drinking ale and awaiting hot pies.

"Enthree? Hey, big bug, are you still with us?"

Enthree tilted her head clockwise through ninety degrees, a gesture of apology that was lost on the young human. "I apologize, Meatbolt. I am discomfited by our lack of activity, that's all."

"Relax, buddy. Vetch and Lily know what they're doing. Anyway…" He took a long sip of his beer. "I'm opening up to you, girl. You could at least open your ears in return."

Enthree was no more female than male, although it had seemed simpler to identify with one of the more common humanoid genders. And she didn't have ears! One day, her patience with the humans would crack, but not with Meatbolt. There would never be the chance. Her hearts ached with the sadness of his fate. So she apologized once more and motioned with a forelimb for him to continue.

"So, I was saying, I never thought I'd miss anyone this way. You know, *have feelings.* Does that mean I'm getting old? Or soft?"

Another head tilt. "Remind me of whom you speak, my friend."

The trooper drew his shaggy eyebrows together in a frown. That was good. He could still generate genuine human emotions. "Linh, big bug. Linh!"

"Of course. Elin Linh." *Lance Company, 2nd Battalion, 532nd Regiment of Militia.* Vetch had been clear that they were not to advertise their

Militia status in public, so she spoke the redacted parts of Linh's identification in her head. "Estimated age: 22 standard Terran years. Height: 1.8 meters. Unladen mass: 196 pounds. Estimated gender: standard female. Oh, that's interesting. Your previous sexual obsession known to me was Green Fish."

"Yeah." Meatbolt rolled his eyes for some inexplicable reason. He looked away in the direction of the stables where Vetch had posted his former mating partner. For a few seconds, he was lost in contemplation. "Green Fish...She's the most beautiful girl in the galaxy, but it was weird. She's just too close, like a sister. I love her, but like a sister, man."

Enthree tilted her head anticlockwise. *I'm not a man, Meatbolt.*

But Elin Linh was. "I thought your mating preference was for females," she inquired.

"It is...I think."

The door to the side of the bar opened and the noise of a busy kitchen flooded out, propelling a Littorane waiter with his upper torso erect like a centaur. He was carrying three plates of hot pie.

First delivery was for Meatbolt who tucked into his steaming meal with gusto.

The smell of the pie helped to mask Meatbolt's own corrupted scent, and that lifted Enthree's mood a little. *He is no longer fully human,* she reminded herself. *His decline is irreversible. Soon, I will be forced to kill you, my good friend.*

"You see," said Meatbolt, licking his lips, "I'm still young. Figure I should take a bite from every pie while I can. Drink from every tap. You get what I'm saying?"

"I believe I do. Enjoy today because tomorrow we die."

"And that—" the human punctuated his words with a chunk of meat dripping with gravy on the tip of his knife, "—is a perfect example of why we're so superior to the Legion. I mean, if they were here in Raemy-Ela, can you imagine them rolling into a bar and rubbing shoulders with the locals? It would be against regulations or something. No, we're utterly different."

"I wouldn't know," Enthree replied carefully. "I have never thought to compare our party of speculative traders to *a military organization*."

"Oh, yeah," Meatbolt said after a moment's confusion. "My bad."

It was all so hearts-rending. Enthree rubbed her shoulders together despondently and looked away from the tragic sight of the innocent young human. *Remember, he's not fully Meatbolt anymore. Soon he'll be lost completely.*

"You all right, buddy?"

"I am," she lied. "About your pie sampling…have you considered intimate interaction with a non-human?"

"Oh, yeah," he sighed with such relish that she looked back at his face, finding it smug and deepening into a grin. "You remember Zec-Huyroff?"

"Juru Zec-Huyroff." *4th Squadron, Rapid Deployment Wing, 2nd Reserve Division.* "Estimated gender: standard female. Race: Kurlei. Wait, you had a Kurlei lover?"

"Yup!"

She'd never seen Meatbolt look so satisfied with himself. "Kurlei are dangerous predators," she pointed out.

"I *know*." If anything, the human looked even more pleased with himself.

"And me?" she countered. "I am the least humanoid person you know. Could you have a romantic liaison with me?

"A romantic liaison? What the hell, Enthree? You speak like someone out of the Orion Era. Where did you learn our language?"

"In a Federation school. Same as you."

He shrugged. "Yeah, well…" Meatbolt sized up his friend, trying to see her from a new perspective. It didn't seem to be working. "I don't know, Enthree. Don't take this the wrong way, buddy, but you might be a bridge too far. It would take a *lot* of beer. I mean, intoxication just shy of respiratory arrest and coma, but…yeah." He shrugged. "Why not?"

They smashed their tankards together to seal the deal, spilling beer over the wooden table.

"Then it is agreed," she said. "At the next opportunity, we both get dangerously drunk and if we survive the poisoning, we shall see where the encounter ends. Imagine what that group of repressed drones you mentioned earlier would make of such a thing."

Meatbolt roared with laughter, but Enthree could not share it with him. Not this time. It felt like a betrayal to be speaking with him of a riotous future liaison that she knew damned well could never happen. She had no data on the effect of the Corruption on human physiology. Even if she had, the rate of takeover was dependent on multiple factors she could not possibly know, but the boy surely had only a few days left at most in which he would still be capable of laughter.

When he can no longer laugh…She shuddered. That shall be my sign. That's how I will know I can delay the mercy killing no longer.

Meatbolt peered at her in mock shock. He poked a finger at her head. "Is that a tear?"

"Yes. It is a natural reaction to cleanse my eyeballs of contaminants. Yours do the same."

He frowned, not fully convinced. "Looks like weepy tears to me." He brightened. "But that's impossible. Must be the smoke from the kitchens."

Humans! They had a strange compulsion to tell themselves that only their species could cry. Despite all the overwhelming evidence to the contrary, not least from their own xeno-biologists, they couldn't bring themselves to believe that other species could weep.

For once, Enthree was glad of the distorted view humans had of reality.

She wept uncontrollably.

* * * * *

Chapter Thirty-Four:
Vetch Arunsen

What was up with Enthree lately? Vetch pulled at his beard braids trying to figure out the bug. Ever since that encounter with the vampire cult of phony jackheads, she'd been sticking close to Meatbolt. The lad had shrugged off the weird encounter, but the Muryani was acting like a mamma bear with a wounded cub.

Aliens! They fascinated him. But he couldn't make sense of them most of the time.

Vetch took another bite of his pie, mopping the gravy off his whiskers with the back of his sleeve. Delicious. And seeing as the alien didn't need to eat...

"Enthree," he called. "Relieve Green Fish, will you? She deserves some of this food."

The big insect twisted her body around and with slow deliberation rotated her head ninety degrees to the left...and kept going until her face was almost upside down.

Please, Vetch, don't make me do this. I'm begging you.

He thought that was what she meant. Admittedly, his insect-to-human gesture translation wasn't perfect, but she was definitely not thrilled by his assignment.

Vetch sucked in his lower lip. He'd have to fix Enthree's sudden attachment to Meatbolt, but there were higher priorities today.

255

"Belay that," he said. "Darant. Finish your page and your dinner, quick as you can. Then relieve Green Fish. It's your turn to look after some beasts. I've got my hands full with Enthree and Meatbolt. At least the beasts in the stables are broken in."

Meatbolt laughed, but Darant didn't. He lowered his book and stared at Vetch as if considering the worthiness of his request.

Damn! Forgot I'm no longer sergeant.

Everyone but the lieutenant acted as if Lily and Vetch still ran the squad between them, just as they always had.

Darant nodded. "Give me two minutes," he said, easily enough, but the challenge had been made.

The trooper held his book close to his face with one hand while shoveling in hot pie with the other. Before he finished, though, Lily and Sward burst in.

Vetch knew immediately there was trouble.

Lily took a moment to give him the highlights in a whispered report before hurrying over to the door with the sign that read 'Reserved for private use' in several languages.

She left Sward in her wake, staring at Vetch with arms crossed.

"Lily says it's time for answers," the Zhoogene told him. "So do I."

Vetch downed his beer while looking longingly at his half-eaten pie. "Guess Lily's the boss now," he said, wrapping his food in a napkin and stuffing it into a fold of his coat. "Everyone! Grab your gear and meet in the stables. Now!"

This time there was no resistance from Darant. They all followed him out into the shocking cold of the sheltered path that led to the stables. After a moment weighing the risk of removing the sentries, he also summoned Deep Tone and Rynter from the shadows. Together they pushed open the insulated double doors to the barn.

It was a different world inside, the cold replaced by—well, not exactly *warmth* but a welcome sense of *shelter*. The layer of wood shavings coating the stalls had soaked up the animal smells before spilling onto the main walkway. Vetch liked the honest feel to the place. It would be a pleasant place to sleep.

"Are we leaving?" asked Green Fish.

Her voice came from above, but Vetch couldn't see her.

"Hey, Sarge. Over here."

Vetch was impressed. The wall opposite the stalls was hung with tackle, feed attachments for a variety of beasts, and sundry other equipment. Above that was a block and tackle with a saddle resting on top. This was Green Fish's perch. How she got up there was a mystery. He swore she must have wings.

"Well done," he said. "You just earned two thousand points. And then lost three thousand for saying a military rank out loud when I told y'all not to. Anyways, Green Fish, don't you keep up with the news? According to Shen, that rank isn't even mine." A few of them laughed at that. "Remember, you lizards, we're not supposed to be advertising who we are. Stay up there for a moment, Fishy, and keep watch, but bend an ear to what I have to say."

"We're not as dumb as you think," said Meatbolt. "We know the lieutenant is on a different agenda from you and Lily. What's going on?"

"Ahhh…" Vetch rubbed a thumb along his lip. He'd been planning a long speech about how they had to choose the right path in their heart over following Shen's orders, or some such drent. But without Lily beside him, he knew he'd screw up trying to put it into words.

"We'll tell you later," he said instead.

"Later tonight?" asked Meatbolt.

"Or later…after we're all dead?" suggested Darant.

"Before we leave Raemy-Ela," Vetch replied. "I need to grab Lily first. Those of you who can trust Lil' and me just a few moments longer, keep the Saruswine company, keep quiet, and try not to kill anyone."

"And the rest of us?" Deep Tone growled.

Vetch shot him a look of betrayal. And shock. He'd expected Deep Tone to back him to hell and back. "If you want to trust your own judgement—or want to suck up to Shen—then go back to the bar. I hear the pies are good. Everyone else, stay here but be ready to move out in case Lily and me come in hot."

"You heard the sarge," said Deep Tone gruffly. "I mean…Hell, he's still the sarge in my book. He's giving you a free choice. I'm not. Anyone but Vetch leaves this barn…I won't forget, see?"

Heart buzzing with the vote of confidence, Vetch grabbed his war hammer from the gear stashed in the stall next to their oldest Saruswine, and hid it within his cloak before heading out.

Without the others, the short walk back to the bar felt very different. Ominous, threatening.

He turned abruptly and scanned the yard, expecting to see assailants but seeing no one. The yard was covered but snow had blown in. He saw no footprints. He must be imagining things.

Idiot! I'm the assailant here. Better get used to the idea of being a murderer, Vetch boy, cause I don't reckon it's the kind of stain that ever washes off.

He cursed himself all the way back to the bar. Even before setting out from Iceni, he knew he'd have to choose between Shen and Yazzie.

And since Shen hadn't conveniently died on the way...He hated this more than anything he could remember, but he couldn't dodge it any longer.

With one hand gripping the haft of his war hammer under his cloak, he pushed open the door to the bar.

* * * * *

Chapter Thirty-Five:
Vetch Arunsen

Inside, the bar was eerily unchanged since Vetch had rounded up the troopers and made them accessories to mutiny.

Crumbled pastry was still scattered around Darant's plate next to his empty tankard. His own table was being cleaned by the waiter.

It looked so normal, but it was not. His heart was pounding, and his hand was sweating as it gripped the hidden weapon that would be the means of his murderous intent.

But he saw no other choice.

He advanced on the door behind which Julius Shen was tucking in to a rich dinner, oblivious to his fate.

"I ordered heated pies to be delivered to the stables," said Lily.

She was standing at the bar. He hadn't even realized she was here.

"Figured we'd be needing them," she explained. "As for you, Vetch Arunsen, come sit next to me and spend a moment before you do something you'll regret."

The waiter cleaning Vetch's table froze.

"Sometimes you have to make a choice," Vetch told her. "I don't like either option, but my people need me to make a decision, and that's what I've done."

Earlier, Vetch had ordered the food and drink via the archaic standard tongue of the ancient Exiles, combined with a lot of pointing and miming. His words to Lily should be gibberish to the waiter, but the Littorane set down the stack of dirty plates and his cleaning cloth and tiptoed away in the direction of the kitchens. Literally tiptoed on all six feet as if doing so waved an impenetrable shroud of invisibility around him. If they were gonna get through this alive, Vetch wanted to understand the Littoranes a whole lot more. First, they had to get through today.

"You're right," said Lily, "but a good leader knows how to get themselves informed first. *Then* they make the big calls. So come here, big fella, and let me inform you. It'll take three minutes, tops."

Vetch looked at the *Reserved for private use* sign, then at the tail of the tiptoeing waiter as it disappeared into the sanctuary of the kitchens.

"Make it quick," he said, and joined her on a humanoid-compatible stool.

"Already ahead of you." She pushed a shot glass of dark liquid across the bar top and revealed an identical glass in front of her.

"Can't let you go ahead with what you planned," she said. "I've let you take on too much of a burden already. You can't have something like this on your conscience. Not yet. It'll eat away at you more than you realize. Besides, you're an ignorant arse, Vetch. There are easier ways. Drink up and follow me!"

He made the mistake of sniffing the drink as he brought his heated glass closer. It looked like whiskey but had the aroma of bitter herbs steeped in hot urine. He tipped it down his throat and slammed the glass down. It tasted as bad as it smelt, but as the warm liquid slipped down his throat, it developed a delicious aftertaste of spicy honey.

"Not bad," he said. "I thought you wanted to tell me something."

"Not tell. Show."

She hopped off her stool and he followed her through an unmarked door, along a wide corridor, and into another bar he hadn't seen before. About twenty human men and women relaxed, drink in hands, standing or perching on benches around a central stone hearth in which a log fire blazed, threatening the wooden floorboards with sparks.

All wore the uniform of the Cora's Hope Division.

Some of the rebels were armed.

And every last one of them was staring at Lily and Vetch.

* * * * *

Chapter Thirty-Six:
Lily Hjon

"Hey, heroes," Lily announced. "I was in the Militia once."

Weapons were readied and leveled at the two troopers.

She put on her sweetest smile. "Yeah, I pointed out that my fellow officers were corrupt slime wipes, and for my troubles got tortured, given five years hard labor, and kicked out in disgrace. So I was just wondering, come the revolution, what are you going to do with the Militia?"

The tension eased a little. One of the rebels eased her way out of the crowd to meet the two strangers. She wore sergeant's stripes on her uniform, and the same scout unit insignia as the rebel Lily had watched the legionaries interrogate and execute a few days before.

"Many of the enlisted Militia troopers are as much a victim of a corrupt system as anything else," said the rebel as she eyed them suspiciously. "Not all, though, and precious few officers have a shred of decency. Naturally, the Militia will be purged. However, those who are blameless will have nothing to fear, and will be invited to join a new citizen's army."

"That's what I was hoping. Well, seems to me that the revolution has already come to this part of Rho-Torkis. So quit whetting your whistle for a few minutes and go visit the private room off the other bar. There's a man in there with an elegant shirt and diamond earrings worth more than you ruffians earn in a decade. I heard him say something about needing to lead his patrol back to Fort Iceni."

The rebels looked at her, incredulous.

"Do you think maybe he might be a Militia officer?" she asked.

The rebel soldiers stampeded for the private room. All except a pair, who stood with their tankards at the bar.

"That's a very convenient explanation, girl," said one, not bothering to turn and look at her.

"Yeah, let me see if I can figure this out," said his friend. "There's a barbarian shadowing you who looks as if his IQ count is lower than the number of my toes. And I just lost half my toes due to frostbite. He looks the embodiment of a serving Militia NCO, which would make you his officer."

"You're wrong," she said, taking two steps forward.

"Maybe you fooled Fitchy and Grunvalt," said the first rebel. "They're late reporting in. But you don't fool us."

Both the rebels went for their pistols. But Lily was quicker, closing the distance at a sprint and throwing rapid-fire punches to their throats.

"Do I really look so unintelligent?" Vetch asked as he grabbed the men's heads by their hair and rammed them against the bar until they went limp.

"Yes," replied Lily. "You see? This is a more merciful way of ditching Shen. You should be more creative in your thinking." She frowned at Vetch. "Is that *really* necessary?"

Arunsen was working efficiently through the downed rebels' jackets, pilfering anything of value. "Old habits die hard," he said.

"I forget sometimes that you were a prison recruit."

A Littorane barkeeper appeared, carrying a crate of beer bottles. If he noticed the change in clientele, or the two rebels slumped on the other side of the bar, he made no sign.

"Excuse me," Lily asked. "Do you know if our pies have been delivered yet?"

"Yes," hissed the Littorane. "Pies to stables. Delivered. Done."

"Thank you."

Vetch placed a handful of credit chips on the bar. "For excellent service," he explained.

Within two seconds, the barkeeper had swept the chips out of sight.

"You go now?"

"Yeah. Soldiers. We don't like them."

"I agree. Soldiers no good. Rude. Poor tips. And guns! In Thousand Sorrows. It is an outrage."

"So true," Lily added. "Why, there are two of them passed out at my feet. Disgusting."

She gave a circular bow to the Littorane, as she'd learned to do in her previous posting here.

He was astonished that she knew their customs so well and gave an exaggerated bow in reply.

The formal farewell concluded, she hurried out of the bar with Vetch in tow.

"Oh, stop seething," she told him on the way. "Spit it out, Vetch."

"You call that being merciful?" he accused.

"Sure. Julius will probably soil his pants, but he'll be fine. The man can smooth talk his way out of most things and has loyalty only to his own comfort. The rebels will probably recruit him. And if not..." She shrugged. "Do you really care?"

Leaving Vetch to digest that, she pushed through the door to the covered walkway and walked straight into an ambush.

* * * * *

Chapter Thirty-Seven: Vetch Arunsen

"Sybutu!" boomed Vetch, hoping his voice would travel to sharp Zhoogene ears in the barn. "What is the meaning of this?"

The ambushers were in partial cover and further concealed by tattered white cloaks. They could be anyone, but he'd counted three blasters and the cannon of one hoverbike aimed at the doorway. Yeah, Vetch felt his money was securely placed on these being the jacks.

"Good," said Lily, still walking toward the stables. "Saves us the bother of picking you up."

"There are rebels in town," said Sybutu, breaking cover and pulling back his hood.

"We know," said Vetch. "Most of them are inside having a beer. Why not join them? See if they can guess who you are."

"I don't think so," said the legionary. "We killed two rebels half an hour ago."

That stopped Lily in her tracks. "Oh, you stupid dumb jacks!" she cried.

Vetch clenched his hands, wishing he was crushing one of the stupid man's vital organs.

"You can't help yourselves, can you?" she berated Sybutu. "I mean, why? *Why* would you do that?"

270 | TIM C. TAYLOR

"Because they'd been tracking you and your Zhoogene friend, and were about to bring you in."

She took a step back. "Really?"

"Really," said another jack. Vetch remembered his name was Bronze. "They had the drop on you, and you had no idea."

"There's irony for you," said a Zhoogene voice.

It was Sward who'd taken a firing position just outside the barn. Rynter was with him.

"Our green friend," said Vetch, "is probably the finest sniper on Rho-Torkis. Unless anyone is in the mood for a shootout, I suggest we lower our weapons and make a strategic relocation to the hell outta here."

"The lieutenant?" asked Sward. "What's his status?"

"He's more or less alive," Vetch answered. "Probably. If anyone wants to check on Lieutenant Shen, feel free to go back in there. Say hi to the Cora's World soldiers from us. Everyone else, saddle up and ride out. We'll meet up 10k east of town at coordinates I'll agree with your sergeant. Get there and everything will be explained to everybody. I swear."

"Do it!" said Sybutu, motioning to his team to mount their bikes.

They obeyed like the jack-headed automatons they were, but while Vetch was jogging across to the barn, he overheard an unexpected hint that not all legionaries were mindless drones.

"What are we doing, boss?" hissed one of them. "We can't be lumbered with those pirates. May the colonel's ashes recombine and kick you in your hairy butt if that's what you're intending."

Vetch didn't wait for the answer.

He'd find out soon enough.

* * * * *

Chapter Thirty-Eight:
Osu Sybutu

S even klicks east of Raemy-Ela, heavy rain began lashing the four legionaries on their hoverbikes, turning their cloaks into fast-flowing rivulets and whipping the upper layers of snow into deep slush. It was the late afternoon of what had been a sunny day, but now the skies were dark with anger. Osu had his glacier goggles raised up on his head, but he could see little beyond the curtain of raindrops dripping off the front of his hood.

The slush beneath the bikes looked a surefire way to both slip over and lose your feet through frostbite, but cruising as they were, about a foot off the ground, they made good progress to the rendez-vous coordinates he'd hastily agreed with Arunsen. They had to put their trust in the forward terrain sensors and autopilots, but the bikes had proven their worth.

The Militia party was another matter. The troopers were mount-ed on huge shaggy beasts who'd plodded surefooted across sheet ice, happily munching on the huge canisters of feed pellets carried on their backs. They slithered and squeaked in distress at this new ter-rain.

Arunsen's troopers had fallen behind, but Osu could still hear the angry cries of the Saruswine in the distance. They sounded like the squeak of a rat de-tuned by several octaves; it made his skin crawl.

Osu wasn't the only one.

271

"I don't like it," grumbled Stryker over the radio after the loudest chorus of Saruswine cries yet. "I don't like those creatures following us. As for the animals they're mounted on, they give me the creeps too."

Despite his attempt at humor, Osu could tell the sapper was serious. Mutinous, even. *Better he kicks off now than later.* They were just three klicks from the rendezvous, and this time Osu was determined to make it. He'd come to accept that with Urdizine out of action—and hopefully keeping his green head down in Raemy-Ela for them to retrieve at a later date—he needed Militia help to give them the best chance of completing their mission.

His team, though? They weren't so convinced. None of them. Better to lance that particular boil within the next three klicks. And who better to do so than Tavarius Stryker, a SOTL who was never shy about telling you to your face exactly what he thought.

"None of us have forgotten what the Militia did to us on Irisur," said the disgruntled sapper.

"Do you think I have?" snapped Osu. He cursed inwardly. *Got to keep my tone measured. They're supposed to look up to me as their leader.* "I know they look like degenerate bandits, but they're useful. Frankly, some of them disgust me, but I think that Viking sergeant of theirs has a spark of honor, and he's under orders from the officer who runs Fort Iceni. They'll help us get to Bresca-Brevae."

"Possibly that detachment riding the shaggy beasts through the rain and snow isn't so bad," said Stryker reasonably. "But the Militia as a whole is rotten and can never be trusted. You know that."

"Hey!" snapped Bronze. "Drop it! If the Sarge says we use these Militia clowns, then that's what we do. End of."

"It's okay, Bronze," said Osu. "Give him a chance to speak his mind."

"Speak his mind?" Stryker roared. "Has everyone here forgotten that the Militia is responsible for the LT's death? Why don't you ask Lieutenant Szenti to speak *his* mind, Zy Pel?"

Osu gripped his bike's handlebars so hard, he threatened to snap them off. He tried to keep his cool enough not to punch out the loudmouth idiot, but it wasn't working. Osu was about to explode. No one felt the loss of Lieutenant Szenti more keenly than him. How dare Stryker imagine he had a monopoly on grief?

Through the rush of hot blood, and the drumming of the rain, the sound of shouting reached Osu's ears.

"Quiet," he told his team, and listened.

He missed his legionary's helm. Its directional auditory sensors meant he could pick out sounds from the background noise and locate their position. Swaddled as he was in scarf, hat, and dripping cloak, the shouts diffused through the downpour. They could have come from any direction, but he was sure of their nature. The initial shouts had been of surprise, but they had rapidly shifted first to warnings and then to orders being issued.

"They're to our north," said Zavage. "Human, I think."

Osu's mind shifted into a different gear. The Militia was to the west. Whoever they had heard would not be friendly.

"Tactical formation," said Osu. "Form on me and orient due north."

Tactical formation. With their numbers reduced to four bikes, it was a hopelessly optimistic description, but they had pre-programmed the formation into their bike computers, which rapidly organized them, despite the limited visibility.

Zavage was twenty feet away to Osu's right. Bronze and Stryker took the flanks, another twenty feet out to the side and twenty to the rear. Their awareness of what was behind them would be minimal. They just had to hope Zavage's ears had them pointing the right way.

Through the rain curtain, Zavage drifted in and out of vague visibility; the other two had completely vanished from Osu's sight. He relied on the four red dots showing in his bike display's terrain grid as they took up position. Four? The emptiness of the formation made his breath catch in his throat. He had set off from Camp Faxian as part of a Legion operation on this planet that counted thousands of personnel. To the best of his knowledge, only four effectives remained on Rho-Torkis.

Osu tried the radio channel he'd hastily set up with Arunsen, but the Viking didn't respond. Damn! Should've given Zavage the problem of how to arrange comms with the Militia. He was the squadron's signal genius after all.

The dots turned green, the bikes registering that they were now in the pre-programmed formation.

Just four legionaries.

Pride chased away Osu's doubts. It wouldn't have mattered even if there was just one of them. They were Legion. They would hold the line, no matter what.

The order to advance was on his lips when the world was interrupted by a horizontal flash of lightning and a scream of brutalized air, as a heavy blaster bolt hit a point a few hundred yards to the west, drawing a howl of inhuman pain from what Osu guessed was a Saruswine.

A fusillade of much smaller bolts followed, their energy severely depleted by the driving rain by the time they reached their targets.

That first shot, though, had come from a seriously big gun, not a handheld blaster rifle.

What were they up against? Time to find out.

While he was painting a route in the bike computer that he hoped would take the flank of that big gun, the map screen changed. Four dots became three; green changed to red.

Stryker had dropped out.

* * * * *

Chapter Thirty-Nine:
Vetch Arunsen

Blaster bolts sizzled through the rain over the heads of Vetch's troopers, instantly vaporizing the raindrops as they passed. In theory the impact energy would be reduced, but with enough hits, even the armored troopers lying prone in the slush would die.

But no one was dead yet. The enemy fire had mostly gone high overhead, which suggested they were relying on visual targeting, and weren't sure what they were facing or where.

Good.

After a quick check on the channel he had shared with the legionaries—naturally, the jack-heads weren't listening—Vetch rose from the freezing slush and jogged over to the Saruswine who'd taken the heavy blaster bolt in the belly.

The entry wound was two fists wide. The bolt had burned straight through the bulky animal before blowing a deep trench out of the ground, leaving an exit wound that was...messy.

It was a lucky shot.

Though not for the beast.

The Saruswine was one of the docile adults, but it wasn't calm now, thrashing its head in agony. With its bulbous eyes mounted on each side of its huge head, its gaze never seemed to leave Vetch.

He rested the muzzle of his blaster on its head. "Rest now," he said and put it out of its misery.

A fresh volley of blaster bolts whined over their heads. Its origin seemed a little closer, but at least the heavy-caliber blaster fire had ceased.

"The gunners don't want to hit their own soldiers," Vetch said to no one in particular. Then he took charge.

"Hold your fire and listen up," he said over the squad channel. "I expect the enemy to pin our front while they probe our flanks. Drop your blasters and switch to slug throwers. Darant, you're with me by this dead Saruswine. Green Fish, Meatbolt, set up an SFG twenty yards to my left. Rynter, Deep Tone, SFG twenty yards to my right. Lily and Sward, watch our rear. Enthree, you're in reserve. When I give the signal, Enthree, you're to stampede the juvenile Saruswine through the enemy ranks."

"Stampede, Sergeant? I don't think they do that."

"Then think of something, Trooper! I've ridden on them, and I can tell you for a fact that they're excitable. Bite their asses. Read them Muryani poetry. I don't care, but I want them running at full pelt when I tell you. Got it?"

"Yes, Sergeant."

Vetch hesitated a moment. He'd forgotten he wasn't officially a sergeant. So, it seemed, had everybody else because they were racing to follow his orders before the enemy overran their position.

Two dark humanoid forms loomed out of the rain toward the dead Saruswine, slithering through the slush.

"Here they come," Vetch growled into the radio and squeezed off three bolts with his light blaster, having forgotten to follow his own orders to switch to a slug thrower. The two soldiers screamed in pain, splashing down to the ground, but one got a shot off first.

Darant fired back, briefly. Wildly too. Vetch looked over to see his comrade jerking in pain, his chainmail glowing with the energy from the blaster bolt he'd taken. But it quickly dissipated into the wet ground.

"I'm all right," said the trooper shakily. "Problem is, *they* might be too."

Vetch fired three shots from his rifle into the downed enemy. One twitched, and then both were still.

"Anyone else sighted the enemy?" Vetch asked his squad.

"Negative."

"I see only rain."

"Nada."

"Nothing."

"Now they know where we are," said Vetch, "they'll be back in force. Stay alert."

He checked the legionary channel again and got zilch for his trouble. Suddenly, worried that they'd shot their allies by mistake, he scrambled across the Saruswine corpse for a closer look at the downed soldiers.

They were Cora's World regulars. He didn't recognize the unit insignia, but it was different from the rebels he'd seen in Raemy-Ela.

"Hey, Boss," called Meatbolt as Vetch made his way back to Darant. "When are the heroic Legion reserves going to rescue our asses?"

Vetch raised his hand to the selector switch on his headset, intending to try the channel to Sybutu once more. He thought better of it. He'd only be wasting his time.

"Forget those damned cowards," he said bitterly. "If they were coming, they'd be here by now. We're on our own."

"I see something," said Green Fish.

"Me too," confirmed Rynter.

"Here they come," said Vetch. "SFG teams, on my command, left gun aim low. Right high. Aim for the center and then sweep your fire cone to the flanks so Enthree can do her cavalry charge. Ready..."

He'd switched his blaster for his war hammer. Lucerne was ready and eager, his hold firm on her high-grip haft despite the drenching. They didn't need the Legion. They were Militia and they were ready.

* * * * *

Chapter Forty:
Osu Sybutu

"That's serious opposition," said Stryker after the heavy blaster gun had fired. "If they're to the north, then we should head south to get away. If the Militia wants to assist, they can do so as our sacrificial rearguard."

Osu hesitated on the cusp of ordering them forward. Yes, the Legion's honor said they shouldn't abandon the Militia. But the Legion had another reputation: one for getting the job done, no matter what. Colonel Malix had ordered him to deliver a message in person to a contact in Bresca-Brevae. There were four of them left. If he took them to meet these rebels head on—assuming they were indeed rebels—then four could become zero within moments, and then who would deliver the message?

"The troopers aren't our people," said Zavage.

"They came to Raemy-Ela to help us," Osu answered.

"We didn't ask them to," said Stryker. "We don't want them."

"But we need the assist," said Bronze.

"Have you forgotten what it is to be in the Legion?" Osu cried, his doubts gone now. "Honor! We tell ourselves that it's our honor that makes us the best, and we *are* the best. We hold the line, and we don't let our brothers and sisters down. Listen to me, sappers. This is what Arunsen and I were going to tell you if we'd made it to the rendezvous. We are more than the Legion now. The 27ᵗʰ Independent

281

Field Squadron has been wiped out. And our brothers and sisters back there under fire—they're no longer just Ravens either. We're something more. Something new. An idea that matters in a galaxy collapsing around us. We are Chimera Company now. Arunsen. Hjon. That Muryani trooper and the others. They irritate the hell out of me, but they're one with us. Are you willing to abandon them, Stryker?"

"No, Sergeant." Three dots became four once more. "We hold the line." The dots turned green.

Osu led them north.

* * * * *

Chapter Forty-One:
Vetch Arunsen

"Fire!"

At Vetch's command, the suppression fire guns on either side of his position lit up, throwing lines of segmented metal slugs into the zone in front of the dead Saruswine. Operating like machine guns in this firing mode, the SFGs were firing blind, but screams pierced the icy drumbeat of the rain as they began to register hits.

A lone rebel charged past the dead Saruswine, firing blaster bolts into the Militia position. Behind Vetch one of the juvenile beasts squealed in pain and rage.

Vetch made the intercept, swinging his hammer horizontally to smash into the enemy's chest.

The rebel was knocked backward by the heavy blow, staggered back a few steps and landed on the Saruswine's corpse, gasping for air that would never come. Darant finished him off with a shot through the head.

To either side, he could see from the pattern of chaos whipped into the slush that the two SFGs had walked their firing cones out from the center to the flanks.

It was time to send in the cavalry.

A fusillade of blaster fire flailed the Militia position, sending him diving into the ground. He heard a groan to one flank and angry cries from the Saruswine. Darant seemed okay.

Vetch grabbed his blaster rifle one-handed and sent some bolts into the bad guys to give them something to think about.

"Enthree," he said over the radio.

He never finished his order because he once again threw himself into the freezing slush as a column of three Saruswine leaped over their dead elder and the two humans sheltering by its corpse. The animals bounded into the enemy.

"Enthree, you were supposed to wait for my signal!"

"I did, Sergeant," replied the alien. "But the Saruswine wouldn't."

The three animals chattered angrily with their long rows of back teeth, setting Vetch's on edge. The hinged fronts to their jaws with the cutting teeth at the front snapped open and closed, biting into human flesh.

Rebel blaster fire poured into the Saruswine, but the biting—and the screams—kept coming. The beasts' thick shaggy fur drenched with rain—Vetch realized it must be providing some protection against blaster bolts.

And still the rebels advanced out of the rain, but their steps seemed more hesitant now.

Darant fired a burst of segmented rounds and, nearby, rebels went to ground, sending return fire ripping into the ruined corpses of the adult Saruswine and the soldier whose chest Vetch had shattered.

He heard firing from behind and swiveled his head to look. Lily and Sward were occupied with something, but the rain choked his vision, and he couldn't see what.

Then he was hugging the ground as a furious volley of bolts sought him. The wet ground sizzled with blaster fire, and he felt the scalding heat of a near miss on his face, which he'd tilted to avoid drowning in the slush.

Water sprayed over him as grenades landed nearby, shrapnel hitting his side. He tensed, expecting the warning vibration of his chainmail's breach detection system, but it stayed firm.

"Darant, you okay?" he asked over the radio, but his headset was making weird noises he didn't recognize. Probably short circuiting or rebooting with all the abuse of being shoved into freezing water.

"Darant, you alive?" he shouted over the driving rain and the din of battle.

"I'm good," Darant shouted back. "Comms are out. My headset's rebooting for some reason."

A fresh flurry of blaster bolts flew over their heads. This time headed in the direction of the rebels.

Enthree emerged from the rear, tottering upright on two hind legs and firing blasters in each of her other…well, they weren't exactly *hands* but there were four of the hoof-like appendages, and they were pumping blaster fire at the rebels. She looked like a demonic sea creature made to walk on land for the first time, and forced to wear high heels just to add to the challenge.

No matter that she looked so ungainly; she was shooting accurately.

"My comms have failed," she announced, her voice slicing through the din. "So I thought, 'What would the sergeant be saying if he could talk to me?' And I imagined he would be saying, something like, 'Reserves are meant to be used, you big dumb insect. Get your hairy alien carcass into the fight.'"

"I would never utter such racist words," Vetch protested as he and Darant added their fire downrange. "Shame on you for suggesting such a thing. Now, get your enormous alien head down before a rebel blasts the ugly thing off."

The Muryani splashed down beside them.

"Was that humor, Sergeant?" she inquired. "I think it was possibly amusing, but I find the distinction between cynicism, irony, and insults so difficult to unravel with your species."

"Shut up, you pair of buffoons," Darant snapped. "The enemy's turning. Look!"

Vetch tried looking. He squeezed his eyeballs hard but he couldn't see anything through the rain. *Have to face it, old man,* he told himself. *You need to get your eyes checked out.*

"Darant's right," said Enthree, who had eyesight to rival a high-spec sensor drone. "They're crawling away."

Blaster fire converged on her head, missing her by a hairsbreadth. Enthree decided she'd seen enough and ducked down behind the cover of the Saruswine's enormous corpse.

Another burst of rebel blaster bolts crackled to their rear. Lily and Sward returned fire.

There was nothing for it. He'd just have to trust their rear was secure because this was the moment to press the enemy.

"Darant, cover us. Enthree, ready to close assault?"

"Always, Sergeant."

"Good bug. Here we go."

Vetch took two steps back while Darant gave a long burst on auto to make the rebels duck for cover. When the trooper's rifle ceased its chatter, Vetch leaped over the corpse of the Saruswine, war hammer high and screaming the Militia battle cry: "Liberty or death!"

Enthree was close by, bellowing the same words. Having dropped two blasters to redeploy her mid-limbs for locomotion, she covered the ground at a fair clip.

Given the amount of firepower the troopers had poured into their front, Vetch was surprised to see so few rebels, alive or dead. He heard nervous shouting in the distance, and a hesitant blaster bolt fired his way that steamed in the icy water at his feet.

He ceased his battle cry.

"I think they've gone, Enthree," he said.

"No," she replied. "Contact!"

Vetch hurried over to the vague bulk to his left that could only be his Muryani comrade. She was firing blasters with her forelimbs. Her mid-limbs were punching horizontally, which meant she had probably switched to short swords, but all Vetch could really see was the pounding sheets of rain.

A squelch to his right alerted him to a rebel advancing on Enthree.

The splash of his own feet must have alerted the Cora's World soldier because they swung their rifle Vetch's way.

The rebel released an aggressive feminine scream and shot him from the hip as she ducked and rolled out of his way.

The bolt hit Vetch in the upper thigh, but his mail took the worst of the blast. He screamed in pain nonetheless as he ignored the wound and brought the hammer down onto the woman's shoulder as she dove past. The blow pulverized the bone, and she screamed as she thudded along the ground on her unwounded shoulder.

Vetch hooked his hammer up in readiness for another downward swing, but the rebel rolled back a little and lifted the muzzle of her rifle out of the water.

He wasn't going to make his swing in time. Dropping the heavy war hammer in desperation, he sidestepped away, forcing the rebel to shift her position despite the agony evident in her groaning.

Abandoning Lucerne didn't leave him defenseless. He tried to draw his knife but stumbled on the smooth ice hidden beneath the water and went down.

This is it, he thought. I've done you proud, Ma.

But the rebel didn't fire the killing shots.

Vetch pushed himself back upright. Enthree had butchered the rebel, the Muryani's sword blades dripping with fresh human blood.

"Retreat! Retreat!"

The cry spread through the rebel soldiers.

"We got 'em," Vetch roared at Enthree. "We didn't need the Legion cowards."

"Retreat! Retreat! Fall back on the tank."

"The tank…?" Vetch echoed. "That doesn't sound good."

One of the young Saruswine sauntered back from the enemy position, giving Vetch and Enthree a sniff. The animal seemed reassured by the familiar smell and calmly walked to the rear, uncaring that its flanks were matted with its own blood and of the absence of its fellows.

The beast had proven itself surprisingly valuable in this no-visibility battle where your enemies appeared without warning out of the rain. But a creature of flesh, blood, and fur was no match for a tank. And given the power of the heavy blaster that had ripped straight through the adult Saruswine, they were up against a serious main battle tank.

"Time to go!" he bellowed at his troopers, limping back and hoping enough of the Saruswine had survived for them to mount up and get the hell out of there before the tank blew them into atoms.

Suddenly, the dark skies resonated with light.

Vetch assumed the flash meant the main gun had fired again, but there was no bolt of induced plasma. Instead, his eardrums were assaulted by the boom of a furious explosion. Then he felt himself picked up as if by giant hands and thrown headfirst into the corpse of the giant adult Saruswine.

Dazed, all he could do for the next few moments was to lie there as his skull echoed with the aftershocks of the explosion.

But then the fog cleared a little from his brain, and words formed on his lips.

"What the hell was that?"

* * * * *

Chapter Forty-Two:
Vetch Arunsen

"Raven One, this is Bandit 1-5-6. How copy?"

Vetch picked himself up and shook his head, convinced he was hearing voices in his broken headset.

"Raven One, do you copy?"

The voice sounded real. It sounded like that no-good Legion sergeant. Perhaps Vetch was in hell.

The horror of spending an eternity stuck with the jack-heads shocked some sense back into him.

But it wasn't hell. Worse, this was really happening.

"I can hear you, jack. What's your ugly voice doing on my squad channel?"

"Saving your prison rat ass, Raven One. Over."

The explosion…was that the jacks? To the north he heard the legionaries' bike cannons spitting bolts. "In plain language, Sybutu. What have you done?"

"Scratch one main battle tank. An HRT-7 Citadel. Engaging supporting infantry now."

A citadel? That was a powerful machine of war, designed for siege operations and heavy assault. The Cora's mob must want to keep a tight hold on Raemy-Ela.

"Sybutu, how many more citadels do you see?"

"None. We've encountered one tank with infantry escort. Also some enraged animals. One looked like it was on its way to you. Over."

The bike cannons ceased firing, and the noise of battle was quickly swallowed up by the endless drumbeat of the elements. Vetch realized the SFGs had fallen silent too. He thought he heard the groans of the wounded out in the gloom, but that could have been his imagination.

"The enemy has scattered," said Sybutu. "For now. Recommend you keep your position. We have your location through your radio node. Remember, we're the ones on hoverbikes. Try not to shoot us or hit us with your club. Over."

"It's a war hammer," Vetch replied indignantly. "But I'll try not to smash you with it. You hear that, everyone? Don't shoot the mounted heroes. Call out your status and scrub up before they get here."

* * * * *

Chapter Forty-Three:
Vetch Arunsen

"Didn't think you were gonna make an appearance." Vetch shook Sybutu's hand.

The legionary shifted uneasily on his bike. "We're all Chimera Company now," he said defensively.

Now that was interesting. The battle zone was secure for now, the four jacks on their steeds like knights of ancient Earth on horseback, lords of all they surveyed as the peasant Militia levy readied the beasts of burden for the journey.

But that isn't the truth, is it, Osu boy? The only reason you're invoking Yazzie's idea of Chimera Company is desperation.

On the other hand, the way those four had blown up a tank and hacked the Militia comms was impressive. And Major Yazzie would have the Ravens lined up for the firing squad if Vetch didn't escort this jack to the capital.

Vetch sighed. He wasn't being honest, either...with himself. Truth was, he was as desperate as Sybutu.

"Okay," he said, breaking an uneasy silence. "We're all Chimera Company now, although we ought to actually tell my people that before they mutiny. And since we've suddenly become family, I have wounded. Can you spare a ride on the back of your bikes?"

"I'd prefer not to," Sybutu replied. "The weight would rob the bikes of their agility. Can't you sit your people on those animals of yours?"

"The Saruswine are among my wounded. I've got three adults and one juvenile left. They're tough and they're going to be very useful, but they need a chance to heal first."

"How many troopers need transportation?"

"Just me," said Vetch. "I've been shot in the leg."

The legionary's long and painful sigh was audible even through the rain. "Very well. You ride pillion with me, Arunsen."

Neat. Vetch tapped his headset to transmit. "Rose of Rho-Torkis, this is Viking Rover requesting assistance, over."

"Pillock," said Lily, but she was laughing at the call signs he was dicking around with. "What do you need, Vetch?"

Painkillers, brandy, and a warm rub from a hot woman. He grimaced. *If only.* The truth was his leg had stiffened up and he felt rooted to the spot. Worse, his head was still ringing from the blast that had taken out the tank. In his current state, organizing the withdrawal of his troopers seemed as impossibly complicated as plotting hyperspace jump routes while simultaneously walking a tightrope over a bottomless gorge and reciting badly written poetry. Backwards. He needed Lily to take over.

Suddenly, a battle cry rent the air. "Purity! Purity! Death to the other!"

Vetch collapsed to the icy wet ground, blaster bolts lashing the space where he'd been an instant before.

Darant was hit.

One of the legionaries, too; the jack tumbled from his bike.

Vetch couldn't stand, couldn't swing Lucerne. So he dropped the hammer and rolled through the slush toward the enemy.

There were three of the rebels. They'd extended the muzzle blades from their rifles and were stabbing at their foes. One was thrusting down at Vetch, but he hadn't got his weight behind it properly, having expected to stick opponents who weren't already on the ground.

"Rookie mistake," Vetch told him, shifting to the side and reaching up to grab the rebel's forearm.

Over the rebel went, following his rifle to splash facedown into the ground.

Vetch went for his own gun, thinking it was still strapped to his back, but it wasn't there! He'd lost it in the slush.

Flashing limbs, blaster bolts, and blades of metal: the confusion of melee was going on all around, but Vetch had eyes only for the rebel blaster lying nearby in the wet snow.

So did the rebel. And he was closer.

Who would get there first?

They both scrambled for the rifle, but before either could reach it, Enthree kicked it away and skewered the rebel with a short sword held in each mid-limb.

"Thanks," said Vetch and he went for the rebel's blaster on hands and knees. "I think I'll grow an extra pair of limbs next time I'm on leave. They look really handy."

He shook water off the rebel's blaster and retracted the muzzle blades. Now the weapon could fire again, but there were no more targets.

Not at the moment, at any rate. All three rebels lay dead.

Likely they'd been three stragglers lost in the rain who chose the wrong direction to stumble away. Bad luck for them…

"Stay alert!" said Lily. "There could be more."

And bad luck for Darant. The trooper was holding his left arm, inspecting the wound. At least he was on his feet.

"How bad?" Vetch asked him.

"Hurts like hell. Melted part of my glove into my flesh."

"Your glove? I thought you were hit in the arm."

"I was." Darant shook his head sadly. "That bolt fizzled. Misfire. It was the next one. Hit me in the hand. And the left hand, man. Why did it have to be the left?"

"But…that's not so bad? You're right-handed."

"My left hand is what I use to hold my book. Leastways, I did until now."

Using Lucerne, Vetch levered himself up to standing and hobbled over to Sybutu. One of the other legionaries had a med-kit open and was crouching over his comrade who'd fallen from the bike. The remaining legionary patrolled nearby on his bike, using its sensors to sweep for more trouble.

"How's your man?" Vetch asked Sybutu.

The Legion sergeant didn't immediately reply.

Vetch felt a creeping horror. He recognized that awkward pause; he'd used it himself.

"Stryker," Sybutu replied at last. His comrade with the med kit rolled closed the fallen legionary's eyes. "Off duty, we called him Old Guard. One day I'd like to tell you the story of why. His real name was Sapper of the Legion Tavarius Stryker."

Vetch's arm stretched out toward Sybutu. If the other sergeant had been a friend or comrade, then an arm over the man's shoulder would have been the most natural thing in the universe.

But Sybutu was neither. The Legion saw the universe differently and Vetch didn't understand their ways.

He lowered his arm to his side.

"Stryker serves us still," Sybutu announced in a loud voice, "through our memories and the steadfast example he set us. Farewell, brother."

"Farewell," echoed the two other surviving legionaries.

"Go in peace," said Vetch, not knowing where his words were coming from. He meant them sincerely, but he was thinking of his own death.

Would anyone care enough to say fine words for him?

"Not if you carry on like this," said Stryker's ghost.

Through bulging eyes, Vetch saw the man's shimmering spirit sit up from his fallen body and stare at him.

"At this rate, you'll get them all killed," the ghost accused.

"That's not fair," Vetch protested. "I mean, so far…"

Instead of justifying himself to the apparition, Vetch snapped his jaw shut and tapped his commset for transmission.

"Lily. I've got a concussion. Take us away now and keep us safe."

"It's the truth," said Stryker. "Fix it."

The ghost flared with light and was gone.

Vetch had never felt so alone.

* * * * *

Chapter Forty-Four:
Vetch Arunsen

Vetch didn't pass out on the journey east, away from Raemy-Ela, away from the battle scene and those who would seek revenge for the mauling of the Cora's World troops.

He didn't.

But he wanted to.

Sick. Dizzy. Confused. And with a headache of the sort he hadn't experienced since his youth before the first time he was arrested, Vetch kept a loose grip on consciousness and a tighter one on Sybutu. He rode pillion with arms around the legionary's waist, praying that either the universe would end, or his head would clear. Either way was fine with him.

Alongside, Meatbolt rode Stryker's bike, his spot on one of the Saruswine taken by the dead legionary wrapped in rebel coats.

By the time they set down in a slight depression in the ice about two hours later at dusk, the skies had cleared of rain and his head of the pounding. Knowing Lily, she'd kept them going until she thought he was ready to take charge again.

While the others secured the hollow, cared for the Saruswine, or rested while checking both equipment and wounds, Vetch followed Sybutu to the lip of the depression and looked west toward the town of Raemy-Ela, which by now was just shy of twenty klicks away.

300 | TIM C. TAYLOR

A light snow fluttered gently down.

Vetch had his binocs ready, but he didn't need them to see the rebel aircraft circling low around the scene of battle. They stabbed probing channels of light through the snow-filled sky, seeking the Chimera Company fugitives.

"What worries me most," he told the legionary sergeant alongside him, "is how the rebels are able to deploy surveillance aircraft unopposed. Where are our orbital defenses? Where are the Legion aircraft?"

"We have to conclude that…" Sybutu took a deep breath and tried again. "As far as we are aware, my team is the only Legion force remaining in the system. I'm not stupid, Arunsen. With Stryker lost and Urdizine keeping his head down in Raemy-Ela, we're unlikely to prevail alone. We need you."

Vetch had dropped the binocs in shock. "The only remaining…? What about the legionaries at Faxian?"

"All dead."

"I'm…sorry."

"Not as much as I am. And not nearly as much as the traitors will be when I get hold of them. Interesting that Major Yazzie never saw fit to share that intel with you, because I did brief her." Another deep breath. "Talking of sharing, it's time to bring our teams up to speed. We need to tell them we're all recruits to Chimera Company now. My people have heard it, but it wouldn't hurt to repeat it. Together."

"Vetch!" called Lily from the hollow.

"You worry too much," Vetch told the jack. "It'll be fine."

They slid down the slope, fat snowflakes sticking to their goggles. Vetch wiped the snow away with his upper arm, which revealed his

Militia troopers mobbing the two remaining legionaries. The jostling was getting angrier by the second. The sentries he'd posted had more than half their attention on the brewing fight.

Vetch leaned his weight on Sybutu's shoulder and hobbled over to the budding fracas, interposing himself between Legion and Militia.

The arguments fell silent.

"It is something of a perverse notion, I know," he told them, "but our respective officers—the ones we respect, that is—have ordered us to work together. We have a shared objective, a shared destination. Major Yazzie has even seen fit to issue us with a new name."

"What's that?" asked Meatbolt, excited.

"As naught but a humble and ignorant graduate of the Federation penal system, I shall leave the explanation to my far better qualified Legion colleague. Some of you have heard some of this, but everyone needs to understand it all. Sergeant?"

"We've been given a task," Sybutu told them. "It's simple in nature. Deliver a message to a contact in Bresca-Brevae. The contact poses as a smuggler called Captain Fitzwilliam. If you've any sense, you'll be asking who has given us this task and why should we trust them? This world has been betrayed, opened up to forces hostile to Legion and Militia alike. I suspect this is not an isolated incident, either. The Federation is being turned upside down and our message is the signal for those who remain true to their oaths to right it."

"Go on, then," said Green Fish. "Who are these heroes of the galaxy we're supposed to follow mindlessly?"

"I only know a few names. For the Legion, Colonels Lantosh and Malix. For the Militia, Major Yazzie. It's a risk telling you even those names, a confidence you must never betray. In a galaxy where your friends turn out to be your foe, you can go mad trying to figure out who to trust and who not to. So let's start by trusting ourselves. And that's why I've shared those names. They aren't alone. Our message will activate those hidden forces. Let them know what's happened here, that it is time to act. Time to reclaim the Federation from the cesspit of corruption, division, and self-interest it's sunk into, and shake it until it's fit for purpose. Until we—Militia and Legion alike—learn to work together to defend the Federation, because time is running out."

"Why now?" Lily challenged. "I'd throw away Legion and Militia and start again if it were up to me. But you're talking as if there isn't time. What's happening?"

Lily's question prompted the other human legionary—Bronze, if Vetch remembered rightly—to snap his attention onto his sergeant. Immediately, the man eased his focus away, but Vetch had seen it. Enthree had too. The Muryani had tensed and was looking Bronze's way with her head tilted low. If you didn't know her race, you'd think she was bowing, but Vetch recognized the unconscious gesture that deployed the olfactory organs dotted along her swept-back head. She was sniffing him.

Now he thought of it, Enthree had been acting weird around Bronze for a while now.

Oblivious to the reaction he was getting, Sybutu answered Lily's question. "A few centuries before the Amilxi Exiles arrived in this region of space and formed the Far Reach Federation, there was a war across the Tej Sector. We've known this for centuries thanks to the archeological record, but those dusty old theories suddenly became real important to the Legion. At Area of Special Interest 39, they found a ship left over from that war, and I think it's nearly ready to fly again. I think they've found relics on other worlds, too. Maybe they're getting intel on who fought that war because they fear the combatants will come back. And we all know the state of the Federation military. We wouldn't stand a chance against a real enemy."

"That's like thousands of years ago," said Green Fish. "Reckon they're long gone."

"You're thinking like a human," Vetch answered. "Our race is still running around the galaxy like an overstimulated toddler hyped on combat meds and armed to the teeth. We're new. Races who've been around longer are used to thinking on projects with a far longer time frame. Such as the Muryani Expansion. Isn't that right, Enthree?"

The Muryani trooper froze, caught in the act of edging toward Bronze, who was himself taking innocent half-steps that brought him closer to Meatbolt. What in Orion's name was going on?

"A few thousand years," Enthree echoed. "Yes, it is not a long duration. The Muryani Expansion began over a million years ago."

"Then it's not expanding very fast, eh?" Meatbolt drawled.

No one laughed with him. The Expansion had never developed a faster-than-light drive for its ships, and yet over in the Orion Spur of the galaxy its border was not far from Earth. A Muryani vessel would take at least twenty thousand years to fly from Rho-Torkis to the frontier near the human homeworld. By comparison with the vast ancient civilization, the Federation was like a barnacle clinging to an enormous oceangoing vessel. It was not a comforting thought.

"Sergeant Arunsen is right," said Sybutu angrily. "If you're human, never forget that our outlook is notoriously short-term in the minds of other races. Perhaps the Exiles arrived at a time of cease-

304 | TIM C. TAYLOR

fire. It used to be said that our destination in the Perseus Arm was not randomly selected. Perhaps we have been planted here for a purpose."

"Let's ask your Muryani," suggested the Kurlei legionary. "From the perspective of a civilization that's lasted a million years, the old war here has only just finished. What can you tell us about it, Enthree?"

The Muryani tilted her head left and then right. Then left again. Small movements only, but Vetch noticed. She was conflicted.

"I know nothing of this ancient war."

Damn! She was lying!

"I'll tell you what I *do* know," said Sybutu, obviously used to squad members keeping quiet like good little jacks. "You troopers encountered what you called phony legionaries. We met them a few days later and lost a good man fighting our way out. They were headed for that ancient ship. I don't know who they are, but they knew that ship was there, and they wanted it for themselves."

"Perhaps the phony jacks think the buried ship belongs to them," suggested Meatbolt.

"It's possible," Sybutu admitted, but Vetch was far more interested in Enthree's reaction to Meatbolt's suggestion. Her limbs trembled, starting at her flexible hooves and running up to her torso and hips before reflecting back down to her hooves.

She finally noticed his attention and shut down her shaking.

Busted!

"You have not answered Meatbolt's original question," said Enthree. "What is this name the major has given our joint endeavor?"

"Chimera Company," the two sergeants said together.

"Remember, troopers," said Vetch, "this comes from the same Major Yazzie who will determine whether we live or die when we return to Fort Iceni. So let's take her wishes seriously, eh?"

"I like it," said Lily. "Chimera Company. Pristine. But I'd also like to put another ten klicks between us and the aerial search before we shelter for the night. Before then, we have an important task to perform. Burial duty. Volunteers?"

The legionaries looked at her strangely, but Sybutu didn't protest that she was usurping his duty. Not after his we're-all-together speech. All three raised their hands.

The Militia troopers didn't. They just looked on awkwardly.

"Former Ravens!" Vetch bellowed. "Did you not hear? Trooper Hjon asked for volunteers."

Vetch stretched his hand high.

Tentatively…they all did, even the two sentries who were supposed to have their attention on what was happening outside of the perimeter.

Maybe it was the mental and physical fatigue, but Vetch shook and not with the cold.

This felt like an important moment.

A start.

It isn't much. It probably won't last. But all journeys start somewhere. How far will Chimera Company's journey take us?

He made a quick mental calculation. They were five days' travel from Bresca-Brevae, four if the Saruswine could pick up pace. Would Chimera Company hold until then? He would soon find out.

* * * * *

Chapter Forty-Five:
Osu Sybutu

All night long, a hurricane of freezing wind and driving snow had blown from the west, picking up the barren essence of the Great Ice Plain and hurling it spitefully at the Chimera Company party.

The legionaries joked that Rho-Torkis was finally rallying to their side, putting a wind at their backs to hurry them toward their destination. Bresca-Brevae lay just 100 klicks to the east.

The Militia troopers were unconvinced, wrapping themselves in heated snow masks and plastic sheeting to ward off the ice planet's caress.

Even the one surviving Saruswine juvenile appeared cowed by the relentless wind, pushing into the middle of the line of adults, sheltering within their bulk and their confidence. Indeed, so sure-footed were the adults that, after a while, the legionaries stopped scouting ahead to check the terrain was clear and settled at the rear of the column. With one legionary on watch at all times—to keep an eye on the Militia as well as other potential threats—the other two slept in the saddle.

With the Militia remounting the Saruswine, who had recovered with amazing speed from the pasting they'd received in the battle, an empty hoverbike took the rear of the column on auto-follow.

They pushed on relentlessly, telling themselves of the need to distance themselves from Raemy-Ela and the battle scene before the weather cleared. That need was true enough, but the prospect of resting in such a harsh environment filled them with horror. They had lived in the icy hell for many days since setting out from Faxian and Iceni, and by now they were stinking, soiled, and suffering from exposure. However exhausted they were, the survival instinct they had built up on their journey insisted that if they stopped, their flesh would become ice, merging into the landscape like a wintering Tallerman.

And so they drove onward, every call for a halt bringing howls of frightened protest.

But they had no choice. They had to stop for their mounts.

The beasts had won the admiration of first the troopers and then the legionaries. However, they could only endure when properly fueled, and the Saruswine needed to eat frequently, crunching away at the feed pellets stored in canisters piled high over the backs of the adults.

The Saruswine feeding halts were the pitstops from hell. The placid beasts would not tolerate riders when they fed, nor would they feed on the move. The feed pellets were scattered on the ice and the beasts left to their business. Meanwhile, the team crowded around the heated bikes in a mob that shuffled through the snow and wind, hunched over like undead polar creatures, never daring to halt but lacking the energy to do more than tramp the snow as they slowly circled the warm bikes.

Even the bikes needed their rest stops. In the extreme cold conditions, their batteries required frequent rebalancing and toxic waste gases needed venting. When the legionaries powered down their bikes, the Chimerans huddled around the dying embers of their residual heat, all the while turning their heads away to avoid choking on noxious fumes.

At Osu's insistence, they improvised nose bags so the Saruswine could eat on the move. But like all the species who had survived nuclear winter on Rho-Torkis, the Saruswine had a ferociously stubborn streak. They considered the plastic sheets folded around their mouths to be intolerable burdens. They nipped at them with sharp front teeth and dipped their heads so they could rub at them with their forelimbs.

And when they finally succeeded in ripping the bags open, scattering the feed into the snow, they would halt until they'd eaten their fill.

It was inefficient. Infuriating. But the only way was to scatter the pellets into the snow and halt every three hours or so. The Saruswine foraged by battering the ground with their furry heads, throwing up great mounds of snow that scattered most of the pellets and wasted the precious food.

"They're like bulldozers," Zavage observed at one halt.

"That they are," murmured Green Fish. She was a little taller than the Kurlei legionary, but nonetheless she had leaned in against his chest, using him for what little warmth and shelter she could extract from his place in the outer layer of the ring of half-alive bodies circling the warm bikes.

"Imagine the possibilities!" The heat of Zavage's excitement awoke some of those nearby from their torpor. "Berms, ramparts, walls, and channels through drift snow—imagine what we could train them to do."

"That's…not bad thinking," Green Fish admitted.

"No," Zavage replied proudly, "I'm a sapper of the Legion. It's thinking like an engineer."

His excitement had been a brief spark of life in the grim struggle for survival, quickly swallowed by the cold and wind, but it hadn't gone unnoticed.

"Your alien has a point," Arunsen told Osu. "Although what's truly amazing is that I never imagined Green Fish could speak to a legionary without spitting on them. Maybe this Chimera stunt will work."

Maybe.

Osu didn't reply. It looked more to him like the love-hungry Kurlei SOTL was hitting on the female trooper.

If the wind ever relented, and the cold eased—as it would do if they ever reached Bresca-Brevae—then Zavage was going to be a problem. Osu should nip that in the bud now.

The cold, though, said otherwise. He shivered in his thermal coat, wondering how it could be that the extreme weather gear was proving so inadequate, and concentrated on placing one foot in front of the other as they trudged around the bikes. It was all he could do.

Keeping going meant staying alive for the next five minutes. Osu couldn't focus on a future beyond that.

In silence, he pushed his body to move, cursing the Saruswine for their need to feed.

* * * * *

Chapter Forty-Six:
Osu Sybutu

As day broke, so too did the storm. In the orange skies of a Rho-Torkis dawn, they saw aircraft flying a surveillance pattern to the west, too far away to spot them but looping ever closer. To the north, the black sky warned of a blizzard rolling their way, but it wouldn't hit for hours, leaving them dangerously exposed to observation.

Which left the Chimera group looking to the east and the edge of the Great Ice Plain.

Beyond the high ice escarpment, a snow-covered lowland plain rolled out toward the coast. Beyond the horizon, around 80 klicks away, Bresca-Brevae lay nestled in the shelter of a natural harbor.

For as far as Osu could see, the escarpment dropped hundreds of feet down to the lowlands. They had known they would eventually face this barrier unless they spent a couple of days detouring to the south, but the brutal reality of the plunge was terrifying this close up.

"We lost our best rider," Osu told Arunsen as they contemplated the descent. "You helped to bury him. I think Stryker told us enough to give us a fighting chance with the bikes, but your Saruswine? We hadn't planned on encountering followers riding snow camels crossed with giant rodents. We can take a few of you on the bikes. It will increase the risk, but I'm prepared to take that. Once down,

312 | TIM C. TAYLOR

there will be no way back up for us. The rest of your party will have
to head south and hope to meet us in Bresca-Brevae."

When Osu glanced at the Viking for his response, the big man
laughed and slapped him on the shoulder.

Osu brushed him away. "I don't like being touched."

That only made Arunsen laugh louder. "On this, at least, you
mean well, but you don't know much, do you?"

"Some things aren't worth knowing, you barbarian oaf. If I need
advice on cosmetics or jewelry for facial hair, I admit I have something to learn from you. I can't imagine needing your advice on any
other topic, unless you are going to tell me your beasts can sprout
wings."

The big man stroked his beard braids thoughtfully. "Watch."

They sent the juvenile over first.

Lily was riding him.

They'd found a section of ice cliff a few klicks to the south where
the drop wasn't quite so sheer, and snow had drifted against the base
of the cliff, reducing the drop somewhat.

Even so, anyone sliding off the edge of the cliff would hit with
such impact that they would shatter every bone in their body.

The Saruswine, though, were tougher than that. Better adapted
too.

Whatever Lily did to the snowy white beast she rode, she never
let on, but it made the creature squeal in panic and run off the cliff at
a sharp angle.

The legionaries looked on, incredulous. It seemed at first that the
animal would scamper a diagonal path all the way down, but the
smoothness of the ice proved too much, and the creature began sliding on its side.

The Saruswine squealed in terror, but powerful survival instincts took control. Its limbs folded away against its belly, but its feet dug into the ice, acting as brakes.

Lily was screaming too. Hollering in excitement at this ultimate extreme sport.

Perhaps egged on by the distress call of the youngster, the adult Saruswine followed, sliding down on their flanks and using legs and feet to arrest their fall.

"Urdi won't believe me when I describe this." Zavage shook his head in wonder.

"True," Bronze replied. "We'll just have to put him onto one of those oversized rabbits and push him over a cliff."

"*If* any of them survive," said Osu, "then feel free to put it to the green guy. Rather him than me…ewwww! That's gotta hurt."

Lily's Saruswine had crashed into the snowdrift at the base of the cliff, hurling up a white plume and throwing off its human rider. The beast's momentum kept it rolling down the slope and onto the plain like a shaggy-pelted barrel.

The legionaries tensed as the first adult hit the bottom, its riders and stores still on its back.

It plunged through the snow, having retracted all its limbs into the thick folds of its belly immediately before impact. The troopers riding this beast were not thrown off but went down beneath the snowline with their mount.

For a few moments, only their heads were visible above the snow, slowly sliding away from the cliff base. Then the Saruswine stood and shook its fur clean, scattering the riders and load that it had kept secure during the descent. One of the food canisters hit the

314 | TIM C. TAYLOR

ground and burst open, much to the Saruswine's delight. Completely uninterested by the arrival of the other two adults, it began grazing.

"Our turn," said Osu when he was sure the troopers had survived.

They mounted their bikes. To avoid crashing into the Militia below, they rode a short distance away from the edge and two hundred yards to the south. Line abreast, with Stryker's bike at the far left on auto-follow, they waited on Osu's signal.

Should have requested a trooper to ride the spare bike, Osu told himself, but it was too late now. He glanced back and saw rebel surveillance aircraft getting dangerously close. Much too late.

"Remember what Stryker taught us," said Osu.

"Yeah," Bronze responded. "Basically, we channel some of Lily Hjon's madness."

"Skragg it, man!" Osu admonished. "Don't ever let her hear you say that. But, yeah, that's what we need. A touch of Lily madness. Three...two...one...let's ride!"

They charged off the cliff. Maximum acceleration.

Osu found himself imagining he had a rose tattoo and an industrial-scale attitude problem. It helped. A little.

On the last few inches before the ice precipice turned to thin air, the legionaries boosted power to the front gravitic motor.

Osu was flying.

It wasn't like the steep slope they'd descended near Camp Faxian; this was a two-hundred-foot drop through emptiness. The gravitics wailed loudly, searching for a floor to push against but finding nothing.

Quieter, but more pitifully, Osu whimpered as he fought to keep loose and balanced. The three of them had agreed that this drop was survivable so long as they didn't tip the bikes. If the base of the bike was facing anywhere but down when they landed...survivability rating: zero.

The borrowed spirit of Lily Hjon kept his terror of heights at bay until fifty feet before impact. Then his body tensed, and he screamed in fear.

Ever so slightly, he felt the bike tilt forward. It was probably just a fraction of a degree, but the lurch in his gut felt as if he were a ship tipping off the crest of an ocean swell.

He threw his weight back, and he corrected the forward tilt.

Overcorrected. Now he was tipping back.

He was going to land head first, his neck vertebrae acting as a shock absorber for the impact.

Blind panic pushed him to accelerate away, instinctively opening up the rear engine to speed away from the danger.

Over level ground, that's what he would have done.

As it was, the burst of power accelerated his flip, cartwheeling all the way back over.

Suddenly, the ground was just yards away.

He pushed the gravitics to maximum and eased into a thumping impact that bounced him back up six feet before coming to rest a few inches above the snow.

Osu sat there, staring ahead at the endless white and gripping his bike so tightly, his hands had probably melted through the handlebars.

A distinctive animal squeak made him look up into the face of the young Saruswine. The beast contemplated him from a short distance away. "Nice backflip," said its rider. "Shame about our spare bike."

Scattered across the snow to his left, Stryker's bike had shattered into hundreds of pieces.

"The auto-pilot was supposed to have coped with the landing," Osu murmured. He shivered, realizing how lucky he had been.

That had been close.

* * * * *

Chapter Forty-Seven:
Osu Sybutu

"We cannot stay here!" Osu resisted the desire to punch the ridiculous man in his hairy Viking face.

For now.

"We're lucky the aerial reconnaissance hasn't already spotted us. Let's not wager our lives on that luck holding."

"We wait here," Arunsen replied as if making the decision that could cost them their lives was as everyday an occurrence in the life of Militia troopers as which dumpster kiosk to eat from that day and which brothel to visit that night.

The big man frowned, surprised that Osu didn't accept his judgement without question. "The lea of the cliff face will be the best shelter when the storm hits. I want to give our injured Saruswine a chance to heal too."

"The chance to heal?" Osu tore the air in front of him. If Arunsen hadn't been shot in the leg, it wouldn't have been the air but the Viking's beard getting ripped off his face. "The animal has two broken legs. Shoot the beast and shift its load to our bikes and get out of here already. The forest starts just ten klicks away. It will shelter us from the storm and from observation, but every second we dally makes both less likely."

Arunsen tilted his head back a little as he appeared to consider the suggestion. He looked as if he were sniffing for answers.

He's Militia, thought Osu. That's probably exactly what he's doing.

"Too risky." Arunsen looked to the northern horizon which had been swallowed by the angry storm cloud getting close now. "I don't want to be caught in the open. Better to stay here."

"Hey!"

Osu followed the angry shouts and saw a fracas brewing between Bronze and Meatbolt, the trooper who looked like a junior version of Arunsen.

"What's going on?" asked Lily. Troopers stopped what they were doing and backed up their man against Bronze.

Zavage hurried over across the snow to do the same with his.

"Don't you ever—*ever*—say that again!" Bronze was screaming in fury. He must have lost it completely. Osu had never seen the man like this.

"What? You ignorant, jack-wipe arse filter." Meatbolt punctuated his words by shoving the legionary.

Bronze hesitated before laughing at the young trooper's cack-handed insults.

Then he tore at his opponent, flicking back Meatbolt's hood and half ripping out his scarf.

The trooper backed away, curling in on himself and pulling up his hood and settling his hat that had become dislodged. But in so doing, he exposed himself to Bronze who had discarded his gloves in the snow and came at Meatbolt with open hands, which he plunged down the trooper's neck, throttling him.

"Sapper Zy Pel! Stop that immediately!"

Osu's words were redundant. Troopers had rallied around their comrade and kicked Bronze to the ground. His hands were already shockingly pink with cold, but Zavage had the man's thick winter gloves back on in seconds.

"If you insult a legionary like that," said Bronze, "expect them to kill you with their bare hands. It's not a metaphor, tramp soldier."

"You're insane." Meatbolt gave Bronze a half-hearted kick in the shins but allowed himself to be led away.

"Flee for the trees if you like," Arunsen told Osu, "but we're staying here. And if your man tries anything like that again, when we head off, he'll stay here under the ice in a grave that I will make you dig. Sort him out, Sybutu."

Osu fumed. Brawling was the last thing he needed right now, but Bronze was not like Stryker or Heidl. Everything he ever did was calculated.

"We are in greater danger than I realized." That was the only explanation Bronze offered when Osu pushed for one. He didn't say it in the common tongue, either. He used BDZ—Battle Dialect Zulu.

He's worried about Sward, Osu realized. Even in a whisper, the Militia Zhoogene might overhear, but BDZ was a secret the Legion didn't share with anyone. Certainly not the Militia.

"Better have a good explanation," Osu replied in BDZ. "We'll have time to talk later when the storm hits." He regarded the skies. Now it was much too late to reach the forest. "Looks like we're staying put."

* * * * *

Chapter Forty-Eight:
Osu Sybutu

They hadn't much time before the storm crashed against them.

It grieved Osu to make the admission, but the violent weather hit so quickly that they would never have made it to the forest.

Under Osu and Zavage's direction, they set the uninjured Saruswine to work bulldozing snow into two berms that angled out from the cliff and met in the middle as a bastion against the elements. The beasts, of course, thought they were being treated to copious amounts of free food, and when they had eaten their fill, nothing could convince them to push up more snow. The troopers and legionaries worked at adding to the height of these berms, angling their sides at forty-degrees to maximize stability and deflect the shrieking winds.

When they'd built them six feet high, they punched a step through the point where the two walls met and brought the animals and personnel inside. With moments to spare, they pulled across sheeting they had attached to the cliff face and secured it to the ground.

Then the blizzard hit.

322 | TIM C. TAYLOR

One moment they were being buffeted by winds like icy daggers, and then in an instant they were flung into the pitch-black. Nighttime in hell.

One moment they were being buffeted by winds like icy daggers, and then in an instant they were flung into the pitch-black. Nighttime in hell.

Ice demons whistled and roared as they assaulted the shelter. In the light of glowbulbs screwed into the ground, the sheets overhead dimpled violently under ferocious wind punches.

Suddenly, a sheet tore loose from the cliff.

"Take it down!" Osu bellowed, but his voice was drowned by the blizzard's anger. He stood up and tried pointing to the flapping sheet, but before he could extend his finger, the wind ripped the sheet away and it was gone.

The effect was instantaneous. The snow blowing through the gap in the wall became a stream of white, blasting inside like the anti-version of a plasma flamer. The remaining sheeting, however, shook less violently now, and the wind seemed to be blowing the snow up over the walls and safely over their heads. Very little descended through the gap left by the missing sheet.

The flow of snow through the gap in the wall was another matter. If they didn't stop that, the shelter would fill and they'd suffocate.

Enthree fixed that problem.

The Muryani trooper had developed a special affinity to the Saruswine. She roused the two uninjured adults, who had pushed themselves against the cliff, and led them to the gap in the wall, parking them line abreast.

The seal was far from perfect, but over the next few minutes, the snow piled up against the animals, sealing the hole. So long as Enthree remained nearby, the Saruswine seemed unconcerned by their vital new role.

As long as they were well fed, they would go where led and perform the duty required of them without complaint.

They would make perfect legionaries, thought Osu.

* * * * *

Chapter Forty-Nine:
Osu Sybutu

"**M**eatbolt is one of *them*." Bronze was squatting next to Osu, with his head inside the sergeant's hood. Against the howling wind, and the snow bombarding the walls of the shelter, it was the only way to be heard.

Even so, Bronze spoke in Battle Dialect Zulu.

And that made translation tricky. Bronze wasn't making sense.

"A rebel?" Osu queried.

"No. What Stryker called the vampires. He must have been infected for days."

"Days? You thought Stryker would change within hours."

"I don't know why Meatbolt's taking so long. Could be the cold, could be natural resistance, or perhaps the infection is weak because whoever infected him is too many iterations removed from the source of the outbreak. But I'm absolutely certain. Meatbolt is one of them."

"What makes you so certain?"

"When I appeared to choke him, I felt the skin on his neck. He's growing feathers."

"Feathers!" The notion was so surreal that Osu broke out into the standard tongue.

From the corner of his eye, he saw Enthree's head swivel in interest at his exclamation.

Holy Azhanti! I must be hallucinating. Despite the intense cold, the Muryani had undone the front of her coat and was baring her hairy torso at him.

Osu decided to pretend he hadn't noticed.

"In humans, feathers started to grow in the final phase of the infections I saw," Bronze explained. "Whatever he is now, he's no longer human…although he thinks he is."

"And so do his former comrades."

"Indeed. But we must regard him as an enemy."

"Bronze, you still haven't leveled with me about who *they* actually are."

"Best for your sake that you do not know."

"Is it? As far as we know, the three of us here, and Urdizine hopefully safe in Raemy-Ela, are the only Legion survivors in this system. We're way past 'need to know.' 'Need to survive' is where we're at. Spill!"

"I know only what I've experienced myself and…" Bronze hesitated. That didn't bode well. "And briefing from temporary allies who may have been unreliable. Those allies called them the Invaders. I saw them hit two worlds. Trying to quietly take them over, it seemed to me. I've heard there were takeovers on other worlds too. Some successful, some not. My allies thought the Federation is experiencing an invasion that barely anyone knows about. I think they're right."

"You told the Legion what you found?"

He shifted uneasily. "Most of it. It's why I'm here. Although why I've not simply been eliminated…To be honest, that's an even bigger mystery to me."

"It seems the galaxy is a stranger place than either of us expected," said Osu. "Do you know where they come from? They have to be invading *from* somewhere."

"No idea."

"I bet that Muryani does." Osu shifted his gaze; Enthree had them under observation and was not troubling herself to be subtle about it.

"Agreed," said Bronze. "Secrets, secrets…everywhere I see secrets and mysteries, but before we can get anywhere, we've a mission to carry out and that remains priority one."

"After you attacked Meatbolt today, those troopers will be watching you. If I can engineer an opportunity for you to have another argument, can you kill this…this Invader and make it seem an accident?"

"I can. But that's no guarantee the Militia will treat it as such."

"Understood." Murderous plans began circling in Osu's mind. His ma would not approve, but the mission was all. "Leave it with me."

"Good." Bronze spoke with finality, reached into his deep pockets, and drew out his pipe. A short while later the shelter began filling with the sweet aroma of his synth-bacco.

How does he switch off like that? Osu wondered. He had no such skill himself. With his spirit growing more stained by the second, he honed his plans for murder.

* * * * *

Chapter Fifty:
Osu Sybutu

"What did I tell you, Arunsen? We should have buried your injured animal and run for the trees. They've found us."

The Militia sergeant peered down at Osu from his mount but said nothing.

The Saruswine he rode through the trees was the same beast that had broken two legs in yesterday's wild descent. Now it carried Arunsen, a half load of supplies, and Green Fish—the woman who seemed to be forming an attachment to Zavage. The beasts were magnificent, and Osu had grown proud of Chimera Company's Saruswine contingent, although it suited him to pretend otherwise for now.

"I left a motion sensor at the shelter after we leveled the site. Built out of parts salvaged from the bike wreckage. It's showing multiple contacts. Looks like vehicles there. Probably attracted by the sheet that wasn't properly secured."

"You were there." Arunsen growled. "We wouldn't have made it to the trees before the blizzard hit."

"We would have if you hadn't wasted time with your pets, and your Militia thugs hadn't picked a fight with my man."

The gap narrowing between the trees, Osu had to break contact for a short distance to thread his way through the forest before pulling alongside again when the route widened once more.

It was only a short detour, but it was enough to observe the tension in the party as the Saruswine-mounted troopers stabbed barbed comments down at Bronze and Zavage. The legionaries for their part remained aloof, not deigning to respond to their inferiors.

The insults were becoming angrier by the second.

"Chimera Company is fracturing," Osu warned Arunsen on his return.

"Yeah, and whose fault is that?" Arunsen swallowed his anger. "We don't have to work together," he said after a long pause. "I just have to make sure you fulfil your mission and be present at the photo opportunity so I can say we were there. But…although it tastes like mud to say this, if we do work as a team, we're more likely to reach that point alive."

"Agreed. But it's not working so far. In the Legion, when we have two people who can't tolerate each other, we stick them in a room or cave for a few days and leave them to sort out their issues. If all goes well, they come out as brothers or sisters. Second best outcome: only one emerges alive. Third best: they both die. At least that way they no longer endanger their comrades."

Okay, so Osu was exaggerating, but the Militia sergeant seemed to buy it wholesale. He tugged at his beard inside his cloak and then joined in. "Fourth best," said Arunsen. "Leave the discord to simmer away. If two troopers are at war with each other, the entire team is imperiled. I agree that we are sparring with each other, Militia and Legion. I myself would feel more relaxed after burying my knuckles in your face, Sergeant Sybutu. What do you propose?"

"You and I should settle our differences in private. Everyone else, lock them all in a room for a day to get it out their systems. Kill or cure, Arunsen. Anyone who survives that bloodletting we take with us to Bresca-Brevae."

The big man pulled again on his beard. Osu began to suspect it was a deliberate attempt to wind him up. What could be a less appropriate look for a professional soldier than eyeshadow and bejeweled beard?

Nonetheless, Arunsen's tone became almost soothing. "I misjudged you, Osu. You're arrogant, a complete arse, impaled on your bigoted self-importance, and strangled by your solipsism. Yet you're not as ignorant as I assumed."

"Thank you. And you, Arunsen, are ugly, fetid, and about as unprofessional as a soldier can get and still fire a rifle. I wouldn't trust you to run anything of financial value because you are a king of thieves, ruling an infinitesimally petty kingdom. And yet…"

The Viking laughed when Osu was lost for words. "This is the part where you say something nice."

Osu shook his head, the task beyond him. "What the hell does solipsism mean, anyway?"

Arunsen shrugged. "Fucked if I know."

The whole conversation had been a lie, but there was nothing fake about the laughter that tumbled out of Osu's chest and into the snow-laden trees.

Arunsen joined in with his deep guffaws. Mounted a little further up the same Saruswine, Green Fish turned and regarded them both with disgust.

"Lily knows the ground better than any of us," said Arunsen when they'd settled. "I'll ask her to suggest a place."

"Agreed. But after the blizzard blew itself out, the air's been still. Without our tracks healing up behind us, we have to assume any pursuers will follow straight into the forest. We need to shake them first, and I have an idea how."

* * * * *

Chapter Fifty-One:
Chimera Company

After another hour's journey headed east through the forest, Chimera Company met the river Beythu-Los flowing south toward the sea. The waist-deep water was clear and fast flowing. Fish with fins like brightly colored ribbons darted playfully in and out of sharp rocks.

The Saruswine proved their mettle again, stepping into the cold water and navigating the uneven and slippery riverbed with only the occasional stumble.

Instead of crossing, they remained in the river and followed its course downstream, the Legion bikes carving a foaming channel as their gravitics churned the water. The animals remained as unconcerned with the cold of the water as they were with the snow and ice.

After a couple of hours journeying this way, and with the Saruswine growing restless for a feed, the trees thinned and then gave way to open plain. The party scanned the horizon for trouble and found none. However, they did see scattered signs of habitation: a radio mast here, a storage silo there, and along the crest of a low range of hills on the far eastern horizon, an occasional wheeled vehicle moving along an ice road.

Rho-Torkis remained fiercely untamable, but it was yielding crude signs of settlement.

Since setting out from Fort Iceni, Enthree had developed such a connection to the Saruswine that by now they would follow her anywhere. She led them to the east bank to feed, urging them to hurry. The beasts tore great furrows in the snowy riverbank in their obedient haste to get to food.

Enthree, Vetch, and Lily rode the Saruswine back into the Beythu-Los and resumed their journey downstream, while Rynter, Darant, and Sward joined the three legionaries in tramping east through the snow, pushing the riderless bikes with them and making as heavy a trail as they could without being too obvious about it.

After cresting a hill three klicks out from the river, Osu judged it too risky to carry on. He really had left a motion sensor at the blizzard refuge, but it was a crude affair. There was no way of telling whether it had detected a flurry of snow blowing past or a division of heavy armor, but he deemed it better to plan for the worst than hope for the best.

They mounted the bikes, troopers riding pillion, and pressed on for a few hundred yards, moving slowly so as to minimize the evidence they left in the snow. Then they circled around in a wide arc before picking up speed to rendezvous with the Saruswine plowing through the river.

Reunited, Chimera Company followed the Beythu-Los downstream until they reached the sea an hour before dusk. By nightfall they had arrived at their destination, the location Lily had recommended to thrash out their differences. It was a small island out across the frozen sea. It was an uninviting place with a boulder-strewn beach rising to aggressive cliffs, but snuggled within a fold in those cliffs was a cave accessible via a series of rocky ledges. The Saruswine jumped up them without a problem. By the time the legionaries and their bikes had been lifted up to the cave with ropes, the troopers had already lit the interior, a barrel of brandy had been tapped, and the plasma weapons had been used to heat a circle of stones built up within a large metal trivet they had found there.

Clearly, they weren't the only ones to use this cave as shelter, but for tonight, the island belonged to Chimera Company.

Though whether there would still be a Chimera Company by morning remained to be seen.

* * * * *

Chapter Fifty-Two:
Vetch Arunsen

Across the cave walls flickered shadows of the troopers and jacks sitting around the glowing stones in the fire-pit.

Chimerans, Green Fish had started to call the group. As if they were ever going to be a single unified team.

No one else felt a need to use Green Fish's new name.

But then she had eyes for the fish-jack with the plump head tentacles. If Vetch ever discovered that the Kurlei had been using the lumps on his head to plant ideas into Green Fish's heart, then he'd slice them off and roast them over the fire. Probably go well with onions.

He found himself staring at this Vol Zavage. He'd never seen a Kurlei's face this close before. On the trek here, heads and faces had been covered, but in the cave the goggles and hoods were off, and he could look his temporary allies in the face.

Sybutu, he'd seen before, stretched over a rock for Lily's amusement. Vetch was sitting next to him now but felt no compulsion to study the jack's features. Osu Sybutu looked the same as pretty much every legionary he'd ever met. Sometimes he wondered whether the legions were stuffed with clones imprinted with false memories, and a random selection of skin tone and gender from a limited range of factory options.

Bronze was not such a clone. For a jack, his build was slight and his features pinched and even more pale than Vetch's own. Yet he radiated far more danger than Sybutu. He moved with the grace of a jungle cat who could extend a single claw and sever your artery with a casual flick.

The legionary said something to make the troopers around him laugh. Vetch couldn't make out what they were saying on the other side of the hot stones, but he picked up the cruel edge to the laughter. It was bloodthirsty. Impatient.

Drink had been consumed by all but Enthree and Darant who were on watch. Food shared. Clothing stripped down to the underlayers. It looked as if Sybutu would get his wish to scrap it out, because now that the troopers and jacks had been given their chance to get the measure of each other, there was an expectant air as everyone waited for the mood to switch.

Who would move the group on to the next phase?

"Hey, Sybutu!" called Lily from behind the two sergeants. "How're you feeling?"

Oh, this is gonna be good, thought Vetch as he watched Sybutu ignore Lily's greeting.

Lily, in turn, ignored the slight and waved at Vetch to shuffle along the smooth rock they'd dragged near to the heated rocks to use as a bench.

"You know," she said to the unresponsive jack, "I had you chained to a rock a little like the one we're sitting on. Isn't that funny?" She sat down, her lengthy sigh suggesting she was settling there for the night. "I even warmed it up for you with a plasma flamer, pretty much like the girls used to heat these cave rocks."

"Go away."

Vetch grimaced at the way Sybutu spoke. On the surface it was calm enough, but dig a little deeper and the legionary was boiling with resentment. He couldn't fault the man. Lily *had* played rough with him, after all.

"I'm sorry, Osu, but if we're to work together, then there are some things I need you to know. Major Yazzie ordered me to loosen you up before she talked with you. Sounded like she wanted to play good cop, bad cop, and I'm very good at being bad. As for flames, when we captured you, I planted a sub-dermal tracker while you were paralyzed on the way to Iceni. The incision I made was covered up by the burn scars."

Now that's odd…

Vetch had a theory about what made legionaries tick. They made good soldiers, that was true, but that was only because they sucked so badly at everything else. Such as hiding emotions. Most Militia troopers were graduates of the gutters, sink-cyls, and prisons: they knew how to lie.

Sybutu was the typical Legion open book. So when Lily's jibes failed to fill him with righteous indignation—instead Sybutu looked guilty as hell—Vetch wondered what the man had done.

Or what was he yet to do?

"So," Sybutu responded, "what are you saying, Hjon? Are you telling me you did bad things for good reasons? Do you expect my forgiveness?"

"Don't judge me too soon, Sergeant. I haven't finished. Not quite. I wanted to make it clear that, yes, I was torturing you under orders, but I also want you to know that as I was hurting you, I was thinking only of myself."

For the first time, Sybutu looked at the woman sitting beside him, his face hard with disdain. "You're not making any sense."

She grinned. "What I mean to say, Sergeant Jack, is that the main reason I tortured you for so long is because…" She leaned her head against his shoulder. "Because I enjoyed it."

Sybutu spun about and shoved Lily hard in the chest.

She flew off the back of the stone and made a hard landing on the floor of the cave.

"You asked for that, Lil'," Vetch murmured. Some of his troopers got to their feet. He doubted they would be so understanding.

Lily sprang up and jumped back onto the stone, pushing her face up against Sybutu's. "Didn't like that, did you, jack? Is it a fight you want? You're bigger and uglier than me, but I'll take you on if you're brave enough."

A pair of arms slid beneath Lily's shoulders and pulled her off her seat. Vetch glanced up to see Green Fish wrap her arms tightly around Lily's chest and whisper something in her ear.

He couldn't hear what was said, but Lily walked off into the shadows and Green Fish took her place between the two sergeants. Meatbolt hovered nearby like a storm about to break.

"What can I say?" Green Fish gave Sybutu a half-shrug of apology. "Lily's tastes can run to the extreme."

"I just don't get it," said Sybutu. "The madwoman took a dislike to me before I even spoke to her. The first thing I said to Lily was an incoherent scream when she tortured me. Why does she hate me so much?"

"That's sweet." Green Fish laughed. "The first word you ever spoke to her was *arggh!* You're really not getting it, are you? You're her type. She doesn't hate you. It would be so much simpler and easier for you if she did. I think she's a little in love with you."

Sybutu raised an eyebrow. "That's...disturbing." The eyebrow pushed to the limit. Sybutu was genuinely astonished by this revelation of the obvious. "And highly inappropriate."

"*Highly inappropriate*," she echoed. "You're *so* Legion."

"Her deviancy...is that why she was busted?"

"In a manner of speaking." Green Fish's eyes beamed with pride for her friend. "Honesty is her deviance. She's too decent to avoid doing the right thing. That was her downfall."

Sybutu screwed his face up. "I don't buy any of that. How can you extoll her virtues when she's just told me how much she enjoyed torturing me?"

"It wasn't you as such," said Vetch. "You represent the Legion. In messing with you, she was sticking it to jacks throughout the Federation. She has plenty of justification for that. We all do."

"And this from the same Lily Hjon who said she wants the Legion and Militia both gone to start over again." Sybutu shook his head. "She's crazy."

"Don't go using words like crazy," said Vetch. "My theory is that she's got Jotun blood in her. I'm serious. When our distant ancestors were slaves to Jotun Marine officers, they were brutalized and culled by the aliens who placed no value on individual human life. And yet the same big, shaggy aliens risked their entire race to aid us in the War of Liberation. Hell, they'd started laying down the logistics for our war back when the longbow and lance were the cool new military tech on Earth. They're generous and open-minded in principle; they just don't care about individuals. When it comes to Lily's strategic outlook, she's like a cultured fleet admiral adhering to higher

342 | TIM C. TAYLOR

principles. But in her one-on-one tactics, it's not just her tastes but her morality that's…well, *filthy*."

"I've met my share of filth," said Sybutu. "Blaster bolt through the head is usually the best treatment."

Green Fish bristled. "Attempting that would be a fatal mistake."

"Relax, Trooper," said the legionary. "If Hjon stays away from me, I'll leave her alone. It's not easy to forget torture. It's impossible to forgive. But I'm a legionary and that means the mission comes first."

Lily came from nowhere and yanked Sybutu back off his seat, spilling his precious brandy into the ground. She'd toppled him over, but she'd had to dig her heels in hard to the bottom of the heavy stone to lever him back.

And when he went back, she toppled too. They landed in a heap, Lily laughing and Sybutu on top. The look of shock on his face was priceless.

"Hey!" someone shouted.

Lily had pushed Sybutu too far. He had her pinned beneath his weight and had his arm back to strike. Unlike Lily, he wasn't playing.

Two pairs of hands grabbed the legionary's arm before he could bring it down. They belonged to Green Fish and Bronze.

"That's not going to help matters, Sergeant," advised the sapper. "Chimera Company. The beacon of hope that Legion and Militia can work together. Remember that? You're the one who signed us up to it."

Sybutu shifted his weight, and Lily scrambled free. He seemed to notice Lily's face for the first time. Her rose tattoo had grown fresh blood drips, and these ones were not black but a vivid crimson.

Lily stood and crossed her arms. "Do you have a problem with women, Osu?"

Still staring, Sybutu replied, "No. I have a problem with *you.*"

Lily's face softened into a pretty smile. "Good. So fight me."

"Gladly."

* * * * *

Chapter Fifty-Three:
Osu Sybutu

That damned Militia woman was infuriating.

Worse than that, Hjon was dangerous. It had taken Osu a while to figure out, but Hjon was still torturing him, still jerking him around by his chains, just more subtle ones now.

And Green Fish—the pretty one who was stirring Zavage's head fronds—had said this was all because Hjon felt a perverse form of attraction to him.

Osu believed it. Anything was possible with the deviant Militia scum he'd been forced to ally with. And that was putting the mission at risk. The whole reason Osu had engineered this detour to the island was to carry out his agenda of murder. As foul as that prospect was, his duty to the Legion said he needed to find a way to get rid of Meatbolt fast, before whatever was taking him over endangered the mission.

But it was Lily who was taking things over, shifting the evening onto her own agenda.

A cowardly part of him wanted to thank her for that.

"I got this, Lil'," said Meatbolt stepping in front of her. "I know you can hold your own, but you shouldn't have to sully yourself scrapping with a jack. Besides, I'm more his size."

"No." Osu stroked his chin as he considered the young trooper. Bronze was certain Meatbolt had been infected by these Invaders. If he was wrong, then they were contemplating a terrible crime, but Bronze hadn't been wrong about anything so far.

Osu made the call. He backed his own man.

"Hjon's beneath my notice," said Osu. "Both sergeants will stay out of it today. Arunsen and I will have our chance when his leg wound heals."

His decision made, he squared up to Meatbolt. "We have two sappers waiting to take on anyone who impugns the Legion's honor."

"I'll take on this one."

Osu heard Lily challenge the slighter figure of Sapper Vol Zavage to a fight, but that was not a matter of importance. It was all about Meatbolt from this point.

Meatbolt's death.

* * * * *

Chapter Fifty-Four:
Bronze

B ronze settled into a low fighting stance: subtle, responsive, and able to deliver the fatal blow.

His opponent preferred to whip up the crowd as he strutted along the far side of the ring marked out by loose rocks and the detritus left by previous visitors to the cave. The ring made no sense to Bronze. It wasn't as if there were any rules in this brawl. Beat the hell out of the other guy; that was about the extent of it.

A roar went up from the fight on the other side of the heap of glowing rocks where Hjon and Zavage were the main attraction. Only Green Fish, Enthree, and Osu were on this side of the cave, but only Osu realized that this was where the main event was about to take place.

A light squeeze of his right palm reassured Bronze that the poison tab was in place. A slap against Meatbolt's skin and in a few hours, he would suffer massive hemorrhaging and die.

His opponent was ready to fight now, rubbing his hands in glee.

Clearly, he still thought of himself as Meatbolt.

But he wasn't. Meatbolt had died before Bronze had even met him.

Shock and confusion suddenly wrote themselves across the face of the man who had been Meatbolt.

It's starting.

The last veneer of Meatbolt's essence was being erased in front of Bronze's eyes. His DNA had been infiltrated and rewritten in service to…

Invaders. That's what Bronze called them, but it was just an empty name. He still had no idea who they were facing, what their purpose might be.

A roar of excitement came from Green Fish; she'd probably mistaken his hidden weapon check as a sign of fear.

Meatbolt made the same mistake and stormed toward him. Head down like a charging animal, and swaying drunkenly, Bronze judged him an easy take down.

Waiting in a loose stance until the last moment, Bronze jabbed at Meatbolt's face with his poisoned hand.

Meatbolt's face had vanished…along with his drunkenness. Suddenly he was impressively nimble on his feet for such a bear of a man. The infected trooper skipped away, sidestepping past Bronze's attack and getting behind him.

Bronze threw his weight forward trying to roll out of danger, but he was too late. Meatbolt was wise to him and had leaned with him from behind, pinning Bronze's arms behind him.

Come on, Zy Pel! he screamed inwardly. You picked a bad time to get suckered. Sort him!

He bucked and wriggled, trying to win his hand free to deploy the poison.

No joy.

Not only had Meatbolt pinned his arms too securely, but he lifted Bronze off his feet.

Bronze smacked his head backward.

Meatbolt dodged his head away to the side and rammed his forehead against the side of Bronze's skull.

"You lose, jack." The joy of victory infused the trooper's words.

You haven't won yet, oaf!

His head still ringing in pain, Bronze first went limp, and was about to hurl himself forward and then throw his head back once more, hoping desperately to smack into a nose or eye and loosen the hold on his arms.

Before he could, Meatbolt surprised him again by releasing his bearhug.

Stumbling on the ground, and jarring his ankle painfully against a ringside stone, Bronze expected a stunning blow at any moment as he wasted precious moments he didn't have to regain his balance and ready himself to counter the attack he was sure was incoming.

But it never came.

Confusion and guilt wiped away Meatbolt's fighting snarl. He began lolling about the ring like unsecured gear on an ocean freighter, and Bronze didn't think he was faking this time.

He squeezed his right palm, but the poison tab was still there: undeployed.

"You…" Meatbolt pointed at Bronze, shaking his head in disbelief. "You…" He reversed his finger. "Me!"

The trooper sank to his knees. "Forgive me. Forgive me, please…*elder*."

The last word didn't come easily to Meatbolt. Poor skragg. When the last remnants of your mind realized your body had been taken over by something else, it couldn't be easy. That had so nearly been Bronze's fate, but he'd had access to nano-meds.

There were none for Meatbolt.

The best Bronze could offer him was a quick release.

He lifted the trooper up by his greasy dark hair. "Do you yield?"

"Yes. Yes, of course."

"Are you drunk, Meatbolt?" called one of the troopers.

"Thought you were doin' this for Lil'."

The audience had shifted across the cave to take in Meatbolt's fight. And his submission.

That's what this was. Whatever manner of creature had bitten Bronze two years ago was much higher up the hierarchy than whoever had passed the infection onto Meatbolt. Maybe it had been one of the Invaders themselves he'd encountered at Azoth Zol. Whatever it was, its seniority had transferred to Bronze.

Bronze's heart melted a little to see the astonishment and shame in Meatbolt's face, but he readied his poison hand to strike.

Then the man inside his flesh rallied and the young trooper thought he was back in control of himself.

"What's the matter, Meaty? Going soft?"

Bronze took a step back. He couldn't hit Meatbolt now. With all his friends watching, they would jump to their comrade's defense. And when Meatbolt died a few hours later, they would know who to blame.

Meatbolt rose to his feet and crossed his arms. "Lucky escape for you this time, jack. Must be something I ate. Expect a rematch next chance we get."

"I'll be waiting," Bronze replied. Helplessly, he watched as his opponent merged into the crowd of Militia spectators who shifted their attention back to the other fight.

Only Osu and the Muryani trooper remained with Bronze.

Bronze stared at the alien. He had no idea what was going through Enthree's head, but his gut told him the big insect knew a lot more than she was letting on.

* * * * *

Chapter Fifty-Five: Lily Hjon

The Kurlei glanced across at the commotion on the other side of the cave. Whatever the hell was going on with Meatbolt worried at Lily's mind, but she put that aside; she had a job to do first. After dancing a couple of steps toward the cave wall, she swung a left hook at the distracted Kurlei's face.

It was as if he had read her thoughts.

Funny, that.

Hands around her wrist, he yanked her down. She could feel her center of balance go, so she threw all she had into kicking into the gap between his knees, tangling their legs.

They went down together, landing with a bone-punishing impact onto the unforgiving stone floor.

When her head cleared of the spinning suns, Lily found herself on her back with Zavage on top of her, their hands locking together like lovers and their faces inches apart.

She'd never seen one of his species so close up before. His angular face—with a pointed chin that looked like it could pierce armor—had such hard planes that he looked like a sheet-metal sculpture. But if Zavage was sculptured, then the artist had finished off the stone with a coating of fish scales and powdered riverbed mud. And as for the plump appendages on top of his head pulsing obscenely in her face. What was that all about?

353

And what would they feel like to touch?

She decided to recategorize. Osu was cute and hateful. Bronze was dangerous. But Zavage…he was worthy of further investigation.

"You can touch them if you like." Zavage grinned inhumanly.

Could he read her mind, or did he just want her to think that?

"Of course," he added, "you'll have to concede first."

"Don't get ideas, fish-jack. I was just getting started battering you." Lily tried rolling free, but he had her pinned.

"You flatter yourself."

"I think we've given them enough of a show." She tried flicking her hands free. She failed. "Seriously, I can hand your fishy ass to you if you prefer. You do realize I was holding back?"

Zavage lowered himself until his…fronds? *What are they called?* Until his fronds brushed her hair.

"You held back a lot," he admitted. "I could sense it in your mind. But I held back *more*."

Lily found she could no longer give a damn. Electricity arced between them, her head filled with hiss and swash. She couldn't actually see sparks flying through the air, but it felt like nothing she'd experienced before. Actually…that wasn't quite true. On a dare, she'd once shoved her head inside the shunt conduit of an active hyperjump engine. Being near Zavage felt like that.

"Psychic feedback," he explained.

That smug jack! He's loving my reaction.

Lily had to admit, though. So was she. "And Kurlei girls? Do they have the same equipment up top?"

He nodded.

Lily blew out a breath, imagining Kurlei lovemaking. "That must be wild."

Subconsciously, her mind had secured an easygoing flirtatious connection to Zavage. The alien snapped it abruptly, leaving her in silent isolation so complete it was wounding. The Kurlei was now remote and alien beyond comprehension.

"Wild?" he said, "the word you're looking for is *fatal*."

Now, that, Lily told herself as Zavage rolled off, is a story I'm going to enjoy worming out of you, pal.

She watched him walk over to the crowd around Meatbolt, liking the fact that he could sense her attention in ways no human ever could.

She had no doubt that this Chimera Company business was going to get them all killed, but the journey was shaping up to be a lot more fun than she'd thought.

* * * * *

Chapter Fifty-Six:
Osu Sybutu

On a surface level, the brawl in the cave had been a great success because the bubble of tension had popped for the time being. With the troopers bewildered by the way Meatbolt had conceded, the heated pile of rocks had transformed into a timeless campfire around which stories had been told, tasteless jokes made, and some probing questions asked.

The Militia had poked fun at the Legion for separating the two most common genders into different battalions. The Legionaries had mocked the troopers for mixing them up.

Zavage had asked without rancor how the troopers felt about their officers when so many were without honor or competence. Lily responded by wondering aloud how it felt to learn that your commander-in-chief was in the pay of a foreign power.

The scandal of Legion First General Clarke had broken a decade before, but the mere mention of the traitor's name hit all the legionaries with a stunning blow of shame.

After that, the banter subsided for a long while, yet it eased back slowly. Simply being able to remove glacier goggles and scarves and see each other's faces had gone a long way to make the unwilling allies feel like people.

Osu knew all of that was important, but there was another level on which the night in the cave had been a disaster.

Meatbolt still lived.

The only positive Osu could draw from the cave brawl was that he'd seen Meatbolt's humanity slip away to leave behind a confused creature inhabiting his flesh. There was no doubt in Osu's mind anymore: Meatbolt was morphing into something else, and the transformation seemed almost complete.

Meatbolt sounded as if he'd been a real character, a young man with a lot to offer the galaxy whose story had been tragically cut short. Osu had already seen far too much death, but the loss of this one trooper twisted his guts nonetheless.

In the morning, they had set off on the last leg of their journey to the capital, and whatever fate awaited them there. Cultivated trees, fish farms, religious icons mounted on high poles, farmsteads, ice roads—the signs of Littorane habitation were all around, and as the klicks to Bresca-Brevae ticked down, so the land grew more firmly inhabited.

They passed other convoys of travelers and vehicles driven by citizens going about their daily lives. Only once did they see evidence of the invasion: rebel aircraft appearing beneath the clouds had aligned their flight path to the road they were traveling. Every member of Chimera Company felt a strong temptation to break for cover in the trees lining the ice road, but the two sergeants decided that the best defense was to look as if they had no reason to run.

The aircraft could easily have been lining up for a strafing run, but not on this occasion. The rebels flew overhead with weapons silent and followed the road to the east.

There had been a nuclear strike just days before, and presumably a battle for orbital supremacy that must have been hidden by the clouds. None of that seemed to touch the people of the coastal plain.

It felt so surreal to Osu that sometimes he had to remind himself of Sanderson, of De Ketele and Yergin, and all the others who hadn't made it this far.

A day out from Bresca-Brevae, they stopped for the night at a small town. Little more than a few homes huddled around an inn and a trading post, Pattex-Nio was a much more modest place than Rae-my-Ela, where hopefully Urdizine was holding out for their return. It was time to stop spending the nights in trees and ditches. On the following day, they planned to pass through Bresca-Brevae safely and locate their contact. By comparison, it should be easy to book rooms for the night in Pattex-Nio without getting shot. Plus, any intel they picked up here could be vital to the success of their mission.

Osu agreed with Arunsen that the three surviving legionaries would play the part of mining wildcatters and land traders, while the Militia would be the escorting mercenaries, laborers, and caravan managers.

In a jovial mood, the Chimera Company caravan tramped into the stable yard of the town's only inn. Osu looked bemused at the inn's brightly colored sign showing a beaming human face underneath the name Terra Infirma written in human script.

"It's a human-themed bar," said Lily. "Get used to the idea. Last time I was here, humans were fashionable among the coastal Litto-ranes. Better that than the reception we got in the interior."

With Green Fish organizing stabling of the Saruswine with the Littorane staff, the others pushed into the main bar, splitting up to avoid overwhelming the few patrons inside.

And the drinkers! It wasn't just a human-themed bar; there were several actual humans drinking here.

The ambience was warm and welcoming. The floor was carpeted, and the drinking lounges divided by polished wooden posts that ended in glow globes without ever reaching the matching wooden beams that traversed the ceiling. Fabric partitions divided the rooms further into drinking pods consisting of a large table surrounded by benches and stools.

Pictures were hung on the walls, mostly of humans as, presumably, the Littoranes saw them: androgynous with horizontal slits for eyes, extra-long spindly legs and hair in vivid shades of blue and purple.

For one evening, at least, it felt possible to forget for a while the mind-controlled legions, rebel aircraft, endless cold, and all the other threats straining to end his life.

With Arunsen, Enthree, and Rynter, Osu approached a table occupied by a lone, reclining Littorane and gestured whether it would be all right to join it.

The newt reared up from its couch and bowed deeply, gesturing with its arms to please take stools and couches and sup drink together.

Osu might have judged the body language incorrectly, of course, but when they joined the alien at its table, it didn't display anger. In fact, it didn't display any reaction at all, ignoring them completely.

"Thine welcome is most meritorious," said Osu. The Littorane had seemed lost in thought—possibly lost in drink to be more accurate—but it looked up from its contemplation and considered the human's attempt to speak in the archaic dialect of the ancient Exiles.

"How so?" The Littorane flared its nostrils. It was tricky with the wall lights flickering through yellows and oranges to resemble flames, but Osu judged that the Littorane's snout was orange, and made a working assumption that she was female.

"Thine fellows in the interior of this land, way yonder, dost harbor evil thoughts and wouldst rend our flesh if we traveled unescorted by our stout defenders."

The Littorane waved a hand in a dismissive gesture that could pass for human if not that she'd used a mid-limb. "You don't need to worry about that here. I'd heard some of the fundamentalist clans in the deep interior were getting worked up about something. Isolation and cold will do that, you know. Though I've also heard someone was deliberately stirring up ill will against all humanoids. That kind of crap is bad all round, but it won't wash with the more progressive clans in the civilized part of Rho-Torkis."

"Thank you," said Osu.

"No thees and thous?" Rynter queried. "We don't need to talk like an old book?"

"Not in a human bar," the Littorane told her. "You will find many eager to speak with you, to practice the wider Federation languages. Rho-Torkis has cut itself off, choosing to be a world of isolation for so many centuries. We know that period is drawing to a close. There will come a time when Bresca-Brevae will be a hub of financial speculation and industrial activity. Which, I'm sure, explains your presence here today. So, please, speak easily, especially as I can tell from your accents that you are not long on this world."

Being able to speak easily would prove useful, but Osu was more interested in the Littorane's comment about trouble being stirred up. What had that RIL told Bronze under interrogation? A name...*Khallini.*

362 | TIM C. TAYLOR

"Does the name Khallini mean anything to you?" he asked the Littorane.

The alien swept her head from side to side, thinking deeply before answering. "There's the famous Battle of Khallini back in the Orion Era, of course. A great Littorane naval victory."

Rynter cleared her throat. "I thought it was the Legion who won that battle."

"No, I don't think so. The original Human Legion was born out of that Littorane victory, but…let us not quarrel over misleading histories. Let us instead agree that in those ancient days the alliance between humans and Littoranes was essential to both our peoples. Though we rarely meet in the modern Federation, that is not so with Bresca-Breveers."

"Khallini." A bearded human slammed a nearly empty tankard onto their table. "I know him."

The man was dressed in a ragged cloak that had originally been a rich blue. His muddy calf-length boots hadn't been cleaned for a very long time, and the smell assailing Osu in waves indicated that neither had his body.

"Well?" the interloper challenged, grinning on the edge of drunkenness. "Don't you want to hear what I know?"

Osu had seen his sort on a hundred worlds. The kind who could spin a story out of an overheard half whisper. It was simply an act to cadge free drinks and a hot meal off anyone stupid enough to believe their tales.

Before Osu could tell the rogue to clear off, the Littorane issued a flurry of hand gestures and a stream of instructions in the local tongue to a passing waiter.

"Please," she said to the drunkard. "Will you join us and tell us your tale?"

"I'm Kidson." After a theatrical bow, Kidson took a chair on the side of the table. It was only then that it occurred to Osu that he himself looked every bit as shabby as this man, and the idea of washing before entering the bar hadn't entered any of their heads.

Kidson sucked in a long breath. "Khallini, eh? *Lord* Khallini, I should say. Sticks his beak and fingers into many people's pies. On the outside he's respectability personified: a tiny man with a fancy cane, white gloves, and a genuine aristo-hat dripping with jeweled chains. Acts as if he spends his life sipping fine wine with presidents, senators, admirals, and the finest singers, poets, and sculptors. Maybe he does. Or maybe the man who lets himself be seen is a front for the *real* Khallini who operates in the shadows. All I know is that if Lord Khallini asks a little favor of you, you drop everything and do his bidding. Either that or you run and hide in the most desolate wilderness of an uninhabited planet, and stay there for the rest of your life."

Osu whistled. "Quite a guy!"

"That's for sure."

Osu frowned and leaned aggressively toward the story-spinner. "So explain this. Why have I never heard of Lord Khallini?"

"Be grateful for your ignorance," Kidson shot back. The Littorane began tapping on a handheld device. "Lord Khallini is not the kind of person who allows himself to be traced. And don't try looking him up." The Littorane froze. "In the first place, you won't find information about him. More importantly, if you seek him out, Khallini will start to take an interest in *you*."

The Littorane fled. Just left her drink and scampered away noisily.

Kidson defied Osu's expectations. Instead of basking in the triumph of his story's power, he looked saddened by the Littorane's swift departure. "Probably for the best," he muttered. "I should never have spoken so openly."

A change came over the man's face, like golden sunlight breaking over a rain-drenched land. "What a pleasant sight you are." He spread his arms wide. "Two arms and legs. I've never seen so many fellow humanoids ashore before." He gave Enthree a sidelong glance. "Begging the pardon of your insect companion."

Kidson guffawed, banging his tankard on the table. Evidently, he was drunk enough to find himself hilarious. He rapidly settled, though, and gave Enthree a more sober appraisal. "What's your name, my Muryani friend?"

"Ndemo-327-Cerulian. The humanoids call me Enthree."

"I see." Kidson's apparent drunkenness vanished. "Then they are fools because yours is a beautiful and honorable name. Your people are extremely rare on Rho-Torkis, but now you have shared your name, I start to perceive the reason for your presence. Yours is a trading caste name, if I'm not mistaken."

"You are correct." Enthree tilted her head. "Indeed, you are particularly well informed for a human."

"In my line of business, it pays to understand those with whom you might wish to trade."

Enthree advanced a forelimb toward the man, who allowed her to lift up his unruly cascade of blue-tipped hair. She rose from her Littorane couch and peered at his neck. "I see a ridge of hardened skin over the nape of your neck, such as develops after long wear of a heavy helmet. Implication is that your line of business involves prolonged exposure to the vacuum of space or the pressure of an underwater environment. You work on the deep sea auto miners, yes?"

He gave a half shrug. "Most humans do on this world. And you, trader?"

"We've come from the interior. Scouting possible mining sites and negotiating rights trades."

"Then you are my competitors." The man steeled his spine...and then broke out into more guffaws. "Or you will be in a century or so. Let us drink to friendly competition. In a decade or two, things will become less friendly. Mark my words. And don't let the Littorane clan system fool you. They unite when they have to, and the Littoranes know how to drive a hard bargain. It will be the big newts who play the humanoids off against each other, not the other way around. I suppose that's how it should be."

"Change is coming to Rho-Torkis," said Zavage. "Do you ever wonder what Bresca-Brevae will be like in a hundred years?"

Kidson grinned. "In a word, no. Oh, I admire those with grand visions, but it's a distraction. It's not safe to be distracted, not in these dangerous times. There's rebels been seen near the capital, and I hear rumors of strange goings-on. Dark stories. Don't like to repeat them. Say, you're not rebels, are you?"

"No," Zavage replied, "but we saw aircraft with rebel markings."

Why is Arunsen so uncharacteristically silent? Osu glanced at the big trooper. Something was eating him.

"We don't understand," said Zavage. "How did the rebels get past the Legion defenses?"

The man blinked. "Well, isn't it obvious?"

The Chimera party looked at each other. "No," they chorused.

"Think about it. Let's start with the Militia. People's Army, they used to call 'em." He laughed. "That's a sick joke. 'M.A.P. Militia and the Amilxi People'. That's what they stamp all over their monuments to themselves. Indivisible with the Senate and the Council. All sounds fine except those fine federal institutions are run for the benefit of the aristo-hats. All that idealistic guff about liberty and tolerance sounds good when it comes out of a politician's mouth, but if you don't agree with their way of thinking, then the Federation will decide it is better off without your continued existence."

The wall of blank expressions he faced roused Kidson. "You're not listening hard enough," he insisted passionately. "Those who set themselves up as our leaders and moral betters are either corrupt or totalitarian extremists. Only the office of the president was trustworthy...until First General Clarke. After him, the Federation has been a lost cause. The Rebellion's heart and instincts are in the right place. So too are the Legion's. I know at first it seems ludicrous for the Legion and the rebels to be anything other than sworn enemies, but the more you think about it, the more you realize they're natural allies."

Osu's ears were popping with the treasonous words passing through them. He made himself picture Colonel Malix who'd put his trust in him. And of the LT and Colonel Lantosh he'd lost on Irisur. He owed them to keep calm. Getting angry was a luxury they couldn't afford.

Doing his best to act as if he were commenting on the weather, Osu said, "So you're saying that after a quick civil war to clear the scum away from the top layer of society, the Legion will set itself up as the loyal servant of a renewed Federation, and hand over political power to the Rebellion."

"With the president supplied as always by the Legion," said Kidson. "A proper one, like they managed in the three millennia before Clarke. Yeah, that's it. How else could the rebels arrive on Rho-Torkis with such ease if not that the Legion waved them through?"

"But what about the Cora's World troops?" Osu pressed.

"Cora's World!" Kidson spat on the floor. "That hellhole of totalitarian collectivist puritans. What about those pricks?"

"Those rebel aircraft we saw, they had Cora's World markings."

"They're part of the Rebellion…?" Kidson was so winded by Osu's words that he barely spoke after that and soon left to sit by himself, turning to his tankard to numb the shock of his shattered theory.

The man's dark mood infected Osu. It had been the instinct to follow orders that had propelled him all the way to this bar in a tiny town near the coast.

For the first time, he questioned them.

Whose orders was he following?

The Legion could never be anything but foes to the puritan tyrants of Cora's World, but the moderate wing of the Rebellion was a different matter. Kidson's theory didn't make sense on Rho-Torkis, but it did in the wider galaxy.

Were Malix, Yazzie, and the others planning the downfall of the Federation?

And would that make Chimera Company heroes or traitors?

"Hey!" Arunsen grabbed his wrist. "Don't get the wobbles on us now, Osu."

Osu? The trooper had never called him that before. What was he signaling?

Arunsen gave him a pointed look. "I think it's time to retire for the night."

* * * * *

Chapter Fifty-Seven:
Osu Sybutu

On the way to their quarters in a separate wing to the bars, Arunsen took Osu to one side. "On Lose-Viborg. I saw him. Khallini. He...*touched me.*"

"Touched?" Osu looked askance at the big man. "The little old man felt you up?"

"No! He touched me, but not physically."

"Make sense, man!"

Arunsen's voice sank to a whisper. "Khallini is a sorcerer."

The intensity in Arunsen's dark-rimmed eyes captivated Osu for a moment. Then he laughed so hard at the credulous trooper that some of the others turned to check everything was okay.

"I swear," Arunsen hissed.

"Magic? Sorcery? Now I've heard everything."

"No, Sybutu, you've not heard *enough*. Magic is real. I've seen it on remote worlds. But that was small beer compared with this. Khallini is a powerful sorcerer."

Osu arched an eyebrow. "I'd like to see this sorcerer square up against a Legion platoon."

Arunsen's face darkened. "I've seen him do precisely that, and you would *not* have enjoyed the sight." He checked himself. "Come to think of it, you wouldn't have the chance. You'd be dead, same as all the other legionaries at Lose-Viborg."

Osu forced himself to keep a straight face. During the trek along the ice, Osu had developed a rudimentary respect for the man, but Arunsen remained a simple dope. "Impossible. If such a threat existed as you describe, Arunsen, the Legion would have been briefed."

"Don't be naive! There was a cover-up. There always is. Scapegoats made. In fact, the Legion's traditional scapegoat practically served itself up on a silver platter."

Previously unconnected facts and suppositions suddenly knotted together in Osu's head. He looked up in shock. Maybe *he* had been the dope all along. "The Militia. Raven Company was made the scapegoat. That's why you're here. Because of this Khallini."

The big man nodded, plucking absently at his beard, as if trying to draw strength.

"This encounter," Osu pressed, "were you observing from a distance?"

"I was close enough that I swung my hammer at his head."

"I don't get it. How can it be that the legionaries were killed and yet you are alive to tell me this?"

Arunsen looked away, but he couldn't hide the guilt he felt. "Khallini told me he liked me," he murmured.

"He *liked* you?" Osu had no idea how to take that. He stopped at his door and fished for his room's key disc. "This Khallini jerk must be insane."

Storm clouds gathered over Arunsen's craggy face. Osu regretted sounding so flippant.

"Scoff all you want," said Arunsen. "Good people died that day. Some of them legionaries I'd grown to admire. More continue to die. Didn't you lose anyone you cared for at Faxian? Khallini was funding the Rebellion on Lose-Viborg. If he's behind this chaos on Rho-Torkis, then think how he's hurt you too."

The trooper strode away to set the watch on the rooms, leaving Osu with scorched memories of Nydella Sanderson laughing. Of making love within sight of the alien ship left behind in an ancient war.

The ship…. he'd almost forgotten. Was all this death so that Khallini could lay his hands on that ship? Was this a rich man coveting a priceless antique? But that would mean the Invaders, as Bronze called them, were under Khallini's command too. And when he forced himself to examine the memories of that day outside Camp Faxian, he was sure the phony legionaries had not expected the rebel attack on his home.

Too many questions, still.

He desperately wanted answers, to make sense of this mess so he knew who deserved to die.

But that wasn't his mission. His orders were to deliver a message, and even though he was no longer sure whose orders he was truly following, that was what he would do. But the instant his task was complete, he would be demanding answers.

* * * * *

Chapter Fifty-Eight: Chimera Company

Nestled in a sheltered natural harbor within the Bay of Ablation, Bresca-Brevae was a big step toward proper civilization for the Chimerans, Green Fish's name for them that was now in common usage with both sides.

Only a few tens of klicks earlier, they had been impressed to see outhouses and clusters of Littorane homesteads. Here was a proper city with heated streets, parks, well-lit pleasure lakes, and a protective pressure dome to keep out the rain and snow. Buildings of more than one story became the norm rather than an occasional extravagance.

The bay was mostly frozen, but a clear channel allowed marine shipping to service the burgeoning offshore mining industry. But it was the spaceport that excited them the most. There it was: under a pressure dome protecting leveled ground outside the city proper stood freighters, shuttles, pleasure yachts, and utility vehicles, all lined up in stacked rings of landing bays. There were also bays secured from prying eyes by wheeled screens that hooked in underneath the higher landing pads. If any rebel war craft were present, then that's where they must be because none were on open display.

After so many days trekking through the icy wilderness, and so many trials and challenges that not all of them had survived, the sight of this, the destination they had fought so hard to reach, would have felt like sweetened nirvana if not for one thing.

Great gouts of flame leaped from the windows of the tallest buildings in the southern sector of the city. Out on the harbor, fuel slicked along the surface of the ice, and someone had set it alight. Flames stretched toward the ships, sending up choking black clouds. Ship masters were desperately trying to get their vessels out into the clear channel and away, but with so much of the Bay of Ablation iced over, the flow of traffic was jammed solid.

With a crack of thunder, the fire caught one of the unlucky ships which exploded into a fireball, spreading the flames to the upper decks of the nearest ships.

From the west and north of the city, refugees were streaming out into the deep cold.

Chimera Company had finally reached their destination.

But Bresca-Brevae was burning.

* * * * *

Chapter Fifty-Nine:
Osu Sybutu

Wanting to slip into the city unnoticed, they left the bikes and the Saruswine stabled at a small farm just outside the city, Enthree parting with an assurance to the animals that the Chimeran party would return soon. The Muryani had developed such a tight bond with the beasts that Osu half-believed the Saruswine understood every word.

As they descended the hills on foot, the sense of apocalyptic doom wreathing Bresca-Brevae hit so hard that he began to doubt whether their mounts would be waiting for their return. He mentally pushed that problem into the far future as they encountered the first wave of refugees streaming from the burning city. They were Littoranes in tightly packed formations of a dozen or more. Those on the outside carried hammers, knives, and makeshift clubs. Youngsters and a few objects of high value were protected in the middle.

The Chimerans asked for news of what was afflicting the city, but the fleeing Littoranes either didn't understand or didn't want to. Whatever it was, the flames were deliberate. From the low hills surrounding the bay, they'd seen shadowy figures carrying burning torches.

The closer they drew, the louder the sounds of chaos became. Shrieks and screams filled the air, punctuated by occasional gunshots.

It was too much. The team had intended to split up in the search for Fitzwilliam, but Osu declared the situation too dangerous and ordered them to stick together.

He knew there would come a moment of crisis when his leadership of the Chimerans would be challenged. With seven troopers matched against the three surviving legionaries, Chimera Company was unbalanced. Arunsen seemed to think that gave him a natural authority, but this remained a Legion operation. The Militia were here only as escorts.

But that moment of crisis was not yet upon them. When Osu told them to stick together, Arunsen mulled over the instruction and then grunted—apparently the standard Militia way of acknowledging an order.

Since they would pass close to the spaceport on the way to the city proper, Osu diverted the Chimerans there first. If Fitzwilliam's ship was registered in his name, locating him there should be easy.

Should be. Osu doubted it would be so simple. Nothing had come readily so far, except the punishing blows as he lost another of his friends.

When they were only a few hundred yards from the main spaceport gate—which thankfully had an armed guard not wearing rebel uniforms—a column of human refugees who had been heading for the gate suddenly switched direction and ran headlong at the Chimerans, pursued by a murderous mixed group of humans and Littoranes wielding swords and weaponized tail tips. The pursuers howled bloodcurdling battle cries from mouths bubbling with foam.

"Dust them as they pass," said Arunsen.

"SOTLs," Osu told the legionaries, "the troopers are playing the part of the mercenary escort. We keep our arms concealed and let this ugly lot do their jobs."

Leaving the shooting to the Militia felt like a gamble, but the risk paid off. The pursuers terrifying the fleeing civilians turned out to be strictly amateurs. They made Arunsen's rabble look like elite troops.

The Militia separated into two clumps, allowing the civilians to pass between them, then caught the pursuers in a crossfire of blaster bolts and rifle slugs.

If these were the Invaders Bronze had encountered before, then they were not much of a threat. At least not yet.

The human survivors dropped to their knees in the snow, chests heaving, and eyes wild in faces unprotected against the cold.

"How could you?" one of the men gasped, his gaze on the Militia masquerading as mercs. "Murderers."

Still fighting to regain his breath from the icy air that must be burning his lungs, the man walked back to the heap of fresh corpses, searching among the bodies.

Osu followed, curious. "What you mean, murderers?"

The civilian ignored him as he sat down beside a bloodied corpse, lifting the dead man's head gently onto his lap. He cradled the would-be killer's head, stroking his hair. "He was my husband."

A cry of sheer delight escaped the survivor's lips as his husband gasped in pain and opened his eyes. The dying man reached up with a bloodied hand and stroked the neck of the person cradling him, leaving a bloody trail.

Osu buzzed with horror because he'd seen what had really happened. The infected man had gasped with pain because he had deliberately dipped his fingers inside his own stomach wound, coating them with infected blood before scratching the neck of the man he'd been chasing with a sword.

He hadn't given a last gesture of affection; he'd completed his murderous task. The victim just didn't know it yet.

"Keep away from us!" Osu pointed at the man holding his husband. "This man is infected. He'll turn too. Nobody let him touch you."

"Infected with what?" inquired one of the other survivors. Some of the troopers also gave Osu a questioning look.

"A blood-borne infection that drives you into a homicidal state," he explained. "I've heard of it consuming other worlds. I think that's what's happening here."

The man paid no attention to Osu's words, but when Arunsen leveled his blaster at him, he looked up from his fallen husband to see death staring him in the face.

"What do we do about this one?" Arunsen asked.

More bloodcurdling screams rent the air. With all the panicked bodies streaming from the city, Osu couldn't tell where the noise was coming from, but what they had just witnessed was clearly no isolated incident.

"If he comes close, shoot him," he instructed Arunsen. "Otherwise, leave him be. We can't save the entire city."

The screams were getting closer.

"Let's get to the spaceport gate. Double time."

"Wait!" snapped Lily. "Where's Meatbolt?"

Everyone looked around. It was the sharp-eyed Zhoogene trooper who saw him.

"He's heading for the city," said Sward. "No...Damn! I lost him in the crowd."

"I'll look for him," said Enthree.

"Me too," Bronze added with a little too much eagerness.

"You two can't go by yourselves," said Arunsen. "Sybutu said it was too dangerous and, for once, he's right."

"If it were any other pair," said Osu, "I would agree. But these two? They're safer than the rest of us put together."

Arunsen didn't look convinced but he waved the pair of Chimerans away and they sped off in pursuit of Meatbolt.

The others made for the spaceport, under the watchful gaze of its garrison.

* * * * *

Chapter Sixty:
Vetch Arunsen

wall fortified by watchtowers enclosed the spaceport, and armed guards manned the heavy main gate. The defenses were not enough to delay a serious military assault, but looked sufficient to guard against the rampages of over-excited religious extremists and petty criminals. Given the preponderance of PPR-3 blaster rifles, the humanoids who looked like nervous vagrants were a Militia detachment, and the even more nervous-looking Littoranes were armed citizen volunteers wondering how their home had descended into a hellish pandemonium over the course of a few hours.

The main gate was sealed, but a smaller side door opened, and a man approached the Chimerans in a velvet cloak and self-heating leather boots that repelled snow, water, and dirt. He was flanked by a pair of troopers on either side.

Remember, I'm playing the part of a mercenary, Vetch told himself.

Unlike the Legion, the Militia didn't go in for uniforms much. If your unit commander thought the expense of outfitting worthwhile, you would wear blue above the waist and cream or white below. Underneath their outer layers, the Raven Company troopers did indeed wear blue smocks bearing an embroidered Militia emblem of a silhouetted hammer raised against a star, a reminder of the Hammer of Democracy incident in the early days of the Federation.

But unless they were ordered at gunpoint to strip, none of that was on show. All they'd had to do was leave their Militia-issue PPR-3s behind at Fort Iceni and no one would ever know they were serving Militia troopers.

"We request passage into the spaceport," stated Sybutu.

Request passage? Who did the jack think he was? A medieval herald?

The Militia officer ignored Sybutu, pushing past the two remaining legionaries and on to the troopers beyond.

"You..." He pointed at Vetch. "And you." He indicated Lily. "I know you."

"You're mistaken." Vetch shook his head as he spoke, adopting a gruff voice.

"I don't think so." A crawling sensation up his spine told Vetch that the officer's voice did sound a little familiar. "You're the reason I was sent to this craphole world to die, Sergeant Arunsen."

The man lifted his glacier goggles.

Vetch sucked in a chill breath. "Hello, Lieutenant Kulm."

Yeah, this is kinda awkward.

"Shite!" muttered Green Fish, and with good reason. Kulm had been their platoon commander when they were exiled to Rho-Torkis.

"I thought I was well rid of you scum," said the officer. "Mind you, here in Bresca-Brevae, I thought it was as good as it would get on the Rho-Torkis posting. Right up until this morning when that mob of maniacs tried to seize the spaceport. They weren't in uniform. No one knows who they are, but they'll be back." Kulm stood straighter. "They weren't expecting resistance."

"You fought them off?" said Vetch. He tried to keep incredulity from his voice. Really, he did, but he failed. Throw untested people into a crisis and you could never be sure who would crack and who might prove to be an unlikely hero.

But Kulm?

"Of course." Kulm's voice shook but he spoke with real pride. "We played a critical role. So did the citizen volunteers…As you can see, a madness is afflicting the people here, driving them to burn down their own city. Some say it's Littorane religious mania, but humans have been seized by the same form of crazy. I think it's bio-warfare. Nasty business."

"We were sent here by Major Yazzie to check your status," Vetch informed him quickly while the officer still seemed to be in a good mood. "We can't connect to any global comm system. Radio signals go unanswered."

"Yeah. Comms are down. Funnily enough, Trooper, we noticed that too. And if anything, that's the part of this steaming pile of drent that bothers me the most. I've even pinged a few satellites. They're still there, just not talking to us. How can I ping a satellite in orbit, when I can't transmit a radio signal to Fort Iceni? Last I heard, that was impossible."

Kulm's face settled back into its usual callous look. "And talking of impossible, I thought Lieutenant Shen had been given the dubious pleasure of herding you dogs. Major Yazzie wouldn't trust a punishment company like the Ravens to wipe their own butts without an armed guard of reliable troopers. Now tell me the real reason why you're here, and why I shouldn't have you shot like the rogues I know you to be."

"We're escorting two humans and a Kurlei. I don't know who they are, but the major wants them off planet before the Rebellion closes its grip on Rho-Torkis."

"Rebels, you say? We did see a fighter craft two days ago. *Rebels.* You talk as if they're going to conquer the planet."

"Rho-Torkis is already lost, and the rebels are mopping up the last resistance."

Kulm didn't reply at first. If the rebels really were in a mopping up phase, then Bresca-Brevae would probably be the next major objective. "Bugger!" he said with feeling. "I wouldn't be on this planet if not for you and the mess you made on Lose-Viborg, Arunsen. And now I have to defend the spaceport with thirty troopers and armed newts in plastic swimsuits against a rebel invasion that was prepared to take on Camp Faxian. What news of Faxian? Tell me that the Legion is going to save the day and brag about it for centuries. I wouldn't begrudge them that on this occasion."

"Faxian was completely destroyed, Lieutenant. The Legion's been wiped out."

Kulm gave a bitter laugh, his legs trembling. It was the kind of laugh a man gave when his only other option was to curl up and weep.

"The military situation is hopeless," said Vetch. "Wouldn't it be better to surrender to the rebels rather than go down against the madness infecting the city?"

"You know nothing, Arunsen!" Kulm was screaming in fury, his face purple with rage. "How could you, ignorant prison scum?"

Vetch fingered the haft of his war hammer. He'd had it up to here sucking up to arse-skragg officers. Between the rebels, the RILs, Lord Khallini, and the phony legionaries, the planet was about to be overrun, and *still* the lieutenant thought the best use of his time was to throw insults at the enlisted ranks.

With comms out, who would be left alive to report Vetch if he accidentally buried Lucerne's head in his former platoon commander's skull?

"Easy, Vetch." Lily's calming voice stayed his hand. "Kulm was promoted from the ranks without having to purchase his commission," she explained. "It's rare, but it happens. And all of his fellow officers are waiting for the opportunity to point to him and say his promotion was a mistake, that Kulm has no breeding and could never have any honor because he was always just a guttersnipe. His family, his entire town would be made to suffer. The only way out for Kulm is to make a brave but futile stand, dying as a result."

Vetch softened. "I'm sorry, Lieutenant Kulm. That sucks royally, but the major gave us orders, and from what Lily says, if you're seen to help us achieve our mission, that would benefit your family in the long run."

"I'll tell you what would make me look really bad, Arunsen. Being seen within a hundred klicks of you and your Raven rabble. Maybe the major really did give you orders, but she certainly didn't give *me* any to let you through. She did, however, issue standing orders that deserters are to be shot on sight. Go! Go now, and don't come back. If you do, I'll have you shot."

* * * * *

Chapter Sixty-One:
Bronze

The instant Bronze passed through the city's force dome, the heat of conflagration hit him so hard he staggered.

A strong breeze of chill air buffeted his back, sucked in by the flaming city from its frozen hinterland. The wind's strength was much reduced by the force dome, but the air inside was so much warmer that the breeze felt unnatural. A perversion of nature.

From the outside, the dome that stretched over the city was made visible by a cloaking of light mist and smoke, and by the way the snowflakes that had begun to fall danced away from its surface. Here on the inside, the air was too choked by the smoke trapped inside the dome to see it arcing overhead.

Damned thing is going to choke Bresca-Brevae to death.

The municipal dome was not like the military force shield the RILs near Camp Faxian had used in their ambush. This was a much gentler shield designed to retain heat and deflect rain and snowfall. Howling gales out in the bay were diminished to gentle breezes as they passed through.

"We need to kill the dome shield," he told Enthree.

"If the dome fails, there will be a massive increase in the supply of oxygen to the fires. They will accelerate beyond control. The

387

smoke is irritating but is currently well short of lethal concentrations for healthy individuals."

"You're right," Bronze reluctantly agreed.

Both of them dodged out of the street and took shelter behind a colonnaded portico to allow a mob of Littoranes to pass out of the dome to the safety of the snow. The newts at the front stalled on the other side, shocked by the encounter with the raw cold and wind. Those behind bumbled into them, unleashing a flurry of vicious tail whippings as the frightened city dwellers lost their civility.

"Never get in the way of an angry Littorane," Bronze murmured. *Talking of which…*

Two hundred yards up the street in the direction of the city, a line of six Littoranes guarded a junction, their low-slung silhouettes backlit by an angry orange glow. The details were difficult to resolve in the hazy air, but Bronze had the impression the line was watching the other Littoranes flee, drawing satisfaction from chasing them out.

His augmented eyes began cleaning up the image and he saw the watchers had their tails up aggressively. In their fore-hands they carried improvised clubs, and metal torches from which sprouted orange flames that reflected off the dark orbs of their eyes.

"They aren't closing to kill," said Bronze. "Nor was the group of infected we dusted outside the spaceport. They're herding."

"What makes you think they're infected?"

Because I've seen it before, Bronze said to himself, and forced the memories of Azoth Zol back down into the depths of his soul.

What do you know about it, Muryani? More than you're letting on, that's for sure. I've not come here to chase Meatbolt. He's already dead. I want to learn what's really happening in the city, but I also want to know more about you.

"You should learn to trust me," Enthree told him. "It's the only way to save Meatbolt."

"And you should learn to be more observant, Muryani."

Bronze shot a meaningful look at the infected enforcers, who were now advancing on the two Chimerans with a menacing Littorane stomp.

"Indeed," Enthree replied. "They are what I was talking about. You need to trust me, so start now by grabbing a secure hold across my shoulders."

To say the idea didn't appeal was an understatement, but Bronze's philosophy was to try everything at least once—and certain things every time he got the chance.

Enthree placed her four front limbs on the ground and knelt on her hind legs, presenting her back. She drew her limbs in a little beneath her body like an ambush spider readying to spring on its prey.

Worked for him.

He leapt onto her back and grabbed around her shoulders.

Skragg!

Her back was as bony as a stegosaurus, but before he had time for second thoughts, she was away, scrambling up the colonnades like an insect. She wasn't fast, but her climb was assured, and they soon reached the roof of the building, watched by the line of Littoranes in the street below.

Enthree picked up speed as she bounded across gutters, domes, and tiling to the far end of the building.

As she was turning around to descend back end first, Bronze told her to wait up. "I can use this vantage point to look for Meatbolt."

"Human eyes cannot penetrate the smoke and flames," she countered but didn't protest as he slid off her bony back.

Bronze looked into Enthree's eyes, dark slits heavily shielded by eyelashes and fronting a narrow head that stretched back almost as long as his arm.

"Okay," he told her. "Let's kick off the trust campaign. When I was younger, I was badly injured. Those who repaired me used ancient med-tech, which means my eyes are artificial." He set his gaze over the ruined city, identifying zones blocked by infected mobs, or made impassable by the fiercest flames.

"Thank you for trusting me with your secret."

Trust? You're Muryani. I can trust that you're the Federation's ultimate enemy. I know some of your secrets too, pal.

Bronze kept his thoughts to himself. "Sure, we can be best mates, Ndemo-327-Cerulian. Maybe by tonight the two of us will be sitting around one of those burning buildings singing Kumbaya."

That seemed to do the trick, shutting up the annoying alien while Bronze surveyed the city. He felt sure there was a pattern to this chaos, if only he knew what to look for.

"What is Kumbaya?"

Bronze sighed. He'd seen as much as he was going to from this position. He needed to get down into the action and see what was happening close up. "Kumbaya? No idea. Just an ancient human saying, its origin lost to time."

Maybe it was the talk of campfires, but the heat of the city finally got to Bronze. It was like a furnace in here, and he was dressed for the deep freeze. He'd already loosened his outer coat and switched off its heater, but it wasn't nearly enough. He threw his coat onto the roof and began ripping away the shirt underneath. It was halfway off when he stopped and felt a creeping chill.

What was he doing?

The Muryani was studying him. Down at street level, the infected Littoranes they had run from had followed the Chimerans to their side of the building and were looking up at Bronze too. They didn't look threatening any more, though. They seemed to be waiting. Waiting for what?

For him to join them?

The city pulled at him. An irresistible summoning. Here in Bresca-Brevae, a beautiful new beginning was being born and he longed to be a part of it. No, it wasn't a summoning. It was an invitation. A precious offering to become something new that was beyond the dreams of any mortal.

Enthree stared at him in silence.

Bronze swallowed hard.

Should he level with Enthree? Warn her of what he feared he might be becoming?

No. He'd seen the strategic briefings. Muryani should never have been admitted as Federation citizens.

He needed to find out what was happening and that meant going farther into the city. If he was pulled into the mania so deeply that he lost himself, he would just have to trust Enthree would kill him.

"Over to the northeast," he told the alien, pointing in the direction from which he felt the pull the strongest. "Make for that domed building in the plaza about half a mile away."

"Do you see Meatbolt there?"

"No, but the plaza seems to be a center of activity. Maybe your friend was drawn there."

She accepted his answer without question, stooping down to present her back once more.

392 | TIM C. TAYLOR

He hopped on, expecting to ride his spiderlike mount down the far side of the building.

Instead, she circled back and raced off the edge, easily jumping fifteen feet to the roof of the neighboring building. From there, she hopped onto one of the curved ornaments that arced over the street, spinning around the metal pole before climbing to its ornately sculptured top. She jumped through the smoky air from one pole to the next, flinging limbs out to keep her balance as she teetered each time on the point of falling forty feet to the troubled streets below.

The journey was more terrifying than a dropship descent and felt more suicidal than taking point on a hull breach into an enemy battleship.

"Thank you," he whispered.

He'd just discovered that the infection he'd picked up on Azoth Zol might still claim him. Riding piggyback on this crazy Muryani was the only thing in the universe that was even more terrifying.

* * * * *

Chapter Sixty-Two:
Ndemo-327-Cerulian

Humans were cunning. The one on her back had hidden his foul scent beneath a cloying perfume that Enthree suspected was undetectable by others of his species.

When a compulsion had seized him to strip off and reveal his pheromone code to the Corrupted thronging this damned city, Enthree's suspicions had been confirmed.

Bronze was a part of the Corruption.

And by the way fear gripped his face, the man understood his doom.

Shame.

She had disliked this one on sight, but had been eager to learn his secrets so she could weave them into intricate stories of exotic alien intrigue.

All that remained was to absorb more of his pheromones so she could discern which strain of Corruption possessed him. Human sweat brought on by fear was particularly rich in pheromones and so she flung him from post to post, terrifying the alien to bring on the fear sweat.

She couldn't identify the strain herself, but that was not unexpected. She solidified a recording of his scent in the form of a memory pearl that would harden on its journey to the outside of her head, where it would join the other pearls that the humanoids mistook for warts. If she survived to make the next contact with her handler, then, eventually, on a distant world within the Muryani Expansion, an anonymous archivist would identify Bronze's strain and a new nugget of information would be added to the Expansion's understanding of this latest invasion by the Corruption.

Task complete, she corkscrewed down an ornamental pole—not to wring more sweat and fear from the Corrupted human, but because dancing like this through a burning city was a delightful pleasure—and proceeded at ground level in the direction Bronze had indicated, bounding over burning obstacles and scampering up the walls of buildings to avoid parties of the Corrupted.

The destination was obvious from the overwhelming stench of Corruption. She paused a short distance from the plaza to allow the human to drop off her back and regain his feet.

Should she kill him now or postpone his execution to see what he would do next?

Having spent a lifetime around humanoids, she felt sure she would recognize the wide-eyed confusion and temporarily impaired motor control that would indicate the Corruption taking over. She thought she was alert to whatever he might do next, but the human surprised her.

Bronze sat cross-legged on a soot-stained sidewalk and brought a smoking pipe out of an inner pocket.

"We have to go back for my coat," he informed her as he tamped rough-cut strands of synthetic tobacco into the bulb. He lit its contents by means of a button on the stem. "It's got my best pipe and baccy. Not to mention it's cold outside the city, have you noticed?"

No matter how much she tilted her head first one way then the other, she could make no sense of him.

"Truth now," he said, "why did you really come into the city, Ndemo-327-Cerulian?"

The human's question made no sense.

Was this a sign that the Corruption was consuming him? He didn't appear dangerous at the moment, so she answered. "To retrieve my friend."

Bronze took a long draw and then looked up from his pipe, shaking his head as if disappointed in her. "We both know the Meatbolt who was once your friend is never coming back. I've seen you watch over him. Part nursemaid. Part friend keeping a death row vigil. Part executioner in waiting. You lost Meatbolt the day that Invader bit him, and you know it."

The archivists of the Expansion had much to say about the Corruption, but she'd never heard of a victim who was aware of their own fate, let alone one who faced their extinction so calmly. The humans had surprised and outwitted far older races in their birthplace of the Orion Spur. Would this enclave transported to the Perseus Arm repeat that achievement, despite their seeming inability to prevent the Federation from descending into ruin? Their ability to adapt and prevail was, after all, the reason humans had been brought here in the first place.

She brightened up. She adored humans and loved when they exceeded her expectations.

"Corruption," said Bronze. "You've used that term to describe the threat we face. What does that mean? Why the Corruption?"

"You will never learn the answer."

"Really, is that a threat?" The human killed his pipe, deflated it, and returned it to an inner pocket. "I was bitten by the Corruption—is that how you phrase it?—but I got better."

"Impossible. Your civilization lacks the technology."

"I hope you noticed that we're still doing the trusting thing, Muryani. You're wrong about that. This civilization—of which you claim to be a member, let us not forget—has deep reserves of ingenuity and…" He shrugged. "We like to hoard stuff."

Enthree took a step back. The human had spoken of trust in a sarcastic mode, but his secret was potent with implications. "You used ancient technology from the Orion Era! Who are you really?"

"I'm the guy who was issued wafers of nano meds. That's all you need to know, pal, because that's how I carry the Corruption's scent even though it does not control me."

"I saw you. On that rooftop. It was claiming you."

"And that's why I'm leveling with you, buddy. I figured I'm the reason you came deeper into the city, not Meatbolt. He is only one of thousands now, so let's leave him be. Watch me instead. You're right, I felt a pull stronger than I've ever felt before. If it pulls me too far—"

"Then I shall kill you."

The man nodded. "Just make sure I really am a goner first, okay?" He put a finger to the headset still in place beneath his hat but paused. "The Corruption—Meatbolt—all of this we-are-doomed stuff—let's make that our secret for now."

"Sybutu, this is Bronze. How copy?"

"Go for Zavage," came the Kurlei's voice over Enthree's own headset as well as Bronze's.

"Is Sybutu hurt?"

"His comms took a blow to the head, but he's too thick skulled to be badly hurt. What's your status?"

"We've penetrated a mile into the city. Meatbolt is dead. Have you located the contact?"

"No. We couldn't enter the spaceport. We are searching for news of the contact with everyone headed that way."

"Then we shall search for this Captain Fitzwilliam in the city. The environment is dangerous but the Muryani is providing excellent assistance in evading obstacles and hostiles. If the going gets too hot, we shall turn back and rejoin you."

"Copy that. Shame about Meatbolt." Zavage paused. The sound of sudden exertion came over the radio. "Contact. Wait out."

Bronze cut the link. "Sounds like our friends will be busy for a while. Let's use this chance to root out what's really going on in Bresca-Brevae."

* * * * *

Chapter Sixty-Three: Bronze

Thicker than the pall of smoke, a horrific sense of impending atrocity hung over the plaza like one of the fresh skin rugs the Gorgantheletta once sewed together from captured Federation civilians.

Terrified citizens mostly milled around the open area. Some screamed in rage at those who had herded them there with clubs and swords and stood now in deep formations guarding the exits. Nevertheless, the guards had proved no barrier to a human–Muryani pairing prepared to enter the plaza by crawling down the outside of the buildings that ringed it. Other trapped civilians begged for mercy from friends and neighbors who had turned so suddenly on them.

Many chose to spend their final moments in prayer, and it seemed to Bronze that they had lucked out with the perfect place to pass their final moments before death, in one sense or another, took them. In peaceful times, the architectural showcase of the plaza was the enormous stone building that fronted one side of its square and was topped by a huge copper dome that reflected the flames. Bronze statues of Littorane deities ringed the dome's base like a crown.

He peered more closely at one of the statues that stood out from the others. It was a lone humanoid in a pantheon of Littoranes.

"Some do still honor the old alliance, after all," he said to himself. "That's the Empress Indiya."

399

400 | TIM C. TAYLOR

Unconsciously, he found himself touching the tips of his fingers to his heart: a deep spiritual habit from his youth.

If the likeness of the Empress was displayed here, then this was not just a temple. It was probably the first permanent structure built when this planet was settled. Bresca-Brevae would have been constructed around this temple, and it was no wonder that its frightened citizens now fought for a place of sanctuary beneath its enormous dome.

The sight of Littoranes praying outside on the plaza told them there was not enough room inside for everyone. As Bronze and Enthree approached the throng outside the temple, they saw that there was no room at all for any who were not Littoranes.

Humanoids were being forcibly ejected, some with heads dripping fresh blood.

"Take it easy," said a human male tossed out like an old rug by a pair of Littoranes. He picked himself up and dusted down his leather jacket. "I was on my way out, anyway. Place stinks of fish. You should really get it cleaned properly, you know."

Most of the humans they had encountered in the city had dressed like Kidson, the offshore worker from the inn. Not this man. He wore a brown leather peaked hat adorned with grubby silver braid, dark sunshades, and a brown jacket so old and worn that it probably came from the era when prehistoric humankind first thought to lash sharpened stones onto the end of sticks and go hunting for clothing.

The man in the jacket muttered something into his collar, which was precisely where the secondary microphone pickup was usually placed on a ship suit.

"Stick close to the human spacer," Bronze told his partner.

"Which one is that? Do you mean the one with the droid?"

Droid?

Bronze scanned the area. He didn't see a droid. "I mean the one with the leather jacket who looks like he's on vacation."

"There is none who matches your criteria," said the irritating alien, but followed Bronze anyway as he inched toward the spacer.

It would be so tempting to kick the big bug in the shins, but if Bronze was reading the situation correctly, Enthree's ability to climb like a spider was going to come in handy real soon. So instead he hissed, "Brown leather jacket. Brown leather cap. Can you really not see that, or do you just get a kick out of annoying people?"

"That's the individual I pointed out," Enthree replied. "The one with the droid. Your criteria are contradictory. You said he was human."

Bronze frowned. "Just how *not* human are you suggesting this guy is?"

"Close, but I've encountered many thousands of humans and never smelled one like this."

Not quite human. A mutant, perhaps? I wonder...

A hush suddenly clamped down on the plaza. The citizens guarding the exits squashed themselves to the sides to allow passage for a column of...

Oh, no. No! No! No!

A platoon of legionaries in battle armor marched with good discipline into the plaza and began deploying into a single rank facing the silenced citizens.

A knot of horror pulled in Bronze's guts. Not at what was about to happen—though that was terrible enough—but what the battle armor was telling him. The legionaries wore a variety of armor model variants and made no attempt to unify on the camo pattern or insignia. On the far end of the line, waiting with blasters at the low ready, were a half dozen legionaries in Type C night-camo pattern with shoulder patches displaying not only the crossed lightning bolts of the 62nd Brigade, but the color flash and numerals of Bravo Company, 3rd Battalion. Insignia and camo-variant he'd worn himself when his old squad had entered the caves of Azoth Zol.

He'd thought his captured comrades had all perished. If these legionaries removed their helms, would he recognize the faces?

"Bronze! Snap out of it. Time to go."

He looked up into a Muryani face. "I'm okay. Bad memories, that's all. Let's grab this guy and get out of here."

"What do you mean we're not leaving?" the spacer shouted into his collar.

Bronze grabbed a small disc from his pocket and slapped it onto the man's jacket. "Leaving is exactly what we are doing," he told the spacer.

"Okay, hotshot," the guy said, unimpressed. "Surprise me. How are you planning on getting out of here?"

Blaster bolts suddenly screamed through the air, burning through the Littoranes at the edge of the crowd. Silence crashed into screaming panic, and the scene switched into pandemonium.

A Littorane with a fancy gold collar began shouting and pointing, not at the legionaries—most of whom were still deploying and not yet opening fire—but at Bronze, Enthree, and the spacer.

Bronze got the gist of the message. The burning of the city and the scourging of its inhabitants was divine punishment for the blasphemy of permitting filthy alien humanoids on their world.

Filthy aliens like him.

Angry Littoranes joined in. Never mind the blaster bolts whizzing through the air, bringing death and maiming with every shot.

"I don't have the time for this," Bronze said. "You in the brown jacket, grab onto me."

"Seriously, kid?"

With a quick draw of his blaster pistol, Bronze put two bolts through the rabble-rousing Littorane. Center mass.

That got the spacer moving. He grabbed Bronze around the waist just in time for him to cling on to Enthree who whisked them away from the temple steps.

They cut a diagonal across the plaza. It was only as they neared the buildings facing this side of the square that they heard frantic orders from the line of legionaries, followed by blaster bolts that kicked chips out of the pavement at their feet.

Enthree zigzagged as she scaled the side of the building, flinging the spacer out like a streamer. He was a heavy man, but the Muryani's neck seemed to be made of reinforced ceramalloy because even with the weight of two men hanging off it, she barely seemed to notice.

After hurling themselves onto the roof, they took shelter behind a low ornamental wall, which concealed a gutter. The occasional blaster bolt whined over their heads, but the full fury of the Corrupted legionaries—if that was what they were—was being unleashed upon the civilians.

The blaster volley was so fearsome that the shrieks of the bolts flying through the air almost drowned out the screams of the dying.

Almost.

To Bronze's surprise, Enthree popped her head over the parapet, holding it out in clear view for over a second before dropping down under cover. An answering blaster bolt slammed into the wall in front of her, shattering the stone.

"Bug out!" shouted the spacer.

No kidding.

They dragged themselves by their elbows across the flat roof, the sounds of the massacre hitting them harder than the blaster bolts that passed harmlessly overhead.

"Why?" said Bronze, not expecting an answer, nor receiving one. "Why herd civilians safely out of the city but murder those trapped inside?"

The two humanoids took a firmer grip of Enthree this time, and together they descended the far side of the building.

"Perhaps they have corrupted enough for their current purposes," Enthree said when they reached the ground. "Which is unusual. I suspect they have an urgent objective we do not yet discern."

"Who does?" said the spacer. "The Rebellion?"

"Of course," said Bronze.

"Who else could we mean?" added Enthree. Unwisely.

They put a couple of blocks between them and the massacre. The screams were a little quieter there and they paused to catch their breath by the edge of a miniature version of the main plaza.

The spacer turned on Enthree and threw his hands to the sides. "Wow!" he said. "Hell's Fire, you big insect. That was some getaway. I know a captain who would hire you in a heartbeat. You ever thought of a life of adventure sailing the star lanes?"

Bronze pushed in front of Enthree and stared at the spacer. "Do you know the location of Captain Tavistock Fitzwilliam?"

Behind the spacer's sunshades, Bronze could tell he was rolling his eyes as if he was asked this question a hundred times every day.

"A helluva time to be asking questions, kid. What are you two, debt collectors? No, don't answer. Let's get out of here first."

"Not until we have located Captain Fitzwilliam," said Enthree.

"Figures. You and a thousand others want a piece of him. Look, guys, you did me a good deed back there and the ship's chaplain is always telling me to repay such favors, so I'll tell you what I know. I heard he was in Sector 12, hunting cargo."

When the others looked blank, the spacer shook his head. "Oh, come on, stop kidding me. You come looking for Fitzwilliam and you don't even know the lay of the land? Sector 12, children. It's the northern shore of the seaport. Escaped the worst of the violence so far."

"Thank you." Bronze studied the man. He didn't trust a word he said, but his accent was a unique mix of the Coreward Marches and old money aristocracy. Bronze couldn't tell where the lies were falling. "Did you hear *where* Fitzwilliam was in Sector 12?"

"I might have done, but…I'm sorry, my young friend, but my ears aren't what they once were. They need…Aargh!"

Bronze's straight blade knife was drawing a thin line of blood down the back of the man's ear. But Bronze offered temptation as well as threat. In his other hand he held a small pile of high denomination credit chits.

"I'm sorry, my spacer friend," said Bronze, "but my patience isn't what it once was. It needs…Satisfaction."

"Okay, okay. You make a compelling argument. Fitz was angling for a deal with Polar Blue Logistics. Their main warehouse is on McCarthy and Elmes." Face screwed up in pain, he pushed away Bronze's hand with the credit chips. "He was supposed to meet me in the Vortex Plaza to discuss the deal. Never showed up. What a jerk. Look, son, I could take your coin, but I've been around this galaxy long enough to know that people who smell as bad as you don't take kindly to being given bad intel. If he's still in the city, then my money is on Sector 12, but I don't know that for sure. Good luck finding him. If you do, ask him to tell Izza hi from Pendog, and remind him that he owes me two thou. And if you happen to break a few of his teeth in your discussions, so much the better."

Enthree yelled out, "Meatbolt!"

Bronze turned and saw the corrupted trooper leading a group of humanoids and Littoranes armed with clubs.

But Meatbolt had entered the city armed, like the rest of Chimera Company. He drew a blaster carbine and shot Enthree in one of her mid-limbs.

The Muryani hissed like a high-pressure boiler about to blow.

"Cease fire!" Bronze bellowed. He stormed over to Meatbolt like a general approaching an enlisted soldier who'd just royally pissed him off.

Meatbolt held up his hand and his Corrupted mob lowered their clubs.

"Leave the insect," said Bronze. "She's not important." He breathed deeply of the air and sensed the pull of summoning was strongest to the northwest. In the direction of the spaceport?

"Follow me," Bronze said and led them away in that direction.

Poor Meatbolt, he mused. *Why couldn't you just fade out of the picture?* He drew his crescent poison blade and steeled himself to finally resolve the problem.

* * * * *

Chapter Sixty-Four: Tavistock Fitzwilliam

"Ah there you are," Fitz said to the trash can mounted on hover skirts as it caught up and matched his owner's fast jog. "I'd begun to think I'd lost you, Lynx."

"Would you miss me?" asked the droid, whose correct designation was L1-iN/x. He added a pitiful groan from his gravitic repulsors for effect.

Fitz shot out a door lock with his pistol and kicked his way inside what he hoped was a deserted building. "I'd miss you more than that pair who snatched me away from Vortex Plaza, just as I was about to get us both out of there." The two of them scanned what appeared to be the entrance lobby of a municipal building. They were alone at last.

Fitz lowered his blaster. "What took you so long?"

"Self-extraction from the plaza was more challenging than you might expect. I didn't get to ride piggyback on a Muryani."

"Don't expect one now, either. The big insect's been shot, and the human ran off without so much as saying goodbye. He's the one who's giving me heartburn, though. The human. Did you see him shoot that Littorane near the temple? Double tap with that ridiculous 'C' clamp grip. The man might just as well have sat himself down and started smoking a clay pipe. He's a Special Missions operative or I'm a shaved Jotun."

The droid tilted up its body and regarded Fitz through its slowly pulsing red eye slit. "Do you think SpecMish is behind this mayhem?"

Fitz blinked in shock. *Is Lynx right? It would certainly be SpecMish's style. Hell, I should know.*

He beckoned Lynx closer. Questions later. Ass saving now. "Secure comms to Izza, if you please, Lynx."

"Yes, master," the droid drawled in a sultry feminine voice.

"And will you stop with the 'master' thing? Izza is convinced I taught you to say that, and in that sexy voice too. I'm about to be in enough trouble with her as it is."

"Oh, your impending marital difficulties are *such* a shock, Captain Fitzwilliam. Do you intend to deceive Lieutenant Zan Fey this time, or merely break some of your promises to her?"

"You, droid, have a serious attitude problem. And for the record, I have never deceived my wife."

"No, master. I understand. You merely elide the universe for her benefit. You have explained this at length."

"Better. I can have you rebooted, you know."

"Rebooted?" said Izza's voice out of Lynx's smooth metal head. "Is Lynx toying with you again? Darling, it's good to hear your voice. Are you safe?"

"For now, my lady. We need to bring forward our departure."

"How far?" she growled.

Fitz winced. Izza liked to pretend that she hated being called my lady, but this time it wasn't proving enough to distract her from what she hated most in the galaxy: missing out on a contract fulfillment payment.

"Spool the engines," he said. "We need to take off the second I get back on board the *Phantom.*"

"Fitz!" she snapped. "Grow a pair, why don't you? If we wait, our contract payout is lucrative, and we have more than enough people in this galaxy wanting us dead. We can't afford to make an enemy of our client too."

"I want nothing but sweetness and soft kisses for our client, my darling, but I've encountered some troubling old friends."

"How many times do I have to tell you? Nyluga-Ree is the most dangerous being in the sector, but she wants profit first, second, and last. So what if Ree sends a few ruffians to keep you on your toes? If they hurt you a little, I'll kiss your bruises better and then kill your attackers myself. No, Fitz, we hold our nerve and pick up the client when he's good and ready. The fee will be enough to get Nyluga-Ree off our backs for good."

"I wasn't thinking of our Commerce Guild friends."

"Then who?"

"Not so much who as what. Legion Special Missions."

Only the blue light on the side of Lynx's head indicated that the secure link was still active. Izza remained silent for two full seconds before the words spilled out rapid-fire.

"Run, Fitz. Run! Run! Run!"

* * * * *

Chapter Sixty-Five: Bronze

O pen mouthed with horror, he stared at his trembling hands in front of his face.

What have I done?

The smooth surface of the crescent blade in his right hand reflected the flames from distant fires. Its poison remained in the reservoir. Its surface was clean.

There was no blood on his hands either.

He'd let Meatbolt go.

He'd ordered them all to the spaceport and let the Corrupted bodies live.

Which made him a failure.

Why had he done it? Meatbolt was already dead. He knew that. Hell, even Enthree understood that. He'd hardly known the trooper anyway.

Sucking at his lower lip, he sheathed his blade.

No, this wasn't about Meatbolt. This was still about Sarah. All that he'd gone through since and still that damned woman wouldn't get herself out of his head!

He'd let himself become weak. No wonder SpecMish had cast him to the outer reaches of the Legion.

Bronze slapped himself in the face repeatedly, trying to shock himself back into action.

Come on, Zy Pel. You still have living comrades who need you. Get over yourself, you selfish piece of shit!

"I'll kill you next time," he announced to the deserted street, but he no longer trusted himself to know what he'd do if he met Meat bolt again.

He sprinted back to the location where he'd left Enthree and the humanoid spacer who was either Captain Fitzwilliam or knew more about their contact than he was letting on. It was only a few hundred yards away, but when he got there, he saw no sign of either.

There was a splash of alien blood on the ground where Enthree had been winged, and that was it.

Bloody marvelous.

He was about to call in over the radio when approaching foot-steps made him shrink into the deepest shadow he could find with his blaster ready.

It was only Enthree, favoring one side heavily and with one mid-arm of her jacket cut away and a wound pack doing its business where the bolt had winged her.

But it wasn't *her* jacket that caught his attention: it was the ragged coat tied around her middle. The same coat that had kept Bronze alive on the trek from Fort Iceni.

"You, Muryani, are a revelation. I hope we don't go to war with your people in my lifetime."

She gave him an angry tilt to the head but threw the coat to his feet. "You said your garment was important, so I made use of the time and retrieved it."

"I appreciate my coat back, but shouldn't you have been guard-ing the spacer?"

"No. I thought we had finished with him. He left while I was dressing my wound and you were...called away."

Bronze hung his head. The Muryani assumed he'd killed Meatbolt and he was too ashamed to put her straight on that.

"I also contacted Sergeant Arunsen," Enthree said. "The Chimera group is headed our way."

"Then maybe it's best that Pendog—if that's really his name—set off on his own."

He activated his headset. "Zavage, this is Bronze. Do you copy?"

* * * * *

Chapter Sixty-Six:
Vol Zavage

"This is Zavage. What's your status? Over."

"Enthree's walking wounded. City's on a one-way jump into hell. And I might have found our contact. He's in disguise and going by the name of Pendog, but it could be our man. I've planted a scent tracker on him."

"The city air is choked with heavy smells. I doubt I can track him. I have your location now, and if you'd planted a radio tracker, I could have tracked *him* too."

"No go. He would have detected it."

"I'll give it my best shot, Bronze. What scent did you use?"

"Female Kurlei sex pheromone. High strength."

"You bastard."

"Can you track him, Zavage?"

A shudder went through him. "You know I can," he whispered.

Just the idea of a female of his race in a frisky mood felt as if a chain of toxic addiction had been passed through his nose. From there it tugged at the back of his throat and descended deeper to pull at his stomach from the inside.

Some joined the Legion because they wanted a life of glamor and adventure, not realizing that both were exceedingly rare in the careers of most peacetime legionaries. Others joined because they liked blowing shit up, or from a sense of duty to family and Federation.

415

Vol Zavage had joined the Legion to avoid women. Specifically of the Kurlei variety.

With his kind, once a relationship had passed beyond the fascination and irresistible pull of the rituals of attraction—admittedly a more concentrated burst of pleasure than most humans would experience in a dozen lifetimes—the pairing would be unbreakable until the bitter end. And once one pairing was established, Zavage would himself become irresistible to other Kurlei women. Irresistible, in the sense of being a target they would fight tooth and claw to claim favors from that he would be unable to resist offering up. In a big enough community, once a pair formed, it could attract a score or more women to form a miniature tribe that would last for generations.

The first male might last for a year or so, but his doom would be inevitable, worn down until he was no longer able to satisfy his mates, upon which either they would disperse, abandoning his worn-out husk to die, or one would kill him and become male herself, taking her turn to share his fate.

No wonder the Kurlei race was almost dying out in their transplanted home of the Federation. No thanks. Loving was something Vol Zavage would reserve for other species as long as possible.

Green Fish. Why would he ever wish for more than her?

"Zavage. Zavage! Answer me!"

He saw a blurry image of Green Fish, but when the details came into focus, it wasn't her pretty human face staring back at him but the angry visage of Sergeant Sybutu.

Zavage shook his head. "Sorry. The scent…it's so overwhelming. You humans don't understand what it's like, and I have it in my nose. The man Bronze thinks could be our contact is close by. I can smell him."

* * * * *

Chapter Sixty-Seven:
Tavistock Fitzwilliam

"**S**ir, please halt. We are being hunted."

"*Sir*, is it? Azhanti! This must be serious. Who is it this time, Lynx?"

"Unknown." Flaps opened in the droid's head dome through which he launched three short-range sensor drones. "I suspect a group we have not encountered before."

"Perfect," said Fitz as he watched the drones circle overhead like bats on a length of string. "Izza's always saying we should have more guests over."

The drones dove back inside Lynx's head. "We are being enveloped," warned the droid. "Follow me!"

Lynx tilted forward, wobbled like he was going to fall, and then shot off down the street they had just jogged up. Fitz sprinted after the annoying tin bucket but couldn't catch him.

The little droid seemed to have decided that stealth was no longer a viable option, because he was pushing his gravitics so hard that the ground was throbbing, making Fitz feel sick to his stomach.

Or maybe it just hadn't occurred to Lynx that anyone not currently being massacred would hear his gravitics from five blocks away.

Fitz's money was on the latter. Ever since the emergency recoding job he'd performed on Lynx after acquiring him in *unconventional* circumstances from Nyluga-Ree, sinkholes sometimes appeared in the droid's common sense.

A grenade exploded fifty yards ahead of the droid, the shrapnel on the edge of the blast wave rattling his metal body.

Lynx took a sharp right through a shadowed archway and into an interior courtyard.

Fitz followed, slamming into Lynx who had stopped suddenly.

"How nice of you to drop by, Captain Fitzwilliam," said a voice Fitz had hoped never to hear again.

Thanks for nothing, Fitz mouthed at the droid who'd led him here, and then turned and faced the SpecMish man, trying to flash the classic Fitz grin that had won Izza's heart and secured a hundred deals throughout the Federation. He was everyone's favorite rascal of an uncle, the ever-so-slightly wayward son. No one would dream of harming a man wearing a smile this charming.

Mr. SpecMish was sitting with his back against a wall. Deploying the full unoriginality of his order, he smoked a clay pipe. Beside him, his Muryani companion was bunched up against the same wall, looking suspiciously at a pipe of her own as if she'd never held one before.

While keeping his grin going, Fitz sighed inwardly. The man was SpecMish. They always knew everything, and that included his identity.

Fitz bowed his head and joined them. "Please, my friends call me Fitz. Do you by chance have a pipe to spare?"

"As a matter of fact," said the SpecMish man flicking open an inflatable pipe, "thanks to my Muryani companion, I have exactly that."

Fitz sat against the wall alongside the SpecMish man and accepted the pipe. It had a telescopic stem, inflatable insta-light bulb, and real synth-tobacco, not the cheap stuff they grew in dirt. Smoking was still a filthy habit, though.

"So." He took a tiny draw of smoke into his mouth. "What does SpecMish want with me?"

The man considered him for a few moments before shaking his head. "Nothing. I no longer work for Special Missions."

Liar!

"I can see on your face that you don't believe him," said the Muryani. "I didn't either at first, but I now believe it's true. At least on the surface. Probably they still have him on a very long leash, but we don't know why."

Either the Muryani was lying, or she was an idiot. Fitz didn't care for her race. For sure, the individuals he'd encountered had been perfectly respectable scoundrels, but always with the Muryani lurked the threat of their home empire next door. The Muryani Expansion scared the boots off him.

The wall at his back began to shake, the vibrations rapidly picking up strength and throwing him forward.

He looked up in time to see a formation of fighter craft passing overhead. He only caught a glimpse silhouetted against the red-tinted sky, but the atmospheric tail fins were distinctive. Then the banshee wail hit, confirming they were Falcons. Two centuries ago, they'd been the best multi-environment fighters. They weren't now, but that made little difference armed as he was with only a talking tin can and a travel pipe. He needed to close down this encounter and get to Izza and the *Phantom*. Fast.

422 | TIM C. TAYLOR

"Let's assume what you claim is true," said Fitz. "What do you want from me?"

"Nothing," said the allegedly former SpecMish man as if he had all the time in the world.

The Falcons had circled around and climbed away. Now they were returning, diving onto the city at attack speed.

"In that case, I shall bid you, adieu—"

"Sit down, Captain Fitzwilliam. We won't detain you long." The man took another puff at his pipe but then—thank goodness—he switched it off and began packing it away. "To be honest, we don't need you at all." He pointed a finger at the archway. "But *he* does."

Explosions rang out from the center of the city. Falcons were raking ground targets with their nose cannons, but the whoosh of short-range surface-to-air missiles meant that someone was fighting back.

Into the courtyard, abandoned by the city's inhabitants, stepped a handful of scallywags. Commerce Guild pirates by the look of them, especially the Viking with the beard. One came forward and removed his hat.

A look of proud duty about to be performed was broadcasting from a face colored in one of the darker shades of conventional humanity. Looked like a legionary who'd missed his last few appointments with the hair-clippers. In fact, it looked as if he'd been away from the Legion altogether. Why, he was even smiling! Did they really permit such liberties these days?

* * * * *

Chapter Sixty-Eight: Vetch Arunsen

"Captain Fitzwilliam?" inquired Sybutu of the man in the brown jacket smoking with Bronze and Enthree.

Vetch could hear the relief in the jack sergeant's voice and understood how much this meeting meant to him.

The man had lost a lot of friends. His purpose, his unit, and the base where he was stationed—all gone. All he'd had left to cling to was this strange assignment to pass on a coded message and to keep safe the handful of comrades who'd left Faxian with him.

Sybutu hadn't actually made a good job of the latter. Half his original team had been lost along the way. No wonder the legionary's voice was trembling.

"Can't a guy enjoy a smoke during some downtime?" asked Fitzwilliam, who seemed—erroneously—to think he was lightening the mood.

Realizing he'd misjudged the situation, Fitzwilliam instead raised the shades above his eyes.

It was their contact, all right. Vivid lilac eyes regarded Sybutu.

Vetch shuddered. In the shadows against the courtyard wall, Fitzwilliam's eyes glowed with their own inner light.

The man's mutant ancestors had strutted around the early Federation as the closest thing to an aristocratic class in those far-off days.

Not anymore.

These mutants were descendants of the earliest Legion Marine heroes, but they themselves had been artificial creations. Alien xeno-engineers had made handcrafted modifications to their genetic code. Purple eyes were not the reason mutants were hated and feared. The mutie look was merely the harmless side effect of alien DNA analogs that had been gene-spliced into the selected Marines to give them inhuman powers. And all to an alien agenda. Who could tell what purpose might still be programed into those freaks? No wonder they weren't trusted.

Those eyes…they were so richly colored! He'd never seen such powerfully mutant characteristics. Did that mean the man also possessed some of the arcane powers of those long-dead heroes?

"It's a long way home," Sybutu said slowly, "but I'm setting off tomorrow."

Fitzwilliam's face drained of blood.

"The tide is going out," Sybutu continued. "We need to slip our moorings."

The mutant focused on some distant point, his mind lost in memories.

They didn't look to Vetch like they were pleasant ones.

Fitz's eyes seemed to burn in their sockets. "Tell them to roast in hell," he shot at Sybutu. "I'm retired."

"But…" Sybutu's voice stumbled. Vetch found himself actually feeling sorry for the jack. "We came cross-country all the way from Camp Faxian because Colonel Malix insisted we reach you. The colonel put his faith in you."

"Malix?" Fitzwilliam got to his feet, laughing. *"Cisco* Malix. He's a colonel now? Well, well, well. He'll be loving that...What? What's wrong?"

"The colonel is dead," said Bronze. "They're all dead. We think there are maybe four legionaries left alive on the planet."

"Malix...? No, I don't believe you."

"There was a rebel strike," Bronze explained. "The Legion base of operations was taken out with fusion bombs. We were betrayed, Fitz. Would you like to see the image captures?"

The spacer's eyes glowed even brighter and his easy grin hardened into a snarl. "That won't be necessary." He paused to catch his breath. "Malix was a good man. We used to...Hell, you kids have no idea what we used to get up to." The grin returned. *"And get away with.* If I ever find out who did this, or get my hands on anyone who helped to end my friend Cisco, then I swear their deaths will be long and hard to watch."

"Then you will help us?" asked Sybutu.

Fitz regarded the legionary sergeant somberly. "No. I already told you, I'm retired. Now, off you fuck and leave me alone. I've got a ship full of people to keep alive."

With that, Fitzwilliam summoned his dented old service droid and walked off, leaving Sybutu staring into space.

* * * * *

Chapter Sixty-Nine:
Vetch Arunsen

In a deserted courtyard on the outer limits of a city descending into hell, a heavy look passed between Vetch and Lily. Were they going to chase after Fitzwilliam? They could still bring back the man for whom they had tracked across the Great Ice Plain while being shot at, frozen, and forced to work with a party of jack-head legionaries who'd had no idea how lost they really were. But with every moment that slipped by...

Lily and Vetch looked down at the floor simultaneously. The moment had gone.

He felt bad about Sybutu. Truly. It had all been for nothing, but Vetch had to think about what happened next. They all did.

"You completed your mission," he offered, putting a supportive hand on Sybutu's shoulder. "You played your part and did your best. No one could ask for more."

"That's the difference between us," growled Sybutu, still staring at the empty air near the courtyard wall where Fitzwilliam's absence almost took on a physical presence. He shrugged Vetch's hand away. "The Legion doesn't dish out participation trophies."

"Give him a moment," said Bronze. "Please."

The ground shook with a sequence of rapid thumps. A few seconds later, the sound of explosions hit them from a few klicks away to the northwest.

"If that's the spaceport under artillery bombardment," said Lily, "then neither Fitzwilliam nor anyone else is getting off this planet."

"Enthree," Vetch pointed to the fluted spire that threw its shadow across the courtyard. "Climb that tower and see what's going on. I need to know the best exit route. Go! Everyone else, weapons check. We're about to head out."

Vetch pulled at his beard, trying to figure out which of the three surviving legionaries had enough sense between their ears to confer with.

Sybutu was clearly in shock. Bronze had always struck him as the unflappable one, but something had happened while he had been in the city with Enthree looking for Meatbolt. The man had cracked somehow. It would have to be Zavage, who was standing so close to Green Fish that they brushed arms as she finished up her weapon check.

And this bunch of shell-shock cases and lovebirds was supposed to be the most elite fighting force in the universe!

"Legionaries," he said, nodding at Zavage and winning his attention. "Are you coming with us?"

"Chimera Company is disbanded," stated Sybutu who had finally gotten himself out of his funk enough to look Vetch in the face. "We worked well together, but Chimera's purpose is at an end. I wish you all safe passage back to Fort Iceni, but we're staying. We have to try to get the message out through Legion channels now. The Legion needs to know what's happened on Rho-Torkis."

Green Fish gasped. Vetch looked up to see her and Zavage together like teenage sweethearts gazing into each other's eyes. They brushed each other's faces with their fingertips.

Luckily, before Vetch had to embarrass himself by breaking up the pair, Enthree jumped down onto the courtyard and made her report.

"Rebel ground forces are attacking in strength. One column is about to enter the city from the west, and another, supported by light tanks, is trying to seize the spaceport ahead of the...I don't know the correct term to use. I shall call them *bad legionaries*. They are racing each other to gain control."

"Let's see if I've got this right. The bad legionaries—the ones we saw marching through the snow outside Iceni—are enemies of the rebels."

"Correct. They are firing at each other. As is Lieutenant Kulm's detachment who holds the gate for now, but surely will be overrun within minutes. Also, on the hills above the city where we made observations this morning—"

Enthree's report was interrupted by a piercing shriek. Rockets arced over their heads, heading west. Scores of them!

"On the hills," shouted Enthree, "the rebels have positioned an artillery battery. I don't think they were expecting counterbattery fire, but looks like that's what's headed their way."

"The main battle is to the west of us," said Vetch. "Kulm doesn't want us, and his fate is sealed anyway. We'll head to the docks and commandeer a boat. If we can't get one, we'll find a way onto the ice and get out that way. Shame to lose the Saruswine, but they're as dead to us as Kulm. Sure you're not coming, Sybutu?"

The idiot shook his head.

"We'll watch for you, but we won't wait to die with you in the city."

430 | TIM C. TAYLOR

"If you change your mind," said Enthree, "the route is clearer and the fires lighter to the north of the port area. Remember, the north shore. Sector 12."

"At least come with us out of the city," Vetch begged Sybutu. "You can do your Legion thing once you're clear."

"No. We've got this. Go, Arunsen. Don't delay further."

The man was a fool, and Vetch had no more time to reason with fools. It was too bad about the jacks, but he had his people to look after. And they would always come first.

Vetch marshaled his troopers and set off for the docks without looking back.

* * * * *

Chapter Seventy:
Vol Zavage

When Green Fish and the other troopers left, Zavage looked to Sybutu for leadership. Instead of supplying fresh orders, Sybutu sat down with his head in his hands. Bronze was no better. A darkness had broken loose in his mind while he'd been hunting Meatbolt and then Fitzwilliam. Now that darkness was consuming him.

Intense artillery and missile exchanges were ongoing outside the city. The rebel air attack was shifting its attention, raining down cannon fire on targets of opportunity that seemed to be without any more air defenses. Screams of terrified citizens mixed with volleys of blaster fire and the moans of the wounded.

Zavage was used to that backdrop. What made him struggle to even think was the despair seeping out of the two humans he respected the most on this world, combined with the raw memory of the human he most wanted to be with, but who had followed her Militia comrades to the docks.

"If we reach the spaceport before it's seized by the two fighting factions," Zavage suggested, "maybe we can smuggle ourselves out on a civilian ship."

It was a crazy plan, but they had to start somewhere. If he could get the others to engage their brains, he prayed they would soon realize that a far better idea was to follow Green Fish while they still could.

He got nothing for his troubles. Bronze turned away, unable to face him, and Sybutu was still lost with his face in his hands.

"Snap out of it! But hey, I get it. You, Bronze—the enigmatic Hines Zy Pel—have just come out of remission from a chronic case of survivor's guilt. And you, Sergeant, had locked away the horror from the destruction of your home and loved ones until you completed your mission. Now that Fitzwilliam's gone, it's hitting you all at once, and you can't deal with it. I know you're both hurting, but you're legionaries. We hold the line because the Legion is the only thing between civilization and eternal darkness. Right now, holding the line means sucking up your pain and figuring a way to get out of here so we can warn sector high command. Grieve later. Act now."

"We could ask Fitzwilliam to take us off-planet," said Bronze, though without conviction.

"There's got to be government buildings or corporate headquarters with system-wide comms," said Sybutu. "Maybe interstellar comms. You got a message out of Irisur, Zavage. Maybe you can work your magic and defeat whatever's blocking our signals on Rho-Torkis?"

Zavage raised a fist and then gave rapid hand signals. *Hostiles overhead. Two of them.*

A pair of humans were clambering on the roof above their heads, whispering to each other. They sounded calm and disciplined. Probably rebel scouts.

His human comrades could hear none of this, of course. Earth must have been a strange world indeed to have produced a species so deaf, half blind, and unable to smell a foe hiding two yards away. It was part of humanity's charm: despite the many natural failings of their race, they had a remarkable knack of getting things done anyway.

Sybutu quickly signaled orders, and the three legionaries backpedaled as silently as they could, their weapons aimed high.

Zavage almost froze. The humans on the roof were firing a rapid burst of blaster fire, not into the courtyard, though, but at targets deeper into the city.

Stepping up the pace, Zavage was first to get far enough inside the courtyard to see up to the roof. They were rebels, all right. Cora's World regulars.

He shot them both. They didn't see it coming.

"They should have checked the area was safe," Sybutu noted grimly, but the tension had left his face, and Zavage could feel his friend's spirit regain its sense of purpose. "Fitzwilliam is our contact," he said, sounding like a Legion NCO once more. "We'll persuade him to take us off-world."

"The man wanted nothing to do with us," Bronze pointed out.

"He was desperate to get back to someone," Zavage said. "A lover, I think. I know I've told you a million times that I can't read thoughts, but the man's need was so strong that I could sense it. If we can convince the partner, then perhaps they can convince Fitzwilliam."

"How?" Sybutu frowned at Zavage. "Are you suggesting you'll seduce this man's partner?"

"I am. With charm and the promise of money. You have no idea what I'm capable of, Sergeant. And whatever Fitzwilliam once was, if he's captaining a smuggling ship, they will always feel the lure of profit. The Legion *does* have funds."

Zavage tried to look defiant. He meant every word he said. Being able to sense people's emotions could boost his powers of persuasion to preternatural levels, but he was still hoping Sybutu would see sense and order them to the docks.

"Very well," said Sybutu. "Your plan is a starting point. We head for the spaceport and hope we think of a better idea before we get there."

Damn! Sybutu wasn't supposed to buy his idea. "And the warring armies we'll have to fight through?" Zavage queried.

"We'll slip through in the confusion. I know you want to follow Arunsen's troopers, but the Militia are heading back to Fort Iceni, and we already know Iceni's comms have been suppressed."

"Zavage is right," said Bronze thoughtfully. "Any course of action will be highly dangerous. However, all of them would be more likely of success if we were equipped with Legion armor."

"Don't tell me." Sybutu rounded on Bronze. "You want to top Zavage's crazy plan by walking up to those...*infected* legionaries and asking them to hand over their armor?"

Bronze sucked in his cheeks. "Yeah. That's about the strength of it. It worked with Meatbolt."

Osu narrowed his eyes. "You told us Meatbolt was dead. No, never mind that. Will it work?"

Zavage couldn't believe what he was hearing. Nor what he was sensing through the kesah-kihisia organs on his head: Bronze and Sybutu were serious about this.

"It *might* work." Bronze sounded less certain now. His mind was seeping doubt too.

Zavage couldn't stand it anymore. He backed away from the mad humans and kept watch for any more rebel scouts.

"If it doesn't work, then I'll be dead or captured," said Bronze. "But you can stay away at a safe distance. But if it *does*, then everything else from that point is much more likely to succeed. Look, Sarge, if you want minimum risk, then we follow the Militia and hope we catch up with them. You want the maximum chance of making a difference, then let's see if I can rustle us up some proper fighting armor."

* * * * *

Chapter Seventy-One: Bronze

"Hold the line," Bronze murmured.

It seemed like the kind of thing he was expected to say, but he'd been so many different people over the past twenty years that it felt like someone else's words.

"HTL," whispered the other two, and Bronze headed away from the entrance to the pleasure pool a block away from Vortex Plaza.

When they had arrived and quickly scouted out the civic amenity, Zavage had heard noises beneath the water of the entrance pool. They had decided to hope these were the sounds of Littorane citizens trying to hide from the massacre of Bresca-Brevae.

Bronze put the noises from his mind. The biggest dangers to be faced over the next few minutes were all his own.

Seeking cover as best he could, using the poles that curved over the streets like giant naganita, he made his way back to the plaza.

Bodies were strewn along the streets. Most of them were Littorane civilians, both Corrupted and those for whom death had spared them that fate. There were also a few rebel corpses in light armor and one Corrupted human legionary slumped against a wall that had been mostly demolished by heavy blaster fire.

Bronze made a quick inspection of the corpse that had once been a man. The armor and the flesh within had been holed by heavy caliber slugs, which meant there was no point stripping this armor. The helm looked undamaged, but Bronze couldn't bring himself to remove it. He feared what he might see inside.

He guessed that rebel light armored vehicles advancing through the street had used a vehicle-mounted gun to deal with the Corrupted man. The sounds of battle, however, were coming from the spaceport and the western approaches to the city. All he could hear from the plaza were screams and keening wails; they were more than enough.

Thankfully, the mobs of Corrupted Littoranes who had guarded the entrances to the plaza had dispersed, allowing Bronze to slip inside and spy out the area from the blasted ruin of a building that fronted the open area.

The smoking ruins of three rebel armored hover carriers stretched in an arc across the plaza's center. The infantry squads they had transported hadn't made it far from their vehicles before being cut down, but they'd taken a terrible toll in Corrupted legionaries. He felt the bile rise in his throat at the way the dead from both sides had been abandoned. Some of the downed legionaries were groaning in pain, wounded but seemingly left to die alone by their own comrades, now that their usefulness was at an end.

Bronze fancied himself a worlds-weary cynic, but he was sickened by the way these travesties of human beings dishonored the Legion armor they wore. Of course, they were victims of the Corruption themselves, but seeing the way they abandoned their wounded made it personal.

But then, it had always been personal. Ever since Azoth Zol.

What made it worse was that Bronze could do nothing for the wounded either; to try would jeopardize his already near-suicidal plan.

Littorane screams from the temple pierced his red shroud of rage, and he assessed the scene more carefully. If he survived to make a report, what he saw here could be vital in learning to defeat the Corrupted, because they evidently did not operate as other soldiers.

Civilian bodies were heaped around the steps to the temple, the grim result of the massacre he had witnessed with Enthree and Fitzwilliam, but the temple still thronged with terrified civilians seeking sanctuary within. Frightened, but unhurt.

Now that the legionaries in the square had other objectives, they were no more interested in the civilians than in their own wounded. They bunched behind and on top of the ruined hover carriers with rifles trained on the western approach to the plaza.

It was as if they had room in their minds for only a single task at a time, and they had forgotten the order to murder the civilians.

That wasn't all they had forgotten. Smoking craters contained mangled anti-air guns and SAM pods, together with the ruined bodies of the crews who had served them. But some of the anti-air assets still looked functional, their crews lying dead around them and the legionaries behind the hover carriers uninterested.

If the men and women inside the armor had originally been legionaries, then they would have been trained in the use of all but the most specialized equipment. And real legionaries certainly wouldn't wait in the open for the return of rebel aircraft while ignoring their air defenses standing idle just yards away.

It made no sense.

But, Bronze reminded himself, they only *looked* like legionaries. Behind the helms were mindless drones who had expected to encounter only defenseless civilians.

What's more, he knew he wasn't actually facing the Invaders. This was a softening-up operation to disrupt an enemy before the *real* invaders made their move.

He shivered at that thought, but he couldn't help that now. Besides, he desperately wanted to be wrong.

Eyeing Corrupted marksmen positioned on the rooftops looking down on the plaza, Bronze readied himself for the gamble he was about to take.

Act as if you own the place.

HTL. Oorah!

He strode out into the open.

Immediately, rifles shifted to cover him, but the legionaries weren't sure what to make of him.

Could they detect the scent of Corruption upon him?

It was with the group of legionaries sheltering behind the farthest hover carrier that he saw what he wanted. Several of them wore the insignia of the 62nd Brigade, his old unit.

He made it to the ruined carrier without being shot into a smoking ruin, but behind their opaque legionary helms, he felt every pair of eyes upon him. A hush came over citizens sheltering in the temple, as they too waited to see what would transpire.

"You, you, and you." Bronze pointed out three individuals in 62nd armor. He knew that each invader left a unique odor with the individuals they corrupted. He hoped those who had been captured at Azoth Zol would be attuned to his own scent.

"Come with me."

A single legionary took a step toward Bronze. Then another step. Then a third that brought it close enough to lean forward and bring its helm an inch from his face. It seemed to be sniffing him.

After passing his head over Bronze's face like a security guard using a threat-detector wand, the Corrupted straightened up and gurgled in its throat.

It sounded as if the once-human voice had seized up from disuse, almost gummy with resin. If their airways were really like blocked sewer pipes, did that mean they no longer needed to breathe?

"Yougghh. Ouughhh. Youuuhh. I. Know. You. Bronnnnnze."

"I was Bronze. Yes." It was ironic how this name from his past would not release him. "You have not seen me for a long time because I have served our purpose elsewhere. Follow me!"

He walked back the way he'd come as if he expected instant compliance.

The confidence he projected was entirely false, but three pairs of armored footsteps marched behind him nonetheless.

His plan had worked.

So far...

* * *

"We need to go incognito," Bronze told the former human legionaries when they had reached the temporary safety of the pleasure pool entrance. He felt Zavage's mind touch his, but Sybutu and the Kurlei remained out of sight. "Remove your armor."

"Yes, Bronze."

They obeyed without question.

The helms came off first, revealing hideously disfigured faces of what had once been men. Their canines had grown into miniature curled tusks and their concave noses looked as if they had been melted into their heads. Instead of hair, their skulls were entirely covered in downy feathers like a human duckling.

One of the three looked familiar…

Obscenities though they had become, they clearly remembered some of their training, because gauntlets, arm segments, and torso armor were rapidly stripped off in the sequence mastered by every legionary during basic training.

Bronze had eyes for only one of them. "Empties?"

The Corrupted man grunted ambiguously. But it *was* him. This was Empties, his squad mate when he'd played the role of Jonathan 'Bronze' Marquez. Or rather, this had once been Empties. Now his friend's body was twisted into an S-shape that made him wonder how he still fitted into the armor. If he were human, a malformed spine like that would make him an invalid, but though his shape was distorted, Empties looked strong and ready for his new instructions.

"Empties, lift up your shirt."

Bronze wanted to retch at the sight Empties revealed, but he needed to see if he'd changed like the first to be infected on Azoth Zol. Sure enough, his chest was coated in a plumage of dark feathers patterned with bright rusty chevrons. He'd *known* this man. Called him friend.

Empties had been captured with Bronze and one other legionary: Redwing. Bronze looked into the faces of the other two, but they were too far gone to tell whether he'd once known them.

I must have known them once, he told himself. They're wearing the same camo I did.

It would have been easier if all three had remained anonymous monsters, but he kept searching the features of the other two, trying to find familiar features. He owed it to Redwing and the others to try, so he could honor their memories properly.

And then the armor was off, and Bronze was forced to consider the three Corrupted legionaries as a dangerous liability that had to be removed.

It had been the case since they'd removed their torso armor. If they had turned on Bronze after that point, Zavage and Sybutu would have shot them from cover. But the creatures who had once been men were as compliant as good-natured babies.

"Face the plaza," he told them.

They gave no indication they had heard.

"Turn around!"

This time, they complied.

"I won't make the mistake I did with Meatbolt," Bronze whispered.

He drew his crescent blade—a relic from an ancient era in which his distant ancestors had known only war—and dispatched all three, slicing their throats so they lacked the ability to cry out.

The blade ran thick with blood that soaked his sleeve. He stared at it for a while. It looked like human blood, but he told himself it was not.

"I know how difficult that was for you," said Zavage, startling Bronze who hadn't noticed the other two appear.

Bronze felt the Kurlei put a hand on his shoulder and attempt to smooth his mind, but they lacked a deep enough connection for it to work.

"When this is over," Zavage said, "you can talk to me about what you just did at any time. Just one thing, brother. Don't ever tell me it was no big deal, because I could sense what you felt."

"One day, maybe I will." Bronze tapped his head. "Locked away in here I have a lot of tales I'm not ready to face and are too dangerous to unleash now." He drew a deep breath and regarded the fresh corpses. "Their tales are finally at an end. Help me, Vol."

With Sybutu standing guard, the two of them laid the former legionaries out respectfully.

Bronze took a moment to stare into the face of the man who had been Empties. "Go in peace and honor, brother." He closed his comrade's eyes.

He repeated the words over the other two, trying and failing to recognize the person they had once been before shutting their eyes.

In silence, they put on the discarded armor and set off for the spaceport.

* * * * *

Chapter Seventy-Two:
Vol Zavage

B y the time the three of them left the city, they'd switched their captured helms to a supplementary comm channel over which Sybutu told them to speak openly. Not that the other channels were exactly cluttered with chatter. They'd heard a few grunted phrases on Channel Zero, the default wide area Legion signal, but even that had sounded more like a sick person talking in their sleep than the kind of orders and reporting you would expect with a battle raging.

"Bronze, you're the one who's partway on the journey to being one of them," said Zavage. "They're meant to be an army. How are they coordinating when no one's talking?"

"I don't know. Enthree said she could smell the infection—the *Corruption*, she called it. My guess is it's some kind of pheromone control. Like ants. That's my guess, but being sealed up in armor with a legionary helm ought to kill any pheromone control dead. Makes no sense in a way, but these were once legionaries and carry a memory of what it was to be a legionary."

"You mean that even though it cuts them off from orders, they don't want to take off their armor for anything."

"Precisely. The habit is too ingrained."

They jogged away from Bresca-Brevae, piercing the city force dome and emerging into air that was bitingly cold and clear after the smoky atmosphere they'd left behind. But their armor rapidly adjusted its heating and insulation settings, and their helms increased their visor polarization against the white glare.

With their HUDs identifying battlefield objects of interest, they quickly pieced together the situation as they merged with streams of other legionaries headed without any apparent coordination toward the spaceport. They were not challenged.

The Rebellion had clearly made an attack on the spaceport. Probably they had expected only token resistance but had hit a Corrupted advance reaching for the same objective. The rebels had been repulsed, but it looked to Zavage as if they were only regrouping before throwing in a fresh assault.

Corrupted dead and wounded lay scattered around the snow, ignored by their comrades who rushed to join the force milling around the spaceport that was exchanging sporadic fire with Lieutenant Kulm's garrison.

"What are they waiting for?" asked Zavage.

"Those perhaps?" said Bronze. He pointed to a heavy weapons squad headed on a parallel course about thirty yards away. There was more of a sense of purpose to this squad, perhaps because they had been given specific instructions. They'd been supplied with special weapons, too: four partially dismantled MM-7s, which would be plenty enough firepower to obliterate Kulm's main gate.

The MM-7 was an infantry support gun from the post-Orion Far Reach era, but it used alien-designed components from before even the days of the Human Legion, components whose design secrets had been lost long before. If Lord Khallini was supplying the rebels, who was supplying the Corrupted with these treasures?

"We need to move away from them," said Sybutu. "I want at least 150 yards separation from those guns."

They pivoted east. Sybutu didn't need to explain his reasoning. If a Corrupted squad ever deployed those guns, it would become target number one for any enemy in range.

"Anyone have experience firing MM-7s?" Zavage asked.

"Virtual simulation only," replied the sergeant.

"Same here," added Bronze.

"And me," said Zavage. "But I've fired MM-17s on the range, which is basically the closest the modern Federation can get to making an MM-7. As for GX-cannon, I've fired them in an anti-air role for real."

"Is anyone suggesting we steal those guns?" Bronze sounded unconvinced of the idea.

"I don't like it either," Zavage replied, "but it's the only weapon I can see nearby that could defeat an army on its own. An uncoordinated army of zombie humans, at any rate."

"Fair point," said Sybutu, "but keep your distance from them until I say otherwise."

Suddenly, the edge of Zavage's helm visor flashed red, and a very specific warning tone sounded. The one for incoming missile attack.

He tensed. *Calculating impact zone…*was written across his HUD.

Run or drop? Come on…what's it to be?

The HUD showed its calculation, adding red hatching to the ground over an area several hundred yards across.

"Drop!" he shouted and flung himself at the snowy ground.

He did his best to screw himself into the snow in the remaining moments before impact.

Then all he knew was noise and heat as he was flung through the air in a spray of snow and steam, cosseted inside his armor by automatic impact buffer foam.

"Call in," said Sybutu. It wasn't until then that Zavage realized he had landed.

The HUD was showing minor damage to his armor. Despite the buffeting he'd suffered, and the static stuffing his ears, the armor didn't find any damage to Zavage's body worth reporting.

Of course it doesn't, he cursed. His armor was set up for a human legionary. He had to hope it didn't misread healthy Kurlei life signs as a critical injury and pump him full of drugs designed for a different species.

"I'm good," he reported over the radio.

"Just a cracked rib," said Bronze. "Armor's injecting painkillers."

"I'm unhurt," said Sybutu. "Stay down and play dead. I see the rebel attack coming in. Let it pass. And…good call on grabbing the armor first, Bronze. You just saved our lives."

Zavage shut down his armor into passive mode. He retained ultra-low power, short range radio link, and nothing else. The buffer foam had softened into a sticky mess that was growing cold. It would get even colder real quick. Everything would. But his life signs were shielded by the armor and he would appear dead.

Just so long as we get back up before I freeze to death for real.

The helm's enhanced vision display and HUD had shut down too, but in this mode the polarization of the visor had reduced so he could see through clearly. It didn't help much. The glare from the ice and snow was now blinding without the helm's assistance, and the view to the spaceport was blocked by a curtain of debris from a creeping barrage of artillery shells sent out by the rebel battery on the hills.

A heavy beat shook the ground, growing louder by the moment. Zavage stopped worrying about the cold and started fighting back the powerful urge to vomit as sickening waves of sonic power pulsed through his stomach. The prospect of drowning was another worry, as the snow was melting all around.

A cylinder moved into his field of vision, lengthening into a tube that became a battle tank's main armament.

Keep. Absolutely. Still.

His guts churned. If he retched, even if the tank didn't spot him, it surely had supporting infantry that would.

Keep calm...

The heavy grav tank thundered past, just yards away, pounding the snow beneath it, and having pretty much the same effect on the inside of Zavage's head.

He couldn't identify the tank model. Sybutu was so obsessed about these details that he could probably tell the year of manufacture from the pattern of the blast shields that hung down into the snow like rigid curtains over its flanks, there to protect against infantry like him getting close and firing rockets at its underside. Zavage didn't need to know. It was a tank with a damned big gun, and if it saw him as a threat, he'd be dead.

The behemoth passed him, the spray of snow it threw behind showering him and providing additional cover just in time for the support troops to arrive.

A cloud of hover darts followed fifty yards behind the line of five tanks. These were nimble light air vehicles that would hang in the air for a few moments before flitting to another position like hoverflies with nose cannons. Behind each pilot sat a heavy infantryman in armor similar to the Legion's, armed with heavy weapons and det packs.

The heavy tank rumble was now a bass note almost overcome by the high-pitched buzzing of hover darts. But the formation was moving fast behind its creeping artillery barrage, and it soon left Zavage behind, dismissing him as just another corpse rapidly cooling to ambient temperature.

By pure chance, he had landed at such an angle that he had the perfect view of the rebel attack as it rolled in. It was hoping to punch through the disorganized Corruption troops and mainline straight through to the spaceport. It seemed to Zavage that the rebels had learned from their earlier repulse, and were using the creeping barrage not to destroy the enemy so much as to hide from them.

So far, the tactic was working. A few of the Corrupted were firing through the curtain of destruction thrown up by the artillery barrage at where they thought the rebels might be, but most of them jogged toward the spaceport, oblivious to the threat steaming up to their rear flank. They were almost at the main gate.

Neither faction expected much resistance from Kulm's spaceport garrison. Zavage hadn't either.

This proved a mistake.

The Militia officer had been waiting for the moment to make his presence felt; that time was now.

A volley of missiles shot out from the spaceport's watchtowers, screaming through the air above Zavage. It must have been aimed at the rebel guns on the hills because the battery fell silent and didn't resume fire.

Kulm's troopers shot more missiles through the debris screen thrown up by the creeping barrage. Two detonated beneath one of the tanks. Secondary explosions rocked the behemoth's underside as its hardworking gravitics blew out. The beast of metal and ceramalloy crashed deep into the ice.

And there was more to the spaceport's defenders than missiles.

They sent out a fusillade of blaster bolts that burned brightly through Zavage's inactive visor, hitting several hover darts.

Smooth, reflective armor in the aircraft nose cones protected the vehicles, but two deflected bolts hit pilots of other darts, sending them tumbling out of control to the ground, taking out another dart on the way down.

The parvenu officer had made his mark, but the spaceport garrison had only managed to tweak the nose of the rebel juggernaut, making it angry.

The tanks replied via their main guns. Even the grounded tank that had sunk hull-down into the ice had traversed its turret and joined the CAEM shells hitting the gate. Controlled Area Effect Munitions made a big bang but reined in the explosion—great for blowing shit up with minimal collateral damage.

The watchtowers were obliterated and—it seemed—the garrison along with them. The only damage to the spaceport beyond was to receive a light covering of dust.

Kulm's brave soldiers had taken care not to fire on the Corrupted, and now the reason for that tactic became clear. With the artillery barrage silenced, and not having themselves taken heavy fire from the spaceport, the infected legionaries finally saw the rebels as a deadly threat and pivoted their attack to face them.

With Corruption and Rebellion exchanging fire, and the darts dancing through the air to stab down blasts of automatic fire at ground targets, no one was paying attention to the dead men in legionary armor that had been overrun by the initial advance of the tanks.

Sybutu's voice came over the comms. "On my mark, we get one of those MM-7s together and x-skragg those tanks. Zavage is gunner. Bronze, load feed. I set the tripod and command. Three, two—"

"Break. Break," Zavage interrupted. "I do not see the MM-7s. Over."

"You're practically lying in them," Sybutu replied. "There's a main barrel ten yards from your feet. Three, two, one, go!"

The armor was a stiff encumbrance that was almost impossible to move, not least because the human stink inside was a reminder that it had not been set up for a Kurlei. But by the time he'd pushed himself to his knees, the armor's power functions had restarted. So had its internal heater. With the muscle enhancement fizzing through the armor, Zavage leaped into the air.

Together, they swiftly assembled the gun components that had been buried in the churned-up snow, but which their helm HUDs clearly highlighted.

Bracing his lower back against a mound of snow, Zavage snapped the holo-sights onto one of the mobile tanks with his left hand and readied the firing stud with his right.

"Light 'em up," said the boss.

"You got it."

Despite the many components of the gun's Firing Stability Platform, Zavage felt an urgent power surge through the MM-7 as it came to life and threw x-shells downrange.

Brrrpppp! Brrrrpp!

Spent cases fountained into the air as rounds clattered against the tank's armor. Some bounced off, peppering the snow, but many fragments stuck onto the tank like half-melted licorice.

"Switch target," Osu ordered.

With no obvious damage to the tank, Zavage traversed the gun to take in its nearest neighbor. He checked load feed was good and targeting locked. Then he opened up once more.

Even the MM-7 would struggle to penetrate a main battle tank's armor with conventional rounds, but Bronze had loaded x-ray rounds, another technology whose secrets had been lost, but Zavage didn't need to know how to manufacture an x-round to point and shoot them.

"Switch target," Sybutu said again.

As the x-round came into range of its target, a miniature fusion bomb ignited, its enormous power channeled into a nanosecond pulsed x-ray laser that hosed the target, focusing its energy beam on the inside of the vehicle. The tiny amount of unconverted energy often melted the round casing, but that was nothing compared to what the x-ray beam was doing to the tank's crew. As for its electronics, unless the tank was properly shielded, they would be turned to slag.

The three tanks Zavage had raked with the x-rounds had gone dormant, but the other two were traversing their turrets to exterminate this threat from their rear. Hover darts banked around and blew small craters into the snow around the gun team as they sought to take out the MM-7 gunners first. But in exposing their vulnerable flanks to Corrupted blaster fire, the aircraft began taking heavy losses.

Which would be no consolation if the sappers were blasted to hell.

"Switch targets." Osu sounded as cool as if ordering his lunch in the Faxian chow hall.

Zavage's heart was pounding louder than the noise of the gun, and he was glad of his high-grip gauntlets because his hands were slick with fear. Nonetheless, he set the target lock on the turret that looked in the holo-sights to be almost aiming its barrel directly at his face. *Target lock. Ammo check. Fire!*

Brrrpppp! Brrrrpp! Booooom!

Something unyielding slammed into Zavage's face and he was thrown hard against his icy back rest.

He was sliding backwards on his butt. Two pairs of hands were dragging him.

"Move it!"

He willed his feet to work.

"Come on, you ugly sack of squid meat!"

Zavage found his feet and ran with Bronze and Sybutu. He was too disoriented to know where he was headed—just away.

Then he looked over to the rebel attack wave and saw the last tank with its barrel pointed directly at them.

Fear drove an additional burst of speed, but the world suddenly fell away, and he was falling. Sliding. Landing with a bump at the bottom of a shell crater. Sybutu and Bronze toppled onto him.

"Stay down," said the sergeant.

Zavage was okay with that for a while. "What happened?"

"One of those dart fighters got our number," Sybutu answered. "The MM-7 took most of the impact. That and your face."

"Lucky it wasn't the tank gun," said Bronze who had already scrambled to the lip of the crater, peering out at the battle. "That would have delivered more than just bruises."

The sounds of battle washed over them for a few seconds as they got their breath back. Zavage realized he'd lost his rifle. It had never truly felt his, having been stolen from a Corrupted corpse, but he sure missed it now. The furious exchanges of blaster fire taking place just a few hundred yards away meant there would be plenty more rifles lying around to be picked up. If he didn't get killed getting there.

"They were main battle tanks," Sybutu mused aloud. "No one designs resistance to energy beam munitions anymore." Zavage understood why the man sounded so unhappy about a fact that had saved their lives. The modern-day military had lost so much. They wouldn't have stood a chance against the Legion of the Orion Era. What if they had to face an enemy equipped with higher tech weapons? Perhaps those who had created the Corruption?

But that was a problem for tomorrow.

"Any sign of life in that last tank?" Zavage asked.

"No," Bronze replied. "Reckon it had zeroed in on us only to discover we'd zapped its fire control system."

"We left it too late to bug out," said Zavage.

Bronze looked down at him. "We would have timed it just right if we hadn't lost time dragging away a fish-head who'd decided to go all sleepy on us in the middle of a battle."

"That's enough," said Sybutu, but Zavage could sense Bronze's good-humored grin even though he couldn't see it behind the opaque helm. Whatever psychological crisis had overwhelmed the SpecMish man back in the city had resolved itself for now.

"The Corrupted are going to win this round," said Bronze, returning to his observation of the battlezone. "The hover darts are taking a pasting. Whatever they might once have been, their soldiers aren't legionaries. They're drones with no coordination that I can see, but they remember how to take a knee and lay down accurate fire."

Sybutu joined Bronze at the lip. "Any sign of the spaceport garrison?"

"Negative."

Zavage got to his knees, intending to join the other two, but Sybutu waved him back down. "You took a knock, Zavage. Use this timeout. In any case, you've made your presence felt in this battle. Scores of the Corrupted are carrying det packs over to the stranded tanks. Others are carrying them to the spaceport gate. They're not acting as brainless zombies as much as I'd like. They still look like an unruly mob divided up into separate packs, but those packs are tactical elements operating independently to provide fire support for the assault element going in with the det packs."

"So what you're saying," said Zavage, "is that they're acting as if their legionary brains have been scooped out and replacement Militia ones dolloped in."

"Yeah. I guess that about covers it."

Sybutu sounded amused by his reply, but Zavage's words had sounded dumb as soon as they had escaped his mouth. That morning they were still talking of Chimera Company. Were they back to Militia versus Legion so soon? Had none of this meant anything?

"It's all over," said Bronze, who had never shown any interest in smacking down the Militia. That was interesting: the former Special Missions man had probably seen far more of the galaxy than any of them. Were the two facts connected? "The hover darts are fleeing. They know they can't save the tanks now."

A series of explosions proved Bronze's point a few moments later as the charges laid by the Corrupted blew up the tanks.

By then, Zavage was intent on a new task: reconfiguring the helm comm system to throw a signal far enough to snap into the headset net used by their former Militia comrades—to send a signal that could connect with specific headsets.

Sybutu might not have changed his opinion of the Militia troopers, but Zavage had. Of one trooper in particular.

Text appeared in Zavage's helm in a disapproving shade of red.

Connection to external comm node active. Warning! Link is not secure!

"Green Fish, it's me. Just checking in."

"Vol," she said breathlessly. "Could do with your help about now. We're pinned down by rebels near the docks."

"Hang tough, Green. We're near the spaceport. The Corrupted have beaten the rebels back. Twice. Maybe the rebels will think again and pull back from the city."

Instead of Green Fish's sweet human voice came heavy breathing and blaster fire. Sounded like she was clearing out from a position that had gotten too hot for her.

Meanwhile, back in the crater, Sybutu was reporting on what he was seeing in the battle zone but didn't appear agitated. Zavage kept him on half-mute.

"Don't think that's going to happen," said Green Fish. "We're not going to make it. And that's a shame. Spend a night of passion with a Kurlei. It was the only item left on my ten things to do before I die. So close. It would have been great, Vol. Remember me."

"It still will be. Hang in there, Green Fish. You'll get to complete your list. I swear it."

"Zavage!" Sybutu shouted.

"Yes, Sergeant."

"Are you fit to go?"

Zavage cut the external link. "Yes, Sergeant."

"Time to move out. We merge with the Corrupted entering the spaceport, find Fitzwilliam's ship, and persuade him to take us off-world. Then we report in to Legion high command before coming back for Urdizine. Any questions?"

"Yeah," said Zavage. "Can you find us something difficult to do next time? I could do with a challenge."

Sybutu laughed. Zavage hadn't heard that sound since they'd left Camp Faxian.

They scrambled out of the crater and back into the battle.

There was one impossible objective Sybutu had left off. They had to get to the docks and rescue their friends. It was bad enough leaving Urdizine to fend for himself. They couldn't leave the others behind to die. Zavage wouldn't allow it.

* * * * *

Chapter Seventy-Three: Bronze

"Captain Tavistock Fitzwilliam. Owner-operator of free trader *Phantom*. Bay 27-Gamma." Bronze flicked through the console log in the abandoned spaceport control center. "Port fees paid in advance for the next month...refueling and resupplying...they booked some minor repairs. According to this, they're still here and ready to go."

"Good work," said Osu.

Damn! He *was* good. This, at least, he could still do well. SpecMish had backdoor access to many systems, and Rho-Torkis Main Spaceport was no exception. But something was not right. "Fitzwilliam's ship has been here eight weeks. Time is money for a free trader, and I've never known one yet who felt comfortable with an empty cargo bay, because I've never known one who didn't have debts to pay. Financial or otherwise. Why have they been here so long? And why haven't we seen ships fleeing the battle?"

"We can ask them that ourselves," Osu replied, "after we secure passage off-world."

"Get real," said Zavage. "It's not going to be easy."

Bronze stared at the Kurlei. What was bugging him?

Zavage looked away, ashamed.

"No, it's not," said Osu. "But we're Legion. We do it anyway. Let's go."

"Wait," said Bronze. "The ships are on lockdown. All of them. A security override was issued in the early hours of this morning. They're clamped and tethered. I'm downloading the override code for the *Phantom*'s bay."

"Can you countermand the lockdown throughout the port?"

"Yes."

"Do it. But then re-clamp Fitzwilliam's ship. We don't want him slipping away too easily."

When Bronze had unlocked every ship in the port bar one, Osu led them down the port control building. Bronze noted half-drunken coffees still steaming and holo-screens showing uncompleted mayday messages pleading for assistance. Where were the staff now?

Rho-Torkis had become a planet of mysteries, and that was one more that would have to wait.

* * *

Once the Corrupted forces had taken out the rebel tanks and driven away the hover darts, the survivors—about three hundred of them—had entered the gaping holes where the gates had once stood and seized the port without resistance. Once inside and back on script, a renewed sense of purpose and organization took control. Teams of legionaries armed with heavy weapons ringed each occupied bay, making doubly sure no ship could escape.

As the three genuine legionaries jogged to Bay 27-Gamma, they saw covered trucks scream through the service roads, headed for the northwest corner of the port. Something was going on there; yet another mystery. But as far as Bronze was concerned, it was a good one, just so long as it stayed in the far corner of the port, attracting the attention of whoever or whatever was controlling the Corrupted.

When they finally made it to Fitzwilliam's bay, Bronze's heart sank. Weapons were trained on all the ships around, but the *Phantom* had been singled out for special treatment. The circular pad at the center of the bay was ringed by twenty troops. Equally spaced around this ring were a plasma cannon, mobile SAM system, and two Corrupted legionaries standing near the closed lower hatch with heavy blasters on tall pintle mounts.

If they had faced fewer heavy weapons, they could have pulled this off. Or even if the big guns had been bunched in one spot, they might have had a slim chance.

But this…No, it was impossible. The only way the *Phantom* was getting out of here in one piece was if the Legion remnant of Chimera Company somehow managed to change the facts on the ground.

"Ship looks like your head, Zavage," Osu commented.

Normally, the Kurlei would be impressed by the protuberances that swept back from the *Phantom*'s cockpit like the kesah-kihisia organs on his head. Not today, though. Zavage merely grunted.

Actually, Bronze thought the strange appendages to the ship more closely resembled horns and tusks. Whatever their function, they were tethered to the landing pad now, a part of the security mechanism that could physically clamp down a ship the port authorities didn't want to leave.

Following Bronze's plan, the three of them were waiting at the edge of the bay, with Bronze in the lead performing a gas flush of his armor so the Corrupted could get a good sniff of him. The soldiers guarding the ship had noted their arrival and seemed to have decided they were not an immediate threat.

"Here we go," Bronze said over radio comms. "Act like them. It doesn't matter if you're soiling your underwear, so long as they don't realize."

Flanked by Osu and Zavage, he marched over to a spot beneath *Phantom*'s lower hatch from which the hatch camera could get a good look at him. He raised a gauntleted fist. "Open up," he demanded through his external suit audio.

"I've nothing more to say to you freaks," Fitzwilliam's voice replied from a hidden speaker in the *Phantom's* hull.

"If you won't see sense, Captain Fitzwilliam, then let me speak with someone more intelligent. Your hovering tin can, perhaps. Or Izza."

The hatch slid open and the boarding ramp unfolded, lodging against the landing pad at Bronze's feet.

"No need to bring Izza into this," said the captain, "you had me at tin can. Which one are you? I can't tell with that stupid bucket on your head, but I'd put money on the pipe smoker."

"That's me."

The three sappers marched up the ramp, feeling the heavy blasters trained on their backs.

Once they were aboard, the ramp retracted and the hatch snapped shut, but Bronze still felt the blasters' lethal attention.

* * * * *

Chapter Seventy-Four:
Osu Sybutu

The grinning smuggler captain stood beside a female Zhoogene a little way inside the ship, bathed in blue light that diffused from the overhead. Passageways led away to either side of the entrance in which the three legionaries stood. In one of them lurked a big Pryxian with a gun so heavy Osu doubted he could lift it even in his powered armor.

He dismissed the show of force. Fitzwilliam wouldn't be fool enough to fire weapons that could penetrate Legion armor. Not inside his own ship.

The *Phantom*'s captain was also making sure his new arrivals could see the custom heavy blaster slung low on his right thigh, and the confident grin on his face.

It was the unarmed Zhoogene standing next to him who registered as the most dangerous in Osu's assessment. She wore a burgundy leather jerkin over a gray ship suit stuffed into calf-length leather boots.

Osu had clocked up many thousands of hours aboard navy ships, and he'd never seen shipboard footwear like that. Probably a smuggler thing.

Other than her clothing, she was still the strangest Zhoogene he'd ever seen. Her figure was too curvaceous, the green skin lacked the normal waxy texture, and instead of the golden eyes he'd seen in every other Zhoogene face, hers were marbled in ribbons of pink and blue.

Whatever their color, the most striking aspect of her eyes was the way they sparked with anger. She glared at Bronze with pure hatred.

Fitzwilliam himself noticed and whispered something that Osu's helm picked up but couldn't translate.

His meaning was clear, though. The Zhoogene released Bronze from her angry stare.

And redirected it at Osu.

"We wish to renegotiate." Osu directed his statement at Fitzwilliam, but he wondered who was the real captain of this ship.

"Nice job of walking in here without being blasted full of holes," said Fitzwilliam, "but it's the same answer, kid. I'm retired."

"So you say. Your lack of cooperation is noted, Captain Fitzwilliam. For now, though, we seek only extraction and transport to a safe planet with a Legion presence."

"You can call me Captain Fitz like everyone else. And you can call my first officer here Lieutenant Zan Fey. You've earned that much. But off-world transport comes at a premium in these troubled days, and I don't offer lifts for free."

"We'll pay."

Fitz made a show of rubbing his chin, unimpressed.

Zan Fey entered the negotiation. "The price to take one person off-world is a fortune. To take three...?" She raised a golden eyebrow. "How would you pay?"

"Not just three of us," interrupted Zavage. "Our entire team. The others are pinned down at the maritime docks."

Bronze winced, expecting Osu to unleash hell onto Zavage over his intervention, but Osu's next words were to Fitz and his partner.

"The deal is simple. We're the only ones who can get you off this planet. If you refuse, every ship's captain stuck at this port would beg to take our offer. We're getting out, the only question is whether it's your ship we'll be leaving on."

Fitz glanced uneasily at Zan Fey. "One moment while we consider your offer."

* * * * *

Chapter Seventy-Five:
Izza Zan Fey

Fitz activated the privacy bubble.

"We're wasting time," he suggested, but she noted the uncertainty radiating from those wide human eyes of his. "If they convince me they can get us off this landing pad, then we jump out system and take them with us."

She knew damned well it was this Special Missions skragg making him nervous, and when Fitz got nervous, he made some very bad decisions. The evil man Fitz had let into their ship was an unwelcome reminder of Fitz's past. Her human had always hated SpecMish on principle, but he'd once confided in her that after a joint training exercise with them in an earlier life, he'd learned to fear them too.

"I don't like it either, my dear," he tried to reason, "but they may be our best route off this mad world."

She ignored the unprofessional endearment. He couldn't help himself when he was nervous.

"Leave now," she reminded him, "and we won't be able to pay off Nyluga-Ree. If we hold our nerve and stay, we might still collect our fee."

"No, Izza." He shook his head, his near-permanent grin slipping away to reveal a look of revulsion. "The city's burning, and its people are being twisted into monsters by a malevolence far worse than Ree.

468 | TIM C. TAYLOR

I don't know what's happening, but we aren't sticking around to find out. We've gotta ditch our client and get out of here."

"What if our client is behind all this?"

Fitz rubbed at his chin. He hadn't considered that angle. "You think this is Khallini's doing?"

"Perhaps. Lord Khallini didn't hire us to smuggle him in to play charades at the local newt orphanage. And if we leave now, we make Khallini our enemy. I do not want that."

"No." He put the swagger back into his stance. "No, Izza. There are things I might not have mentioned to you about Khallini because they were need-to-know. He's funding the Rebellion, for one. The Panhandlers, I mean, not this zombie plague. The most likely scenario is that he's already dead, or already gotten off-world and left *us* for dead."

"You don't know that."

"No, I do not. If you want a career with certainty, Izza, qualify as a tax accountant. We're free traders, my lady. Unfettered by customs duties and monopolistic trading restrictions. That requires a certain aplomb. I have decided to negotiate a deal with these legionary gentlemen."

Fitz doused the privacy bubble, revealing Izza shaking her head in dismay. *Aplomb!* Fitz was using pompous words in place of reasoned arguments. That was a bad sign. It meant they were screwed.

* * * * *

Chapter Seventy-Six:
Osu Sybutu

Before facing the ring of soldiers outside the *Phantom*, Osu looked over the robot in his new combat attire and felt his confidence surge. When Fitz had said the little droid would give them the additional firepower to take out the Corrupted guards in the landing bay, Osu had thought the smuggler was joking. Then Fitz casually mentioned he'd come across a Legion-surplus combat frame and ordered his crew to fashion an adapter so the droid could operate it.

The bot was housed inside an armored sphere mounted on four legs. Three blaster barrels poked out from a domed mini turret while two arms stretched from either end of the body. One was fitted with a percussion spike to penetrate armor, and the other held a blaster cannon with an extra-large power pack.

If the bot hidden inside could control all these systems simultaneously, then it would be a fearsome weapon of war. But there was more to being a good fighter than having a big weapon: you needed to fit into the team.

The notion made him think of Zavage. Was the Kurlei still thinking of Chimera Company as his team? The alien clearly had a passion for one of the human troopers in particular, but in the years Osu had known Vol Zavage, the alien's colorful romantic life had never compromised his professionalism.

Osu wondered whether he needed a few lessons in teamwork himself, especially if they really were going to pick up that Viking oaf and the others.

Before he could worry about that, they had to escape the space-port.

One impossible challenge at a time, Sybutu.

He nodded at the droid. "What is your designation?"

"L1-iN/x. Humans rarely trouble themselves with words of greater than three syllables. I think it causes them pain. So the captain calls me Lynx."

"Humans champion brevity and conciseness," Osu countered. "The better ones, at any rate. We are very smart at some things, droid. War is one of them. I have less faith in combat droids."

"Charming!"

"And I particularly lack faith in you, Lynx. Tell me, who are you going to kill out there?"

"Corrupted, sir."

"And who are you not going to hurt at all?"

"The three heroic legionaries."

Osu sighed. "Did Fitz program you to have all this attitude?"

"No, sir. But he did reprogram me, a task for which he is not remotely qualified."

"Azhanti! I didn't sign up for this, but you'll have to do. Follow at the rear and remember to obey the plan."

"Of course, sir. I have always remembered. I remember *everything.*"

Frowning at the emphasis the bot had placed on its final word, Osu tapped the door release and led the party down the ramp as soon as it had unfurled.

Throughout the bay, Legion helms suddenly snapped their way, but it was the reaction of the two Corrupted with the pintle-mounted heavy blasters that worried him most.

Both of them tracked him as he descended the ramp, and he sensed fingers about to ease into triggers.

If they opened fire, he would barely have a chance to register that it was all over before he was vaporized.

He felt a shove from behind as Bronze pushed to the front.

Did the two Corrupted ease off their triggers or was that his imagination?

Expecting oblivion with every step, they walked down to the landing pad and formed a wedge behind the two gunners; Lynx took one flank, Bronze and Zavage the other.

The gunners had relaxed as soon as the party exiting the ship had passed them by. Osu guessed their assignment was to cover the *Phantom*'s hatch for any sign of escape. Now that they had moved beyond their perimeter, the gunners no longer considered Osu and the others to be leaving the ship.

For an agonizing couple of minutes, the legionaries waited silently in their wedge. Osu ignore the sporadic blaster fire elsewhere in the port and the screams drifting on the wind over from the city. Then, judging the Corrupted had settled sufficiently, the three legionaries moved around the ring of guards, leaving Lynx positioned behind the two gunners.

Osu stood behind the SAM operator while Zavage and Bronze placed themselves to strike the plasma cannon gunner.

"On my mark," radioed Osu when the others had all confirmed they were ready. "Make it fast. Make it certain. 3...2...1...rip 'em!"

* * *

The SAM operator wore the form of a woman, but that was all. The thing inside was alien now, all humanity overcome. Telling himself that made what he was about to do a little easier, because Osu wasn't about to kill her. How could he? She was already dead. He was about to release a sister from an obscene violation.

He raised the barrel of his blaster rifle until it was four inches behind the back of her head and put three rounds into her.

At this extreme short range, the bolt had yet to fully induce plasma before it hit the target. Consequently, it wrapped around the back of her helm before fully activating and slicing through like high-energy cheese wire. The result looked sickening, but her brain would have been obliterated before she knew what was happening. It was the most merciful way to go about this gruesome task, but for all that he justified his actions to himself, it wasn't easy. And it didn't feel like the right thing to do.

"Rest in honor, sister," he whispered to the corpse as it sank to its knees, but he was already firing at the nearest Corrupted Legionary, sending a flurry of bolts to his head.

"Rest now," he said to the brother he had released. He jumped sideways, curling into a roll as crossfire howled into the landing pad where he'd just been standing.

He took a knee and snapped off a bolt at another Corrupted, only to realize his adversary had been shot by someone else.

With the barrage of blaster fire and the plasma cannon loud in his ears, Osu jumped away using all the power his armor could add to his legs. Rolling as he landed, he came up behind the cover of one of the *Phantom*'s landing struts.

He poked his head out from behind the strut and saw the battle was already over. Zavage had cooked half of the Corrupted with the plasma cannon, and Lynx had wrought carnage with the gore-coated drill spike that left jagged holes in the enemy heaped by the droid's feet.

"Go in honor," Osu said to the fallen while shuddering at the thought of how easily the droid had torn through the same armor model he wore himself.

"Check in," he said over the team channel.

"I'm good," said Zavage.

"Me too," added Bronze. "Cover me while I release the docking clamps."

"I suffered minor damage to one leg," said the droid. "Nonetheless, I find I rather enjoyed that brisk melee."

A psychotic droid. That's all I need, mused Osu as he and Zavage provided overwatch while Bronze busied himself inside the small kiosk that housed the controls for the bay.

Lynx, meanwhile, picked up the plasma cannon and its fuel drums.

"Hey, droid! What are you doing?"

The bot ignored Osu's challenge and carried the cannon around to the *Phantom*'s landing ramp.

"Leave that!"

"I'm afraid I can't, sir. Captain Fitzwilliam would have my guts for garters if I left such valuable equipment behind. Besides, I suspect the near future will see an increased incidence of combat activity for all of us."

The clamps released, and the additional security tethers fell away from the force keels that swept back from the *Phantom*'s cockpit.

They were good to go.

"What are you waiting for?" Osu barked joyfully, not quite believing they had gotten this far. "Jump in our new ride before it forgets its passengers."

They hurried past the droid salvaging the battlefield and passed into the relative safety of the *Phantom*.

Osu made straight for the flight deck.

* * *

"What the hell is that?" Zan Fey cried from the copilot seat.

"A paying passenger not strapped down," Fitz growled.

But that wasn't what Zan Fey meant. She was pointing out of the cockpit at something on the ground. She was pointing to the northwest.

The *Phantom* tilted radically as it made its escape from the spaceport, but the anti-gravity kept Osu from falling, even though his stomach warned him that if he didn't stop tumbling, he'd lose his lunch.

"It's a ship," said the copilot.

"My lady, we *are* lifting off from a spaceport."

"Shut up, Fitz. The ship looks...*alive.*"

"You're right," he said as he jinked the *Phantom* away. "It looks...*valuable.*"

Osu stumbled over to the seat behind Zan Fey, bracing himself on the seat back so he could see what she was pointing at. It was a starship. A cylindrical front section with three sweptback wings gave way to a hundred-meter rubbery tail that ended in a spiked club. The last time he'd seen this ship, he'd been with Nydella Sanderson.

This was the reason the Legion had come to Rho-Torkis. It was the reason the Corrupted were here too, most likely.

"I'll tell you what that is," he said as the *Phantom* urgently sought altitude. "It's dangerous. These zombies who had you shackled to the spaceport think it belongs to them. Or, rather, to whoever is controlling them."

The *Phantom* leveled out and spiraled back down to the city.

"Belongs?" Fitz commented. "As in, Team Zombie paid for it?"

"Not exactly." Osu stared at Fitz. "That ship was damaged in a war that ended before the Exiles ever came to Far Reach. I think whoever's controlling the zombies built the ship."

He watched as the smuggler captain ground his jaw. The man could sit back and watch a city burn and do nothing, but the mention of that ancient war had gotten through to him. Maybe Colonel Malix had been right about Captain Fitz after all.

"Nice backstory," Fitz said with a grin. "Sounds even more valuable than I thought. Lieutenant Zan Fey, kindly put your delightful head together with the crew to figure out how we can steal that ship while I'm busy picking up the rest of our passengers."

Zan Fey turned to regard Osu with a smile that oddly reminded him of Lily Hjon. "You do realize my husband is teasing us?"

Osu said nothing. He wasn't so sure. Unlike Zan Fey, he'd seen the conflict fight over Fitz's face.

"He's doing nothing of the sort." Fitz sounded indignant. "But seeing as you've seen fit to grace the flight deck with your presence, Mr. Legionary, perhaps you can tell us where you left the rest of your team."

476 | TIM C. TAYLOR

"North side of..." A red alert light flashed, and a pungent alert odor was released.

"Pickup will have to wait," said Fitz. "Which of you has the best gunnery skills?"

"Bronze."

"Mr. Bronze!" Fitz announced over the ship-wide PA. "Kindly get your ass into the dorsal turret. We have company. Move it, Legionary!"

* * * * *

Chapter Seventy-Seven:
Osu Sybutu

In less than two minutes, they had dispatched the pair of rebel Falcons with ease. Bronze had fired at the attacking fighters from the dorsal blister turret that had popped out of the hull, but he hadn't made the kills. He had reported back to Osu, though, that the human-AI gunnery setup was so good that SpecMish operatives would have given their arms for a ship like this.

The *Phantom* swept down upon the docks from the north. The Cora's World rebels held this area, but they themselves had been left stranded by the speed of their advance into Bresca-Brevae. Before Fitz had begun the descent, Osu had seen a flotilla of light boats racing up the coast for the bay. Probably the rebel naval component coming in for extraction.

The monitor by the lower hatch offered a stabilized view of the ground below for the battle-ready service droid and three legionaries waiting to drop. The docks were a mess, shelled into oblivion for the most part. A single jetty remained that looked fully functional, the access route from the bay not blocked by sunken ships and the approach from the city not yet engulfed in fire. But if the rebels were to get away on the boats, then they had a problem. Only one warehouse still stood nearby, and it commanded the approach to the jetty. Someone had fortified the building and was using it to resist the rebels. If those someones weren't led by an ignorant oaf with a beard and a furry coat, then this was going to be a very embarrassing way to die.

Rebels were massing in the approach roads. Scores of them. If Osu was observing Arunsen's troopers holding out, then they were about to be overwhelmed.

The *Phantom* plummeted, leaving Osu's stomach behind in the clouds.

By the time he'd recovered enough to scream, the ship was hanging in the air like a hover platform, nose dipped at the mass of rebels as if in respectful greeting.

Azhanti! What kind of a ship was this *Phantom*?

Whatever else it might be, it was clearly a warship. Twin front cannons opened fire, not with eye-searing blaster bolts but kinetic rounds. Bullets, flechettes, explosive-tipped micro rockets…hell, he didn't know what Fitz and Zan Fey were firing but whatever it was pulverized streets, buildings, and rebel troops, turning them into a cloud of powdered debris.

What kind of smalltime smuggler flew a ship like this?

His mouth wide open in shock, Osu suddenly had to grip onto the handhold for dear life as Fitz accelerated away, tearing through the street before rising up in a loop that brought them back to their starting point above the street.

Lynx hit the door hatch. "I'll go first," announced the droid. He curled his outer combat frame into a ball and rolled out the ship.

"Go! Go! Go!" screamed Bronze, following the droid out into the air.

Osu and Zavage looked at each other. All they could see below was dust. It would be a great way for Fitz to divest himself of his troublesome passengers: convince them to drop out the ship from two thousand feet and then come back to pick up the droid unscathed.

Zavage leaped out the hatch.

Osu had no choice. He jumped too.

* * *

The drop was only ten feet. His armor absorbed nearly all the impact, but none of the shame of Osu's continued trepidation with heights.

Through the clearing debris clouds, he saw a metal ball rolling away down the street.

"Follow that droid," he ordered.

"I always wanted to hear that," Zavage replied, laughing.

They'd advanced a hundred yards toward the Militia troopers when blaster fire lashed at Lynx from ruined buildings to either side of the street, deflecting off the smooth body he was wearing.

Lynx returned fire against one side; the sappers directing their reply against the other. The dust still hanging in the air glowed red where the rebel blaster bolts had passed through, pointing a finger back to the positions of the shooters.

They took out the rebels, but if the hot dust had acted like tracers for the rebel fire, it would too for their own.

"Move!" yelled Osu, but he didn't need to because the other legionaries were already shifting their butts.

Not quickly enough, though. A bolt took Zavage in his torso.

"I'm okay," said the Kurlei, but Osu wished he had a properly set up squad net that would report his legionaries' status automatically.

While the legionaries took cover behind the heaps of debris littering the street, Lynx pulled himself out of the building he'd assaulted.

In one hand, the droid held a human leg, in the other, he directed a heavy blaster toward the shot that had hit Zavage.

"Wait!" Osu shouted. That shot had come from directly ahead. From the defended warehouse.

"Chimera Company!" he shouted through an amplified speaker in his helm. "Chimera Company."

"Identify yourself," yelled a female voice out of the air.

"Who do you think it is, Lily?"

"Oh, my. It's the pretty boy come to rescue me. How dashing."

"Stow it," he retorted. "If it was up to me, I'd have abandoned you. This was all Zavage's idea." But he had to admit, it was surprisingly good to hear her voice.

They shouted a coordinated plan to each other. A rebel attack on the Militia position along a parallel road had stalled without the support from the main force obliterated by the *Phantom* and mopped up by Osu's team. With a little help from Lynx's powerful limbs and blaster, the legionaries cut through the buildings to one side, emerging into the street behind the rebel pocket.

Most of them had already fled, hearing the plans for their doom being shouted from the rooftop. Those that didn't were ruthlessly dispatched.

But not without cost.

Bronze was down. Hurt bad.

Vetch raced out of the battered warehouse to help Osu haul Bronze to safety. One of the other troopers came too, assisting Zavage and Lynx to cover their retreat.

"Nice entrance." It was Green Fish. Of course it was.

"Yeah," Zavage replied. "Not bad. But it's the *exit* I'm hoping to get right."

Once inside, they carefully lifted Bronze onto a freight box. Zavage checked the external suit diagnostics to see what was going on in the inside.

Two troopers were laid out on similar boxes nearby.

Arunsen shook Osu's hand. "Thanks, brother. We lost Rynter, and Deep Tone's in bad shape. We're low on charge packs and ammo too, but we're still fighting for an out. We saw that ship scream in and thought our number was up. You would put my ignorant, uncouth Militia mind at rest if you told me it was coming back for us."

Doubts began creeping up Osu's spine. Wrapped up in his combat frame, Lynx was a one-bot army who could easily roll out the city and be extracted by the *Phantom* from safety. There was no reason for Fitz to come back for his passengers.

"Lynx?"

"Yes, sir."

"Contact Fitz and request immediate extraction."

"I can't do that, Osu."

"Don't call me Osu. And you, Arunsen, stop tugging at your beard. I got this." He took a breath. "Lynx, why can't you talk with the *Phantom*?"

"Out of range, sir."

"But you do trust Captain Fitz to come back for you?"

"The only one Captain Fitzwilliam can be trusted to come back for is Lieutenant Izza Zan Fey, and she for him."

"Are they actually in love?"

"Apparently so. Also, they display a level of synergy unparalleled in my experience of humanoids. Each functions better in partnership with the other, and they both know it. It would be impertinent to speculate whether it is romantic infatuation or the efficiencies of synergy that causes them to reunite with such frequency, despite their many and noisy fallings out."

Zavage interrupted with his report. "Bronze is stable. His armor's keeping him under for now, but he'll need proper medical attention soon."

"If Captain Fitz and Lieutenant Zan Fey do return for us," continued Lynx, "then it will be because they have a desperate need for us. If we leave the planet, then our client will be left stranded here, and he is not a person one crosses lightly."

"He? Who is your client?"

The droid kept silent.

"Lynx?"

"I'm sorry, sir. I am not at liberty to say."

"Then you're no use to me here. Get on the roof and add to our overwatch. If your smuggler lovebirds do come back for us, your job is to cover our extraction. You're to be last to board the *Phantom*."

"I understand and comply."

The droid moved off, leaving Osu staring at Green Fish and Zavage, who had united in a loose embrace.

Talking of lovebirds…

"Plenty of time for cuddles when we're on the *Phantom*. For now, I want you two apart and minds focused on the job."

Green Fish shot him a lingering dirty look but joined Enthree guarding one of the warehouse entrances.

"Zavage, check your weapon and then make yourself available to Arunsen. I'll stay with Bronze and make sure he gets on the ship."

"Roger that."

Osu had nothing to apologize for. He felt bad nonetheless. Splitting Zavage and Green Fish was the right thing to do, even though they all understood the *Phantom* might never return. As far as Osu knew, these few snatched moments of peace might be the calm before the storm of steel and plasma that could come at any moment and end them all. He was denying the two their chance to enjoy that moment of calm, and it was his job to do so. He had to keep everyone fighting to get out of here and brutally crush any other thoughts. Arunsen was doing the same: issuing orders and checking in with his team. So was Hjon.

Osu found himself alone with the comatose SOTL. "I don't know whether that bot is playing games," he told Bronze while he carried out a weapons check, "or whether its circuits are fried. Either way, we've just been given a clue to explain why the *Phantom* has been waiting on Rho-Torkis so long. When you wake up, you'll figure it all out. I guess that's the kind of thing you used to do, Hines Zy Pel. Make it through, brother, and solve me this puzzle."

"Incoming!" came a shout from the roof.

Osu took his rifle off safety. It gave a satisfying whine as it charged its first shot.

"Hey, Sybutu," shouted Arunsen cheerfully as he came over. "It's your taxi service. They're late. Does that mean we get half-price fare?"

"Shut up and move your team out."

The Viking laughed and picked up his wounded man, Deep Tone, in his arms.

Osu felt the same imperative and lifted Bronze over his left shoulder.

The warehouse's main entrance faced the dockside road and beyond that was the jetty. Osu could see the water churning into a white vortex on one side. Then the *Phantom* came into view, making a vertical drop onto the water, coming to a halt ten feet above the waves.

"With me, Zavage." The Militia on the roof were making their way down, but Osu was getting out now with the two surviving legionaries.

After hanging in the air for a few moments while the water calmed, the *Phantom* aligned itself parallel to the jetty and gently touched down on the water. Cables shot out from its hull and secured themselves to mooring posts.

The ship was just two hundred yards away. Osu hurried out of the warehouse as fast as he could with an armored man over his shoulder.

The *Phantom's* hatch opened, and a stubby boarding platform emerged, coming to rest on the jetty.

Fitz's grinning head poked out. He waved at Osu. "Sorry we're late. I confess, I can't resist a good dogfight."

Osu laughed. If they were going to spend the next little while together, Fitz might be an amusing distraction from all he'd lost on Rho-Torkis. "Zavage! You there?"

"Coming, Sergeant," said the alien's voice from a short distance behind.

They were going to make it.

Fitz's grin disappeared, and he leaned out the hatch to look at something at the rear of his ship.

Whatever it was, it could wait. Osu picked up the pace. Getting Bronze to safety was all that mattered for the moment.

Then Zavage shouted the words Osu least wanted to hear. "Contact! Newts in the water!"

Osu was almost on the boarding platform now. He put everything he had into a final dash for the *Phantom*.

"Sniper!" cried Zavage. "I'm hit!"

* * * * *

Chapter Seventy-Eight:
Ndemo-327-Cerulian

"No! No! No!" Enthree screamed in rage. They had survived so much. To be cut down now would be unjust.

She shot at the sniper. The human had lodged in a window frame set high up in the only wall still standing in what had been the neighboring warehouse.

She missed. But the war bot didn't. It leaped across from the warehouse Enthree's team had defended and landed on the sniper. Then the droid punched a spike through the Corrupted human before the wall collapsed in a cloud of debris.

One sniper, dusted.

Elsewhere, Corrupted Littoranes were emerging from the water onto the bank, the jetty, and even clambering over the curved structures that swept back from the *Phantom*'s main hull like horns. They were armed with primitive and possibly ornamental melee weapons. They did not appear friendly.

Captain Fitzwilliam shot one, his oversized handgun barking once with no apparent recoil. Now, that was interesting. The impact of his shot was so devastating, it hadn't so much hit the Littorane as disassembled it. The technological principles behind his weapon were unfamiliar to her but merited further investigation.

She shot one rushing at her from the road, but there were too many and coming from every direction. The war bot was supposed to be covering the retreat. What had happened to the wretched machine? She drew her swords and beat off the attack, deflecting blows, stabbing and slashing, never standing still.

Swordplay was her greatest combat skill, but she was picking up too many wounds. She was slowing. Her swords were getting heavier.

Blaster bolts flew toward her across the jetty, one coming so close that it seared the side of her head crest.

The attacks ceased coming, though, and Littoranes fell to the ground.

Up ahead on the jetty, Vetch, Lily, Sward, and the Legion sergeant knelt with rifles pointed her way.

"Hurry up, you great, hairy insect!" cried Vetch.

This was good. Vetch must have safely deposited Deep Tone on the evacuation craft and appeared to be in good humor. For a human.

She hurried over to her friends, realizing that now the war bot had fallen silent, she was the last one to make it onto the jetty.

To volunteer for the rearguard was the Muryani way, of course. Everyone wanted to sacrifice for the greater good. Her brood sire used to tell stories of a Muryani military unit left behind on a hostile planet because when the rescue mission arrived to evacuate them, the soldiers had been so intent on fighting each other to see who would be last out that they forgot to board. A joke, of course—probably—but even as an infant, Enthree had sensed the underlying truth.

That sense of service powered her legs, and she sprinted for the floating spaceship. The most important service she could perform today was to survive and report what she had seen to the Expansion.

More Littoranes yelled war cries behind her. A volley of bolts from her friends cleared them away.

Yet more jumped out of the water and into her path.

Strange. They seem to be concentrating on me.

With a shock, she realized that the Corrupted really were directing their attacks on her. She was the only Muryani around, and they would not permit her to escape. They wanted her silenced.

Yes, the Andromedan Corruption knew she was their greatest threat. And they were right. She knew what they truly were.

She turned and fended them off with her swords, but only barely. Her limbs shook with fatigue.

Green Fish waded in and dispatched two with her plasma pistol at point-blank range.

Then a Kurlei distress cry pierced the air. Green Fish's attention switched to Zavage, who was lurching around the jetty a short distance ahead.

"Vol!" cried Green Fish, but the Kurlei waved her away. The sniper's bolt he'd taken a short while before had clearly hurt him, but not critically. Green Fish was displaying excessive concern for his well-being.

Interesting. Enthree began to wonder whether this implied a strong emotional attachment between the two.

"I'm all right. Seriously, Green. It's this damned armor. Thinks I'm human. A badly wounded human who…Shit! It's injected me again! Gree…I shle shlll…."

490 | TIM C. TAYLOR

Zavage staggered drunkenly, but Sward had come back to help, and an array of Chimera Company rifles were covering their retreat, as was Captain Fitzwilliam with his mysterious handgun. Even the little service droid came bobbing back over the jetty, though why it had decided to abandon its combat frame was unclear.

Enthree sheathed her swords and kept her blasters covering the water, but she could finally relax. Fittingly, she would be the last one back.

Or so she thought. Dripping with water, a pair of human hands grabbed onto the side of the jetty, just hanging there for a moment. Most likely this was a Corrupted human who'd swam out with the amphibious Littoranes and only now made it to the target area. There was an audible sigh and then the human hauled himself onto the jetty.

Meatbolt!

An exhausted Meatbolt—or, at least, the obscenity of Corruption that wore his form—drew his blaster pistol. Water dripped from the end of the barrel, a barrel aimed at Zavage.

Would the weapon work after its soaking? Possibly. Such weapons were designed to be robust.

"Meatbolt," she called to the creature wearing the form of her friend. "Please."

"You wouldn't," said Sward.

"He would," Enthree insisted, feeling a twinge in her arm. "He shot me only a few hours ago."

Meatbolt took a half step forward but his face was a storm of confusion. He didn't appear to know why he was there.

Enthree strapped her blasters over her back and drew two short swords.

Green Fish interposed her body in front of Zavage. "Meat, it's me. Greenie."

Meatbolt's open mouth trembled. "Gr...Green?"

"Yeah." Green Fish smiled. "'Course it's me. Remember when we broke into that restaurant and made love in the kitchen on that steel worktable?"

Meatbolt halted. He blinked. "Green Fish?"

"Yes, Green Fish. I know you're still in there, Meat. I love you. Always will. Whatever you've done—whatever you ever do—I will always forgive you. I don't have the room in my heart to hate you."

The Corrupted man looked in astonishment at the blaster pistol he was holding. He dropped it, snapping his hand open as if the weapon were white hot. It clattered to the ground harmlessly.

Green Fish took a tentative step toward Meatbolt.

"Stay back!" Enthree warned. "You cannot cure him." Swords aloft, she was ready to step forward and decapitate the perversion of her best friend. She had been ready for some time. For many days now, she could have and *should* have ended this obscenity.

That's how the Corruption wins. It makes us weak.

But even now, doubts stayed her hands. Green Fish opened her arms and took another step toward their friend who, amazingly, smiled sheepishly beneath a dripping moustache of feathers that had grown in only the last few hours.

The Expansion archivists had recorded the Corruption that preceded the last Andromedan attack. In those far-off years, humans had not yet been brought here. They were a race of many surprising abilities. Could some of them have resistance to the Corruption?

Enthree stayed back and said nothing as Green Fish closed the last couple of steps and embraced Meatbolt.

Sward must have been too intent on the drama playing out to keep a proper hold of Zavage. The Kurlei slid from his grip and fell lifelessly onto the jetty.

The noise spooked Meatbolt.

He pushed Green Fish away and reached behind to pull at the back of his neck.

Enthree jumped at Meatbolt.

"Meat?"

Green Fish's plea found no purchase in Meatbolt's Corrupted mind as he drew the death needle he'd strapped beneath the back of his shirt. It was a traditional Littorane underwater weapon: a barbed spike he'd probably picked up from a temple.

He slashed at Green Fish. She blocked him, but his move was a feint. His real attack came in beneath her arms, piercing her flesh beneath her sternum and driving the barbed metal through the cavity within and out the other side.

Green Fish gasped and slumped into Sward's arms.

Enthree's sword sliced through Meatbolt's weapon arm, and her momentum carried him away from his victim. She grabbed him tightly and spun them both around to topple off the jetty.

"Green?" Meatbolt questioned pitifully just before they splashed beneath the water.

Enthree wrapped a limb around an underwater post and grabbed Meatbolt's head, holding it before hers. "I'm sorry," she told her friend through the water.

He was panicked. Fighting for air. He no longer recognized who she was or why he was here, but she explained anyway. "This is my fault. You were my best friend, and yet in my weakness I failed you. I shan't be weak again."

She ended him. With her sword.

* * * * *

Chapter Seventy-Nine:
Tavistock Fitzwilliam

"Haven't you forgotten something?" asked Fitz without looking up from the monitor showing the awful scenes on the jetty.

"I have forgotten *nothing*, sir," replied the hovering droid.

"I don't see my combat frame. Have you any idea how much that thing cost?"

"1.34 million credits. I processed the transaction myself."

"Less of your lip, droid."

"The frame's power always drained too fast," whined the bot. "That's why the military paperwork said the frame had been destroyed as faulty."

"Now you're nitpicking. It's an annoying habit you've picked up from Izza."

"Fitz!" warned Izza from the copilot station. "I know you can't bear to watch people suffer, but distracting yourself by annoying Lynx isn't helping. You have to hold it together. Whether we're moving to a safer location on Rho-Torkis or flying these chumps off-world, we're not safe yet."

The passengers embarked, two of their number having to be carried: a bleeding woman and an unconscious legionary. A corpse and a severely wounded trooper were already aboard and strapped into the med-bay by the crew.

Fitz looked across. Izza was biting her lip, saying nothing, but he knew exactly what was going through that green head of hers.

She wanted to stick it out and wait for Lord Khallini.

"I've made my decision," he said.

"Just fly us out of here, Fitz."

He flicked on the ship-wide PA. "Okay, people, listen up. I want one of you refugees in the dorsal turret. Preferably the pipe smoker from before." The *hatch secure* indicator lit. "Everyone else, strap in tight." He spooled the lifter motors. "The good news for our new gunner is that anyone up in the skies is trying to kill us, so you don't have to mess with that friend-or-foe malarkey. The bad...well, you figure it out."

"Shield deflectors angled for atmo-assist," Izza announced. "Weapons hot."

"I love it when you say that," Fitz drawled.

The lifters roared, drowning out Izza's reply and sending water spraying over the cockpit. The *Phantom* tottered in the air, rising slowly. Then the gravitics found purchase and the ship corkscrewed for the heavens in a near-vertical climb.

"Any signs of bandits?"

"A flight of four atmo-craft diverting to intercept. They're too far away. We'll outrun them."

"Of course." Fitz grinned. "This is the *Phantom*. The fastest free trader in the galaxy. And with the most charming crew."

The missile lock alarm sounded.

"SAM launch. SAM launch," Izza reported. "PS4s. Two launches. Fire pattern is...piecemeal. We have eleven missile locks, but most aren't firing. It's as if they forgot to."

Fitz leveled out the *Phantom* and sowed a confetti corridor of false targets over the path of the SAMs. The missiles exploded against the decoys, but the operation had robbed them of precious time and altitude.

"Bandits closing from east. Vertical stack. Sixteen thou."

Damn!

"We need a diversion," said a very annoying voice.

Double damn! It was Sybutu on the flight deck.

"Get aft, you dumb jack."

"We released the docking clamps for every bay in the spaceport."

"Except us?" said Izza.

"Except you."

Fitz sucked in a breath while he patched through to the public comm frequency. Sybutu was making a dangerous enemy of Izza. "To all pilots trapped at Bresca-Brevae, this is Captain Tavistock Fitzwilliam of the *Phantom*. Your clamps are released. Your guards are dangerous but can be evaded. I repeat, your clamps are released. You are good to go. Be safe. Be fast. Be gone!"

"Why are we not experiencing extreme g-forces?"

"Azhanti!" Evidently it was now the Viking's turn to enjoy an unauthorized tour of the flight deck. "I'm trying to fly a spaceship here!" Fitz ignored the passengers and tilted the nose down in readiness to punch out of the atmosphere and break orbit.

"Our three wounded are stable," said Arunsen. "But gee-stresses could kill them. That's what I came forward to warn you about."

"Diversion is working," said Izza, ignoring the big human. If *Phantom*'s inertial bubble failed, it wouldn't just be the wounded passengers who would die. "Multiple ship launches. Not all are making

496 | TIM C. TAYLOR

it. Explosions on the ground. SAM launches. Another ship gone. They're fighting back. We're losing missile locks."

"And the bandits?"

"Too slow," Izza replied with relish.

"Oh, yeah! Nothing outruns the *Phantom*."

"Ship launch," she said. Fitz didn't like the tension in her voice. "It's the ship the zombies were after. Bylzak! It has a tail…I think it's alive!"

"Relax, my lady. Whatever it might be, it can't hope to catch us now."

"Why does he keep calling you *my lady*?" asked the Viking.

"Fitz! It's fast," cried Izza. "*Real* fast. Forget your flight plan. Just get us far enough away from this gravity well, and I'll make an emergency jump."

Lights started flashing all over the flight deck. Notification alerts chimed.

"What's happening?" asked Fitz.

"Comm blanket has lifted," Lynx explained. "The *Phantom*'s reconnecting with the rest of the galaxy."

"Energy spike forming on that living ship," warned Izza.

Fitz threw the *Phantom* sideways, missing an energy discharge that cut through the air where she'd just been. It was an energy tunnel eight feet in diameter with an edge marked out by coruscating green light. He'd never heard of anything like it. "What the hell was that?"

"Death," Izza answered. "But there's a reply. Legion fighters launching from orbital defense array. Spikeballs. Lots of them."

"Legion?" said Sybutu. "I thought they were all dead."

"So did I," said Fitz. "Sorry, Sybutu. Turns out you're not the only legionaries on the planet anymore."

Lynx made a sound like a humanoid clearing its throat. "Sergeant Arunsen, with my owners otherwise engaged, it falls to me to answer your question. Captain Fitz uses the *my lady* honorific because he likes to put about that he is of noble birth."

"Is he?" Arunsen asked.

"I regret to inform you that after some research, I can attest that he is indeed," replied the disloyal trash can.

"Yeah," said Fitz, "the dark side of the family. Now quit yapping, or I'll have you flogged and force you to call me Lord Fitz."

As they pushed through into the safety of the black, one squadron of Spikeballs tunneled down into the atmosphere, racing to engage the alien craft. A second squadron flew an interdiction pattern at the interface between atmosphere and the void. They sure didn't want that fancy ship getting away.

He'd heard rumors. Of course he had—Fitz was plugged into more secret networks than he cared to remember—he'd just never believed the stories.

Until now.

They could get away today, but what that ship meant to the Federation was not something that could be dodged.

He glanced across at his beautiful wife, hunched over an array of screens, fascinated by this new and dangerous thing in her universe. They'd been good together. Oh, more than good. The lord and lady of illicit trading in this sector, they had made the perfect team. And they would again one day.

But the galaxy had just called time on their adventures for now. He would once again have to consider motives other than fun and profit. For a little while, at least.

The question was: would Izza join him?

498 | TIM C. TAYLOR

"No. It can't be." Sybutu's denial was awful to hear. "Someone in the Legion let the rebels through the orbital defenses to bomb my home into ash. Where were these Spikeballs when the rebels landed unopposed on the planet?"

The holo-comm activated itself and a ghostly miniature figure appeared, projected in the air between Fitz and Izza. It was an elderly gentleman holding a fancy walking cane.

"A good question," said the holo figure. "But one I can answer. It is I who locked up the Legion orbital defenses. And now I have released them."

Fitz cleared his throat. "Good afternoon, Lord Khallini, sir. We were just talking about you, wondering where and when you might need pickup."

"I have heard every word spoken on your flight deck."

Rewinding the memories of the past hour or so did nothing for Fitz's peace of mind.

"Yeah, well, about stranding you on Rho-Torkis, Lord Khallini. We were about to die."

"You were about to die when I offered you the contract!" spat that old man indignantly. "I know of your troubles with Nyluga-Ree." He calmed and smoothed his thinning hair. "I am magnanimous, Fitzwilliam. I shall forgive you your disloyalty and pay you our originally agreed fee, plus an additional fifty percent bonus, on condition that you track that ship and report its location back to me. Are we agreed?"

"We are in agreement," said Fitz in his most trustworthy voice.

"*Our* agreement is to get off-planet to a Legion system," Sybutu insisted.

"And *my* team's post is down there in the Great Ice Plain," said the bearded Militia NCO.

Khallini raised an eyebrow at Arunsen for a reason that escaped Fitz.

"Be quiet," Izza snapped to the backseat drivers. "Both of you."

Fitz almost retorted that after Khallini's change of heart, Rho-Torkis still *was* a Legion system. But the Spikeballs were being blown apart by the alien ship that looked as if it were swimming out of the atmosphere and then diving back from space, eager to swipe a foe from the sky with its tail, but settling for forward-facing fire.

When Izza announced that a rebel flotilla was jumping in system, it was obvious that Rho-Torkis was lost.

The alien ship reached orbit with a flick of its tail that looked joyful. No longer pursued by the Legion fighters, it held a steady bearing. It no longer appeared interested in the *Phantom*.

"Space is distorting in front of it," said Izza. "Massive energy spike."

Fitz glanced out the cockpit, but he could see nothing in the visible spectrum except a very valuable ship that was even more dangerous than it was precious. But when had anything of genuine interest not also been perilous?

"Is it jumping?" he suggested.

"I think so."

The *Phantom* angled her force keels like a high-dimensional rudder and came about. Aiming for the mystery ship.

"You can't be serious!" Izza stared in horror.

"It's the find of a lifetime. Nothing in the galaxy is more valuable than that ship."

"You're gonna steal it?"

"Maybe. I'll learn about it and report what I choose back to Khallini. Come on, my lady. Have you never taken a chance? You can trust me—I take risks for a living."

"I know you do, Tavistock. That's what bothers me."

Fitz bit his tongue. No one seemed to appreciate superior flying skills anymore. For his own amusement, Fitz put in fishtail waggles while spinning the old girl like a coin on a bar top as the *Phantom* intercepted the alien ship's path.

"Incoming fire," announced Izza, an instant before the front shields flashed.

"Kinetic darts," she said. "Tungsten."

"I thought that ship was supposed to be special," said Sybutu. "Tungsten darts? That's pre-Contact Earth weapon tech."

"It is," said Fitz in awe, and maybe a little in love with this magnificent vessel. This...this *space dragon*. "I think the length of the entire ship from tail tip to nose is used to power its main weapon. If we'd faced that, we'd be atoms."

"Energy spiking further," said Izza.

Fitz seized his chance, putting everything the *Phantom* had into an intercept course with a point just ahead of the alien ship.

"We're going to crash," screamed Arunsen.

"Not with Fitz at the helm," said Izza, the pride in her voice warming his soul. "He's a fool, but he's a fool who knows how to fly like no other."

The stars stretched away to infinity. The familiar sight of the moment before a jump was enough to convince him that the alien ship was using a crazy form of hyperjump. If *Phantom* jumped at the same moment, they should be able to follow. But there was only one person in the galaxy who could produce jump calcs on the fly like that.

"Can you do it?" he asked Izza.

"Yes."

"And *will* you?"

Her voice went husky. "You know I will."

The distortion tunnel before the alien ship shifted. The vanishing point of infinity suddenly got farther away, which made no sense, but it was the only way Fitz's brain could encompass the impossible sight.

In the same way that he wasn't entirely human, Izza was more than mostly Zhoogene topped up with an old dash of *Homo sapiens*. Patterns designed by ancient biowarfare engineers flowed through both their veins. Hers allowed Izza to understand hyper-dimensional trajectories.

They allowed her to do *this*…

"Engaging jump drive," she said.

Following a slight jump in his stomach, the stars disappeared. They were in jump.

"Thank you, Lieutenant Zan Fey. You are a marvel."

He meant every word, but Izza wasn't buying. "You'd better be right about this, Fitz."

"Since when have I—"

His mouth clamped shut as every screen, light, and indicator flashed warnings across the flight deck.

Tidal forces were wrenching the ship apart. It was on the verge of melting. And the jump drive warning messages were using words he hadn't seen before, but all of which looked exceedingly bad.

Even the infinite void, which was all one saw outside the ship during a jump, wasn't an empty void anymore. It looked as if they were jumping into the inferno of the Five Hells.

He hadn't been right at all. And this time, even Izza wouldn't be able to pull him out the fire.

The *Phantom*'s jump was about to fail.

Fitz's limited perception felt the universe stretch and warp in abhorrent ways.

"This trip is about to get interesting," he said as the cockpit view shifted to blazing white. "No one's ever survived an emergency drop to normal space before."

# # # # #

Appendix 1: Timeline of the 6th Legion

= Highly Confidential =

Ferrata Fidelis Constans
"Iron clad, loyal, and constant."

Home base: Wandrine-Callos, Tej Sector.

Battle Honors: Tej Sector, Zhoogene, Taegi-28, Core-7.

Battle Cry: "Hold the Line!"

Current Status (FL-3030): Strategic Legion Reserve for Tej Sector, Theta-Zanovis Sector, and Ishgen Spine.

Timeline of key events:

Note: Dates are given in standard Far Reach calendar, commencing (Year FL 0) with Far Reach Landing. In the old Orion Era Calendar, FL 0 corresponds to 2745.

FL 71: Sixth Legion is established on Wandrine-Callos/Tej Sector during the Nine Systems War, in which rebellious political factions allied with existing nearby civilizations to crush Far Reach, attempting to reduce it to Nine System colony status. In its motto, the Sixth is awarded the name 'Ferrata:' 'iron clad' in Latin, a part of the name awarded to a Sixth Legion raised 2868 years earlier by a famous Orion Era general named Julius Caesar. At a time when the continued existence was in doubt of the Far Reach Federation and its population of Amilxi exiles, many of the new legions raised in this period stress their links to renowned military forebears of Earth and other Orion Spur worlds.

FL 262: Supports Legion Reserve Fleet in the Tej Sector Counterattack that defeats the self-styled 'Supremity.' In reality, the Supremity is a bandit warlord commanding a vast armada of armed vessels: the dregs of a hundred civilizations that has drifted in from the Interspiral Wastes intent on despoilment, plunder, and murder. A motley pirate raid it might be, but both the Fourth Legion and the Militia system defense forces in 21 planetary systems are routed before the counterattack, and Legion losses are heavy. After the joint operation, the Admiral of the Reserve Fleet, the most renowned organization in the Legion, shares blood with the Sixth Legion's General Weygrunth, and conveys on her command the right to use the Reserve Fleet's famous battle cry: 'Hold the Line!'

FL 291: The Relief of Zhoogene. In FL 288 the Multiplicity Alliance was facing invasion and assimilation by the supremely powerful Muryani Expansion. Despite the lack of a formal military treaty between the Federation and the Multiplicity Alliance, which at the time constituted 52 systems, the Sixth Legion feels honor-bound to come to the aid of the Zhoogenes, having conducted a cultural and military exchange program over the previous decades. After seeking and winning approval from Federation President Weygrunth, herself a former general of the Ironclads, the Sixth attempts to break the Siege of Zhoogene. They fail, being repulsed with catastrophic losses. But the Muryani besiegers themselves are severely weakened, and within a year, Alliance forces sweep away the siege and other invasion forces, resulting in a humiliating peace settlement imposed on the Muryani, who have hitherto appeared invincible. The Zhoogene are so impressed by the loyal support of the Ironclads in a conflict that wasn't theirs that they soon persuade the Multiplicity Alliance to join the Federation. In acknowledgment of the Sixth's action around Zhoogene, the second segment of their motto is added: *fidelis* or loyal.

FL 291-296: First Reconstitution. The Ironclad's responsibilities are temporarily handed over to the First and Third Legions while the shattered Sixth is reformed.

FL 450: Operation Orion Rearguard. The Sixth Legion and Third Fleet combine to provide military support to Operation Orion: a project to re-establish communications with Earth and the Orion Spur by establishing a corridor of colonies and trading posts across the 12,000 light years from Federation space in the Perseus Arm. Initially penetrating nearly 600 light years with relative success, Operation Orion turns into a disaster when it awakens a Gorgonthola. After a fighting retreat over 257 light years, the Sixth Legion makes a rearguard stand at Taegi-28, determined that the Gorgonthola will not follow the fleeing colonists back to Federation space. Only one ship, *FRS Wavefront*, survives the action, filled with wounded, civilians, and prisoners captured from the Gorgonthola's serf armies. Only 47 legionaries survive the expedition. In recognition of the Sixth's steadfast action, another portion of the ancient Roman Legion's name are applied to the Legion, even though it has ceased to exist as a functioning unit. Henceforth, it is to be known as *Ferrata Fidelis Constans*: 'Ironclad, loyal, and constant.'

FL 451-469: Second Reconstitution. The Sixth is reformed. The renown of its action at Taegi-28 means that only a small fraction of the multitude who volunteer can be enlisted.

FL 903: The Razing of Core-7. For the Federation, the war against the Grunvalt Gestalt that begins FL 887 goes from bad to disastrous, and then to existential crisis in FL 901 with the Siege of Wutan-Scala-7, the first capital of the Federation. Employing the technique of 'vacuum replenishment' for the first time and to devastating effect, the Ironclads arrive without warning deep inside enemy territory at the principle Gestalt hub-world of Core-7. Here they annihilate all defenses within hours and force the Gestalt to surrender unconditionally.

In a controversial decision that to this day inspires mobs of chanting protesters to denounce the Sixth Legion of war crimes, the

Ironclad's General Soleb deploys fusion munitions against the underground Gestalt AI spines, reducing Grunvalters to the semi-sentient drones they are today. General Soleb bullishly justifies his action, arguing that since forming the Gestalt means the Grunvalters have effectively cut out their emotions, they have rendered themselves incapable of any sense of honor, meaning any treaty with them would be meaningless. Unaware that while the Sixth was moving on Core-7, the Grunvalters have destroyed all life on the Federation's capital world, Soleb reasons that the only way to keep the Federation safe in the long term is to render the Gestalt permanently harmless.

At the time, his decision is widely backed by Federation citizens still reeling from the destruction of Wutan-Scala-7. Many see it as justified revenge. Within a decade, however, the public mood is soured by the Legion's political opponents. General Soleb himself is ambushed by a group of political terrorists while on vacation with his family and is murdered in FL 926.

FL 3001-3004. The Ironclads crush the 'Sequined Flower Rebellion' on the Muryani border. The causes of the rebellion are still highly classified.

FL 3025-present day. An important archaeological find on the hitherto obscure planet of Rho-Torkis leads to a flurry of archaeological activity throughout the Tej Sector. The digs, the site security and the analysis of the finds are all conducted through the Sixth Legion. The exact nature of what has been uncovered remains highly classified. However, it has been widely reported that many of the dig site locations coincide with earlier archaeological and other evidence

508 | TIM C. TAYLOR

of a war that took place in the sector some centuries before the arrival of the Exiles in FL 0.

Today, the renowned Sixth Legion approaches its termillennial celebration: 3,000 years of proud service to the Far Reach Federation. Whatever threats the Federation will face over the next three millennia, we can be sure the Sixth will be there to hold the line, forever ironclad, loyal and constant.

* * * * *

Appendix 2: Timeline of the Far Reach Militia

According to official Militia records

Mission: To protect the Federation against its internal enemies, and provide system defense to aid the Far Reach Legion against external threats.

Battle Cry: "Liberty or Death!"

Composition: Although the Militia has a visible presence in all Far Reach Federation star systems—comprising army, air force, sea force, system and orbital defense, navy, and dropship infantry—the precise make up of its forces remains a matter of speculation. The

510 | TIM C. TAYLOR

federal budget allocated to the Militia is enormous, and, when combined with the heavy contributions demanded of planetary governments, it is widely believed that the majority of that budget must be spent on something other than the Militia's modest visible presence. Some hint at hidden reserves maintained to save the Federation when its darkest moment comes; cynics point to the lavish lifestyles enjoyed by many Militia officers and federal senators. The truth is known only by the Senior Committees of the Federal Senate, and possibly the President and Militia High Command.

Motto: The Militia declines to invent what it regards as ridiculous slogans for its units, leaving that kind of posturing to the Legion. However, the phrase "The Militia and the Amilxi People" is frequently used in official documents ('Amilxi' is the name used by the original Federation settlers to describe themselves.) In Terran script, this is frequently initialized as M.A.P. Similar compact abbreviations are commonplace in scent or other script symbols.

Symbol: A silhouette of a hammer held proud against a stylized star. This is in recognition of the Hammer of Democracy movement in FL 25.

Nickname: The People's Army.

Chronicler's Personal Notes: Although some Militia officers rise from the ranks, most use money and influence to purchase their commissions and expect to turn a good profit. By contrast, the ranks are frequently the scrapings of the penal and welfare systems. Every year, federal and planetary budgets divert more credits from the Legion to the Militia as the latter's allies increasingly dominate the political sphere other than the presidency, which is still controlled by their arch-rivals: the Legion. Despite this, many rank-and-file Militia troopers serve with pride and honor. Maybe the Militia isn't perfect, but the life they knew before was even worse.

Timeline of key events:

Note: Dates are given in standard Far Reach calendar, commencing (Year FL 0) with Far Reach Landing. In the old Orion Era Calendar, FL 0 corresponds to 2745.

-41 FL: The First Schism.

During the War of Liberation in the Orion Spur the ancient Human Legion undergoes the First Schism: a decisive split in which a disaffected group of senior commanders and military units breaks away, rejecting what they see as the dictatorial tendency of the Legion high command. It is this faction that conceives the goal of establishing a Far Reach settlement outside the region in which the war is being fought.

FL 25: The 'Hammer of Democracy.'

When a campaign for democratic representation of the people declares an unauthorized election on the capital world of Wutan-Scala-7, workers in the orbital shipyards put down their tools and descend the orbital elevators. They intend to vote for their representatives in the Federal Council, whether the election is official or not. Units of 3rd Assault Marine Division—a formation that was one of the earliest to detach in the First Schism—form a protective shield to prevent the authorities from arresting the shipyard voters.

Workers grab hammers as an emblem of their impromptu movement, and stand side by side with the Marines as they are surrounded by the ultra-loyalist 119th Armored Division and buzzed by aircraft of the 5th Shock Wing. The tense standoff lasts eight days before ending in a non-violent resolution that pleases nobody. The Hammer of Democracy incident polarizes the Federation. Civil war seems inevitable.

FL 25-31: The Battle for the Future.

A cold civil war sweeps the early Federation. The leaders of the two factions during the First Schism quickly lose control of the situation. Factions split further and recombine in new combinations, each with their own shifting agenda. Centers of power and influence are seized and exploited by rival factions. There is rioting, cyber war, and armed skirmishes. Disgruntled and terrified citizens launch a wave of settlement outside of Federation territory.

FL 31: The Great Settlement of Wutan-Scala-7.

The remaining leaders from the Orion Era avert full-blown civil war by agreeing to a settlement between themselves, and they present it to the people of Far Reach over the heads of the new warring factions. On the edge of disaster, the Federation blinks and steps back from the brink.

The two Orion Era factions acknowledge each other as core pillars of the Federation, with distinct and inviolate traditions. They are to be known henceforth as the Militia and the Legion. A separation of roles and responsibilities is agreed, as is a new political settlement that leaves the Militia with stronger political influence over the Federal Council and Senate, and the Legion with counterbalancing influence over the presidency. The people of the Federation are to remain the ultimate sovereign power.

The Militia adopts a military hammer as its emblem in remembrance of the Hammer of Democracy. It also adopts the convention of describing itself as 'The Militia and the Amilxi People,' emphasizing that it draws its legitimacy through the sovereign people of the Federation.

FL 69-82: Nine Systems War.

Treacherous factions within the Legion ally with foreign powers to seize control of the Federation and rule it as a vassal state. The Militia blunts or repels attacks from the rebel Legion and Nine System forces, rallying loyal legionaries and raising new legions based on elite Militia cadres. After the Federation is eventually victorious in the Nine Systems War, the Militia wins the nickname of the People's Army.

FL 622-643: Private Wars.

Three corrupt alliances of senior Militia commanders, federal senators, and organized criminal networks compete with each other in what are later called the Private Wars. The situation drags on for many years, devastating both the lives of innocent citizens and the reputation of Federation institutions. The long-running scandal is finally defeated by the Militia Independent Task Force established by the Anti-Corruption Senate Committee, and supplied by the Outer Torellian Commerce Guild (OTCG). The latter is a legitimate and patriotic trading organization, which nonetheless profits greatly from the action and hugely extends its commercial network. Until this time, the OTCG has sometimes been smeared by its rivals who call it the 'Smugglers Guild.' The use of this objectionable term is made an offence against the Purity Act.

FL 1120: The Samarian Reforms.

Recruitment and organization of the Militia is reformed to improve recruitment, discipline, and to re-instill a military ethos after a long period without external wars. Key reforms are:

- The *Indentured Service Program*. Rather than wasteful penal incarceration, individuals convicted under the criminal or purity systems can now pay their debt to the Federation in the form of service in the Militia.

- *Officer Commissioning.* Most Militia officer commissions are now purchased, and units run on a commercial basis. Commissions are not simply handed out to the highest bidder; applicants are vetted carefully so that only the right sort of people take on these vital roles.

- *Per-capita Funding Formula.* Militia units are now funded on a per-trooper basis. Militia numbers soar. Cynics allege that the number of troopers claimed by officers in funding assessments vastly exceeds the number of real troopers present in barracks and even further exceeds the number of troopers who are properly trained and equipped. It is evident to all right-thinking people that these allegations are unfounded because the 'paper' strength of the Militia, on which funding is based, is highly privileged information unavailable to the public.

FL 2866: Gorgantheletta Eruption.

No one knows who or what the Gorgantheletta are or how they came to invade the world of Breda-Anthemis. Some say they poured through a hyperspace portal to emerge beneath the foothills of the Eunzler Mountains. Others say they came from a hell dimension, or that they were always there but only recently woken. Armed with serrated short swords, cruel maces, and venomous fangs, the humanoid creatures swept over the planet, relishing every opportunity to kill in cruel and imaginative ways.

When the Militia's initial attempt to stem the flow of invaders is overrun, the local commander evacuates her personnel into orbit, to the fury of the planet's citizens. Then the Gorgantheletta seize jump-capable starships and make for orbit themselves. The Militia rallies, flinging its forces against the enemy to win time for the fleet of system defense boats to mount an effective blockade.

When the enemy makes a concerted effort to leave the planet, their commandeered vessels are disabled by Militia warboats ramming their jump drives in suicide runs. Meanwhile, a scratch force of troopers on a one-way dropship descent into hell destroys the spaceport facilities on the ground before being overwhelmed.

Before the Gorgantheletta can repair the facilities and launch fresh ships, the Legion 3rd Fleet arrives and sterilizes Breda-Anthemis.

With the voices of the citizens abandoned on the planet's surface silenced by the murderous foe, the Militia finds itself—somewhat to its surprise—celebrated across the Federation as heroes. The name People's Army is spoken once again with pride.

FL 3020: First General Clarke.

An unlikely alliance of Militia Commandos and Legion Naval Intelligence seizes the Commander-in-Chief of the Legion. A crack Legion Special Missions squad immediately launches a successful retrieval mission, but on the return flight the Legion acknowledges the awful truth: First General Clarke is a traitor in the pay of a foreign power. Legion morale is badly shaken. There is also a deadly new intensity to the long-standing rivalry between Naval Intelligence and 'SpecMish' (as Special Missions is unofficially called; officially it doesn't exist).

FL 3030 (present day)

With the rise of the Pan-Human Progressive Alliance (the self-styled *Rebellion*) from protest group to armed insurrection, the Militia is more vital to the survival of Far Reach Federation than at any time in its history. Not everyone has the wisdom to understand the strength of its leadership and funding mechanism, but the People's Army exists to protect and serve all citizens of the Federation, whatever their beliefs or political philosophy.

The Militia and the Amilxi People. M.A.P.

Together, the Federation's future is assured.

* * * * *

ABOUT THE AUTHOR

Tim C. Taylor lives with his family in an ancient village in England. When he was an impressionable kid, between 1977 and 1978, several mind-altering things happened to him all at once: Star Wars, Dungeons & Dragons, and 2000AD comic. Consequently, he now writes science fiction novels for a living, notably in the Human Legion and Four Horsemen Universes. His latest project is an adventure serial called Chimera Company, which has been described as Warhammer 40,000 in the style of Star Wars. For a free starter library of stories from all the worlds he writes in, join the Legion at humanlegion.com.

* * * * *

Looking for the Latest in Scifi Goodness?

Come join us on the Factory Floor on Facebook!

Meet us at: https://www.facebook.com/groups/461794864654198/

* * * * *

AUTHOR' NOTE

Get More Chimera Company!

If you want to keep up with the news on the latest season, you can check out the Chimera Company page on https://humanlegion.com/, where you can also download prequels and join the Legion to get the latest skinny on my stories and learn about the Chimera Company Insiders.

There are three prequels so far, featuring the Militia, Legion, and Special Missions (with Vetch, Osu, and Bronze on the covers). You can download some for free from the Chimera Company page, and the rest by joining the Legion at humanlegion.com.

I'm going to write at least two more Chimera Company novels. I would love to write more, but for that to be a reality, the series needs to sell well. Spreading the word and leaving positive reviews are things you can do to help it succeed.

Thanks for reading.

Tim Taylor—June 2020.

* * * * *

The following is an

Excerpt from Book One of the Revelations Cycle:

Cartwright's Cavaliers

Mark Wandrey

Available Now from Seventh Seal Press

eBook, Paperback, and Audio Book

Excerpt from "Cartwight's Cavaliers:"

The last two operational tanks were trapped on their chosen path. Faced with destroyed vehicles front and back, they cut sideways to the edge of the dry river bed they'd been moving along and found several large boulders to maneuver around that allowed them to present a hull-down defensive position. Their troopers rallied on that position. It was starting to look like they'd dig in when Phoenix 1 screamed over and strafed them with dual streams of railgun rounds. A split second later, Phoenix 2 followed on a parallel path. Jim was just cheering the air attack when he saw it. The sixth damned tank, and it was a heavy.

"I got that last tank," Jim said over the command net.

"Observe and stand by," Murdock said.

"We'll have these in hand shortly," Buddha agreed, his transmission interspersed with the thudding of his CASPer firing its magnet accelerator. "We can be there in a few minutes."

Jim examined his battlespace. The tank was massive. It had to be one of the fusion-powered beasts he'd read about. Which meant shields and energy weapons. It was heading down the same gap the APC had taken, so it was heading toward Second Squad, and fast.

"Shit," he said.

"Jim," Hargrave said, "we're in position. What are you doing?"

"Leading," Jim said as he jumped out from the rock wall.

* * * * *

Get "Cartwright's Cavaliers" now at:
https://www.amazon.com/dp/B01MRZKM95

Find out more about Mark Wandrey and the Four Horsemen Universe at:

https://chriskennedypublishing.com/the-four-horsemen-books/

* * * * *

The following is an

Excerpt from Book One of the Salvage Title Trilogy:

Salvage Title

Kevin Steverson

Available Now from Theogony Books

eBook, Paperback, and Audio Book

Excerpt from "Salvage Title:"

The first thing Clip did was get power to the door and the access panel. Two of his power cells did the trick once he had them wired to the container. He then pulled out his slate and connected it. It lit up, and his fingers flew across it. It took him a few minutes to establish a link, then he programmed it to search for the combination to the access panel.

"Is it from a human ship?" Harmon asked, curious.

"I don't think so, but it doesn't matter; ones and zeros are still ones and zeros when it comes to computers. It's universal. I mean, there are some things you have to know to get other races' computers to run right, but it's not that hard," Clip said.

Harmon shook his head. *Riiigghht,* he thought. He knew better. Clip's intelligence test results were completely off the charts. Clip opted to go to work at Rinto's right after secondary school because there was nothing for him to learn at the colleges and universities on either Tretra or Joth. He could have received academic scholarships for advanced degrees on a number of nearby systems. He could have even gone all the way to Earth and attended the University of Georgia if he wanted. The problem was getting there. The schools would have provided free tuition if he could just have paid to get there.

Secondary school had been rough on Clip. He was a small guy that made excellent grades without trying. It would have been worse if Harmon hadn't let everyone know that Clip was his brother. They lived in the same foster center, so it was mostly true. The first day of school, Harmon had laid down the law—if you messed with Clip, you messed up.

At the age of fourteen, he beat three seniors senseless for attempting to put Clip in a trash container. One of them was a Yalteen, a member of a race of large humanoids from two systems over. It wasn't a fair fight—they should have brought more people with them. Harmon hated bullies.

After the suspension ended, the school's Warball coach came to see him. He started that season as a freshman and worked on using it to earn a scholarship to the academy. By the time he graduated, he was six feet two inches with two hundred and twenty pounds of muscle. He got the scholarship and a shot at going into space. It was the longest time he'd ever spent away from his foster brother, but he couldn't turn it down.

Clip stayed on Joth and went to work for Rinto. He figured it was a job that would get him access to all kinds of technical stuff, servos, motors, and maybe even some alien computers. The first week he was there, he tweaked the equipment and increased the plant's recycled steel production by 12 percent. Rinto was eternally grateful, as it put him solidly into the profit column instead of toeing the line between profit and loss. When Harmon came back to the planet after the academy, Rinto hired him on the spot on Clip's recommendation. After he saw Harmon operate the grappler and got to know him, he was glad he did.

A steady beeping brought Harmon back to the present. Clip's program had succeeded in unlocking the container. "Right on!" Clip exclaimed. He was always using expressions hundreds or more years out of style. "Let's see what we have; I hope this one isn't empty, too." Last month they'd come across a smaller vault, but it had been empty.

Harmon stepped up and wedged his hands into the small opening the door had made when it disengaged the locks. There wasn't enough power in the small cells Clip used to open it any further. He put his weight into it, and the door opened enough for them to get inside. Before they went in, Harmon placed a piece of pipe in the doorway so it couldn't close and lock on them, baking them alive before anyone realized they were missing.

Daylight shone in through the doorway, and they both froze in place; the weapons vault was full.

* * * * *

Get "Salvage Title" now at:
https://www.amazon.com/dp/B07H8Q3HBV.

Find out more about Kevin Steverson and "Salvage Title" at:
http://chriskennedypublishing.com/.

* * * * *

The following is an

Excerpt from Book One of Murphy's Lawless:

Shakes

Mike Massa

Available from Beyond Terra Press

eBook and Paperback

Excerpt from "Shakes:"

"My name is Volo of the House Zobulakos," the SpinDog announced haughtily. Harry watched as his slender ally found his feet and made a show of brushing imaginary dust from his shoulder where the lance had rested.

Volo was defiant even in the face of drawn weapons; Harry had to give him points for style.

"I am here representing the esteemed friend to all Sarmatchani, my father, Arko Primus Heraklis Zobulakos. This is a mission of great importance. What honorless prole names my brother a liar and interferes with the will of the Primus? Tell me, that I might inform your chief of this insolence."

Harry tensed as two of the newcomers surged forward in angry reaction to the word "honorless," but the tall man interposed his lance, barring their way.

"Father!" the shorter one objected, throwing back her hood, revealing a sharp featured young woman. She'd drawn her blade and balefully eyed the SpinDog. "Let me teach this arrogant weakling about honor!"

"Nay, Stella," the broad-shouldered man said grimly. "Even my daughter must cleave to the law. This is a clan matter. And as to the stripling's question..."

"I, hight Yannis al-Caoimhip ex-huscarlo, Patrisero of the Herdbane, First among the Sarmatchani," he went on, fixing his eyes first on Volo and then each of the Terrans. "I name Stabilo of the Sky People a liar, a cheat, and a coward. I call his people to account. Blood or treasure. At dawn tomorrow either will suffice."

Harry didn't say a word but heard a deep sigh from Rodriguez. These were the allies he'd been sent to find, all right. Just like every other joint operation with indigs, it was SNAFU.

Murphy's Law was in still in effect.

* * * * *

Get "Shakes" now at: https://www.amazon.com/dp/B0861F23KH

Find out more about Myrphy's Lawless and Beyond Terra Press at: https://chriskennedypublishing.com/imprints-authors/beyond-terra-press/

* * * * *